Praise for *Pyro*

"You will finish this book with a racing heartbeat, and a deepened respect for the fierce complexities that go into the making of a hero."

—*Mystery Scene*

"A fast-paced, smoke-filled, gripping story loaded with plot twists, snappy and graphic dialogue, and firefighting lore."

—*Publishers Weekly*

"Emerson has another four-alarm winner."

—*Library Journal*

Praise for Earl Emerson

"Earl Emerson's plotting is original, suspenseful, so well done that the richness of his writing seems almost a bonus. . . . [He] has taken his place in the rarefied air of the best of the best."

—ANN RULE

"When writer Earl Emerson takes you into a burning building, you believe it."

—*The Baltimore Sun*

"Earl Emerson gives the reader enormous insight into the grueling and dangerous lives of firefighters."

—JOHN SAUL

By Earl Emerson

Vertical Burn
Into the Inferno
Pyro
The Smoke Room

The Thomas Black Novels
The Rainy City
Poverty Bay
Nervous Laughter
Fat Tuesday
Deviant Behavior
Yellow Dog Party
The Portland Laugher
The Vanishing Smile
The Million-Dollar Tattoo
Deception Pass
Catfish Café

PYRO

A
NOVEL
OF
SUSPENSE

EARL EMERSON

BALLANTINE BOOKS • NEW YORK

Pyro is a work of fiction. Names, characters, places, and incidents are the products of the author's imagination or are used fictitiously. Any resemblance to actual events, locales, or persons, living or dead, is entirely coincidental.

2005 Ballantine Books Mass Market Edition

Published in the United States by Ballantine Books, an imprint of The Random House Publishing Group, a division of Random House, Inc., New York.

Ballantine and colophon are registered trademarks of Random House, Inc.

Originally published in hardcover in the United States by Ballantine Books, an imprint of The Random House Publishing Group, a division of Random House, Inc., in 2004.

This edition contains an excerpt from the forthcoming book *The Smoke Room* by Earl Emerson. This excerpt has been set for this edition only and may not reflect content of the forthcoming edition.

ISBN 0-345-46289-0

Cover design: Carl D. Galian
Cover illustration: painting of fire by John Ennis; photograph of match © Mark Sykes/Alamy

Printed in the United States of America

Ballantine Books website address: www.ballantinebooks.com

OPM 9 8 7 6 5 4 3 2 1

For Sandy, who always lights my fire

Everybody ends badly. There's not a damn thing we can do about it. Only the lucky ones get to choose how and when. We all die. It's what vultures are about.

—E. Slezak

1. THE PIANO MOVER FROM HELL

Life has been a rocky road since that morning nineteen years ago when my brother and I killed Alfred. For want of a better term, the police said Alfred was our mother's boyfriend, but we never thought of him as anything but an interloper, not until the moment Neil and I found our sneakers stuck to the floor in his blood.

The morning of the murders my brother was eight days shy of his thirteenth birthday. I was ten.

The papers called it an execution-style slaying, and it was partially due to their distorted portrayal of the event that my brother was tried and sentenced and packed away to a long series of increasingly harsher juvenile detention facilities. We made some mistakes that morning. Not that, given the same circumstances, we wouldn't kill Alfred again. Because we would.

In later years, our memories pasted over with hope and optimism, we decided that last drunken squabble between our mother and Alfred T. Osbourne started because Mother had been on the cusp of throwing him out. Maybe she'd found the gumption to do so. We certainly wanted to believe it. She'd never be able to tell us, since she died that morning too.

We had thought life was about as bad as it could get until Alfred and his stinky feet and seminal flashes of madness came along. He was meaner than a boot full of barbed wire, and more often than not Neil was the object of this meanness. It was a testament to Neil's courage that he didn't run away.

"I'm not leaving him with you and Mother. That is not an option. You just remember where we keep Uncle Oren's Spanish Civil War revolver if we ever need it."

"I know where."

When she wasn't drinking, our mother was too fragile to look out for the family, and when she *was* drinking, she was too drunk. Neil was the one who looked out for us. He'd been in that role for years.

It was mystifying how our mother ended up with two men of such differing temperaments as Alfred and our father, but then, she had always been a sucker for a uniform. Our father had been a Seattle firefighter; Alfred, a former King County cop, although by the time we met him, he'd traveled a good distance downslope and was working as a part-time piano mover.

There are things people never recover from, and for Emma Grant Wollf, it was the on-duty death of her husband six years earlier at an arson fire. Some people bend with adversity. Others break. Our mother fell solidly into the latter camp.

During those years after my father died, our mother struggled with a string of minimum-wage jobs that seemed to disappear as quickly as the gin she spilled on the carpet, the three of us moving into and out of a dozen apartments and as many schools in half as many years. It wasn't long before she began going through men as fast as she went through jobs, hooking up with a series of drunks she met in bars and, in one case, at the driver's license bureau. Mom met Alfred in the Blue Moon Tavern. She frequented the Blue Moon because it was close to the University of Washington campus and she'd heard a rumor that published poets hung out there.

Despite the cataclysmic change it produced in our lives, or perhaps because of it, that last morning together was so vaguely installed in memory, I found it difficult to bring back details. Odd, considering how much time I spend thinking about the past.

My brother Neil ended up celebrating his thirteenth birthday in the youth detention center off East Alder, where he became an immediate celebrity in that palace of losers and lost souls, the only thirteen-year-old in the United States to have slain a former cop. "People leave me alone," he told me during a visit. "They're afraid of me."

The first decade of my life, Neil had been closer to me than anybody, yet for most of the next twenty years the majority of our communication constituted ten-minute collect phone calls from one prison or another.

One thing I learned early on—happiness is elusive. You learn that when you're ten years old and your brother's in the clink and you're being passed around from relative to relative. It's elusive.

Here are the facts as they stand today:

I'm twenty-nine years old, the same age my father was when he died, the same age Alfred was when we killed him right after he killed my mother. I have one sibling, Neil. For the past eight years Neil has been picking up his mail at the State Penitentiary in Walla Walla. It's the sixth time he's been in lockup. You probably should know that in the law enforcement community, Neil is considered unpredictable and dangerous.

I'm the brother who went straight.

These days I work for the Seattle Fire Department, just as our father did. Until recently I believed I had a reputation for integrity and probity, and when other firefighters seemed wary of me, I told myself it was because they'd heard about Neil. Obviously there was more.

For instance, the night I cold-cocked Chief Hertlein.

It's not something I'm especially proud of—impulsive violence.

Say some jerk in a movie theater keeps rattling the cellophane wrapper on his candy. I turn around and object. He objects to my objection. I stand and block his view of the screen. He stands and tells me I'm an asshole. Next thing I know I'm walking out of the place in the middle of the picture and the cops are on their way. Mr. Cellophane goes to the hospital, where they wire his broken jaw shut. I know I'm bad. I can't help it.

I escape that one. I escape them all through happenstance

and a remarkable string of good fortune. Eventually I won't escape. Eventually I'll be in prison with my brother.

For years I've known where I'm headed. I've known it and thus far have been unable to do anything to stop it.

Before I punched out Chief Hertlein, I was assigned to Station 32 in West Seattle at the top of the hill near the YMCA. The station housed Attack 32, Medic 32, and Ladder 11. I was the lieutenant on Ladder 11.

Even though his home base was miles away at Station 29, most days you could find Hertlein in our beanery bullshitting, eating our food, and throwing his weight around. Because he protected us from other chiefs and rarely drilled us, we tolerated his bad jokes and around-the-clock presence, though I found him annoying and boorish. He was a bully and a butt-kisser, and in our department the latter made him a fast-tracker. It was rumored he was up for a deputy's position.

The day it happened, the entire house was dispatched to an alarm at 1048 hours—the engine, the ladder truck, the medic unit, and the chief all swooping down off the hill to Pier 28 on the Duwamish waterway, just about a mile due south of downtown, where we found black smoke billowing from the hatches of a three-hundred-foot oceangoing ship.

By noon there were fifteen engine companies, six trucks, and God knows how many chiefs in the dock area. While other firefighters poured water onto the fire, we pumped the excess accumulation out of the holds lest the ship sink from the added weight. In the end we sealed the hatches and filled the holds with CO_2, beginning a process that would take days to complete.

An hour before we were sent back to the station to clean up, a captain named Bill Coburn tripped on a hose line and fell down a gangway. In his mid-fifties and married to a younger female firefighter, Coburn was somebody who'd worked with my father and told me things nobody else ever did. I liked him. A lot. The fall killed him.

I was in a pretty bad mood when Hertlein arrived back at

the station just after we did and made a tasteless joke about Coburn's voluptuous wife needing a fireman to "comfort" her now that she was a widow, illustrating with a crass sexual gesture involving his meaty hand and thick hips. It was the type of thing Hertlein did all the time, though not usually under such dour circumstances.

I was the only one who thought to slug him. Or maybe we all thought of it and I was the only one with the guts to follow through.

You get an opportunity for a freebie with a guy like Bill Hertlein about once every hundred years, so I gave it everything I had.

Turned it into a work of art.

Hertlein, who was six feet and almost three hundred pounds, stagger-stepped away from my right cross, eyes rolling into his skull, his bulk striking the floor with a sickening thump that sounded like a waterlogged sofa falling off a truck. One member of my crew let out a barking laugh and then caught himself.

Flat on his back, Hertlein began snoring.

"He went down like a tree in a windstorm," said one of the medics, spitting a plum pit into the nearby garbage can.

"You really whacked him," said the other medic, sipping his tomato soup.

"It was a good one, all right," Donovan added, through a mouthful of mashed potatoes.

Rostow, who'd been out of the room when it started, felt the chief's body shake the building and rushed back to find five of us standing over Hertlein. "Tell me you didn't hit him," said Rostow. "Jesus. Boy, this is sure going to be the end of your career. Please tell me you didn't hit him."

I picked up my salad and walked over to the table with it.

One of the medics knelt to attend the chief and said, "It'll be interesting. Yeah, it'll be real interesting to see what they decide to do with this one."

2. THE GOD BLESS AMERICA FIREHOUSE AND LOUNGE

Chief Hertlein wanted to call in the cops but was soon talked out of it. The administration didn't want his comments about Coburn's widow to be made public. The witnesses were sworn to silence, in some cases threatened into it.

While the story changed from telling to telling, everybody knew I was now the department bad boy. For months afterward I was transferred from one station to the next. Perhaps because he'd been promoted and was using his newfound power to bounce me all over the city, to the rank and file Hertlein had become the goat and I the hero. The bad boy hero.

My current assignment was one I could walk to, Station 6, on the corner of Twenty-third and Yesler, catty-corner from the Douglass-Truth Library and directly west of the Catholic Community Services building. Six's was an Art Deco style firehouse with a stubby flagpole above the center of two bright red apparatus bay doors. At night neon lightning bolts above the doors dazzled children and drug addicts alike.

The building housed two units, Attack 6 and Ladder 3. I would be working on Ladder 3, my first truck assignment since June. I was ecstatic.

The north side of the bay housed the engine, the south side the truck, both pieces of apparatus stuffed into their tiny spaces like bratwurst into a glutton's mouth. From outside it didn't look as if either rig could squeeze through the doors.

I was placing my turnout boots-and-pants combo, coat, and helmet on the officer's side of the truck in the tight, shadowy quarters up against the south wall of the apparatus bay when a woman in uniform edged around the front of Ladder 3.

"Cindy Rideout," she said, sticking out her hand. "I'm here for my probationary truck work."

We shook. Her grip was soft and damp. "This your first shift in the station?" I asked.

"Yes, sir."

"Mine too." I smiled. Rideout was a Native American, five-eight or -nine, with black hair, eyes so dark they too looked black. She was pretty enough that the other guys in the barn were sneaking looks at her. "How long have you been in?"

"Almost four months, sir. I've been up at Thirteen's."

"Is that your permanent assignment?"

"It *was.* It looks like it might be up in the air now. Any special place you want me?"

Jeff Dolan, the driver, had just stepped up onto the running board alongside his seat and was making silly smiles at me across the engine compartment while pointing to a spot between us in the front where *nobody* ever rode.

"Ride behind me in the number three position," I said.

After we signed into the daybook in the watch office, Rideout and I inventoried the compartments one by one. The barn was humid and filled with the sounds from Twenty-third Avenue. A passing bus. Squawking kids on their way to school.

In the six months since the Ocean Pride fire and Coburn's funeral, I'd worked on all four shifts and in seven different stations, which had to be some sort of department record. I might have appealed for clemency to the chief of the department, but Hiram Smith, an alcoholic, was a man who surrounded himself with people whose job it was to keep him from looking inept, and it wasn't his practice to contradict the orders of the men who were actually running the department. The odds of him interceding were almost nil. Besides, I didn't want to give Hertlein the satisfaction of thinking he was anything but a tick on my thick hide.

And . . . I was beginning to grow fond of the notoriety.

There would be four of us riding Ladder 3. As lieutenant, I sat up front in the officer's seat next to Jeff Dolan, the driver; Mike Pickett, a seven-year firefighter, and the probie, Cindy Rideout, would ride in the jump seats behind us.

Sharing the station with Ladder 3 were the firefighters assigned to the engine, known as Attack 6: Lieutenant Stephen Slaughter, Bill Gliniewicz, and Zeke Boles. Slaughter was their ramrod. He and I had a mixed history. Gliniewicz was the driver on Engine 6 and Boles the tailboard man.

Gliniewicz and I had worked together a time or two. He was one of those people who never met anybody he couldn't say something bad about. All I knew about Boles was that he was rumored to be a crack addict and alcoholic. Slaughter had been my first officer in the department, which meant he'd taken up the approximate space in my life I would be taking up in Rideout's. His father and grandfather had both been firefighters, and he was about as gung ho as you could get and not be in an institution. I was pretty sure he had an American flag stuffed up his ass and chewed red, white, and blue gum. On September 12, 2001, as a tribute to the firefighters who'd died the day before, he'd had the initials NYFD tattooed on his left forearm. It wasn't until later that he learned New York's Fire Department goes by the initials FDNY. Nobody laughed about it, though. At least not to his face.

He was a hard man and intimidated people, including any number of chiefs. For reasons I never understood, he had written negative and what I believed were biased reports on me for a good long while as my first officer.

After the housework was done, I called Rideout into my office. It was a tiny room with a bed in the corner—uncomfortably intimate, with the rain beating on the windows and the dark skies outside. Rideout was a high-breasted, long-legged woman with fine copper skin who made me nervous as hell.

I told her the same thing I told every recruit I worked with. I told her how to stay alive. I told her she could increase her odds by staying hydrated and keeping physically fit. I told her what I expected from her. She listened and seemed eager to learn. Her probation would last another eight months, and for the time being I would be writing daily and monthly reports on her. It was a task I took seriously. If I let somebody through who wasn't right for the job, he or she might end up dead. I didn't want that on my conscience. And I didn't want me or anyone else to end up dead because of them either.

I told her what happened at the Mary Pang fire. What happened at the Leary Way fire. I told her about Coburn and the Ocean Pride fire last summer.

She held my look—confident, self-assured, without any real idea of what she was getting into. She had recently turned twenty-two.

"Any questions?" I asked when I was through.

"Sir? There've been some arsons in the past week. I'm just wondering . . ."

There had been half a dozen small fires in Station 6's district, mostly late at night. So far nobody was overly concerned. "Don't worry about it. We fight an arson fire just like we fight any other fire. We catch the guy. I break his neck. It's that simple." I grinned.

She laughed nervously.

"I just wonder about these arsons. What if it's a terrorist?"

"If terrorists were setting fires, they'd do a better job than these piddly-ass calls. This is just some dingbat."

At that moment Lieutenant Slaughter poked his head in my door, smiled warmly, and said, "Hey, cocksucker."

"What's up, gramps?"

"So you finally decided to come where the action is?" It wasn't until he pushed the door open that Slaughter realized Rideout was in the room. "Sorry. I didn't see you. Excuse my French. Paul and I go way back."

"Steve was my first officer," I said. "He tried to can me."

"Bullshit. I was keeping you on your toes."

Slaughter stepped into the room, making it even smaller, and we all three looked at one another for an uneasy moment. I had the feeling from a fleeting look I saw behind his heavy glasses that Slaughter thought there was something illegitimate about my closed-door meeting with Rideout. There'd been male officers in the past who'd harassed female recruits, and I knew of at least one woman who got her job by sleeping with an officer. There'd been women on the receiving end of bad reports who claimed the officers evaluating them tried to pressure them into having sex. These were by no means common problems, but we'd all heard the stories.

"You'll both like this station," Slaughter said. "We're busy. We do our work, but we have a lot of fun too. We call it the God Bless America Firehouse and Lounge."

Rideout laughed. I said, "We heard you've been having some arson fires."

"Nuisance crap. It's not like when Paul Keller was running around. Or the other one, the one we never caught."

Slaughter was a big man, imposing, six feet, 250 pounds, with thick, black-framed glasses, a shock of brown hair, bushy eyebrows, and a walrus mustache he let creep over his lip. He was a firefighter's firefighter and had the kind of face advertisers slapped on fire appliance calendars.

Before we could continue our conversation, the station alerter went off. At Six's the engine got more calls than the truck, but this one was for us.

It was a water job.

3. FIRST SHIFT AT SIX'S

Cynthia Rideout

DECEMBER 5, THURSDAY, 2331 HOURS

As far as I know, everybody else in the station is asleep. I can hear Zeke Boles snoring on the other side of the lockers. Poor Zeke. Slaughter and Gliniewicz had worked themselves into a lather by the time Zeke finally walked in at 0835, almost an hour late. Apparently this isn't the first time they had to call Zeke at home.

After he got here, some chiefs from downtown showed up and they all went back in the engine office. He ended up working the shift and getting disciplinary charges for a failure to report. Zeke seems to be a gentle, kindhearted man. People say he has a drug problem, but I think they're just saying that because he's always late and he's black.

When they all went into the office, Mike Pickett, my partner on Ladder 3, griped that we were going to catch some of their aid alarms because the engine wouldn't be in service to take them. I never dreamed there were firemen who didn't want alarms.

The unofficial department policy is that firefighters can go to bed after ten at night, but Jeff Dolan, our driver, was asleep by nine-thirty. He's the hardest worker on the crew and pretty much does what he wants. Pickett was on the phone all evening, so I have no idea when he turned in. Pickett seems to be Ladder 3's resident complainer. He and Bill Gliniewicz, the driver on Engine 6, bitch for hours on end.

I can't sleep. I'm in the bunk room tucked up in the corner of my bunk against the wall. I can hear the wind in the bushes outside my window. It's a cozy little walk-in cubicle about the size of a jail cell. I never would have thought a shift with no fires and only two alarms could wear me out, but being a probie is no picnic.

This morning when I got here at a quarter to seven, I ran into Katie Fryer in the beanery. I knew there were women working in the station, but I didn't expect a giant. She's six-three or -four, and I hate to think how much she weighs. After she left this morning, I heard a couple of men on our shift making jokes about her breasts. My guess is they've been making those same jokes the entire eight years she's been here.

Katie has this affected way of speaking that almost makes her seem retarded. It's tricky to describe. She reminds me of someone who's been raised by very old grandparents and has adopted their speech patterns.

"Listen," she whispered. "We've got fifteen minutes before the night watch opens that door, so I'm going to fill you in. This is a man's world, but you can fit in if you take into account a few basics. The first thing you have to remember is you're not a man. I know that sounds moronic, but we've had women here who thought they had to undress in front of men. Thought they had to curse like the men. Always keep your dignity. The second thing—they sent you down here to fire you."

Her last statement shocked me. My first monthly report at the end of November hadn't exactly been glowing, but nobody'd mentioned termination.

Now that I've been moved to Six's, the December report is going to be written by Lieutenant Wollf, and I figured things would get better.

I stared into Katie Fryer's eyes and said, "*Every*body in my class is doing three months on a truck company."

"Listen, honey. Wollf never worked here before you showed up. They brought him in to terminate your sweet ass. That's what he does. Wollf fired a woman recruit last year. They sent you here so he could fire you too."

"But the union. The civil service regulations. They have to be fair."

"That's right. There are rules, and trust me when I tell you they know them a hell of a lot better than you do. You got a bad report from Galbraithe, right?"

"Those reports were supposed to be confidential."

"Nothing's confidential in the fire department. Last year one of the deputy chiefs went to bed with a secretary in the FMO. Wanna know what they had for breakfast? Honey, this is a fire department. It's a gossip factory. I haven't even come to Wollf yet. Paul Wollf is a badass right out of . . . who was that bozo who wrote *The Three Musketeers*?"

"Alexandre Dumas."

"Right. He's right out of one of those comic books. You never met anybody like him. His father burned up in a house fire right here in our district. When Paul Wollf was a boot out at Thirteen's, he saved three lives in a furniture warehouse factory. About the biggest hero we ever had. He beat up a chief last summer and got away scot-free. All you need to know is Wollf eats recruits raw and spits 'em out before breakfast. Hey, listen. I'm not telling you this to scare you. What you have to do here is go out and do the best job you're capable of. That's what'll get you through. And remember. Don't make excuses when you screw up. Somebody asks you to do something, do it. Pitch in whenever there's *any* work to be done. Be aggressive at fires. Push people out of the way if you have to. I mean that. This is one place where polite'll get you fired. They're looking for aggression. People who can prove they're not afraid of anything. Elbows and assholes."

"But if this guy's here to fire me, what chance do I have?"

"Like I said. The two things they're worried about with women is strength and fear. Pretend you're fearless even when you're staring the Antichrist in the eye. Hey. That's not bad. I think I'll write that one down. And trust me, sweetie, that's who you've got for a lieutenant—the Antichrist. You get in trouble, call me. Us girls have to back each other up."

"Thanks, Katie."

Despite what Fryer told me, everybody on C-shift treated me well all day, including Lieutenant Wollf. Then again, they treated me well up at Thirteen's and that didn't stop them from writing a nasty report on me.

Lieutenant Wollf has a direct quality, a way of staring at you with those blue eyes that's almost like a movie star. I mean, he's that self-assured. He's not a pretty boy, but with that curly black hair and those eyes, he has some charm in spite of never showing his emotions. He's six-four or -five and has a large, open face. You can tell exactly what he looked like as a little boy.

The lieutenant on the engine, Slaughter, has twenty-five years in the department, has been to all the big fires, and says things like, "He doesn't show up in a few minutes, I'm going to my locker and get a can of whup-ass."

Station 6 is a small cream-colored firehouse built around a double apparatus bay. On one side of the apparatus bay you have the watch office and the kitchen, which in the Seattle Fire Department they always call the beanery. There's a chrome island with a gas range. Two refrigerators. A TV mounted on the wall.

Crammed into the apparatus bay behind the engine there's a workbench area, the officers' rest room, a storage room for our bunking boots, the two officers' rooms, the hose tower, and a small inspection room with a computer, a printer, and file cabinets.

On the south side of the app bay is a long, narrow bunk room split up into little cubicles without doors. The bunks are separated by tall lockers. My bunk is directly across from the women's head at the front of the station. Bill Gliniewicz is in the corner bunk next to the door to the apparatus bay. On the other side of me is Zeke Boles. He's a whole chapter.

Downstairs is, believe it or not, a handball court. There's a study room with a second computer, a laundry room, and a carpeted weight room with weight benches, dumbbells, exercise bikes, a StairMaster, you name it. I went down there this afternoon and found Lieutenant Wollf working out. The amount of weight he was bench-pressing was obscene.

We only had two alarms today: a water job this morning, where we used the water vacs to suck dry the carpets in an apartment house after a pipe broke, and an aid call this afternoon. Meanwhile, despite being out of service for a couple of hours this morning over the Zeke fiasco, the engine went out nine times, every one either an aid or a medic run. Gliniewicz tells me that's a typical day around here.

Jeff Dolan and Mike Pickett like to say they're saving the truck for the important stuff.

4. TIPS ON APPROPRIATE CONDUCT AFTER YOU GET CAUGHT MASTURBATING IN TIMES SQUARE

According to Earl Ward

You want to be famous, it's simple, all you need is a book of matches and the willingness to spend the rest of your life in prison. Period.

I tell you this, but it's not the way I landed in the Powder River Correctional Facility and then later at the Oregon State Penitentiary in Salem.

I *will* tell you this: If I never spend another second in the august state of Oregon, it will be too soon.

Fire is what I know and fire is what I love, but fire is not why I spent the majority of my sorry life being Nelson's bitch; I almost wish it had been. On the other hand, had I gone into the joint as a firefly, they might have treated me worse.

What I got now, if you stop and think this through clearly, is my mother's 1976 Dodge Dart when she's not at work or out playing bingo or driving her idiot friends to doctors' appointments, a criminal record that keeps employers at bay, and a girlfriend named Jaclyn.

In some ways losing the right to vote is the worst. I think the Republicans are having a hard time, and every vote counts.

If things had worked out the way our dear Lord Jesus intended, I'd be riding one of those big red engines and nobody would have to worry about me walking up a dark alley with a book of matches. It's *their* fault, not mine. What I really wanted to be, from the time I was two, and what I should have been, was first and foremost—a firefighter. You look at things from that perspective, it's their fault. Everything. Period.

Seems like nobody's ever been fair with me.

And now this hassle with Jaclyn.

We were in the caretaker's house, Jaclyn and me, behind the main house, at the back of the garden. It was wet outside but it wasn't raining. From time to time you could see the moon poking through the clouds. Eight days I'd been free. Each day a small miracle.

"Get out of my house," said Jaclyn. "Who told you to come sniffing around here at midnight?"

"It's not midnight. It's eleven-thirty."

"Okay. Who told you to come at eleven-thirty?"

It would be the third time she'd thrown me out of her place in a week.

Jaclyn Dahlstrom. Late twenties, blond from a bottle, sexy like a cheap porno mag you find alongside the road. Likes to write prisoners. Hell, I was the one who got her this job, taking care of the old woman. Mom told me about it and I told her. Then when I showed up last week, all she did was laugh and throw me out.

"You come here at eleven-thirty and bother me when Leno's about to come on. And God help your sorry ass if you woke up Mrs. Pennington. You didn't ring her bell, did you?"

"I didn't wake up anybody."

"Jesus Christ. Look at that. You made me miss the monologue. Now he's going to a commercial."

"I thought we were going to have something between us. You and me. Something—"

"What we had was a bunch of letters. And you lied in those letters. You said you were in for murder."

"I *was* in for murder."

"What? You run over a chipmunk with your mother's car? Listen, punky. There's *nothing* between us. So get out."

"I don't get it. You were flirting with me before."

"I get so tired of people saying I'm a flirt. What did I do that you interpreted as flirting?"

"For one thing, you asked me how much I would pay to see you naked."

"And you said you didn't have any money. That wasn't flirting. That, my friend, was an aborted business transaction."

"Jaclyn." She went over to the dark window where light from the courtyard fell on her hair and about took my breath away. "I didn't have any money. But I do now."

"I'm not going out with somebody who doesn't have two nickels to rub together. How much do you have?"

"Jesus, Jaclyn. How much does a guy need? What if I were to ask my mother for money?"

She tapped her bare foot on the floor and stared a hole through me. Even her feet were pretty, the toenails painted crimson. "How old are you, Earl?"

"What do you mean?"

"It's not a trick question. Just answer."

"Forty-four."

"You're forty-four years old, and you still have to ask your mother for money?"

"I—"

"Do you realize how pathetic that is?"

"Jaclyn . . ."

A minute later I was in the Pennington garden looking up at the lighted window in the caretaker's house.

That's the thing with beautiful women. Their lives are too damn easy. She wouldn't have it too easy if I went back up there and fucked her. I could do that. I could stomp back up those stairs and kick the door in. I know how to fuck somebody. That's one thing you learn in prison. Boy, wouldn't she be sorry? I could wear a mask. I could put a hood over my face. Maybe a paper bag. They'd never prove it was me.

Except I don't have a paper bag.

I walk over to the shadows by the side of the house and wait under Jaclyn's window, the big house behind me dark and quiet.

I'm where I've been many times before, alone, in the shadows, crying.

After a while it starts to sprinkle.

Getting spotted lighting a fire—it's a little like getting caught masturbating in public. *You* know you were doing it and *they* know you were doing it, but when you get hauled up in front of the judge, you're going to say you weren't and they know you're going to say you weren't. It's the nature of the beast.

It's always so simple.

A book of matches and the willingness to light something. That's all *I* ever had.

Period.

I got a whole scrapbook from my merrymaking. A scrapbook and then some. 'Course, I was famous and anonymous at the same time, and that last part hurt. I never wanted to be anonymous. For a while there I had the fire department running around like the Easter bunny with a dog after it. It was funny, though. Not ha-ha funny but funny in a way that makes you put your hands in your pockets and smile.

From my point of view lighting things always makes everything better. Been doing it since I was a tyke.

I look down at my Bic lighter. I flick it open and stare.

Amazing. There isn't anything like it. I mean, take water. You can't start out with a drop of water and end up with an ocean, now can you?

There is a newspaper recycle bin next to the big house, and from this bin I remove last Sunday's paper. I tear a strip off and light it. Then another. The flames are comforting. In the drizzle I feel the heat on my face.

The house behind me is two stories plus, with basement window wells. I step into one of the wells and push the window open with my foot.

The room beyond the pane is dark. I tear off a strip of newspaper, light it, and let it drop inside.

I pull the basement window shut. Looking back at the cottage, I watch the blue light from a television set and wait.

5. NOTHING VISIBLE

It was half past midnight when the house bells and lights woke me. At the front of the apparatus Rideout was getting into her bunking coat when I squeezed past.

It was a "reported Dumpster fire—possibly spreading to the building." Twenty-third and Cherry.

Gliniewicz pulled Engine 6 out of the station and raced down the street while Jeff Dolan held Ladder 3 close behind, bitching that Gliniewicz was driving too fast. At Twenty-third and Cherry we found nothing but wet streets and a minimart on the corner. No smoke or fire. By the look of the streets, it had been raining hard, water puddling in the ripples in the roadway.

Slaughter gave a brief radio report. "Attack Six at Twenty-three Avenue and East Cherry Street. Nothing visible. Investigating. Let's code yellow all incoming units until we find out what's going on."

The dispatcher said, "Okay, Attack Six. Nothing visible.

Investigating. All units responding to Twenty-three Avenue and East Cherry—code yellow."

My father had worked these same streets. He must have felt, as I did, that there was nothing stranger than waking out of a deep sleep and racing down the street on a thirty-ton rig, red lights and sirens blaring. It was one of the reasons I loved the job.

The first call was a false alarm, but before we got back to the station we responded to three more fire calls, all arsons. One was a tree fire. Attack 6 caught a fence fire. We caught a garbage can on fire behind a residence. When Pickett and Rideout came around the truck with pump cans, I watched Rideout make a point of getting water on the fire first. I liked that.

We ended up missing two more fires while we waited for an investigator. There'd been multiple arsons in this part of town over the last week, and the department's investigative arm, Marshal 5, wanted to see every one of them.

"Who do you think's setting all these fires?" Rideout asked.

"Probably some probationary firefighter who wasn't getting enough action," Dolan teased.

At two A.M. Marshal 5's investigator arrived, a woman named Connor. After she snapped her photos and poked around, we headed back to the station, where Rideout and Dolan refilled the pump cans and pressurized them, Pickett went to bed, and I wrote the fire report on the computer in the cramped inspection room just outside my office.

Thirty seconds after my head touched the pillow the house lights came on again, the big bell on the apparatus floor clanged, and we heard the dispatcher over the station amplifier. "Porch fire. Flames showing."

"I get my hands on this arsonist, I'll fuck 'im up," said Dolan, using the steering wheel to pull himself up onto the rig. "I'll fuck him up good. We're supposed to be in bed."

6. YOU BE BURNIN' ME OUTTA MY HOME

Both rigs were fired up and everybody was on board except Zeke Boles. For whatever reason, Boles hadn't reported to the apparatus floor, and now Slaughter and Gliniewicz were shouting his name in an attempt to wake him up.

Their efforts might have been more effective if one of them had gone to the bunk room to get Boles, but they preferred to sit on the rig screaming until their neck veins bulged and their mustaches twitched. Being effective was not their goal. This was about enjoying their rage, and I had the impression they both relished the sight of a black man screwing up.

"Let's go," I said to Dolan, even though by the book we were supposed to follow behind the quicker engine.

It was a porch fire on Thirty-first Avenue South. We were the first firefighters on the scene, but there wasn't much we could do except mark the location and give a radio report. Ladder 3 carried almost no water. We had the hundred-foot aerial built into our truck, half a dozen ground ladders, hundreds of tools, pry bars, machinery of all sorts, ropes for high angle rescue, so much equipment the apparatus compartments could barely contain it, but only five gallons of water in two pump cans.

"Ladder Three at eighteen twelve Thirty-one Avenue South," I said into the black telephone-style handset. "We have a preconnect porch fire attached to a two-story wood-frame residence approximately thirty by forty. Engine Thirty, on your arrival lay a preconnect. Ladder Three is doing search and rescue."

I turned around and looked at Pickett and Rideout. "Make sure everybody's out. Take the thermal imager to see if the fire has spread. Rideout, take the irons."

As I spoke, Engine 30 rolled up from the other direction.

Two men climbed down out of Engine 30's crew cab, ran around to the back of the apparatus to pull out the two-hundred-foot 1¾-inch preconnected line, and tapped the fire, all in less than ninety seconds.

When an elderly Filipino man and woman emerged from the house in their pajamas, Rideout escorted them down the concrete stairs so they would be safe from the hose stream.

My guess was the perp was still somewhere in the neighborhood. Two vehicles had driven past: a station wagon with a family in it, and a young man and woman in a Jeep, who looked as if they were coming home from a date—if people still dated these days. *I* didn't. Not like that.

The fire was out and we were regrouping when the dispatcher sent Attack 6 and Ladder 3 to Thirtieth Avenue South and South Judkins, mere blocks away.

Attack 6 took off and a minute later we found them on Thirtieth South parked in front of a fence fire. Zeke Boles was using a pump can to put water on the flames. Had this been your first glimpse of him, you might have thought he was firefighter of the year.

"Damn! Look at that," Pickett said.

"That's Zeke," Dolan said. "Fall asleep in his spaghetti one minute, save your life the next."

While we were mopping up and talking to neighbors, Engine 30 was dispatched to a residence a block or two west of the original call on Thirty-first. It was clear our fire-setter was still working the area.

"Don't this bastard ever sleep?" Dolan asked.

"I don't get it," Rideout said. "Why would somebody go around lighting fences and porches?"

"So this is how many tonight?" Dolan asked. "Six? Six." He turned to Rideout with a glint in his eye. "Hey, little girl. This the first time you ever had six arson fires in one night? The probie buys ice cream for every first."

"My name is Rideout."

Dolan grinned. "Okay. But you owe us ice cream."

"If you say so."

Engine 30 came on the radio. "Engine Thirty. We have a fully involved car fire. No exposures. Laying a preconnect."

"Okay, Engine Thirty," said the dispatcher. "Fully involved car fire. Preconnect."

"We're going to be up all night," said Pickett. "I got a golf game tomorrow morning."

Minutes later Battalion 5's Suburban pulled up and Chief Johnson asked us to return to the first alarm on Thirty-first to pick up Engine 30's hose line, which they'd abandoned when they got the car fire. We were shoulder loading and draining it when Attack 6 was dispatched to a garage fire down the hill on Lake Washington Boulevard South. Moments later the dispatcher added us to the alarm.

Until now we'd been saved by luck, insomnia, and drivers with cell phones. But there was no guarantee the next fire would be spotted in time. Most of the city was asleep. Any wall fire could spread to the eaves, flash through the attic, destroy a house before the family inside could roll out of bed. What we had here was a murderer looking for victims. The thought made my blood boil. I'd always hated arsonists, but this was the first time I'd run up against one this bold.

Our garage fire was "out by occupant" when we got there.

We were on our way back to the station when we ran into the biggest fire of the night quite by accident. As we were driving past, we spotted some orange light flickering off the walls of a nearby house.

"Sonofabitch!" said Dolan.

As we pulled around the corner and headed down the residential block under the trees, a thick pall of smoke hung in the street. "How the hell did they miss this?" Dolan asked. "Attack Six must have driven right past it."

"They were probably busy yelling at Zeke," said Pickett.

The fire was in a garage directly across from a nursing home on a little-traveled street.

I called it in on the radio, asked for a full response, and told Dolan to park in front of the nursing home, where we wouldn't be blocking the hydrant or any other incoming units.

There were two large houses on the south face of the block, with a garage between them at the top of a long driveway. Black smoke was boiling from under the eaves of the garage.

"I'm going to the roof," Dolan said, as I came around the front of Ladder 3.

"Take Rideout with you. Let her cut the hole." Pickett had rendered himself useless by running up to the fire building for a gander, "scouting," he would explain later when I chewed him out. "You and I'll carry a ladder," I said to Rideout.

Across the street Attack 6 pulled around the corner and Gliniewicz jumped out so quickly he fell onto his hands and knees. I'd noticed earlier he was excitable on alarms. Slaughter was already screaming at Zeke Boles. "God damn it, Zeke! Where the fuck are you? I said preconnect. When I say preconnect that means you get the preconnect. Are you deaf, man? Jesus Christ. Do I have to do everything for you? You want me to wipe your behind too? You like four squares or do you want me to shove the whole goddamn roll up your ass?"

Even though he was already one jump ahead of his officer, you could see Zeke beginning to buckle under the abuse. I had never had that reaction when I was a rookie working under Slaughter. I'd been as close to clobbering him those first few times he screamed at me as I'd been to clobbering anyone. Fortunately I hadn't, or I would have lost my job. His yelling on the fire ground was odd behavior for somebody who prided himself on being so reasonable and measured around the station.

Rideout and I slid the heavy three-section, thirty-five-foot ladder from the rear ladder compartment on Ladder 3 and walked across the street with it. Avoiding both windows on the side of the oversized garage, we dropped the spurs into the flower bed and I steadied the ladder from one side while Rideout stood on the other and tugged on the halyard to raise the sections. I'd given her the fly side to test her strength. A lot of people weren't strong enough to raise the flies on a thirty-five-foot ladder. Others were strong enough during daylight hours but couldn't do it in the middle of the night. Rideout raised it without a hitch.

In front of the garage Slaughter and Zeke were straightening the kinks in a two-hundred-foot section of hose Zeke had laid from the engine. Through the smoky opening I saw two automobiles. You could hear glass breaking, the crackle of fire, a popping sound as a can of paint exploded. Inside sat a Fifties-era Buick, pristine and shiny. Another automobile looked to be a decade older: whitewall tires, running boards, and a suicide door—collector's items.

Taking a lungful of black smoke, I shouldered the heavy door open. Zeke opened the task force tip on his 1¾-inch line and threw a spray of water into the interior.

"What the hell are you doing?" Slaughter barked. "You see any fire? You see anything? You don't just go squirting at smoke. Look for the seat of the fire."

Chief Johnson showed up a moment later, his words muffled by the yowling of the chain saw on the roof. "Who called this in?"

"We did," I said. "We spotted it from the road."

Even if we lost control of the garage fire, which was not going to happen, the only other building in immediate danger was the residence to the west. The larger residence to the east was separated by the driveway and a small garden embroidered with ivy.

"What the hell's going on? I been hearing sirens all night, and now you people be burnin' me outta my home." A large, angry-looking man climbed the slope of the driveway.

"You'll have to go back, sir," said Chief Johnson. "This area is under fire department jurisdiction."

"That's my home next door there. My wife's over there right now coughin' her fool head off 'cause of the smoke. Whatsa matter wi' you people?" He'd been drinking.

"Sir," Johnson said. "We didn't start this."

"You tryin' to say *I* did?"

"Sir, you're going to have to leave this area until we get things under control."

I found Rideout at the base of the ladder we'd put up. "Why aren't you opening the roof?"

"Pickett said we were switching partners."

"He said what?"

"He said we were switching partners, that he and Dolan were opening the roof."

7. I KNEW HE KNEW I KNEW IT

Dolan and Pickett cut a hole in the roof, heavy black smoke pouring out as soon as it was open. They climbed down just as the officer from Engine 10 rushed up to Chief Johnson and said, "Chief, we got a report of a fire on the other side of the block."

"Go check it out," said Johnson, a battalion chief who had a reputation as a nervous Nellie, a man who followed the book so closely that when something came up that wasn't in it he was struck dumb.

While Johnson was mulling things over, a large maroon Chevrolet with three radio antennae pulled up. Chief William Hertlein was driving.

The last time I'd seen Hertlein, he was flat on his back on the beanery floor at Station 32.

For almost half a minute Hertlein didn't look at anything on the fire ground except me. No matter what he said, no matter how much power he thought he had, he was afraid of me. He knew it. I knew it. And he knew I knew it. A muscle under his right eye twitched. I almost expected the scene to start moving in slow motion, a haunting musical score building to a crescendo in the background: department bad boy faces down the chief who wants to oust him.

Hertlein abruptly turned to Chief Johnson. "What's going on, Joe?"

Engine 10 came on the radio and said they had a tapped exterior wall fire on the other side of the block, then asked for a thermal imager. After exchanging looks with Johnson, I sent Dolan and Pickett around the block with our thermal imager. "Radio if you need something," I said.

The thermal imager was a handheld camera that registered heat in the viewfinder. You could direct it at a row of parked cars and tell which had been driven recently by the warmth of the hoods. In fact, the imager was sensitive enough to trace someone walking barefoot across a tile floor by footprints invisible to the naked eye. In a smoke-filled atmosphere you could spot victims or fallen firefighters. These days it was the standard tool for search-and-rescue teams.

An immense, three-story house loomed to the east. A smaller, raised cottage I hadn't noticed earlier stood at the rear of the property behind a courtyard and beyond the smoldering garage. Because of the slope and angle of the driveway, the cottage was invisible from the street.

A blond woman in tight pants and a sleeveless blouse was watching us from the cottage porch. I took a couple of steps in her direction, gestured at the main house and said, "Anybody inside?"

"My boss."

"Just one person?"

"Yeah."

"Is he home tonight?"

"She. I guess so."

The house was dark. "She a sound sleeper?"

"Usually."

I strode through a patch of wet ivy and knocked on a back door. I knocked again. "Let's go around," I said to Rideout.

Lieutenant Slaughter shouted at me as we rounded the corner of the house, "Hey! Aren't you going to help with these cars? We got a salvage job going on here, buddy."

Ignoring him, we walked around to the front of the house and found a covered wooden porch overlooking Frink Park and Lake Washington. I knocked on the front door. The windows were dark.

Chief Hertlein pulled up in the street, waiting for me to do something wrong while drizzle speckled his windshield. Once again I knocked on the front door. Rideout rapped on a window. "Hello. Hello in there," she called.

I looked at Rideout. "You smell smoke?"

"The whole neighborhood smells like smoke."

I put a flashlight up against the window, then stepped back and kicked the front door three times before the frame split and the door shuddered open. Somewhere behind me I heard Chief Hertlein yelling to stop. The foyer was filled with smoke, so we couldn't see more than eight feet. When he saw the smoke, Chief Hertlein announced over his radio that he had located a fully involved house fire just west of the garage fire, that he wanted a second full response.

"Cover," I said to Rideout.

"My mask?"

"Yeah. Cover. The neighbor said there's somebody in there. We have to move."

We were entering the residence when Chief Hertlein approached the front porch. "Stop! You can't go in there. You have to wait for a hose line."

"There's a victim inside. She'll be dead if we wait," I said.

"I'm telling you to wait."

I looked at Rideout and spoke softer so the chief couldn't hear. "It's your choice. Come in with me or stand out here while the lady dies."

"He said to stay out," she replied through her mask.

"I can't hear him."

I'd placed her in an interesting moral dilemma. Obey the orders of her immediate supervisor who was looking for a fire victim, or obey the chief of fire department operations. She followed me.

I had a battle lantern in one hand, was feeling along the wall with the other, doing what we called a right-hand search, going in right, following the wall. In short order I knocked over a table of some sort, heard a vase shattering, then bumbled into what must have been a hat stand. I touched Rideout's shoulder and told her to go left, which she did. I heard more glass breaking on her side of the hallway. The thermal imager would have been invaluable, but Dolan and Pickett had it.

I couldn't see her flashlight and she probably couldn't see mine. The smoke wasn't hot and didn't appear to be moving, and we were breathing compressed air off our regulators, so we weren't in any immediate danger. It was the homeowner who was in trouble.

It was only when I realized how large the house was that I told Rideout we were backing out.

Hertlein was gone when we got outside. "Go get a fan," I said.

Unclipping her high-pressure air supply hose from her face piece, Rideout left the yard at a jog trot while I radioed King Command, as Chief Johnson had designated himself, that Ladder 3 was at the house due east of the fire building, that it was full of smoke, and we were initiating a search.

Waiting for Rideout, I made a couple of quick reconnoiters left and right of the front door, and managed to find a staircase and get back to the door before Rideout showed up dragging the wheeled gasoline-powered fan up the stairs. I helped her get it onto the porch and told her to fire it up. Chief Hertlein must have followed her because he was on the sidewalk looking up at me.

"What are you doing?" Hertlein yelled.

"I think he's talking to you," Rideout said.

"Fire it up."

"I think he's talking to you."

I looked down at the sidewalk, knowing Hertlein wouldn't understand a word I said over the noise of the fan. She fired it up and I said, "He's a fuckin' idiot." Hertlein yelled something long and complicated, but neither of us could hear a word over the fan, which sounded like an airplane motor. Rideout placed the fan an appropriate distance from the doorway and reattached her supply hose to her face piece.

According to common SFD practice, we should have first ensured an exit for the smoke before firing it up, yet there was an easier—though frowned upon—method. Fire up the fan and watch the smoke. An experienced firefighter could tell within seconds if there was an outlet for the smoke elsewhere in the building. If there was no exit, the building didn't clear. But it *was* clearing. So there *was* an open door or window elsewhere in the structure.

Hertlein was headed up the concrete steps with surprising agility for a three-hundred-pound man when I grabbed Rideout and pulled her inside. We found a carpeted stairway and took it up into the grayness. The second floor was huge: three, maybe four bedrooms, two baths, a room that appeared to be a sewing or wardrobe room, a guest suite, all of it empty. There was more smoke up here, but it was moving around now because of the fan. I could see the dim light from a Tiffany lamp in the hallway.

The third floor was smokier, which probably meant our open window was on the second floor.

In a bedroom on three we found an enormous canopied bed with a body in it. Under the glow from my battle lantern we saw a raven-haired woman, nude, a wineglass next to several pill bottles on the night table.

"Ma'am," I said, shaking her gently. "Wake up. Ma'am." She didn't wake up, not then and not when I shook her more forcefully. There was no telling how long she'd been in this smoke.

"Chair carry?" Rideout asked.

"No. I've got her. Just walk in front and make sure I don't trip."

"I can help."

"I have her."

I pulled a sheet off the bed and wrapped her, then scooped her into my arms. Maybe it was because I could no longer direct the beam of the battle lantern, but I had trouble finding my way out of the room. It seemed smokier than it had a minute earlier. Rideout was confused too and opened a closet door thinking it led to the corridor.

The woman was limp and fragile in my arms. I had her under the knees and armpits, carrying her in front of me like a baby. Her heavy head lolled against my shoulder. To her credit, Rideout spoke over her portable radio, "King Command. This is Ladder Three. We're bringing a victim out of the house on the east corner. We'll need a medic unit."

"Ladder Three? Did you say you had a victim?" It was Chief Johnson.

"That's affirmative," Rideout answered.

The smoke was thicker in the corridor as we felt our way down the stairs. Somewhere on the second floor the victim awoke briefly and launched into a coughing fit, then just as quickly lapsed back into unconsciousness.

8. TIG OLD BITTIES

We got turned around on the second floor. It didn't take long to get straightened out, but the woman in my arms didn't need any more smoke. I'd been hoping to be out of the house in sixty seconds, but a minute had passed and we were still goofing around on the second floor where the smoke was even denser than it had been on our way up. The smoke and gases had thickened and we were blind now, working from memory.

At last, with great caution, we found and descended the final flight of stairs, Rideout in front, her hand on the victim, guiding me step by step.

Halfway down the staircase I realized why our visibility had decreased. The fan was no longer running. To make matters worse, the front door had closed on us. By this time the woman was beginning to sag in my arms. We wore close to fifty pounds of gear. This woman weighed 130, easy, so here I was carrying 180 pounds at three in the morning.

When we finally got the door open and stepped out past the dead fan on the porch, it was raining. Huddled under the hoods of their foul-weather jackets, two fire department paramedics waited in the street with a gurney. They had a yellow disposable blanket over the gurney to keep the bedding dry. A civilian with a news camera hustled toward us from Jackson Street. Zeke Boles stood at the bottom of the steps in full turnout gear, looking disheveled and confused.

The sheet had slipped off our patient's shoulders so that her torso was bare from the navel up. Rideout flipped the sheet back over her. I recognized this woman, but I couldn't quite think of where I knew her from.

Judging by the wrinkled flesh of her arms and lower neck, she was in her late seventies or early eighties, though her breasts looked as if they belonged on a porno queen. Her lips had been pumped up with silicone too. You could see where her neck had been tucked and tightened, the skin around her brow and ears pulled unnaturally tight.

At the bottom of the stairs I startled Zeke by placing the victim in his arms—then headed back up the stairs. The cameraman began taking pictures of Zeke with the woman.

Rideout followed me.

"What happened to the fan?" she asked.

I leaned over and checked the settings—it had been shut off. I pulled the cord and it fired up.

We'd searched all of floor two but only one bedroom on three. It would be a lousy deal to save one victim only to have another die somewhere else in the house. Because the smoke was quickly dissipating under the pressure from the fan, we raced through the first floor. In the kitchen when I took hold of the cut-glass knob and opened a basement door, a cloud of dirty smoke smooched my face like a drunken lover. It was the first warm smoke I'd felt in this house. I closed the door. We had a basement fire.

It wasn't much, because a good fire would have blown me across the room.

"Upstairs," I said to Rideout.

"But the fire."

"We'll finish our search. People first. House second."

We raced up two flights of stairs. I was moving as quickly as I could without breaking into a full sprint, gasping for breath. Rideout's alarm bell began ringing just as we reached the third floor landing. Despite the fan, it was smoky enough up here that we had to search each room by walking around it. Two bedrooms, a bath, and some sort of sitting room. All empty.

We were downstairs and back out on the wet sidewalk when *my* warning bell began ringing. Over my portable radio I said, "King Command from Ladder Three. Secondary search all clear."

The dispatcher replied, "Secondary search all clear, Ladder Three. Did you receive, King Command?"

The medics had wheeled our patient away, and now a bewildered Zeke Boles was standing in the lights of a news camera while a woman with a microphone shot questions at him.

Engine 25 was rolling up the street. When the officer jogged up to me to ask what was going on, I said, "Basement fire. Everybody's out. The door is in the kitchen in the back. The smoke didn't seem that hot."

"Okay." The captain turned around and began shouting orders to the three men on his rig.

Rideout and I went back to Ladder 3 to exchange our empty air bottles for full ones. A medic unit was parked catty-corner from our ladder compartment in back, the rear doors cracked open. I stepped inside and spoke to the medics for a few moments, then to the old woman, who had regained partial consciousness.

I was kneeling on the wet street changing my air bottle for a fresh one when I looked up and saw Hertlein beside me. "That was the worst display of firefighting I've seen in ten years," Hertlein said.

"How do you figure?"

"To start off with, you never, *ever,* go into a house fire in front of a hose line. That's how people get hurt."

"If we waited for a hose line every time, we'd never get *anyone* out."

"That's bullshit. I told you not to go into that house."

"Did you? I didn't hear."

"Did *you* hear me?" Hertlein said, looking at Rideout.

Rideout stared at the chief and then at me. It was a few seconds before she replied, her tone apologetic. "Sir. The fan was so loud I honestly couldn't catch what you said."

This clearly was not the answer Hertlein wanted, but there wasn't much he could do about it. I said, "You runnin' that fire over there, or did you bring in somebody who knows what they're doing?"

"If you're such hot shit," Hertlein said, walking away, "how come Boles made the rescue?"

After Hertlein was out of earshot, Rideout said, "But *you* carried her out."

"Don't worry about it."

By the time we got back to the house on the corner, Engine 25's crew was dragging a smoky mattress out the back door of the basement, throwing it down alongside a second smoldering mattress they'd already hauled out. Lieutenant Slaughter was hosing the burning materials down with a limp stream from his 1¾-inch line while firefighters began picking at the mattresses with knives to sort out the burning materials.

There had been two separate fires on this property, as well as a third fire on the other side of the block. We had a pyromaniac.

Steve Slaughter dropped the hose and threw a heavy arm over my shoulders. "By God, don't you and I make a team? Huh? We put out two fires with just our two rigs. And a rescue to boot, eh?"

"I guess—"

"You're just about twice the fire officer that Crocker was. God, he was in your spot two years, and it seemed like all he ever did was laugh like a hyena. I'm telling you, Paul, he just about drove me nuts. He wasn't too bad at a fire, but man, all that laughing."

I wasn't as certain as he was that we were a matched team. I'd been watching him all day and wasn't sure I liked what I saw. Around the beanery table he was calm and reasonable and had a story for every occasion, most of his tales well told and to the point. He wasn't even the hero of some of them. But at each of our fires he'd found a different reason to scream at the same people he worked so hard to charm in the beanery, as if yelling at a fire was the normal thing to do. I wondered if, when he was gracing us with tales of his exploits hunting elk, hooking salmon, and killing cougars, he wasn't leaving part of the story out—the part where he's screaming maniacally at his stunned prey or his hunting partners.

The shouting hadn't touched my crew yet, but I knew from discussions with Dolan and Pickett that it would, and when it did I'd have to decide what to do about it. For me, being around a volatile personality was worrisome, because even though I managed to keep it under wraps most of the time, when it came to the nitty-gritty, I was a lot more volatile than Slaughter ever dreamed of being.

What I knew about fire scenes was this: Yelling tended to

stifle communication. It inflamed the emotions and took the focus off the task at hand. Firefighting was a team effort, and teams worked best when they worked cohesively. A well-drilled crew of firefighters didn't need to be berated in public. Outwardly, Dolan, Pickett, Gliniewicz, Boles, and Slaughter all got along well, but I knew Dolan and Pickett seethed over indignities Slaughter had inflicted on them in the past, even though, as the Attack 6 officer, Slaughter had no real authority over them on the ladder truck.

When Jeff Dolan and Mike Pickett came back with the thermal imager, Dolan was angry because he'd missed the rescue on this side of the block. "It was out before we got there," he said. "They didn't even need an imager. It was just two shingles."

"I coulda pissed and put it out," said Pickett.

Dolan said, "You see the tig old bitties on that old lady in the back of the medic unit?"

Rideout remained silent. I said, "She took a lot of smoke. She might die."

"Oh, shit. Really?"

"You know what Chief Hertlein was doing out here, don't you?" Pickett said.

"What? What was he doing?" Rideout asked.

"Cruising for fires. He's trying to make himself look good in the papers. I never seen a firefighter wanted to be in the papers more than him."

"*We* found that fire," said Rideout. "The lieutenant did. The chief didn't even get out of his car."

"Ain't that a bitch?" Dolan reached down beside the rear duals on our rig. "Who the hell put this here?" It was a Shasta soda pop can, diet black cherry, the liquid sloshing around. He sniffed the opening, made a disgusted face, and heaved the can off toward the north end of the nursing home, where we heard it crash into the blackberries.

"What'd you do that for?" I asked.

"It was full of piss."

"Was it there when we pulled up?"

"No way."

"You sure?"

" 'Course I'm sure. The piss was still warm. I wonder who put it there."

An ugly feeling began to grow inside me.

9. MY BOSS'S BOSS'S BOSS

Cynthia Rideout

DECEMBER 6, FRIDAY, 0930 HOURS

We didn't get to bed until sometime after four in the morning, and then the engine got up at six for an aid call to one of the local nursing homes. Right now I'm running on adrenaline and coffee.

Wow.

Talk about a hayride down a mountain without brakes.

More has happened to me in the last twenty-four hours than happened all last year. I remember one of the lieutenants in our drill school saying not to get antsy about getting fires after we got out in the company, that sometimes a recruit went into the company and didn't get a fire for two or three months. That there were cases of recruits not having a fire their entire probationary year.

Last night we had seven. Granted, they weren't big fires, but Lieutenant Wollf and I made a rescue. My first shift on Ladder 3—A RESCUE!

Wollf took the whole thing in stride. He even thought it was funny the news people got mixed up and gave Zeke credit for the save.

I keep thinking about what Katie Fryer told me about Wollf coming to Station 6 to fire me. Two things worry me. No. Three.

Wollf didn't fill out his portion of the daily report yet. I'm worried the reason he didn't is because he wants to screw me over and he needs some time to think through the wording. He said he was going to wait and fill it out next shift, Sunday. But he also said I did good and that there wouldn't be any surprises.

On the other hand, that's pretty much the same thing Chief Eddings told me at Thirteen's, and look what she wrote.

I've been thinking about it, and here's what he might say. I don't know that he will, but this is what it could be:

(1) That I didn't set up the fan properly. I delayed starting it because Chief Hertlein was talking and I knew the moment I pulled the cord we wouldn't be able to hear him. Wollf seemed irritated with the delay. Then it shut off while we were inside. I suppose that's my fault too.

(2) The second negative Wollf might write about me concerns the rescue. When we got upstairs to the third floor and found the woman, I wanted to take her legs, at least—the easy end—but he brushed me off and picked her up in his arms like a baby.

So what did I do? I got all turned around. I took us into another bedroom and we bumped into things, and all this time that poor woman was getting sicker and sicker.

This morning the medics called and told us her CO readings had been high but not fatally high and that she was going to make it. I'm so glad.

(3) The roof. Wollf told Dolan to let me open the roof. But then Dolan went up with the chain saw before I could stop him! Pickett told me I was Wollf's partner, so I went to join Wollf. Later, I found out he made it up.

Pickett gave me a lot of tips yesterday, but the theme was basically that firefighting's a challenging job *most* people can't do. He never said I was *most* people, but I'm beginning to think that's what he meant.

The more I think about it, the more I think he saw a chance to step in front of me and make me look bad, and he went ahead and took it. I hope that's not true, because I don't want to be thinking bad thoughts about anybody and, in spite of all his pontificating, I was ready to like Pickett.

After the Engine 25 guys came out of the basement with the mattresses and determined there had been no extension to the house itself, Lieutenant Wollf and I finished ventilating the house. Those gas-powered fans have large wooden blades that move 22,000 cubic feet of air per minute. They blow air in a cone that spreads as it leaves the fan blade. The idea is to seal up the entrance point with the largest part of the cone. The house gets pressurized. It amounts to the same thing as trying to blow up a balloon. Except, obviously the walls of a house aren't going to stretch like a balloon. So now all that smoky air is looking for someplace to exit. You open an exit somewhere on the far side of the house and you watch all that smoke go shooting out.

Here's something funny. Wollf and I were in the hallway on the second floor, and he was looking at pictures on the walls and said, "Patricia Pennington."

"What?"

"I thought I recognized her. Patricia Pennington. She's an actress. Her career extended back to the Forties and Fifties."

Pennington had been featured in mostly B movies, Wollf said. She had dated some of the biggest male actors of all time. She'd even gone out with Howard Hughes. I think he was filthy rich.

He started naming her movies. I can't remember any of the titles, but he knew them all and all the leading men she costarred with. John Wayne, Robert Mitchum, Spencer Tracy, Mickey Rooney. Those are the names I recognized. It was weird the sudden surge in adrenaline I saw in him—the excitement—like nothing I'd seen during our fires. He handled those fires like they were piecework. But this!

I followed him to her bedroom, where he pointed out a poster for a movie called *River Brand Riders*. It must have been printed forty years ago. The date was at the bottom in

Roman numerals, but I didn't stop to figure it out. She costarred with John Payne and Andy Devine.

Wollf was examining the pill bottles and wine decanter on the bedside table. "Darvon. Taking this with wine would knock her out for a week. No wonder she couldn't wake up."

"You think there's an Academy award lying around here somewhere?" I asked.

"She never won an Academy award. She *was* on the list of top ten female performers three times in the early Forties. Then her career did a slow nosedive. Had a lot to do with the advent of television and the fact that they weren't making B movies for double bills anymore. She never quite made it onto the A-movie list."

Wollf knew every movie she'd ever been in, her marriages, divorces, costars. The affairs she'd had. Then, right before he clammed up, he told me the first personal information I'd heard out of his mouth all day. He said he had over eight thousand videos of old movies. That he'd collected every movie Patricia Pennington ever made. That he had every movie Marilyn Monroe made. Jane Russell. Clark Gable. Paul Newman. Joan Crawford. Bette Davis. Lon Chaney, whoever he was.

Remarkable. Under all that brawn and fire department professionalism there actually beats the heart of a human being.

We were really starting to get chummy, I thought. Wollf must have thought so too, because he stopped talking.

When we got back down to the first floor, a woman was waiting for us on the front porch. She'd obviously put herself together in a rush. She wore jeans and a white ski jacket and was a couple of years older than me.

"Hi," she said, looking at me instead of the lieutenant. Maybe she didn't realize the red helmet was the boss; the yellow helmet with the big recruit number fifteen on the back was the flunky. "I'm Vanessa Pennington. This is my grandmother's house. I just spoke to her in the medic unit. The chief said you might let me walk through the house?"

"I'd have to escort you," Wollf said.

Looking at her, you automatically thought money. Later we saw her driving a BMW, white to match her ski jacket. She had dirty-blond hair that fell to her shoulders. I could see right away she'd never make it in the fire department. She was too skinny. But she *was* pretty.

10. FIRE

Vanessa Pennington

It was just a good thing it was the middle of the night and there were no police cars around. The drive to Nanna's normally takes ten minutes, twenty if traffic is heavy, but I made it tonight in under seven.

I've been so worried about her lately, and then Jackie wakes me up to tell me Nanna's garage is on fire and what should she do. What should she do? This is just the kind of thing that makes me want to get Jackie out of there. "Call nine one one," I said. "I'm on my way." Later I find out she never did call 911. The fire department discovered the fire on their own. Jackie is such an incompetent. I'll never understand why Nanna doesn't fire her and hire a housekeeper and companion who isn't likely to get her killed.

There were so many fire department vehicles in the street I ended up parking half a block away. I found Nanna's front door broken open, the house full of firefighters and residual smoke. One of them told me I couldn't go in, that the fire department hadn't released the property back to the owners yet. When I asked where my grandmother was, a helpful black firefighter named Zeke told me she was in the medic unit with the man who'd rescued her.

When I got there I told them who I was, and they were kind enough to let me sit with her for a few minutes before they took her up to Harborview. Everybody was so nice. But when I asked permission to go inside and secure Nanna's things, I had to go through the chain of command, just like the army or something. They sent me to a lieutenant named Wollf, the same fire officer who'd been in the medic unit when I first got there. He'd been holding Nanna's hand. Nanna was barely conscious, and he was talking to her as if she were *his* grandmother and not mine. The sight impressed me more than I can say.

Later, he seemed inexplicably tense around me.

"Pardon me," I said. "I'm Patricia Pennington's granddaughter. They said you might take me inside the house?"

He seemed shy and tongue-tied. It was painful to watch—but cute too, especially for such a big, brawny guy. Finally he said if I could wait a minute he'd take me inside and show me what they'd broken. He must have seen the look on my face because he added, "Don't worry. It's not bad. The house is smoked up, but there's no structural damage."

A few minutes later he walked me through the house and explained where they'd found Nanna. He told me they would secure the front door and told me how to get the smoke out of the draperies and clothes. Never once did he mention anything about Nanna being famous, although the woman firefighter told me he knew.

I found myself drawn to him. He wasn't particularly handsome, but he had an open, boyish face that didn't hide what he was thinking. I like that in a man. I've always been attracted to shy men too. Perhaps because I used to be so shy.

After we'd gone down to the basement to check out the damage, I said, "Look, Lieutenant. My grandmother is going to want to do something for all of you who helped her tonight. That's how she is."

"We were just doing our job."

"It might be a job to you; it was my grandmother's life. They told me nobody even knew there was a fire in the house until you discovered it."

Wollf looked at the female firefighter as if she were going to help him out—something he'd been doing all along—but she didn't let out a peep. I think she enjoyed watching him bumble along. It was like watching King Kong trying to play checkers.

"Just doing our job, lady."

"Vanessa. Call me Vanessa. I can tell you right now my grandmother isn't going to give up until you let us do something. I was thinking about a catered dinner at the firehouse? We'll supply everything."

"You know," Wollf said, "this is my first day at the station. What you should do is, you should go around back and find Lieutenant Slaughter."

"But aren't you the one who—"

"Slaughter's the guy you want."

Five minutes later I was behind the house talking to Lieutenant Slaughter when Jackie came out and began flirting with one and all. To my surprise, she homed in on Lieutenant Wollf, and to my even greater surprise, he flirted with her too. In fact, they were like a couple of drunks at a frat party. It was amazing. With me he'd barely been able to get a word out, yet here he was putting on a show with Jackie. I guess I misjudged him. Apparently what I mistook for shyness was actually a distaste for me.

11. CANNONBALLS IN A PILLOWCASE

Lt. Stephen Slaughter AU6/C-3

All day I been watching Wollf and that new recruit of his, and here's what it boils down to. No. This is really what it boils down to. Forget the ifs, ands, or buts. He's going to fuck her. I'm sure of it.

We can say whatever we want about her abilities as a firefighter—and I seen some stuff tonight makes me want to puke—but the truth is, there isn't a man jack of us wouldn't sit her on our lap if she asked.

She just might be the single hottest female in the department. She's got those perky little . . . If she wasn't an Indian and twenty-five years younger than me, she'd be perfect. But here's the deal—and I'm pretty sure about this part: If he *doesn't* end up fucking her, he's going to fire her.

Oh, yeah. He's going to give her the heave-ho so fast she won't know whether to shit or go blind.

Of course, after he gives her the axe, those namby-pambies in the administration will offer her the option of resigning, which they always do, which means she won't take any of our negative assessments with her when she signs up at the next fire department. What a racket these bitches got going. We fired the chief of Tacoma when she was a recruit here. They fired our Battalion 4. Bellingham fired our training officer. We fired their newest lieutenant. They're like dogshit on your boots. You can't get rid of 'em.

Good men line up by the thousands for a crack at the job. They fly in from Minnesota and New York just for the privilege of taking our test. Women go through a special door. No waiting. No fuss. Thank you, ma'am. I know you're a little weak and a little scared, but would you like to be a battalion chief tomorrow? No problem. Just shine up those bugles for your collar and show up on time.

Disgusting ain't even the word for it.

'Course, the chicks can't get through a drill school on their own, so they get a coupl'a weeks coaching prior. Then they come out here to the stations and swish their little butts around, making the officers feel sorry for them, and they end up passing them through. We all know after the first year you can't fire *anybody.* Take Zeke. Lazy bastard should have been shitcanned long ago.

The only swinging dick downtown worth two cents is Billy Hertlein.

He came out last night to watch a couple of our fires, then at the garage fire, he's the first to realize the house next door is on fire. Sharp.

I don't know exactly what's going on between him and Wollf, but Wollf would do himself a favor by making peace. One thing I can tell you about Billy, he's got no forgiveness in his bones. I've never known him to forget anybody ever did him wrong.

I made a big production of telling Wollf we were going to be a team, but the truth is, he keeps a little too much to himself for my taste. Also, he takes chances at fires.

In addition, I heard he's a whorehound, and a whorehound is always susceptible to the charms of a chick, especially one like Rideout.

She made so many mistakes tonight I should have been taking notes. To start off with, why wasn't she the one on the roof with the chain saw? You don't have to think about that too hard. She was scared, scared to climb a ladder and scared to be on a roof over a fire.

This morning I heard from one of the medics that when they came out of the house with the victim, she wasn't even helping. Now I'm hearin' talk she didn't know how to run the fan.

I mighta jumped her shit 'cept I had my hands full keeping Zeke and Gliniewicz in line. Gliniewicz has been smoking so long he gets winded doing a simple hydrant hookup. At that garage fire we stood around waiting for water seemed like five minutes. At the beginning of the shift I was waiting for Zeke. At the end I was waiting for Gliniewicz.

God, if I could just get those two whipped into shape.

The thing I noticed after the Pennington fire was Wollf practically ignored that Pennington granddaughter, even when she was trying to be nice to him. Lordy, but she was fine. I mean, she could have been an actress herself. And

Wollf? When the slut who lives out back showed up, he was on her like white on rice.

Ignored the fox, chased the pig.

Now, why would he do that?

You could tell the old lady's housekeeper had been drinking, flouncing around making comments about how HOT firemen were. You know the kind, never passes up a wet T-shirt contest. Walking back and forth in front of the spotlight on our rig so's we could see through that blouse. Enjoyin' the way the guys on Engine 25 just about swallowed their tongues. Out in the cold dressed like summertime. When she walked, her ass end worked like two cannonballs in a pillowcase.

Wollf was wasting *way* too much time with her. And check this out. *He* kicked in the front door. Not Rideout.

If Rideout did a single blasted thing last night, I don't know what it was.

12. THE RESIDENT DICK

The last thing I remembered about the shabby apartment near the Aurora tunnel in Belltown was my brother and me being picked up by two burly SPD officers and carried bodily from the house, probably to avoid the blood, our shoes confiscated, bagged, and classified as evidence. We never got them back.

It had been a sunny morning, cold and crisp, blue skies. I still remember watching the exhaust fumes build up around the tailpipe on the police cars in the street. I remember trying to form mental pictures from the clouds of exhaust. Elephants. Zebras. The things kids do when they've just killed a man and their mother has just been murdered. We *were* still kids.

After a bit of poking around, they decided Neil had killed Alfred in cold blood.

They couldn't have gotten it more wrong.

We spent the next twenty-four hours shoeless. It was early spring, and what I remember most clearly was how cold my feet got.

We'd been sleeping on a mattress on the floor in a room I'd always remembered as a small bedroom but which I later found out had been a closet. In the early days our mother would have given us the bed and taken the sofa, but she graduated from that and we'd been forced to make do with a mattress scrounged from a vacant apartment next door.

We slept in our clothes, often in our shoes too, and that morning we wore identical PF Flyers our mother bought at Chubby and Tubby. We didn't see new clothes often, and I remember being incredibly vain about those orange sneakers.

Alfred T. Osbourne.

I heard him quarreling with our mother that morning. Then suddenly their arguing was replaced by a silence I remember to this day.

A few minutes later Alfred had Neil by the ankles and was dragging him around the room, cackling and laughing, making fun of Neil's protestations, mocking his squeaky preteen voice. It could have been me. Alfred simply grabbed the first feet he saw. I'd seen him coming and pulled my feet up under the blankets.

Bouncing across the floor like a rag doll, Neil couldn't see Alfred's deranged eyes the way I could. I was across the room wedged into a corner, trying to make myself invisible, wondering why our mother didn't come out of the kitchen and put a stop to the insanity. It was only then that I noticed the bloodstained knife in Alfred's free hand.

"You little shit," Alfred said. "You stinkin' little shit. I'm finally gonna teach you some manners." He threw me a bloodcurdling look. "And *you're* next."

* * *

I think about the past more than I should. I think about our mother, about that morning with the piano mover from hell. People tell me I'm a candidate for psychotherapy, but I tried a counselor once and she only pissed me off. There are things people never recover from, and for Emma Grant Wollf it was the death of her fireman husband six years earlier. For me it was the loss of our mother and the rest of that morning with Alfred.

Walking home on the wet streets on December 6, I could feel that old anger beginning to build in me. There had been random arsons before I got to Six's, but last night we'd been hit by a true pyromaniac.

There was nothing I hated more than a pyromaniac.

I had no doubt our pyro had been watching for at least part of the time, watching our red lights and sirens drive past, watching as we stamped out his pitiful little fires, probably watching the Pennington house too. Pyros sometimes set fires just so they can see the firemen and trucks. The experience of watching the flames feeds a sexual appetite in some pyros, who might stand in the crowd and masturbate. Setting fires is almost never the work of a bold man as, too, it is almost never the work of a woman. Fire-setters are a breed apart—the lonely, the loony, the lost.

I'd been feeling the rage grow all night and knew if I ever ran into this guy I wouldn't be able to control myself.

What made it worse for me was that this pattern of serial random nighttime nuisance ignitions was occurring in the same part of town as the fire that killed my father.

While I have absolutely no recollection of our father's funeral, I recall vividly the weeks and months afterward in the darkened house with our grieving mother, drapes pulled, dishes piling up, milk spoiled. I recall our mother's endless bouts of weeping, the fact that she wouldn't come out of her bedroom for days on end.

Neil was seven. I was four.

Neil pretty much took care of me after the neighbors and relatives stopped coming around.

Mother stopped paying bills, and eventually, about a year and a half after my father's death, we were evicted for the first time. After the eviction, she gathered her strength and moved us into an apartment, and for several weeks Neil and I thought things were going to be all right.

Then, just as abruptly as she'd gathered her strength, she retreated back into her bedroom. On my first day of school Neil walked me to kindergarten. God only knows who signed me up.

We lived two years like that.

Then she started drinking. Wine at first, then gin, vodka, anything with a kick to it.

In many ways her first year as a drinker was our best year with her. She began to regain some of her function. She cleaned the apartment and from time to time took us to movies, even shopped for Christmas presents.

My brother and I often spoke about the pyromaniac. Even then, three years after our father's death, after the hero's funeral I had absolutely no recollection of, even then we both believed the pyro would be apprehended and punished. We believed that the appropriate officials would arrest and convict the man who'd murdered our father.

As it was, nobody ever heard from the pyro again.

I know I made a fool of myself last night with the housekeeper.

I don't know why. If I had to guess, I would say it was because I felt a spark between myself and Pennington's granddaughter, and it scared me. The more I felt the younger Pennington trying to relate to me, the more I had to show off with the housekeeper.

I'm not cruel by nature. At least I try not to be.

The housekeeper kept asking what we wore underneath our bunking pants, and I told her there was only one way to find out. Good God. It was as if we were both in heat.

When we first ran into the Pennington woman, my mouth went dry; I could barely get any words out.

The housekeeper was different. She and I are two of a kind.

Neil is the same as me. All his women have been lowlifes too.

There were so many things I might have said to the younger Pennington. I thought of every one of them on the walk home that morning to my condo on Lake Washington.

On Lakeside Avenue, I retrieved yesterday's mail and went inside the Water's Edge. In every apartment building there's a guy who never says hi. Who never looks at you. Who you always think is a dick. I guess you could say I'm the resident dick at the Water's Edge.

It was starting to drizzle when I walked through the front door and checked my messages—none; my e-mail—none. I took a shower, then put Patricia Pennington's *River of Dust* into the VCR, turned the sound low, and dragged my father's large black trunk out from its hallowed spot in the back of the coat closet.

On the TV a seventeen-year-old Patricia Pennington was being given her first horse by her on-screen grandfather, Charles Coburn. I watched her ride up and down green fields and jump over a fence. It was strange to realize the young woman on film was now the elderly pill-popper I'd rescued last night.

The top portion of my father's trunk was filled with letters and some of my father's fire department paraphernalia. A half-melted firefighter's helmet—the one he died in.

I set the helmet aside lovingly and sorted through the newspaper clippings, picking one out more or less at random.

The yellowed clipping was dated by hand in blue ink. November 3, 1978. I never knew for certain, but I thought my father had penned the dates on these articles himself before he died.

RAMPAGE OF BLAZES CONTINUE

SEATTLE—Areas of Capitol Hill and the Central District were struck again last night by a series of arson fires that continue to baffle fire investigators and are thought to be part of a string of arsons stretching back to last summer. Fire department chief Frank Hanson says, "We believe the same person is responsible for most of the arsons we've been getting since August."

Last night during a two-hour period firefighters fought five blazes, the largest outside a Safeway on East John, which was started in a garbage bin and quickly spread to the outside of the building.

All of the fires have occurred between eleven P.M. and six A.M.

Fire department officials refused to confirm or deny reports that the Bureau of Alcohol, Tobacco and Firearms has plans to assist in the investigation. Total losses last night were estimated at $15,000.

I picked up a pair of family photos from the time period. There were a couple of curly-haired boys roughhousing with their father. There was a mother so beautiful you could actually see a young man in the park turning his head to look at her just as my father snapped the picture, her auburn hair flashing in the sunlight.

13. BANANA SNATCHERS AND RAT SKINNERS

On Sunday I walked to the station, taking the long route down along the lake and up Madrona to Thirty-second and then to Cherry, carrying a rucksack and hiking the uphills almost at a running pace.

I'd spent two days flopped in front of one Patricia Pennington movie after another, a marathon of B movies in the sequence they were made, watching the celluloid woman age before my eyes. It was like sitting next to God.

When I walked into Six's, the beanery was filled with A-shifters mingling with our shift. Having arrived with half an hour to spare, Zeke was standing along a wall, quiet and smiling in that sleepy way he has. Everybody liked Zeke. He was a gentle soul and meant well. Even his officer, Slaughter—when he wasn't yelling at him—liked him.

Gliniewicz was swapping gossip with the driver on A-shift. Slaughter was talking to their officer on the engine.

There were four shifts working in the station, which meant four officers: three lieutenants and a captain for each rig. On Ladder 3 our captain was a man I'd worked with in the past, Frank Keesling. We shook hands and he congratulated me on my transfer to Ladder 3. We both knew I wasn't likely to stay here. Keesling was in his fifties, balding, a grandfatherly sort who didn't take too many things seriously outside of deer hunting and raising thoroughbred house cats.

"There's this rat-catcher thing going on," Keesling said. "I told your chief, Eddings, it was one of those in-house squabbles, but she had to come down the other day and get mixed up in it. Now it looks like it might be headed downtown."

"Rats?"

Gliniewicz and the A-shift driver were making so much noise it was hard to concentrate. In addition, there were at least two other conversations going on, and the television was broadcasting a women's tennis match. I wanted to hear what Katie Fryer was saying to Rideout because it sounded like a pretty good yarn, something about a GSW they'd responded to yesterday. Gunshot wound.

I turned back to Keesling, who said, "We had a rat problem out back. A couple of them got into the station, so I told the guys I'd buy a half gallon of ice cream for every rat they caught. B-shift told us they killed two, but some of our guys accused them of making it up. You know how that goes. They were just having fun.

"So my crew told their crew they had to *prove* they caught a rat to get the ice cream. The next shift we found a tanned rat hide pinned to a piece of plywood downstairs. That's when you-know-who"—he made a gesture at Katie Fryer and continued in a lower voice—"complained to her officer that there's a state law against trapping animals with steel traps. I thought she was kidding. Next thing I know your chief is up here reading us the riot act. Now I'm writing letters. Katie's writing letters. Who knows where it's going to end?"

"Heard anything more about the arsons?"

"Last night the cops arrested a coupl'a homeless guys lighting a Dumpster fire down by the Market. That was probably the end of that." Keesling had a way of drifting off on you, losing interest in the middle of a conversation. "If you're ready, I could scoot out and get home in time for church."

"I'll have your stuff off the rig in a minute."

Even Slaughter, who'd spent years as an investigator with Marshal 5, thought the two guys they'd arrested downtown had started our fires.

Not me. I knew few pyros worked in tandem, and my vision of our pyro didn't include a partner. Our guy was still out there.

That morning before we went out to drill Rideout, I walked into the beanery to eat one of the bananas I'd brought and found they'd vanished off the chrome island in the kitchen.

"What happened to my bananas?" I asked.

Slaughter, Rideout, Dolan, and Boles all stared at me guilelessly. It was the sort of practical joke Dolan might pull, eating four bananas just to get a yuk out of it. Gliniewicz strutted into the room from the watch office and said, "What's going on?"

"Where's my bananas?"

Gliniewicz sat down and picked up the sports section of the Sunday paper. "You leave stuff out, it's fair game."

"You ate them?"

"It's out, it's fair game. Ask anybody." Without looking up from the paper, Gliniewicz patted his stomach. "I was hungry."

Dolan started laughing.

Slaughter joined in when he saw my face. "Next time you better nail those bananas down."

"I'd put a padlock on 'em," Dolan said.

They laughed even louder when I began searching the beanery and found them in the back of the refrigerator.

Banana snatchers. Rat skinners. I guess it was funny when you thought about it.

14. SOMETHING VERY WICKED INDEED

Cynthia Rideout

DECEMBER 8, SUNDAY, 1345 HOURS

News of Patricia Pennington's rescue was in *The New York Times* and *The Washington Post.* Everybody got it wrong, including the local televised news, who interviewed Zeke on camera and made it sound as if he made the save. We saw one of those reports before we left the station Friday morning, and boy did that give everybody a hoot. Zeke was embarrassed, but you could tell he liked it too.

I met Towbridge today. He's a tall black guy around thirty; drop-dead handsome. He carries himself with a princely bearing, lifts weights at a gym five times a week, plays basketball at almost a professional level on about three different teams, and doesn't have an ounce of fat on him. I've actually seen black women around here whistle at him.

For that matter, our driver, Jeff Dolan, is pretty cute too. He's the oldest on the crew—in his late forties. He's got streaks of gray in his hair and spends all summer working on his tan. He's not as tall as the others, but he's still taller than me. They're all taller than me. Pickett has dark eyes and dark hair, a mustache to match.

The whole crew could be on a firefighter calendar, all except Wollf, not unless he was half naked. He's got a great body. Although he's not handsome, there is something interesting about the way he looks, sort of like a boy who knows he's about to get away with something very wicked. Something very wicked indeed.

He doesn't talk much, but I find myself watching him for his subtle reactions to the things people say.

Ordinarily there are four people working on Ladder 3, but because I've been sent here to do my ladder drills, each shift one of the regular people here has to take a detail to another station. The officer never gets detailed out and neither does the driver, so the traveling falls on Towbridge and Pickett. One of them works here one shift, then packs up all his gear and works the next shift at another station. Today Pickett is gone and Towbridge is here.

Towbridge speaks in a kind of an inner-city patois that is hard to understand. His first name is Harlan, but everybody calls him Tow. Or Bridge. As a sign of affection, Gliniewicz and Dolan, the drivers respectively of the engine and Ladder 3, call him Slowbridge.

This morning Towbridge took me aside and said, "The lieutenant's going to take you out there, have you put on full bunkers and a bottle. Then he's going to have you put up every ladder we got from smallest to biggest. Flat raise. Beam raise. Everything you can imagine. We'll work with you on the larger ladders, of course. He's trying to see how strong you are and if you have any endurance. If you want to keep from bruising your shoulder from having those ladders on it for two hours, pin a sock inside the shoulder of your bunking coat. Trust me. I worked with Wollf up at Ladder

Eleven when he was drilling that gal they ended up firing." Towbridge let out a carefree laugh at the look on my face. "Don't worry. She deserved it. I don't even know how she got through drill school. You'll do fine."

Ladder 3 carries a fifty-five-foot ladder that weighs 250 pounds and takes four people to handle. The drill I'm most worried about is putting that up and then climbing it with a roof ladder slung over my shoulder. Roof ladders can get heavy, and if you take one all the way to the top of the fifty-five, you're four stories high and all by yourself. Then you raise it hand over hand and lay it on the roof. It was the worst thing in drill school, not counting the smoke.

At ten o'clock we went out and did the ladder drills almost exactly the way Towbridge described them. Afterward Wollf said I'd done a good job and then showed me what he wrote on my Form 50 for the last shift. His report never even mentioned the fan shutting down. He also said I assisted him with the rescue. It was a *good* report. Yaaaay!

15. THE INCIDENT AT THE RED APPLE

Cynthia Rideout

DECEMBER 8, SUNDAY, 1645 HOURS

We just got back from an aid call to an older gentleman with stomach pain; we sent him to the hospital in an ambulance. Earlier we'd gone to the store to get dinner. Also, I bought ice cream. When you're a recruit, they want you to buy ice cream for every little thing, which is probably why Gliniewicz looks like an overstuffed toy pig. He's not in very good shape for a firefighter. This morning I saw him and Katie Fryer outside the apparatus doors smoking cigars.

Katie Fryer tells me not to act like a man and then does something like that.

So we're in the Red Apple, Dolan, me, Towbridge, and the lieutenant, all of us in the vegetable aisle, when who should show up but the caretaker for that movie star.

She's maybe twenty-six. She's blond, of course, and she's wearing this tacky denim jean jacket with fur on it. Somewhere in there you could see her bare stomach too, which was just a little stupid in this weather. Dolan had trouble taking his eyes off her. I think she has fat thighs, but guys see what they want.

She spots Wollf, lets out this yelp, skips over, and starts hanging all over him. Ignores me. Ignores Dolan. Ignores Towbridge.

None of the women around here ignore Towbridge.

She proceeds to flirt up a storm with Wollf. Hanging on him. Touching him. Following him around the store, walking backward in front of him, bumping into people, laughing.

He answered her questions, which she would ask every time it looked as if his interest was flagging—questions about the fire and how he'd found the old lady and who he thought started it and what were the chances of having another fire and on and on. Why is the gift of gab always squandered on half-wits?

I was the only one who noticed her slipping a piece of paper into the pocket of Wollf's foul-weather jacket.

And this is the evil part, I'm ashamed to admit. After we got back to the station and the lieutenant was downstairs lifting weights, I went into his office and pretended to be cleaning. I looked in the lieutenant's coat pockets, but the note was in the trash. Torn up.

When I pieced it together, it read: "Lt. Wolf [sic], I can't stop thinking about you. Please come and see me. Call 323-3308. You won't be sorry. xxxxooooo—J."

Aren't I terrible?

This is what else happened at the Red Apple.

We're standing in line. The lines in that place are pretty

long. Wollf is in front and about two people from the checker when I notice a middle-aged woman in front of Wollf. She's diaphoretic. I mean really sweating. She's got a hat with a veil and a purple dress and rumpled nylons and these low heels the size of sampans. My God, her feet are huge.

And the sweat's running out of her black wig like somebody's squeezing a sponge on her head. But more than that, she's staring at Wollf. It's almost as if Wollf is holding a gun on her. I'm not exaggerating. This woman is terrified.

There are four firefighters in line, but she's fixated on Wollf.

When her turn comes, she pushes her six-pack of soda pop at the cashier and then doesn't even buy it. She runs out of the store. I mean—runs.

"You know her?" Jeff Dolan asked Wollf.

"Hell, no."

"You sure?"

"God, she was ugly," Towbridge said, chuckling.

"An old girlfriend, right?" Dolan asked.

It wasn't what he said, but the way he said it. We all burst into laughter.

We've been working together two shifts and already we're a family.

About ten minutes after we got back to the station, Attack 6 went out on a single to a Dumpster fire behind the Red Apple. I can't help but think it was that blonde who set it. In fact, I can't help but think the blonde set those fires at the movie star's house on Friday night too. I'm no detective, but you think about it, they were the only fires all night that were started *inside* a structure. And who else had access to the inside of those structures besides her?

16. A SLY SILLY BITCH

According to Earl Ward

If you want to be with a woman, you better know some of the tricks. That kind of tomfoolery is just what you don't acquire in a godderned correctional facility—no sir—not a single one of those profoundly important tricks you need for impressing the feminine mystique.

You especially don't learn about the bitch type.

And Jaclyn is definitely the bitch type.

Maybe that sounds rough, but hey, I'm trying to change my stripes here, and she ain't helping any.

I've only got a couple of hours in this part of town while Mom screws around playing bingo with the blue-hairs, so I drive over here and spot her walking up the street.

Now I'm in the grocery store and I'm following her and she doesn't even know. She looks right at me and doesn't know.

That's how good I am.

You'd be surprised what you learn in the joint. I can walk right up to her, look her in the eye, and she still won't know. I'm that good. Period.

I'm so godderned invisible it's almost laughable.

What's really laughable is I can do all these things, yet I am still no closer to my goal. It's hard to believe. You want to be with a woman, you can *want* it all day and all night, but that don't mean it's going to happen.

So I'm following J, and she don't know it. I'm following her around when in they walk. The bastards in uniform. It's the same jackasses from Thursday night. Jackie sees them and sneaks off and writes herself a note and then runs back to the produce area at the end of the store, where she's all over the tall one.

I mean *all* over him. It was embarrassing.

I observe the bastard up close, and for the first time they all pass me and I think for a second I know him and then I *do* know him and it's all of a sudden all I can do to keep from crapping my pants. I mean FILLING MY PANTIES, brother . . . I'm shivering. And sweating. Cold and hot at the same time. I've never felt anything like this before. All I can think about is that night years ago when I almost fell into the fire. I can feel the heat. I can feel the heat everywhere.

Even when they arrested me in Portland it wasn't like this.

These minutes in the store are the spookiest since I've been outside.

Because this guy is the spitting image—the spitting image, I'm telling you—of the fireman they say I killed back in '78.

Bigger maybe. Taller for sure. But other than that, he's the guy. Period.

I thought somebody was playing a goddern joke on me. Here I was playing a joke on Jackie, and these idiot firemen with their fire bitch come in and all of a sudden the joke is on yours truly.

I recognize the name of course. Any retard can see the tag on his coat.

Wollf. W-O-L-L-F.

WOLLF!

Maybe it's his son. Or his grandson. Man, I was in the slammer for a long time. I come out and people are driving these trucks where the bumpers come right up against the driver's window of my mother's car, and talking on little phones they carry around, talking in the grocery line, walking down the street, driving, it's nuts—who are they talking to? And everybody's got one, even the kids, and I think everything's different, and then *he* shows up and now everything's the same.

This guy's jumped right out of my nightmares.

He's bigger than the original. Same face but bigger. And meaner-looking. You been in prison awhile, you can figure out who the tough ones are just by looking. I never been more scared of a man in my life, not even in the joint when Nelson first told me how it was going to be. In fact, this guy had been inside with us in Salem, Nelson would have been *his* bitch.

And then J is walking over to him and flirting and touching him and he's doing the aw shucks thing like he doesn't need her, but that only makes her more determined, and now she won't stop and she's following him around the store, following all four of them actually, and I'm following them with a cart, but all I got in it is my drink, and J is making a fool of herself and it's all I can do to keep from running over and slapping her silly.

She's so tiny next to him.

And now *he's* flirting. He's flirting with my girl. Damn, I'm in hell. I'm going to punch him out. I'm going to knock him down and kick him senseless. I'm going to kick his eyeballs clean out of his head. God, how I hate him. I tell you, I'm in hell.

We were going to be actors together. Like Tom Cruise and what's-her-face. We're going to be famous together. Mrs. P is going to hook us up with some of her connections. Me and J were going to be rich.

'Course, I don't have the looks. Okay, so I'll be one of those character actors like Kevin what's-his-name or John you-know-who. One of those guys who never gets the girl but has the chicks crawling all over him in real life. We'll be on the covers of the best magazines in the world. *Star. Globe. National Enquirer.*

He's lucky I don't go over and hit him in the head with a can of asparagus. That's what Nelson would do. Cave in his skull.

Him bleeding all over. Me standing over him.

Instead, I get in line.

Quite by accident they get in line behind me, and now I am standing not two feet from the man with devil eyes.

He don't know it, of course, how nervous I am. Nobody knows but me. That's what you learn in the slammer. How to hide your feelings. Period.

I know it can't be the same guy. Not unless there's such a thing as time travel.

17. THE NIGHT SOME OF US POSED FOR PICTURES

Cynthia Rideout

DECEMBER 8, SUNDAY, 2010 HOURS

The caterers showed up with steak and lobster, potatoes that were whipped and then fried with herbs and a butter sauce. They served us at the beanery table as if we were royalty.

Vanessa Pennington was the picture of grace and civility even though you could tell she was nervous. "I'm sorry my grandmother can't be here," she said. "She's still under a doctor's care and won't be up and around for a week or so. She asked me to give her sincere thanks to each of you."

"It was good of you to take the time to do this," said Slaughter. The food was elegant, but as usual we were eating off our mismatched plates and drinking out of an assortment of jugs and canning jars that looked as if they'd been scrounged from the city dump.

"You were all so wonderful," Pennington said. "We're very grateful."

We answered with a host of demurrals.

In most situations Wollf is his own man, but once Pennington and the caterers entered the station, he barely said a word. When the union photographer came in with a camera to take pictures for the weekly newsletter, he bolted. No kidding. He bolted.

She ended up taking pictures without him.

Somewhere in the middle of our dinner Chief Eddings walked in. When she saw the caterers and the photographer, she was visibly upset, but it was the sight of Vanessa Pennington that really set her off. "What's this? A stag dinner?" The room grew deathly silent. I'd seen Eddings do things like this before. "Are you the entertainment?" she asked, staring at Pennington. Eddings was a bad combination of a sharp tongue and no governor on her mouth.

After moments of stunned silence, Lieutenant Slaughter tried to smooth things over. "Chief Eddings," he said, "Vanessa Pennington. Ladder Three rescued her grandmother at a house fire Thursday night while you were off duty. She was nice enough to buy dinner for the station."

"My grandmother bought it, actually," Pennington said.

"How come I wasn't invited?" Eddings asked.

"I apologize. It was my oversight," Pennington said gamely. "We'd love to have you join us now. There's plenty."

"Your grandmother's that actress lady?"

"Yes. Patricia Pennington."

"She must have a lot of money."

"Right now she has a lot of gratitude. These people saved her life." Pennington hadn't lost her composure for a second.

Eddings glanced around the room. "So where's our new lieutenant? Wollf?"

Dolan spoke through a mouthful of lobster. "Probably hiding in his office."

"He got scared of the camera," Towbridge said, dashing my belief that I was the only one who'd noticed.

"So, Rideout. How're you doing here at Six's?"

"Fine."

"Good. You listen to these lieutenants. They'll straighten you out."

"Yes, sir."

"I don't think she *needs* straightening out," said Towbridge. "She's doing just fine."

But Chief Eddings was already halfway through the swinging door into the apparatus bay. One couldn't help noticing her thighs were so fat she couldn't keep her legs together when she walked.

I can't believe I accidentally called her "sir."

18. THE WEAK SISTER

Eddings pushed my office door open with a thunk and stared into the room for several seconds, giving her eyes time to adjust to the light.

I'd met her twice and had heard as many stories about her as she'd probably heard about me. It was said she got excited at fires. I didn't know about that, but I'd heard her over the radio yelling so shrilly into the radio mike that she was almost impossible to understand.

One thing firefighters took pride in was presenting a calm demeanor at emergency situations no matter what was happening in front of them. Anxiety on the fire ground and particularly over the airwaves was fodder for long-running jokes and cruel parodies.

It was said Eddings didn't have many friends inside the department. I thought it sad, but then I realized I didn't have many friends either. Come to think of it, I didn't have any.

"Sorry I couldn't meet you last shift. I was in California at a fire chiefs' conference. How are you liking this station?"

"Good evening, Chief. So far I like it fine."

"Good. Let me give you the short report on these guys. I'll save you some time."

"I don't need—"

"Towbridge is lazy. I don't know how he got in. You'll have to stay on top of him. Pickett is accident-prone. Don't put a chain saw in his hands, and be sure and keep him off the roof. Dolan is hardheaded. I've had a coupl'a run-ins with him."

"We're all getting along fine."

"Yeah?" She leaned against the army-gray file cabinet inside the doorway. "Wollf. I want a team I can count on here in the Sixth. I figured this spot on Ladder Three was perfect for you. You *do* want a truck company?"

"A lot of people want this slot."

"That's not what I asked."

"If I had my druthers, I'd take a truck."

"Well, you play ball, I can keep you here."

We stared at each other for a couple of beats. She was a pasty-faced woman who wore stark eyeliner as her only concession to makeup. Her limp black hair was molded into a crooked pageboy, as if she'd cut it herself. Tonight static electricity glued it to her head like a skullcap. Looking into her faded gray eyes, you could see she might have been a cute kid, but somewhere along the line her personality had begun to put its stamp on her features. Mostly what I saw in her face now was bitterness. That she called herself a bull dyke—not a lesbian or even a dyke, but a bull dyke—was common knowledge. They said she'd been strong as a horse when she first came in, but it looked as though she'd mostly gone to fat now.

"How's Rideout doing?"

"Fine. She—"

"Yeah, I didn't think she'd have an easy time on a truck. Hooking up to that fifty-five and making your presence felt is something damn few women can do. She's probably afraid of heights too. Check it out. Listen, Wollf. I'm going to tell you this straight, because that's how I am. You and I are going to fire Rideout."

"I don't see how—"

"Oh, yeeeeaaaah. She's already had one bad monthly report, which I wrote personally. That's when those dickbrains in the administration thought she should get evaluated by at least one other officer. Fortunately, I was able to make *you* that officer. I talked to Hertlein on the phone but he wouldn't give you to me, so I went straight to Chief Smith. I want you to evaluate her the same way you evaluated Martinet up at Thirty-two's."

"*Martinez.* Her name was Trina Martinez. And all I did was document what she could and could not do."

"Hell, you fired her. You do the same *documenting* on Rideout, and you and I will be copacetic till the cows come thundering home. Catch my drift? She's a weak sister, and she's going to make the other women in the department look bad. Last month I wrote one hellacious Form fifty on how fucked up her work was. So now you come in and you're an unbiased newcomer. You write another report that parrots mine and we'll shitcan her."

I'd never heard a firefighter conspired against in this way. I'd taught drill school where we evaluated recruits once a week for twelve weeks, and the rule—*never* deviated from, not once to my knowledge—was that each officer made his or her own evaluation of each candidate without help from any other officer. Collusion was not part of a fair evaluation. Chief Eddings had worked at training. She knew the rules.

I said, "This conversation is not fair to Rideout. She deserves the same shot at the job you and I had."

"Oh, bullshit. You think they weren't all talking about us when we came in?" Eddings passed me a large manila envelope of the type the department used for interdepartmental mail. "Technically you're not supposed to see this."

"I'm telling you right now, I'm not going to give her a poor evaluation unless she earns it. And I'm *not* going to read this." I handed the envelope back, irked that she thought I was against all women in the department because I'd fired one individual, that she thought I was willing to cheat this young woman out of a career on nothing more than her say-so.

She tossed the envelope onto my desk.

"We both know I'm not supposed to look at earlier reports."

"Sure. Sure. Sure. Nobody's suggesting you aren't going to be decent here."

I tried to hand her the envelope a second time, but she opened the door and backed through the doorway, where she bumped into Vanessa Pennington.

I don't know who was more stunned. Eddings. Pennington. Or me.

Pennington was four or five inches taller, but because of the chief's girth and Pennington's slimness, the disparity in height seemed more dramatic. They faced each other for a few seconds before Eddings said, "What are *you* doing here?"

"I came to thank Lieutenant Wollf."

"Then go ahead and thank him." Eddings waited, arms folded across her chest.

Pennington looked at me for some sort of signal on how to handle this.

"Come in," I said. In many ways she resembled her grandmother at the same age, particularly her gray-blue eyes and shoulder-length hair, light brown in some lights, dishwater blond in others.

Eddings walked away without saying goodbye, but not before surveying Pennington from top to bottom. Pennington pretended not to notice.

I offered Pennington the swivel chair at my desk and took the straight-backed chair across the room as the door swung closed. The only illumination in the room was from the small fluorescent lights over my desk.

"The dinner was terrific," I said. "Thank you."

"You're welcome. You didn't stay long."

"I had some work to do."

"I wanted to thank you personally, since you're the one who carried her out."

"I was only doing my job."

There were a lot of questions I might ask the granddaughter of Patricia Pennington, yet as we sat across from each other I found chitchat, polite conversation, or even the pretense of either almost impossible to squeeze past a tongue that felt like a piece of dried leather.

19. THE SHYEST MAN IN TOWN

Vanessa Pennington

•

"It's not much of an office," he said lamely. He was so nervous.

"Do you sleep here? I guess that's a silly thing to ask. Everyone knows firemen sleep in the firehouse." I don't know why I was having such a difficult time having a simple conversation with this man. Maybe it was because he was embarrassed about the way his chief had been rude to me. Or I was. I hadn't thought it disturbed me, but maybe it had. It surprised me that she was a battalion chief in the fire department. I would think she'd have scuttled her own ship long ago, but maybe the fire department didn't work like that.

In spite of being tongue-tied, Wollf was working hard to make me feel at home. I couldn't figure him out. He'd been so capable and gentle with Nanna. The other firefighters around here seem to view him with respect, yet all that silly flirting with Jackie the other night made me wonder what was going on inside his brain. And now he didn't seem able to string two words together.

"So do you people work a couple of days at a time?" I asked.

It took him a long time to reply, "Twenty-four hours." Eventually he added, "We work twenty-four hours, and then we get two days off. We work another twenty-four and get four days off."

"That must be hard to get used to."

"At first it was."

Another long silence.

"So why did you become a firefighter?"

"Seemed like the thing to do at the time."

More silence. He couldn't hold my eyes, looking around the room instead.

"Cindy tells me you knew my grandmother once had a chaperoned date with Howard Hughes."

"Cindy?"

"Cindy Rideout?"

He shrugged.

I had the feeling he was going to jump up from his chair and run out of the room, but just then the good-looking black firefighter on his crew named Towbridge stuck his head inside the door and said, "I thought you might want to know that lady who ran out of the grocery store just came in for a BP." He made little quote marks in the air with his fingers and wiggled his eyebrows when he said the word "lady."

"Did you get a look at her, Tow?" Wollf asked, clearly happy to see a face he knew.

"Zeke took her blood pressure. I didn't see her until she was leaving." Towbridge didn't laugh outright, but I could see there was some sort of inside joke going on here.

"So she's gone?"

"Yeah."

"The chief leave?"

The door had closed, but Towbridge opened it back up and grinned. "She's gone, all right. I wanted to offer her some lobster, but she eats so fast I was afraid she'd swallow the shell and choke. I wasn't sure we could get our arms around her to do the Heimlich thing." He left laughing.

"Who was the woman from the store?" I asked.

"It was a woman we saw at the Red Apple, who looked like she might have been a man in drag. She looked at me and then for some reason ran out of the store in a panic. The guys have been kidding me about it, but I've never seen her before in my life."

Telling me about the incident at the grocery store seemed to loosen him up. When he finished, I said, "So how is it that you know so much about my grandmother?"

"I'm a film buff. Your grandmother had five marriages and performed in sixty-three movies. She was in a hundred fifty TV shows. She was on *Laugh-in.* She was a staple on *Hollywood Squares.* I was trying to figure out which of her two daughters was your mother."

"Adrienne."

"Your grandfather was the California real estate magnate?"

"Wow." Cindy Rideout had warned me, but this guy really did have an encyclopedic knowledge of my grandmother's life.

"I just recently watched some of her earlier movies. *Blood Harvest. Duel at Water Creek. Pirates of the Blue Seas.* And the Robin Hood movie with Errol Flynn. She had a bit part. I'm not counting the two movies where she did walk-ons before that. One where she was a carhop. And the other where she was the hatcheck girl in the Dick Powell movie."

"She would love to talk to you sometime. When she's up to it, I'll see if I can arrange a—" We were interrupted by the station alerter. "Is that for you?"

He listened for a few moments and said, "It's for the engine." Which told me absolutely nothing. There were two large fire trucks in the garage outside his office door. I had no idea one was called an engine or which it was. "I'm on the truck," he said. "The big one. With the ladders. The truck is an aerial ladder company. The engine is a hose company."

The alarm was for a Dumpster fire behind the Douglass-Truth Library across the street from the station. After the dispatcher stopped talking,.I said, "Actually, the fire department's been there to see my grandmother a couple of times. Wine and pills. I think it's a leftover Hollywood thing. I was sure scared when I saw her in that medic unit."

"How is she doing?"

"She's going to be okay."

"I bet it's tough to be that famous and then have it all disappear."

"I have this theory people get addicted to fame and when they lose it they go through withdrawal. In this country it seems as though everybody wants to be famous. Even the woman taking care of her wants to be an actress."

"Do you?" he asked. "Want to be famous?"

I laughed. It was the first really personal thing he'd asked. "Not on your life. What about you?"

"I've had my name in the papers. I didn't care for it."

As we spoke we heard the sounds of the engine firing up, the men yelling to each other, the bay doors cranking open. The engine roared out of the station, and a moment later we heard them slowing across the street at the library.

"So how many of my grandmother's movies do you have?" I asked.

"All of them."

"Even the film libraries don't have *Rio Cantina.*"

"I bought it from the estate of a collector two years ago."

"You know, that's the one movie of my grandmother's I've never seen."

Silence. I'd given him an opening, but he either wasn't interested or couldn't summon the gumption to say anything. My money was on the latter. It was intriguing that this man, who in the night in his firefighting armor seemed to be afraid of absolutely nothing, was so afraid of me now.

I decided to give it one more shot. "I have an idea. There's a retrospective at the Harvard Exit. They're playing a couple of Nanna's movies. I've been trying to find somebody to go with. Would you like to come with me?"

Before he could reply, another alarm went off, the overhead lights came on all over the station, a bell clanged, and within seconds he was gone. As were the others. It was just me, the caterers, and a garage full of diesel smoke.

20. GEE. LET'S ROB FORT KNOX

Even though I knew she would be gone when we got back, it was disappointing to arrive at the station two hours later and confront Pennington's absence. Like a boob, I ran into my office and scanned my desk for a note.

There wasn't one.

While the four of us sat in the beanery in various states of deshabille, bored by the lackluster play between the Raiders and Chargers, I stewed over the variety of slow-witted things I'd said to Vanessa Pennington.

All my life I've had trouble talking to a certain sort of woman, the sort I might conceivably fall in love with. The women I spent time with, when I did spend time with the opposite sex, were misfits, neurotics, dysfunctional. Like me.

Real women made my teeth go dry and my eyes tear up.

If I'd had my wits about me, I might have invited her to watch *Rio Cantina* with me. I might at least have suggested loaning it to her, which would have necessitated seeing her twice more, once to give her the tape and once for her to return it, but I didn't think of any of these possibilities until afterward.

As we sat watching TV, Joe Williams came in at a little after ten. Joe wasn't due to relieve me until 0730 hours tomorrow. Gliniewicz, Slaughter, Towbridge, and I were watching the ball game. Zeke was in the phone booth.

"What's up?" Slaughter asked, turning from the TV. Slaughter had a manner of engaging people when he spoke to them that I would have given anything to appropriate.

"The old lady threw me out again," Williams said. "She thinks I'm hot for our next-door neighbor."

"Are you?" Slaughter asked.

"Well, yeah. A little. But hell, I'm a guy. Ain't I supposed to look?"

"Get yourself a pair of those mirror sunglasses so she can't see your eyeballs," Gliniewicz said. "It sure saved my marriage."

"What saved your marriage," said Towbridge, "was you bought your wife that Lexus." Gliniewicz ignored him.

"Are you gonna sleep here tonight?" Slaughter asked.

"I don't have nowhere else," Williams replied.

"You gonna double up with Wollf?" Gliniewicz joked.

Williams gave me a look. "I get the outside."

"*I* get the outside," I said.

"Well, hey. If you're going to be like that, I'll sleep downstairs."

"No wonder your wife doesn't want you around," Towbridge said. "You can't compromise."

As Williams left to get his bedding and personal gear, the phone on the beanery table rang. Towbridge picked it up, glanced at me, and said, "You know somebody named Mitzi?"

"I'll take it in my office."

Williams was still in the Ladder 3 office when I picked up the phone. "Lieutenant Wollf."

"Lieutenant? This is Parkinson on Aid Twenty-five. Hey, we got a call down here at the Arroyo Tavern just off Broadway. It's sort of a mess. This woman named Mitzi says she knows you. SPD wants to take her to the precinct and book her, but she says if she gets arrested she'll have to go back to prison. The cops say if you vouch for her they'll let her go."

"What's she being arrested for?"

Across the room, Williams grew quiet.

"Disturbing the peace."

"She okay?"

"I can't prove it, but my guess is she's on smack. We've had a bunch of ODs in this neighborhood today. There's some black tar in town. You know her?"

"Yeah."

"Do you want to come and get her?"

"Hold on a minute." Williams was halfway out the door with an armful of bedding and his shaving kit. "Joe? Think you could work a couple hours tonight? I'll give you merits."

"You got woman trouble too?"

"In a manner of speaking."

"If you clear it with the chief. But I can't work all night. The wife and I been goin' round and round for two days. I ain't had any rack time."

I borrowed Towbridge's Saab and drove two miles to the Arroyo on Capitol Hill, double parking on East John next to the idling aid car.

There were two police cruisers behind the aid car, two more in front. Inside the Arroyo they were watching the same football game we'd been watching at the station. A few neighborhood blue collar types nursed beers. The rest were police, fire, or prisoners.

Mitzi was on the floor in the center of it all with half the buttons missing from her sleeveless blouse. She was in her early thirties, a buxom bottle-blonde in a tight black skirt. Even at her worst, and this was close, Mitzi could seduce a church softball team into robbing Fort Knox.

Parkinson looked up from the clipboard he was writing on and said, "Her vitals are normal and she's oriented times three."

"She's AOB," added his partner, a woman. Alcohol on breath.

When Mitzi heard my voice, it took her a while to find my eyes in the crowd. From what I could see—broken beer mugs and upset tables—there'd been a brawl. I wasn't surprised. Inciting brawls was her specialty. She had a fat lip and a mouse under one eye.

"You know this woman?" one of the cops asked. I'd thrown a Windbreaker on, but he could see my uniform shirt and collar bars when I took the jacket off to cover her.

"I'll vouch for her."

"Oh, baby." She looked up at me. "Come down and give Mitzi a little kiss. Come here, baby."

"You're drunk, Susan."

"Am I?"

"Come on. Get up. I'll take you home." I took one of her hands, pulled her to her feet, and put an arm around her solid torso. "Where's your coat?"

"I don't know. I guess I got robbed, sweetie."

"You want help?" Parkinson asked.

"I can manage."

I walked her outside and put her into Towbridge's Saab. By the time I started the motor, she'd nodded off. "Susan. Wake up. Where are you staying?"

"I'm with a man named Igor."

"Where?"

"I think it was a Motel Six."

"You gotta give me a little more help than that."

"I do?" Then she was asleep again.

I shook her. "Look, Susan. Tell me where you're staying."

"Call me Mitzi."

"Okay, Mitzi. I don't want to hand you back over to the cops."

"Take me to your place."

"We tried that before."

"Okay, then. Take me to your firehouse. I wanna meet your friends."

I secured her seat belt, let the clutch out, and drove down Madison until I hit Twenty-third, then followed it south to Yesler, where we stopped at a red light across the street from Six's. Behind the closed blinds I could see the flickering light from the TV. Gliniewicz had the night watch and would be up until two or three watching old war footage on the History Channel—he frequently lamented the fact that he'd been born too late to participate in WWII.

There was a damp chill in the night air that penetrated through to my socks.

I drove east on Yesler until the dead end, then headed down through Frink Park and the woods. Ten years ago Attack 6 had been returning from a midnight alarm when they saw a man down here. Suspicious, they wrote down his license number and gave it to the police. Later, SPD found the body of a woman in the park and charged the car's owner with murder.

Susan was just the sort of lost soul who might end up in Frink Park.

When I parked the Saab next to my Ford in the parking lot of the Water's Edge, Susan was asleep, head lolled to the side, mouth open. Gathering the folds of my Windbreaker around her, I hauled her out and tried to stand her up.

Mine was the end condo unit on the first floor, with a deck over the water just off the living room. Somewhere high on the hillside I heard a siren and knew my guys were up there working.

"Where we goin'?" Mitzi muttered.

"Someplace safe."

"You gonna stay with me, Paul?"

"I'm going back to work. I'll see you in the morning."

I turned down the bed in the spare bedroom, removed her shoes, my Windbreaker, and tucked her in. She curled up on the pillow like a little girl, her hands pressed together under her cheek.

"Good night, Susan."

"Numm, numm," she said.

21. WOLLF BECOMES LEGEND

Cynthia Rideout

DECEMBER 8, SUNDAY, 2358 HOURS

Tonight I was cleaning up the beanery when Towbridge and Gliniewicz started talking about Lieutenant Wollf.

It turns out Wollf came into the department as a probationary firefighter under Lieutenant Slaughter, that Slaughter actually tried to fire him. He said he was dangerous at fires because he was too aggressive. That's coming from Slaughter, who has a reputation for being one of the biggest risk-takers around.

Then one night about halfway through Wollf's probationary term, Wollf, along with three others on Engine 13, took a line into a furniture warehouse and proceeded to look for the fire, which, unbeknownst to them, was below them in the basement. While they were inside, the warehouse filled up with smoke, and by the time the four of them began running out of air, they were lost. Wollf had been keeping track of which wall they were on while the others laid their line over the tops of furniture, thinking they would tap the fire and follow the hose out the door. The fire grew and they never did find it. After the heat built up inside the building, they were forced to their knees and could no longer trace the line over the furniture. They split up and began looking frantically for an exit.

Three of them got lost and ran out of air while Wollf found a wall and traced it to an exterior doorway. He turned around and found each of the men in turn, walking them one by one out of the building each had believed they were going to die in.

It turned Wollf into a legend.

For various reasons, he's been a legend ever since.

22. BLACK CHERRY DIET SODA

By the time I got back to the station they'd had two alarms. An aid call and a fence fire, both arsons. So much for the theory that the arsonists had been arrested over the weekend.

When the bell hit again, I was putting my gear on board. Williams shouted from somewhere in the station, "You got me?"

"I got you, man. Thanks for covering."

It was another aid call. An elderly woman in a cramped apartment full of ancient furniture, stacks of newspapers, and broken-down walkers. She was having trouble catching her breath, more worried that she wasn't going to get her purse and keys to the hospital than of dying.

It wasn't until we were back in front of the station that we got the full response to Twenty-ninth and East Cherry. This would be Ladder 3's fourth alarm in an hour.

Cherry Street was a haven for hookers and drug dealers, but as we crossed Martin Luther King Jr. Way heading east we found ourselves in a quieter neighborhood of single-family homes. The area had been mostly Jewish until World War II, was mostly African American now, though more whites were moving in all the time, buying cheap and remodeling. Gentrification, it was called.

We found a small fire in a pile of debris between two houses. Gliniewicz ran the centrifugal pump on Attack 6 while Zeke and Slaughter laid a 1¾-inch line and blew all the evidence thirty feet into the backyard with the hose stream.

A small crowd gathered, rather quickly, I thought, given the windchill factor and the looming rain or snow. By the time the chief left, we had maybe thirty people standing around.

I scanned the crowd, looking for faces I'd seen at other fires. If there was a firebug here, I couldn't spot him.

There was one thing.

On the far side of the involved house against the opposite wall, I found a black cherry diet soda can under a bathroom window. Upright and opened, it appeared to have been partially drained. Or filled with piss. The can looked new, but it could have been there for weeks since that side of the house was littered with garbage and detritus.

"People need to clean up," said Towbridge, who'd followed me around the house.

"Black cherry diet soda," I said, shining my flashlight on the can.

When we got our fifth alarm of the night, I hurriedly told Slaughter about the can and left him in charge of the scene. "Engine Twenty-five, Engine Ten, Engine Thirty-four, Engine Five. Ladders Three and One. Battalions Five and Six. Medic Ten. Safety Two. Twelfth Avenue and East Fir Street. Engines Twenty-five, Ten, Thirty-four—" They didn't routinely send this many units unless they had a confirmed fire or an intersection with a huge potential for disaster.

"We're going to be first in," Dolan said.

He couldn't have been more delighted.

23. PICKETT GETS BURNED AND I DIDN'T DO IT—HONEST

Cynthia Rideout

DECEMBER 9, MONDAY, 0935 HOURS

I just got home from visiting Pickett at Harborview Hospital, and I feel so bad about the whole thing. Roper is on my lap purring away. He's about the only consolation I have right now.

I barely had my bottle on when Dolan drove to Twelfth and East Fir and realized the dispatcher had given us the wrong intersection. Dolan didn't even slow down on Twelfth, just kept rolling up the hill as Wollf said something on the rig radio about a corrected location.

It happened that fast.

When a ladder truck is first in, there's not a whole lot they can do. After all, we don't carry any hoses or water, just the ladders and all that equipment.

The fire was in a three-story apartment building on the northeast corner of a quiet intersection. Lots of potential for fatalities. All kinds of people yelling and screaming for us to do something.

A ton of smoke. No flame that we could see.

It was our second fire in ten minutes, and I don't mind telling you it shook me up.

There were a million things to do and only four of us. Three, really. Because Lieutenant Wollf was the incident commander for the first few minutes.

We could hear sirens in the distance, but nobody else was there yet.

So picture this.

We get to the intersection and we see a three-story apartment building with a brick facade, built in a simple rectangle running lengthwise to the east with a flat roof and no protrusions. All the windows are flat against the walls. In the center of the wall facing us is an open stairway with balconies. On either side of the stairway are apartments, nobody in any of the windows.

There's smoke coming from under the eaves. The central open stairwell and landings are obscured by smoke.

Which apartments are burning—no one can say.

To make matters worse, there are two men in their underwear on the third-floor landing. One man is putting his bare foot up on the railing as if he's going to do a header onto the sidewalk.

"Get a ladder," Wollf said. "Be careful they don't jump

onto it before you get the dogs locked. Talk to them. Communicate."

I say, "Yes, sir." Maybe I don't really say it. Anyway, I am thinking the words. Here's the bad part. When I turn around, Towbridge is gone.

Dolan is putting the aerial to the roof, so he's not going to help.

A civilian standing nearby says, "Can I assist?"

"Yeah. Follow me."

We go to the ladder compartment at the back of the rig and he helps me pull the twenty-five-foot ladder out and we start toward the stairwell with it, and when we get maybe twenty or thirty feet from the rig I hear Dolan yelling at me. "Not that one. Get the thirty-five."

So we lay the twenty-five across the sidewalk and go back to the apparatus for a thirty-five. By now at least one other rig has shown up, Engine 25. When I look inside the ladder compartment, the thirty-five is not there.

When the civilian and I put up the ladder we dropped, I know two things:

(1) This ladder isn't going to reach the third-floor balcony.

(2) The people on the balcony are gone. They've come down the stairs on their own and are standing next to us looking up as if there are other people up there, which there aren't.

We still can't tell which apartment unit is involved.

Then somebody with an Engine 25 badge on his helmet shows up in front of me and says, "Which floor?"

"Your guess is as good as mine," I answer. He gives me a disgusted look. Like *he* knows.

Behind us I hear the roar of the motor on Ladder 3 as Dolan puts down the outriggers and prepares to raise the aerial. A hose line begins to fill at my feet with the usual sound of empty cardboard boxes getting kicked, and more people from Engine 25 show up. Somebody is beating in a door on the first floor. Boom. Boom. Two half-dressed male civilians are screaming at the firefighters that the fire is in their unit on the top floor.

I turn around to get directions from Wollf, but he's busy talking to the officer from Engine 25. Pickett appears in front of me.

Pickett is a Ladder 3 man, but today he's been detailed to Engine 10.

"Come on, kid. We'll do some search and rescue. There's probably people in those units."

Since I can't find my partner, Towbridge, I go with Pickett to the fan compartment and help him carry one of our power fans. We head up to the second floor with it.

This is a mess, I think. My partner is supposed to be Towbridge, but I haven't seen him since we got here. You never lose track of your partner. I am thinking of all the ways I can get into trouble for this.

It's a catfight climbing over all the firefighters from Engine 25, as they pull hose lines around their feet and break into the first-floor apartments. These firefighters are all so big with their bottles and bunkers on, we can't get past them. Finally Pickett starts shoving people out of the way and we manage to get the fan up the stairs.

On two, I fire up the fan while Pickett kicks in the door to the apartment on the west side. Unlike the doors downstairs, this one bursts open at once. The apartment is clear. Pickett looks at me.

It's my turn to kick in a door. It takes me four tries and I tweak my ankle doing it, but I say nothing. Pickett gives me advice, but the fan is making so much noise I can't understand what he's said. The door shudders open.

The unit is filled with black smoke. We've found the fire.

Pickett pulls the door closed to keep fresh air from feeding the fire and gets on his radio to tell everybody what we've found. Just as we get covered, two guys from Engine 25 come up the stairs dragging a hose line.

Pickett tells them, “This is the unit. We’re going in to search.”

Meanwhile, more firefighters are trying to push their way onto the landing. There are five of us on the cramped landing, plus the fan.

It has become so crowded I can barely move.

Pickett taps me on the shoulder, opens the door, and crawls in.

I crawl in behind him.

It’s dark and hot. Then, more quickly than I have ever seen it happen, the bubble of clean air from the noisy fan gets in front of us, and all of a sudden we’re standing up and walking around, and it’s like there isn’t even a fire. It’s like we’re just walking into this apartment in the middle of the night, looking for the owners. Looking for kids. The noise from the fan behind us sounding like a small airplane.

I remember we need to find an exit hole for all the air that’s coming in. We can’t just blow fresh air into a box or it will blow heat back out past us. We need an exit hole.

We search the small living room, then move into the kitchen. I find a window over the sink, try to open it, then break it out with my axe. Something is wrong.

Very quickly it begins to grow hotter.

It gets hotter and smokier. Now we are on our hands and knees.

I can hear men talking. It seems like their voices should be straight ahead, but they’re to our left. I don’t hear any hose lines being operated.

We move into an interior hallway. The bedrooms are down here, I am thinking.

Pickett stops dead. We’ve been moving along pretty smartly until now, but he doesn’t budge for the longest time. I get closer, but it is too hot.

Pickett’s face is in the carpet.

And then he is backing up over me, and I tell him to take it easy, but before I can even finish saying it, he’s crawled over me. I don’t know what’s going on.

Has he found a victim? Is he carrying a child?

He stands up and bumps into a wall hard. I pile into him. "What's going on?" I say. "Where are we going?"

He doesn't reply. He just gets low again. The atmosphere at head height is like a firebox.

I'm thinking he panicked. He panicked and is running out of the building. I've seen it happen one other time. In drill school a recruit threw the hose line down and ran out of the building—then got fired for it.

We're crawling over a coffee table, and I'm trying to figure out how it suddenly got so hot in here and why Pickett is taking us in the wrong direction, because the closer we get to the doorway, the closer we should be getting to the fan, yet the noise of the fan is not in front of us. And then a group of firefighters are butting heads with us, crawling smack into us, and I realize we *are* in the doorway.

By the time I get my bearings, Pickett is gone. I step outside and see him vanish down the stairwell, crashing into firefighters who are coming up. One of them looks at Pickett and steps back, as if frightened by what he's seen.

I follow him into the street, past the twenty-five-foot ladder we put up earlier, past Chief Eddings, who is screaming at someone. I mean *screaming,* "Get your fucking ass over there!"

She looks right at me but doesn't see me. This really is the first time I've been to a fire with Eddings, and it's a whole new side of her. My God, she's frightened half to death.

Pickett hasn't taken his face piece off yet. I am surprised when he zeroes in on a paramedic standing across the street from the fire building. A short, gray-haired man.

The medic gets an alarmed look in his eyes and starts helping Pickett with his helmet and face piece. Pickett's been burned. I can see the marks on his face, blistered and black, like dirty bandages where his face piece wasn't protecting him, burns laid out in patches with straight margins; one edge where his face piece didn't cover him, the other where his collar came up and protected him.

It didn't seem that hot. *I'm* not burned.

The second medic springs into action and they put Pickett on the gurney, handing me his equipment piece by piece as they strip him, telling me the department will want to take pictures of the gear.

Half a minute later Chief Eddings is crowding me in the doorway of the medic unit. "What's going on here? What the hell is going on?"

"Just treating our patient," says one of the medics, without looking up from her work. Pickett is joking with them, although you can tell he is in pain.

"Why didn't somebody tell me about this? Jesus. Rideout! Is this your doing?"

"Chief, we were up there, and all of a sudden he had to come out."

"Why didn't somebody tell me?"

I don't know what to say. Finally Pickett says, "Chief? Why don't you blow it out your ass?"

Over the airwaves we hear Engine 25 announce they have the fire knocked down and are checking for extension. Finally the female medic says, "Chief. He's got drugs on board. He's not responsible for what he's saying."

"I'm not?" Pickett smirks. "Good. Chief. Why don't you retire and make room for somebody who knows what the fuck they're doing, somebody who cares about the people they work with, which you sure don't?"

Pretending she hasn't heard him, Eddings gets on the air and yells at the dispatcher who asked her whether she received the report that Engine 25 had knocked down the fire. "Of course I received the report. What do you think I'm doing here?"

After that she began barking orders at various crews. She hollered at Connor and LaSalle, the Marshal 5 investigators. She called LaSalle a "fuckin' idiot." Got into a shouting match with Battalion 6.

Later, I was in rehab in my damp T-shirt, halfway between feverish and shivering, drinking Gatorade and munching chocolate chip cookies the fire buffs had provided, when I saw Eddings staring at me from across the yard. For some reason her look reminded me of the time up at Station 13 when she came into the bunk room after lights out, ostensibly to ask me when I wanted to schedule my upcoming holiday. It had been dark and she sat on my bunk, and before I knew it she had her hand on my thigh, was slowly rubbing my leg and hip. I asked her to stop. At first she pleaded ignorance. "Stop what?" she said. When I picked up her hand and removed it from the blanket, she said, "Oh, that. Don't mind that. It's just us girls here. I do that unconsciously. It don't mean nothing."

But there had been no mistaking the meaning—not then or the second time it happened before I was transferred to Station 6.

Towbridge, who was sitting on the grass next to me in rehab, noticed Eddings staring in our direction. He chuckled and said, "She ain't always like this at fires."

"She isn't?"

"Nah, she gets worse."

This morning when we visited Pickett in the hospital, Towbridge got him laughing so ferociously they threw us out.

Wollf and I had already retraced our path inside the apartment. We knew, because I was behind him, that I had probably taken a great deal less heat than Pickett. It was hard to imagine it had been *that* much less, but hey—Pickett was burned. I was not.

" 'Sides," added Towbridge. "Everybody knows Pickett never goes into a fire without getting hurt."

Dolan looked at me. "It's true. He falls off a ladder. Something hits him in the head. Every time we get a fire call, he starts planning what he's going to do on his time off. You heard him. He's going to work on his boat."

None of this made me feel any better.

24. NOBODY EVER GOT HURT ON ONE OF MY RIGS

Rideout looked at me and wiped a tear off her brown cheek as the medics worked on Pickett. There were black and red marks down the sides of his face in the shape of parallelograms.

You could tell he had drugs on board, because he spoke with the failure of restraint you see in a mouthy drunk.

"We went through the first two rooms," Pickett said. "I guess that's where I heard a window breaking."

"That was me," Rideout said. "I broke the kitchen window."

"I don't know why. We had an exit for the smoke."

"We did?"

I spoke gently. "You turn the fan into the doorway of a place that small and if you don't have an exit you know right away because it comes right back on you. You had one, all right. So you had the fan running?"

"We fired it up and went in," Pickett said. "The hose line was right behind us."

"The hosers never came in. We ran into them in the doorway when we came out," said Rideout.

"So what happened?" I asked.

"We were headed down this hallway toward the bedrooms. It was hot, but then all of a sudden it starts to get *real* hot. My face felt like it was getting burned around the edge of my face piece, you know, like I didn't have my hood sealing the face piece, so I tried to adjust it. When I moved the hood a little bit, I got burned. *That* was when I knew my hood was already in place."

"Are you okay?" I asked, turning to Rideout.

"I'm fine." The upper half of the Ladder 3 decal on the

front of her helmet was singed. Maybe she hadn't been burned, but she'd come close.

"Was there anybody in the apartment?" Pickett asked.

"No," I said.

"I think it was the fan," Rideout said.

"What about the fan?" I asked.

"I don't think it was on when we came out."

"It wasn't," said one of the paramedics.

"Maybe you were too aggressive," said Chief Hertlein, placing his enormous bulk in the doorway of the medic unit behind Rideout. "I'll expect to see that reflected in her report."

"What are you talking about?" I said.

"It's pretty obvious she was too aggressive and got her partner burned because of it."

"That's not what happened, Chief."

"They were way too aggressive. Both of them. I want you to write her up."

"Since when are we looking for timid recruits? When I was teaching drill school, we drummed it into recruits that they needed to be aggressive. First one through the door gets the job."

"There's a difference between being aggressive and being stupid." Hertlein gestured at Pickett. "That's the difference right there."

"Hey, Chief," Pickett said. "Sometimes it's just a hazard of the profession."

"Every time anybody gets hurt," Hertlein said, "you look around, you'll find somebody did something stupid."

"So walls never fall on anybody?" I said. "Bricks never pop out of chimneys?"

"You know what I mean."

"I don't think I do."

"Nobody goes inside in front of a hose line."

Pickett tried to sit up, but the female medic put four fingers on his chest and pushed him back down.

"Nobody goes inside in front of a hose line?" I said. "Are you kidding me? Maybe we better start stuffing hose in that ladder compartment. Then when we go up to a house fire, we can carry a fifty-five-foot ladder, a couple of fans, a generator and light cord, our chain saws, and a couple hundred feet of hose too. That would be terrific."

Towbridge laughed.

Silencing Towbridge with a look, Hertlein swept his eyes back to me. "Listen to me, you blasted idiot. You damn well better learn how this man's fire department operates! To start off with, you never back-mouth a superior officer. Especially one that can move your butt to the commissary warehouse tomorrow morning."

Last summer when I popped him, I hadn't been angry. Violence often erupted out of a deadly calm deep inside me. Now I was so angry I could barely get any words out. What frightened me was that I didn't know what I was going to do. I had no idea.

Sometimes things simply happened. Bad things.

"When I worked on Three Truck," Hertlein continued, his voice growing soft, "we had more fires than you've probably seen in your entire career. In all that time nobody who ever worked for me got hurt." One of his sentences would be whisper-soft, the next shouted. It was as if he wanted you to turn your hearing aid up so he could yell into it. "You're lucky I don't transfer your ass right now, tonight!"

"I been transferred before, Chief. It doesn't bother me."

He turned around and confronted Eddings, whose face was pale and blank. "I want them here after everybody else is gone," Hertlein said. "Make them the last unit to go. Put 'em on fire watch. And don't let them give you any bullshit about wanting to go up to the hospital to see Pickett. By the way, young man." He gave me a long look through his misty spectacles. "I'm going to talk to Safety. There *will* be a report."

Hertlein stalked off. Eddings raised her eyebrows and

gave me a look, then sighed. Maybe I was wrong, but I had the feeling what I was seeing on Eddings's face was respect. She'd been in her share of hot water over the course of her career, and I think she recognized in me a kindred spirit—two shit magnets in the same battalion.

Eddings walked away, rolling on the outer edges of her feet. Towbridge followed for a few feet, mimicking the waddle perfectly.

"You going to be all right?" I asked Pickett.

"Long as they keep shooting me up with morphine. I don't know how I'm going to get my fix when I get back on the street."

"You're gonna have to start turning tricks," Dolan said.

Everyone laughed except Rideout. Nothing in the world could have made her laugh.

"You guys have yourselves a nice fire watch," Pickett said. "I'll be up in the hospital playing footsie with the nurses."

"Look," I said to Rideout after the medic unit left. "It wasn't your fault. It was up to him to know how much heat there was around him."

"He looked so dreadful. I got in his way. I think I delayed his exit."

"Hey," said Dolan. "Like we told you, Pickett gets hurt at every fire he goes to."

"We're not shittin' ya," Towbridge said. "At the potato warehouse fire down on Rainier last year he got his leg caught in a ladder. Was hanging upside down when we found him."

We were side by side replacing equipment in compartments on our rig, standing under the upraised compartment doors to shield ourselves from a chill rain that had started to drop out of the night, when Dolan turned to me. "Maybe he never got anybody on *his* crew hurt, but he sure as hell banged up some other crews."

"Who?"

"Hertlein. I thought he was my friend. Now he goes and keeps us out here all night on fire watch. They don't need no fire watch out here. Why did he have to go and do that? I helped him build the deck on his house."

"What do you mean he banged up some crews?"

"Instead of running the saw up and over the rafters to save the frame and then picking the roof sheathing off with axes, you know, leaving some integrity to what you're standing on, he would dip the saw blade down in and cut the whole thing out, a big old chunk. Roofing, sheathing, *and* rafters."

"Didn't the section drop into the house?"

"You bet it dropped into the house. I kept telling him he couldn't do that. First couple times we got lucky and the roof landed in the attic. Then one night we're on this duplex and there's a good fire underneath us and he cuts this huge piece out of the roof, maybe six-by-eight. It dropped into the house and hit three firefighters from Thirty-three's. All three of 'em went to the hospital. We were lucky they didn't end up quadriplegics."

"What came of it?"

"It got swept under the rug. And you know what else? He hates fans. Hertlein sees a fan at a fire, he turns it off."

"You're kidding me, right? That's like sending a guy down a hole and then cutting his rope."

Towbridge looked at me. "Maybe he turned off Pickett's fan."

"We should ask those Engine Twenty-five guys," Dolan said. "They were in the doorway. They would have seen it."

25. LASALLE, CONNOR, AND FIVE SNOT-NOSED ARSONISTS

It was pouring rain when the two investigators from Marshal 5 showed up, LaSalle and Connor. Our job was to secure the fire scene and provide lights and manpower for their investigation, to secure the property after they were finished, and then sit around for the rest of the night, since Hertlein had ordered us to stay.

LaSalle's father had been mayor of Seattle thirty some years ago, and LaSalle was a paunchy, soft-looking replica of the old man. Marsha Connor was softer than LaSalle. She had what Towbridge called a teacher's underbelly, a mound of flesh below her belt that sedentary people sometimes accumulate in middle age. In fact, now that I thought about it, LaSalle and Connor looked like a doughy husband and wife who'd been eating in the same restaurants for decades. That's where the resemblance ended. LaSalle was as cocksure of himself as Connor was fraught with uncertainty.

"So who's been setting fires up north?" Dolan asked. "We been hearing units on fire calls all night."

"There's at least two of them now," said Connor. "Maybe three."

"Two pyromaniacs?" My voice must have betrayed something, because everybody looked at me. I could feel the poison coursing through my bloodstream like acid.

"Or three," said Connor.

"Three? There's probably five of the snot-nosed bastards," corrected LaSalle.

They both wore jeans and Windbreakers, fire department sweatshirts under the Windbreakers. Connor wore heavy, steel-toed work boots, while LaSalle wore sneakers. Stepping into the fire unit, LaSalle turned back to the doorway and grinned at me, displaying the gap between his front teeth. "Nice work. You got this place lit up like a condom shop at Mardi Gras."

Connor turned around and twitched an eyebrow at Rideout, as if to say, "Boys."

LaSalle said, "I heard Pickett got hisself burned."

"How bad was it?" asked Connor.

"Just a little on his face," said Towbridge.

"A lot on his face," said Rideout.

"Hertlein's going to hang somebody out to dry. You his partner?" LaSalle asked, turning to Rideout.

"Yes, sir."

"Sir?" LaSalle looked at the numbers on Rideout's helmet and said, "Sir. I like that. Can the rest of you guys call me sir too?"

Dolan said, "Sir Asshole or Sir Ignoramus?"

LaSalle laughed.

It was a two-bedroom unit. The fire had emerged from a narrow corridor leading to the bedrooms to the left of the living room. You could see where it had spread downward from the ceiling, the walls charcoal at head height, gray down low, until, a few inches from the floor, they retained their original color. Even in the corridor, where the fire had burned hottest, the bottom few inches on the wall were clean.

Until LaSalle and Connor began pulling burned material out of the bathroom and examining it piece by piece, we assumed the fire had been started by the carelessness of one of the young women who lived here. She had already told us she had lit a candle in the bathroom and left it burning when she went out. LaSalle and Connor decided the fire started in the ceiling fan over the commode. Faulty wiring had ignited the fan motor and set the ceiling on fire. After it burned awhile it weakened the ceiling plaster enough that the fan unit fell onto the countertop, where the fire quickly melted the candle and the false marble countertop.

I turned to Rideout. "Did they teach you how to read a fire in drill school?"

"A little."

"When there was enough smoke and gas built up from the fire in the bathroom, the smoke began following a natural path to the window in this bedroom. When you guys turned the fan on at the front door, the pressurization helped push the gases out the bedroom window. From the bathroom through this bedroom. It was perfect."

"So when I broke out the kitchen window, I changed the air flow and got Pickett burned?"

"That puny little window wasn't enough to do that," said Dolan.

I said, "What brought the fire out toward the living room was the fan getting shut off. All of a sudden the apartment was no longer pressurized, so the heat began heading toward the largest opening. The front door."

"If the fan had been on, Pickett wouldn't have been burned," Towbridge said.

"It don't help," said Dolan, "that we're forced to wear all this damn equipment. This hood. And now they even say they'll write charges on us if we go into a fire without our collars up. What a crock of shit. In the old days, you went in with your ears exposed. When a room got too hot, you could feel it. You backed out. Now your gear gets hot and you don't even know it. You get burned before you can take it off. Did you see those lines on his face? Those were contact burns. His face piece and hood burned him. He got burned by his own equipment."

"You close to nabbing your arsonist?" I asked LaSalle.

"It's just a matter of time. They *all* get caught."

But they didn't *all* get caught. My father's killer was still out there. "At two of the arsons we found Shasta diet black cherry cans," I said.

"You save them?"

"At the last one I had Slaughter mark it for you guys."

"He never said shit to us."

LaSalle gave me a look. Connor said, "Next time try to preserve anything you find in place."

"It's probably nothing," said LaSalle. "There's been a lot of trash around these sites."

The casualness with which LaSalle treated my tip put things into perspective. He was right. There had been a lot of debris at our fire sites. Discarded furniture. Fast-food wrappers. Bottles. Cans.

26. IF YOU AREN'T, YOU WILL BE

When we got back to Six's I could smell floor wax along with the acrid tang of smoke we'd brought back to the station on our clothes and hair.

As I typed up the fire report, I became aware of Steve Slaughter in the doorway. "You guys have a bad night?" he asked.

"I've had worse. Are you still on good terms with those guys in investigation?"

"Sure."

"I was wondering why you didn't pass along my information on the can we found at that fire off Cherry?"

"I don't know. Didn't seem important. It was pretty hectic."

"Have you heard *anything* about diet Shasta cans?"

"No."

"Maybe you could put out some feelers and see what they know that they're not telling."

"I'll swing by on my way home."

"Thanks."

"Paul, there's something I've been meaning to talk to *you* about. You know as well as I do every time we go out there's a chance Zeke is going to get me killed. Then there's Glinziewicz. I like the guy, but he's bullheaded, drives like a maniac, and any time he has to carry any hose, he starts wheezing like an old radiator. Neither of them's going to run in and drag my sorry ass out of a fire." I tried to keep my eyes off Slaughter's beer belly. Like a lot of overweight firemen, he thought he was in shape because he had been once—years ago. "I don't want another weak sister on my crew."

"And?"

"I'm talking about that chick you've been babysitting."

"There's no babysitting going on."

"Oh, come on. You've been nursing her like a sick kitten. You realize if she makes it through probation, she's going to end up on *my* crew."

"You're not telling me to write a bad report on her, are you?"

"I shouldn't have to tell you. She's fucked up two fires in a row. Thursday night and last night. Take last night. She goes in with Pickett—Pickett gets burned. Or Thursday. You go in with her. You bring the victim out by yourself."

"That was my decision. And she didn't get Pickett burned. Listen, Steve. I've evaluated recruits before and—"

"That's why I don't understand this. Everybody sees her screwing up but you. You know how women are. Hell, they don't even have the same gene structure we do."

"What are you talking about?"

"Think about it. A woman . . . she's got all these genes telling her to build a nest and start having babies. Something bad happens, her instinct is to duck and cover. Hide the babies. The whole Bambi bit. Our instinct, something happens, is to grab our spears and kick ass. We see a fire, we get the hose and charge in. A woman, she sees a fire, her instinct is to run. There's no getting around the fact that every time a woman goes into a fire she's fighting her basic nature."

"I haven't seen any evidence that Rideout's afraid."

"Then you're blind. You know what else? And don't tell me this isn't true, because you and I have both been there. Women come in, they're at their physical peak. They're as strong as they'll ever be. Even then they barely pass the minimum requirements. A year later they're weaker. Five years later they can't carry a suitcase through the airport. A guy comes in . . . hell, take Gliniewicz. He hasn't done a thing to take care of himself in eighteen years. What d'ya wanna bet, one on one, he could take Rideout?"

"Look, Steve, I've got a report to finish."

"Would you want her on *your* crew?"

"She is *on* my crew, and she's doing just fine."

"Bullshit." Slaughter chewed on the corner of his mustache. "We could have a good station here. You know that, Paul. We could have one of the best firefighting units in the city. Zeke's going to transfer out, and I would appreciate it if I didn't have to replace him with a woman."

"I'm not going to make up stories about her or listen to anyone else's. So far she's done fine, and that's what I'm writing."

Slaughter stared at me for ten long beats. "You're bangin' her, ain't ya?"

"Get out of here."

Slaughter walked to the engine office door, pushed it open, then looked back at me. "You're bangin' her. If you aren't, you will be."

27. WHEN I WAS FOUR

The walk home that morning gave me time to clear my head. I was pissed. About a lot of things. People coming at me from right and left trying to get me to fire the rookie. The pyro. The senseless fire watch at Eleventh and Fir.

I was pissed at the thought that the firebug might be driving past me as I walked home. That we didn't know who he was. That his fires kept help from arriving at Eleventh and Fir when we needed it. That Hertlein might be turning off fans while my guys were inside. That there wasn't a damn thing I could do about any of it.

The sporadic fires they'd had in the area in the weeks before I arrived at Six's had affected all shifts, but in the past four days most of them had been on C-shift. It would be interesting to see whether the arsonist would wait to strike again until Friday, when we would be working next. It would be even more interesting to see whether more Shasta diet black cherry cans showed up.

I wanted to kill the pyro.

I didn't *like* the feeling. But there wasn't much I could do to get rid of it either. Most people could have shaken it. I couldn't.

There was a lot to think about as I walked home in the chill morning air. Slaughter was widely recognized as a smoke-eating firefighter, a good officer, somebody who knew his business. Yet having worked with him eight years earlier, it was my belief that most of his reputation came from stories propagated by himself. When I was a boot at Thirteen's, he'd been a yeller and a screamer on the fire ground. I'd transferred out as soon as I could, using the excuse that I wanted to work on a ladder company. At Thirteen's he'd been tough on me until the night of the Armitage Furniture Warehouse fire, when I hauled his ass out of the building. After that there wasn't much he could say. It was a night he never talked about, probably because he knew he'd panicked in the smoke. I got an award, and he stopped writing negative reports on me.

Filling the moist morning air with exhaust, two idling cars sat driverless in the parking lot at the Water's Edge. It was eight-thirty in the morning, and I had to remind myself most people were leaving for work, not getting home as I was.

Two miles away across the flat waters of Lake Washington, skyscrapers in Bellevue appeared to sit right on the water. To the south, the floating bridge supported a string of headlights.

"Hello," I said, unlocking the front door. "Susan? You awake?"

I took off my shoes, set my rucksack by the front door, and walked down the corridor past floor-to-ceiling bookshelves filled with videos. I rapped on the guest room door. "Susan?"

No answer. The room was empty.

I scanned the guest bedroom for a note but found only a rumpled bed and a drinking glass on the nightstand, a half-moon of rose-colored lipstick on the rim.

Last time she disappeared on me she trashed my place. That was a year ago. Since then she'd gotten a job but, judging by last night, had fallen in with bad company again.

Her name was Susan, but she'd recently announced she wanted to be called Mitzi. She'd been raised by a stepfather she hated, and being called Susan brought those years back. I hadn't yet adjusted to the name change.

In my bedroom one of the dresser drawers had been left ajar just enough to tell me someone had been in it. I kept my belongings meticulously arranged and folded, every pair of socks lined up facing north and south, the shirts in my closet arranged by color and sleeve length. I liked order.

A careful reconnoitering of the rooms revealed a small metal box in my office that had been jimmied. Of the assorted coins in the box, three Krugerrands were missing. It showed her state of mind that she'd broken the lock on a box that hadn't been locked and then taken only three out of the fourteen gold pieces, as if I might not notice only three missing coins.

In the sink were two empty Red Hook bottles. I hadn't had a drink since I was seventeen and almost killed Rickie Morrison under the influence, but I kept a six-pack in the fridge for guests. Susan and one or two other women were the only visitors who'd been here over the past two years—unless you counted the cable guy or the butt-crack bozos who laid the new carpet in my spare room.

On the walk home it occurred to me how much I depended

upon the fire department for social intercourse, how little social interaction I had in the rest of my life, and how much I'd been looking forward to spending the day with Susan.

Actually, I didn't have *any* social life apart from the firehouse. On a four-off I was lucky to talk to a single person who wasn't a cash register jockey or a telephone solicitor. There was a redhead I saw at the gym, but in three years I hadn't worked up the courage to say more than "Hi." I could tell she thought I was an idiot.

It would be a dream assignment if I could remain at Six's. I liked Dolan's sly sense of fun and Towbridge's ability to see through bullshit and find the humor in any situation. And while Pickett had problems, he certainly wasn't afraid of heat.

I missed the day Susan and I would have had together more than I missed the Krugerrands. We could have lunched down the street at the Leschi Café. We might have taken in the Patricia Pennington flick at the Harvard Exit. It would be like old times. But this was like old times too, getting robbed by her.

I fixed a light breakfast and ate in front of the *Seattle Post-Intelligencer* Internet site, perusing the stories about last night's twelve fires, which had been attributed to three or more firebugs. The chief of the department said we were closing in on the perpetrators and would have them in custody within days. I very much doubted that.

After cleaning up my breakfast dishes and laundering the bedding in the guest bedroom, I dragged out the trunk under the bed in my computer room. An accomplished thief, Susan was unlikely to have missed the large black steamer trunk.

When I opened it, the mass of materials and papers I'd configured so carefully and stored so dutifully was topsy-turvy.

The melted firefighter's helmet was crammed full of newspaper clippings, as if she'd balled them up to get them out of the way. The photographs our mother had saved had been rifled.

Here was my history. My mother's history. My father's. Neil's.

Sitting cross-legged on the floor in my stocking feet, I began sorting. Fire department paraphernalia laid out neatly in one pile. Clippings about the search for the Central Area firebug in another. Stories about my father's fiery death in another.

One small news clipping caught my eye. It was dated two weeks after my father's death. I had been four.

ARSONIST LEAVES SIGNATURE

SEATTLE—Although most of the arson activity plaguing Seattle neighborhoods over the last three months has abated, investigators are still on the lookout for the individual responsible for the death of Seattle Fire Lieutenant Neil Wollf, 29, last month.

Fire investigator William Kerrigan said, "We've got a dedicated staff and we're putting everything else on hold until we nail him."

Last month during a series of nighttime arsons on Capitol Hill and in the Yesler district, Wollf's body was found in a basement fire near Empire Way and Union Street. Several fire companies had been battling blazes in the neighborhood when Wollf became separated from his crew. Approximately thirty minutes later his body was found in the corner of a basement fire in a house belonging to Esther Woods, 67.

Says Woods, "We didn't even know the house was on fire until we heard the firefighters."

Kerrigan acknowledged that fire department investigators remain on the lookout for fires displaying a specific signature left by the arsonist. However, he refused to confirm what some fire personnel have indicated to us: that the arsonist leaves a can of a particular type of soda pop at each crime scene.

Since November of last year the firebug has been lighting fences, garages, and exterior house walls and has been blamed for over $500,000 worth of damage as well as untold dollars in police and fire department overtime.

The most damaging fires occurred in the two weeks prior to Wollf's death. A fire in January caused the death of an elderly resident in the Madrona neighborhood. Officials strongly hinted all these fires were set by the same individual.

Arson fires in the Central Area have come to a virtual standstill since Wollf's death.

"Right now we don't know if he's still out there biding his time or if he's moved on to another jurisdiction," says fire chief Frank Hanson.

I'd heard about the soda pop cans from Neil, who'd been a child when he told me about it, so until this past week I had no idea whether it was true. Now Shasta diet black cherry cans were showing up at our arson sites.

Was it possible that after twenty-five years of silence my father's killer had returned?

I'd been thinking about offing the bastard since I was four. I would too, if I caught him. It felt funny to voice it. Ethicists speculate about going back in time and meeting Adolf Hitler in 1929 and whether it would be honorable to murder him if you knew it would save thirty or forty million lives. I found those moral conundrums boring. I had no qualms whatever about slaying the pyro who killed my father. No second thoughts. It would ruin my life; it might send me to prison. But he would be dead.

There was no overstating what the death of our father meant to our mother. It had obliterated her sense of self and decimated her identity. As kids we blamed ourselves. It was only later that Neil came up with the stratagem of blaming the pyromaniac.

Looking back on it now, I think that had we not been there,

our mother would have killed herself, that she'd been dragging herself through life because the thought of leaving two defenseless boys alone sickened her even more than the thought of staying alive.

We never had a chance to grow up normally. Instead, we became the neighborhood charity cases, outcasts, the kids with the hand-me-down clothes, boys perpetually in need of haircuts and baths, the boys everybody in school either felt sorry for or targeted for abuse. We became thieves too.

Neil and I blamed *everything* on the firebug. Our mother's condition. The lack of money. The missing presents at Christmas. The missing turkey at Thanksgiving. Later, we blamed Alfred's entrance into our lives on the pyro, and still later we blamed him for Neil's incarceration and my bouncing around from relative to relative. Hating the pyromaniac had been our own very personal and private jihad. For me, it still was.

Sitting cross-legged on the floor thinking about the possibility that he'd come back made my hands tremble.

28. ALPHABETICAL ORDER

Neil was seven when our mother became a widow, somewhat precocious in school, reading before kindergarten, skipping second grade, a child with a tenacious ability to grasp hard facts and regurgitate them months later. Even though as an adult I'd grown several inches taller and many pounds heavier than my father had been, people told me I was a dead ringer for him, that I had been since birth—yet it was Neil who'd aped his every mannerism; it was Neil who wanted to *be* our father. I wanted to be Neil, the older brother who knew something about most things and everything about how to survive.

Over the years, most of what I learned of my father and his death came from Neil.

Our father had been twenty-nine when he died, a firefighter for eight years. He'd been a lieutenant his last three years. I was now twenty-nine and had been an officer for almost three years, in the department almost nine.

Our father had been assigned to Engine 7—housed in Station 25. The engine had been decommissioned long before I got in.

When I entered the department sixteen years after my father's death, the old salts told me he'd been gregarious and extroverted, quickly converting strangers to friends and friends into extended family. His ability to make people relax around him was one of the things that hooked our mother, who, even though she'd been class treasurer in high school, had been painfully timid in both conversation and action. She had a kind and loving nature, but people said she was as delicate as a homemade kite.

For years her world revolved around her husband, Neil, Sr., and her two sons.

The night of my father's death was not dissimilar to other nights in the string of arsons. As had *our* recent fires, most had been set between the hours of midnight and five A.M. Most had been fueled with materials at hand, usually garbage or discarded paraphernalia left lying about in yards or carports. Most had been set alongside wooden fences, garages, or the outer walls of houses. Not counting my father, there had been four firefighter injuries requiring hospitalization. Two civilians, both elderly homeowners, had died in the arsons.

Our mother had been inconsolable after our father's funeral. She wept for weeks. Didn't leave her room. Barely spoke to us. Didn't pay the bills. Didn't buy groceries. Didn't eat. In the beginning relatives came over and fixed meals, but after a while even their forbearance petered out.

Later I learned that although my grandmother Grant had

made several efforts to move in with us temporarily, she'd been thwarted by Grandpa, who operated on the theory that helping their daughter would keep her from ever being self-sufficient.

Neil was left to raise me by himself, a seven-year-old raising a four-year-old. He did a pretty fair job of it, considering.

By the time I was eight, Mother had begun to drink openly. For a while she went out during the day, purportedly to look for a job. I thought she was getting better, but Neil, who was eleven by then, filled me in. She was going to taverns. *All* day while we were in school. About half the day in the summers when we were off.

After a year or so of barhopping, we were introduced to a boyfriend named Dean Zaltrow. We hated him.

Zaltrow was the first.

Alfred was the last.

Oddly, she'd gone through men in reverse alphabetical order.

After I'd emptied the trunk, I picked up the red helmet my father had been wearing the night of his death, turned it over in my hands, tried it on, looked in the mirror across the room, and saw, briefly, my father's face of twenty-five years ago.

In later years, especially after he'd done a stretch in Monroe and another at Walla Walla, Neil's attitude of blaming all our troubles on the arsonist changed, and he grew fond of telling me, "Stop blaming things on other people. You have to take responsibility for your own actions."

29. COULDA, HADDA, WOULDA

When the phone woke me, I was asleep on the carpet in front of my trunk.

"Hello."

"Will you accept a collect call from a Neil Wollf?"

"Yes, operator."

"Paul? I finally got a phone. Susan wrote me last week. It was a screwy letter, so I called the Port Authority and they said she hasn't been at work in six weeks. Have you seen her?"

"I saw her last night."

"Was she all right?"

"Yes."

"You sure?"

"She stayed at my place."

"God. I was so worried. Could you put her on?"

"She's not here just now."

There was a long silence. "She's back on the juice, isn't she?"

"I think so."

"Jesus, man. Couldn't you hold on to her?"

"I was working last night. She was gone when I got in this morning."

"How did she look?"

"Tired."

"What was she doing for money?"

"I gave her some to tide her over."

"God, you don't give a junkie money. Are you nuts? Wait a minute. You didn't give her shit. She robbed you."

"It wasn't much."

"So you don't know where she's staying?"

"I don't have a clue."

"Do you know how crazy it can make you to be in here and know your wife's out there somewhere doing drugs and fucking strangers?"

"I think I can imagine."

"Can you find her? Can you do that for me? Find her and get her off the stuff."

"God, Neil. I might find her, but I can't get her off the stuff."

"You're right. I'm sorry. At least she's got you for a safety net."

"I love her, Neil. You know that. I'll do whatever I can."

"I know you will, little brother. Now tell me how you've been. Are you still stationed in West Seattle?"

"I been moving around in the department the past few months. It gives me a chance to meet people."

"You're in trouble, aren't you?"

"Not much."

"Don't you be losin' that job, buddy."

"I'm trying not to. How's everything with you?"

"Same ol', same ol'. I got a tooth filled last week."

"Prison dentist?"

"They got a guy comes in. He's pretty good, actually."

"Glad to hear it. Are you hanging on?"

"Just doin' my own time. Just one more thing about Susan. Was she with a guy when you found her?"

"She was getting herself arrested for inciting a riot."

He laughed loudly. "That sounds like her."

"She loves you, Neil. When she's straight, there's never anybody else."

"I know that."

"Neil? This is off the subject, but remember when we were kids and you used to tell me about the Shasta diet black cherry cans? You said that was how we were going to track him?"

"Track who?"

"The guy who killed Dad."

"Paul, you gotta do something besides hole up in that condo of yours parked in front of old movies. Do you have *any* friends?"

"I've got friends."

"Yeah? Name one." When I didn't answer right away, he said, "Did you *ever* have any friends?"

"In high school. Dick and Bob."

"Dick and Bob? They lived across the street from Uncle

Darin for *three* months, Paul. Make some friends and take the chief's test."

"Captain would be next."

"Then take the captain's test. Make something out of your life. Quit blaming everything on the past."

"I think he's back, Neil."

"Who?"

"The pyro who killed our father. There's an arsonist working the district I'm in now. He's been leaving Shasta diet black cherry cans."

"Jesus. You're not making this up?"

"I need to know who told you about the cans."

"It was Dad. I suppose he was trying to make me feel special. He told me he had a secret and I couldn't tell anybody, not even Mom. He said they found a can almost every night they had fires. When you're seven, a secret like that is pretty heady stuff."

"I've been sitting here going through those old newspaper clippings Grandma Grant saved, thinking about that last day."

"Don't waste your time."

"Our whole family was doomed from day one."

"You're living in the land of coulda, hadda, woulda. I know this sounds cracked because I'm inside and you're not, but you're the one who got the short end of the stick. Moving around like that. Nobody to call family. All those schools. How many were there? Twelve? Twelve schools from fifth grade to high school. Eight different homes."

"Grandpa should have hired a real attorney for you instead of letting that public defender botch things."

"Of course he should have. But he didn't and he's gone and there's nothing anybody can do about it. You know what you've been doing, Paul? You're obsessing. That's why you can't move on with your life."

"You don't see it, Neil. You're not in the slammer because you screwed up. You're there because some asshole set a fire that killed our father and dropped our mother into a clinical depression. Because our grandfather wouldn't shell out a couple of bucks to get his oldest grandson decent legal representation. Because some lazy cops overwhelmed by their first blood screwed up the investigation. Because the newspapers made you look like a child monster, because that's what newspapers were doing that year. *Alfred* was the monster."

"Listen, Paul. I wanted to be out of the concrete mama, I'd be out. I've had plenty of chances since then to get my life together. And if you want to live a happy life, you'd live it."

"Where'd you get that? *Oprah*?"

"Don't be doing anything you'll be sorry for. Listen to me. You're in the spot Dad wanted. The spot I wanted. Don't mess it up because of some misguided sense of justice. Believe me. I been there. A guy hits you in the mouth. You go get a lug wrench and smash him upside the head. You feel better for about ten seconds. That's about how long it takes them to slap the cuffs on you. Don't mess up what you got. I don't want to find out I've been warming up a cell for you. Think about our mother."

"I think about her all the time."

30. SLAM DUNK IN THE PENNINGTON MANSE

I could visualize the big house a hundred years from now, preserved just as it was today, tour guides escorting the curious through in groups of five or less, paper booties over their shoes. A regular museum. The Pennington place.

The movie posters in glass cases were worth thousands to aficionados, as was the personal photograph collection, mostly black-and-white photos taken in the Forties by studio publicity people. Pennington dining with Ray Milland and his wife. Batting a tennis ball back and forth with Spencer Tracy and Katharine Hepburn. With Rosalind Russell. In the pool at the Hearst Castle in San Simeon with Douglas Fairbanks, Jr., Charlie Chaplin, Harpo Marx, Mary Pickford, Norma Shearer, and Joel McCrea.

I said, "This one must have been taken shortly before her death, because Carole Lombard died in a plane crash about the time Pennington was hitting the Hollywood scene, nineteen forty-one, 'forty-two."

"Really," she said, flicking a lock of hair behind her ear.

The mantel over the marble fireplace was packed with photos from Pennington's career and Hollywood life. Beside the fireplace hung a framed movie poster sporting a pastel sketch of Robert Mitchum and a young Patsy Pennington, a poster for a western called *High Riders.* "I suppose you know when that was made," she said.

"Mitchum was still playing heavies in those days. Studios used to loan their contract players out to other studios. They protected their best properties, but up-and-comers were fair game. At the time, she was an up-and-comer. Mitchum really didn't get famous until later when he did *The Story of GI Joe* and got an Oscar nomination for best supporting actor. Nineteen forty-seven. *Nine Lives of the Cat.* It launched her career. *Cat* and *The Green River Valley.* If she'd kept making movies like those, she would have been the next Elizabeth Taylor."

"So why wasn't she?" The blonde across the room from me leaned against a doorway in a skirt and a V-neck sweater. High heels. "Tell me why she wasn't the biggest star ever."

"Some biographers trace her decline to mismanagement and some to lack of talent. Personally, I think her private life got in the way of the image. In nineteen forty-seven she had a husband who beat her in public. That didn't help."

"Would you like a drink?"

"Sure. But I can't have alcohol."

"You don't drink?"

"I can't."

From the other room I could hear the sounds of ice dropping into drinking glasses. "Sit down. Relax. What made you decide to take me up on my offer?"

"I don't know."

It felt almost illicit to be lounging around Pennington's estate house without her knowledge. I was standing near the front door I'd kicked in a week ago, catching glimpses of Jackie Dahlstrom in the kitchen as she mixed drinks. I watched her get a Canada Dry out of the fridge and pour it into two large glasses, observed her reach into a nearby cupboard and remove a small pill bottle, drop several pills into one of the drinks. What the hell? Was she trying to slip me a mickey?

She sauntered back into the room and put the drinks on a coffee table, placing, I noticed, the drink with the pills in it closer to me, the straight soda reserved for herself.

She sat on the couch, motioning for me to sit beside her. She was almost reclining, but not quite, her small breasts thrust upward. She fit my modus operandi perfectly. I never chased anything I had to work too hard for. I always went after the slam dunks, never the demanding shots.

I came around and sat beside her, close, and it was at that moment, without any warning, that she gave me a kiss that had the promise of more to come.

"If the old gal wasn't up on Guemes Island with her brother, I'd introduce you."

"How's she doing after the fire?"

"Considering Mrs. P is seventy-eight, she's doing great. The doctors say she'll be fine as soon as she shrugs off the cold she got in the hospital."

The phone rang. Jackie got up to answer it, leaving me with a whiff of perfume and a glimpse of her legs as she walked away. I switched the drinks and was sipping the clean one when she returned, turning off lights on her way.

"My mother was mentally ill," she said when she returned.

"That's what I think got me into acting. She had these moods, and I would imitate everything she did. Then they took her off to some institution, and she didn't come back until I was eleven. Maybe that helped me get in touch with my feelings. They say actors have to be in touch with their feelings."

"Was that your mother on the phone?"

"No. I don't know who that was. They hung up. I had a boyfriend who was whacko too. Hey! Maybe I'm attracted to crazies. Are *you* nuts?" She laughed, but there was no mirth in it. "You know, I thought working here I would learn stuff from Ms. P. I thought she'd have Hollywood people in and out. All we seen so far is a couple of old geezers. One said he was a producer, so I gave him a knobber in his Cadillac. He said he would call, but I wonder if he ever will."

"He wants another knobber, he might."

My snideness prompted her to look me in the eye. "Those wrong numbers are always so rude. I've been getting a lot of them lately."

"There are a lot of rude people out there."

She straddled my lap, the two of us face-to-face now. I tried not to look up her skirt, which was hitched up her thighs.

I reached around her slim waist and pulled her toward me. I didn't much care for the way she kissed, jamming her hard little tongue down my throat.

"Wet your whistle?" she asked, leaning back and reaching for our drinks. We made a production of clinking our glasses together.

"To us," she said. What a couple of phonies, she waiting for me to conk out, me waiting for her.

We drank, she sipping, me downing half the glass. "That's a good boy," she said. "Have some more." I had some more.

She reached down for me. My palms were on her firm back. Under a layer of feminine upholstery, she had strong legs. I pulled my shirt off. I lifted her blouse over her head. "I've wanted you since I first laid eyes on you," she said.

"Me too," I lied.

She reached behind her one more time and brought the glasses around. I watched the way her breasts flattened and her ribs stood out when she twisted backward. "Let's make another toast."

We touched glasses, neither of us bothering to come up with a proper toast. I drained my drink. She came close to draining hers.

Long ago I'd learned if I was going to keep company with the opposite sex, this was what I would be stuck with: women who liked to party, women who would never make good mothers or wives. Sex partners who knew they weren't keepers, just as I knew I wasn't a keeper. Now I'd reached a new low: women who wanted to drug me.

She was on the floor on her knees in front of the couch, tugging off my shoes. She managed to get one shoe off, then her mouth went slack and she stared into the shoe in her hands as if it contained the solution to life's deepest mysteries.

She tilted against the sofa and fell asleep.

31. DON'T MOVE AND YOU WON'T GET GOT

According to Earl Ward

One time at Powder River the guys smuggled in some videotapes. We sat around one afternoon ogling them. I never saw X-rated movies before.

I certainly never saw nothin' like that.

And not again until tonight standing below the old woman's porch peeking through a window where the shade doesn't quite meet the sill. Seeing what no boyfriend should see his girl do. Period.

Don't think I didn't see him park his little red car in front of Mrs. P's. Why he's driving that new Escort and I'm puttering around in a 1976 Dodge Dart which I have to sneak from my mother is another story entirely. Nothing in life is fair.

Tonight you had a date.

Which pisses me all to hell. That you're with some asshole firefighter when I'm out here in the dark.

Not *any* firefighter either, but the one from my nightmares.

One of these days I'm going into the library to look it up, to make sure the guy who died back in '78 was named Wollf, 'cause I'm pretty sure I'm not mistaken. I get into the library, I'm going to look up the book on crazy guys too. Lately, my brain has been playing tricks on me.

I figure it this way: There's no way I could go to Oregon for twenty-five years and come back and a month later I'm staring in the face of the man they *claim* I killed.

It's all so ass-backwards. *I'm* the one they were trying to throw in. *I'm* the son of a gun they were contriving to fry in that fire, and they say it's *my* fault when one of them takes a dose of flash? Me? A kid against two grown men?

And now this guy shows up looking just like the man in my nightmares.

Sometimes I wonder if this is how you lose your sanity, with just one little idea that couldn't possibly be true. And then one more. And pretty soon your brain is crammed with ideas that couldn't be true.

I guess when they start coming true—like now—that's when you know you're ready for a ride in the four-point restraints.

I've never much cared for the idea that somebody you killed could come back to life. Anytime I see that plot in a movie, I leave the room.

But think about my experience. I had that terrible month when the firefighter went into the basement and didn't come out, and then a few days later I'm in the Portland pokey for doin' Mildred. Okay. Some of that night with Mildred might have been my fault. We got a little carried away. Both of us. She lied and I got upset. But *she* started it.

Can you imagine in this day and age namin' your kid Mildred? No wonder she had problems.

Standing out here in the dark in front of Pennington's place, I wish for one godderned minute I could shut off my brain so it wasn't all the time driving me crackers.

I watch him get out of his red car and step up onto the front porch like some sort of high-vaulter or something, watch as he knocks on the door and turns around and looks out in the dark like he owns the world. People with that much confidence are always assholes.

And then, as he stares into the darkness, I get the feeling he's staring at me.

I'm hidden and it's dark, but still, it's a scary feeling. Don't move and you won't get got. It's what I do now, and it's also, my friends, pretty much my basic philosophy of crime. Period.

Don't move and you won't get got.

The door opens and you appear, bless your heart, and you look so godderned cute, like you did that time you visited me in Salem.

And then he walks in like he owns the place, so tall he's almost hitting his head on the doorway. Nelson used to hit his head on top of the cell doorway. Only he's not as big around as Nelson. But you know what? I saw the way he carried Mrs. P out of there last week and I'm thinking he could take Nelson.

From my hidey-hole I can see through a crack under the blinds.

You're in the living room. He's walking around looking at pictures.

And then he comes over and looks out the window and I hear his voice through the glass. He has one of those radioman voices, the kind I wish I had. He's standing close, and looking out at the dark. He's so close to the window and so close to discovering me I think I'm having a heart attack. He looks so much like the man in my nightmares my heart begins pounding in my chest. Thud. Thud. Thud.

Now you're on the couch.

You plant a smooch on his cheek. I got this cell phone I swiped from a woman in Kmart was slapping her kid around. I start pressing buttons and I kneel in the dark by the base of the house, where it smells like spiders, and I press more buttons and pretty soon it rings and then finally you come on the line. "Hello? Hello?

"Hello?" you say one more time. I can hear you breathing. And you can probably hear me breathing. I'm thirty feet away outside the window. And I'm beginning to get sexed up. Then you disconnect.

I'm looking through the window again and you're coming back into the room, only this time you do something that astounds me. You hike up your dress and sit on him. I mean, sit on him. Then something else happens. I start touching myself. Mother always said it would make me go insane. I guess she was right.

The two of you are taking your clothes off now and I'm thinking to myself, what I need to do is stop this.

And then you've got your blouse off and I'm not thinking about anything now but you. Period.

I'm twenty-five feet away and even though you've turned the lights down I can see everything about you is perfect. Everything except him.

This has to stop!

I pull out the phone. I can't get the numbers in sequence. I'm fumbling and punching buttons and panting, and then I'm back up at the window and I can't take my eyes off you and I never do get the number right. The phone inside the mansion never does ring.

I want to break the window out or maybe bust in the door, but I sit quietly in the bushes playing with myself and going insane.

You sex fiends don't know who you're messing with here.

Both of you are going to be sorry you did this to me.

I know things.

With a dose of flash there's no one better.

I know where that bastard works. That's the thing. I know he works on a truck company. And I know what a truck company does at a fire. Period.

Oh my, oh my.

Yes, mama. I have an idea now. He's gonna be one sorry little cowboy. Yes, sir. By the time I'm done, he'll be a briquette just like his daddy.

32. NAKED AND DROOLING

I put my shirt and shoe back on and thought about the situation. She was young and in apparent good health. After I laid her on the couch, I made a knuckle with my right fist and pressed it against her breastbone, rubbed hard, a sternal rub it was called; it aroused most faking patients. She wasn't faking.

In the kitchen I found the pill bottle, a prescription sleeping pill made out in Patricia Pennington's name. I don't know how many she dropped into the drink, but the directions said no more than one pill a night.

In the corner of the kitchen I found two suitcases, a coat and purse atop them.

She hadn't said anything about taking a trip, but then, she hadn't said anything about slipping me a mickey either. In her coat pockets I found a stick of gum, an eight-foot length of rope, and a pair of handcuffs.

I dumped the contents of the purse onto the countertop.

There was a driver's license issued in the state of Washington under the name of Jaclyn Dahlstrom. Another driver's license issued to a Judith Devlin. Same stats. Blue eyes. Blond hair. Five-two. A hundred thirty pounds. Inside a paper bag wrapped in rubber bands I found thirty-one credit cards issued to seven different males.

Except for an accident of observation, the old woman might have come home to find me drugged senseless in her living room, naked and drooling.

I took Jaclyn's keys and went through the house, across the courtyard, and up the stairs to the bungalow where the floor was littered with dirty clothes. Drawers left open. Dishes on countertops.

In the bedroom I turned down the covers on the bed, then dodged back across the breezy courtyard into the main house and carried her limp body to the bungalow.

After I'd tucked her in, I began cleaning up. I wasn't doing it for her. More for the old woman. Our mother had left messes like this so many times.

As near as I could tell from drivers' licenses and credit card photos, her victims were all middle-aged men, an aggregation of losers I'd been slated to join.

I should have called the cops and turned her in. I should have handed over the pile of purloined credit cards and IDs. I should have done a lot of things.

I didn't.

She was too much like Susan. Too much like my brother. Too much like me.

The next morning I mailed the IDs and credit cards to the Seattle Police Department anonymously, then I called Vanessa Pennington and left a message saying I needed to speak with her. I wanted to warn her about Jaclyn, but I didn't want to leave it on a tape.

Three days later she still hadn't called back.

33. BULL ELEPHANTS AND BIKINI BOTTOMS

Friday the thirteenth we were back at work relieving B-shift. The day was cold, clear, and crisp, frost lying heavily on the grass. We had a lot to think about. Over the past week the fires had been growing steadily in number and severity. Our arsons had hit *The Washington Post* and *The New York Times.* CNN and most of the other network news channels had taken up the story.

Officials from Alcohol, Tobacco and Firearms estimated there were no fewer than six arsonists prowling our Seattle neighborhoods. One pundit suggested the rain made people crave fire.

In a single period between midnight and 0330 hours on Wednesday there had been eighteen fires over several sections of the city. In the University District a citizen vigilante patroller fired shots at another citizen patroller he mistook for a fire-setter. Two of the bullets struck the wall of a home with children sleeping inside. Luckily no one was injured.

Well-meaning citizens had reported fires that turned out to be steam from dryer vents, exhaust from idling cars, smoke from their neighbors' fireplaces, and in one instance a man with a cigar.

The city was careening down a greased slide into full-blown panic.

There had been arsons each of the four nights we'd been off. The worst had been in the north end in a marina, where five pleasure craft sank and one boat owner jumped into the frigid waters of Portage Bay fleeing the flames.

Both Seattle papers were obsessed with the situation. The *PI*'s headline read, FIRES CONTINUE TO THREATEN CITY—MULTIPLE ARSONISTS SNIPE AT REGION. Down the page were more boldface banners. NORTH END MAN SHOOTS AT NEIGHBOR; GUN SALES UP.

It was widely accepted that most of the arsonists in the city were copycats and that our pyromaniac had started it; or *my pyromaniac,* as I was beginning to think of him.

Friday morning when I reported to work, everybody in the station was talking about the fires. After exchanging gear on the rig with Joe Williams, I signed into the daybook and went to the beanery, where I heard Dolan ask, "Who fell off the roof?"

Rideout had just come into the room. "Lagersted. Jon Lagersted. He's from my class."

"Is he okay?"

"He's got a coupl'a broken ribs. He fell about fifteen feet and landed on a new Lexus. I guess he smashed the hood all to hell."

The driver on the truck on B-shift said, "They're sending firefighters out in cars at night. Arson patrol. Takin' one guy out of each battalion."

"They're takin' recruits, right?" Towbridge said.

"They're takin' everyone."

"What are we supposed to do when we catch someone?" asked Dolan. "Are they going to give us guns?"

"It's strictly to discourage people," Lieutenant Williams said.

"What do you think is going to happen when you have unarmed firefighters tackling someone who knows he's going to prison?" asked Dolan. "They might as well have us out there flagging down bull elephants with bikini bottoms."

"It's more of a deterrent than . . . what's the word I'm looking for?"

"Sitting duck?" said Dolan. "Except that's two words."

Everybody laughed. The room was crowded, all seven of the B-shifters huddling together the way crews did after a particularly busy shift, reluctant to abandon the camaraderie they'd honed over the past twenty-four hours.

Slaughter walked into the room and said, "I spent most of yesterday helping out down at FIU. Here's what I found out. In a nutshell, this guy here in the CD started it. Before Thanksgiving it was only little stuff. As soon as it hit the papers and local newscasts, it began spreading to other parts of town. That moron in the Northgate area. Three teenagers in Greenwood." Slaughter was confident in front of a group; even as a recruit I'd admired his magnetism. If my life depended on it, I couldn't stand in front of a crowd and talk the way he was.

"Maybe it's just somebody who knows the north end needs live fire training," said Towbridge. We all laughed at that. Anyone who worked south of the Ship Canal, where most of the city's fires occurred, enjoyed thinking that people who worked north of the canal were rusty when it came to basic firefighting skills. That wasn't always true, but we got a lot of mileage out of it.

"Anyway," Slaughter continued. "The truth is whenever one of these guys gets a little publicity, the kumquats start coming out of the woodwork. Remember Paul Keller in the early Nineties and all his copycats?"

Even though we'd never spoken of it, I was sure Slaughter knew my father had been the sole department casualty in another set of arsons twenty-five years ago.

"You haven't even heard the bad part," said Lieutenant Williams. "They had a chiefs' meeting yesterday and decided some of these people need help cleaning their yards."

"Are you shittin' me?" Dolan asked. "They want *us* to clean people's yards now?"

"It gets worse," said Katie Fryer. "There's a stack of flyers in the other room. They want you to deliver them door-to-door. They want you out there at least eight hours."

"Eight hours!" Towbridge said. "Somebody's got their head up their ass."

"Then tonight they want you out in your rigs driving around," Katie added. "Unless you get tapped for the fire patrol."

Dolan was furious. "Who the hell do they think is going to put out the fires?"

Towbridge added, "We'll be so exhausted we won't be able to put out a match with a size-twelve boot."

"I'm just glad it's *you* guys," Katie Fryer said as she stood up and stretched, pulling red suspender straps tight against the outer rim of each voluminous breast. Towbridge looked away.

In the watch office we found a box of fifteen hundred flyers.

Dolan kicked the carton. "This is going to kill us."

At 0815 hours Slaughter and his engine crew grabbed a stack of flyers and left.

They weren't on the air five minutes before they picked up a medic response to 2611 South Dearborn, a nursing home we visited at least once a week. At 0830, Rideout said, "Are we going out?"

"Soon."

Towbridge, sitting near the window reading a slab of the morning's sports section, gave me an amused look. He knew as well as I did that protest came in many forms—work slowdowns being one of the most time honored.

Dolan said, "This is a feel-good program, so the fire chief can go to a news conference in three days and say he's distributed X number of flyers. Cleaned up X number of yards. It ain't gonna stop anything."

It wasn't as if we didn't have other things to do. Rideout had drills to complete. Towbridge was rusty too. We had EMT recertification coming up and needed to study for that. The previous truck officer on Ladder 3 hadn't finished his building inspections for the year. I hadn't been on a truck in six months and wanted to go over the Hurst rescue tools again. Dolan wanted to take the truck down to the fire department garage to have the alternator looked at.

We went out at 1010 hours. We'd only handed out fifteen flyers when we got our first alarm of the day, our client a four-hundred-pound man who'd fallen off the toilet and gotten wedged between the commode and the tub. Personal service, it was called, putting a guy back on the shitter.

At noon, when we went back to the station for lunch, our fax machine had eight requests for assistance with yard cleanups in our district. During lunch more came in.

I ran into Slaughter outside his office door. "You get a chance to ask the FIU guys about the Shasta cans while you were there?"

"I didn't." He brushed past me as if I were an irritant instead of a coworker.

"Steve, this isn't about you and me. This is about an arsonist who might end up killing somebody."

"No. This is about you and me."

"So what you're saying is if I don't fire Rideout, you and I are going to have a hard time working together?"

"You got it."

34. ALL THE DEAD GUYS ON THE WALL

Cynthia Rideout

DECEMBER 13, FRIDAY, 2011 HOURS

The men are sitting around grumbling. It's the first grumbling I've heard out of Lieutenant Wollf since I came here. Gliniewicz, for once, is too exhausted to complain. Zeke is in the phone booth straightening out his private life, or trying to. I like Zeke, but it's like watching a comic tragedy.

There's a minor battle going on between the engine and the truck. I'm not sure who started it, but the lieutenants are barely speaking. Dolan and Gliniewicz have been snapping at each other.

Towbridge cracks jokes, and Gliniewicz is the butt of a lot

of these. Sometimes he says things that are so hilarious I have to bite my lip to keep from laughing out loud.

Towbridge also likes to mock Slaughter, but only when he's not in the room.

There has been bickering over who's responsible for cleaning which part of the beanery. Over the location of the imaginary line on the apparatus floor that delineates the truck side from the engine side. Dolan says he's not going to mop the engine side and he doesn't want Gliniewicz's mop on his side. Would you believe these are grown men?

The hubbub over who would cook dinner got so fierce the truck boycotted the dinner clutch and drove down to Toshio's Teriyaki on Rainier.

The fires don't usually start until around midnight, so I wonder, after passing out flyers and cleaning people's yards all day, how many of the split-second decisions we need to make on the fire ground are going to be good ones? Dolan says it's been so long since the people downtown have actually ridden a rig they've forgotten how much we do in a day.

The last two shifts wore me out. It's not just the lack of sleep, but you have to factor in the stress.

Here's what else happened today. Attack 28 was reprimanded for chewing out people and telling them the junk in their yards was a menace to the neighborhood. Engine 30 started a rubbish fire in somebody's yard and burned almost a quarter of an acre. Both crews were told not to pass out flyers until next shift.

"That's what happens when you step in the shit," said Dolan. "You get to sit on the bench."

Nobody's happy about these extra duties. Funny, but my image of the fire department before I got in was a bunch of guys sitting around playing checkers and waiting for the next call. Not *even* close. Somebody is working in the station almost all day and a lot of the night. And frequently everybody's working at once. There's the housework, rig maintenance, equipment maintenance, the endless drilling, classes and workbooks, the daily memos, building inspections. Our calls only put us further behind.

Even the relatively sedate north end got into the fray. A captain on Ladder 8 took his crew to his grandmother's house, where they were caught doing his grandmother's yard work by a photographer from *The Seattle Times*.

I noticed some things today. I noticed how hard Wollf tries to be his own man. In a profession where we're all required to dress alike, there are so many little things he does to effect his uniqueness. For instance: He's right-handed, but he wears his watch on his right wrist instead of the traditional left. He walks to work, the only guy in the department I know who does. He brings all his own meals to work instead of eating in the station clutch with everyone else.

Also, and this shocked me, the firefighter who lost his life in 1978 was Wollf's father. "You wanna check, all you gotta do is drive down to Ten's," Towbridge said. "All the dead guys are on the wall down there."

After three shifts the guys around here know more about me than they'll *ever* know about Wollf. They know I have five brothers and two sisters. They know I have relatives who live on the reservation. That my family lives in Yakima. That I have two brothers who are alcoholics. That I went to junior college and trained to be a dental assistant before joining the department. They know I love field hockey and tennis but can't swim.

Almost everything we know about Wollf is rumor, innuendo, or guesswork.

Tonight we spent an hour and a half at what they call a postfire critique held in the classroom upstairs at Station 25, a big, concrete-walled fire station at Thirteenth and Pine. Before we went upstairs, Wollf made a point to seek out the crew from Engine 25, and after some hemming and hawing, the captain and two crew members confirmed Chief Hertlein had turned off the fan at our last fire.

"When Pickett and the boot were still inside?" Dolan asked.

"You got it," said the captain on Engine 25.

I'm too new to know the department protocol on such matters, but Dolan insists Hertlein is either a criminal or an idiot or both.

A postfire critique is run by a proctor, in this case Chief Eddings. First thing, she had somebody draw the intersection and building involved. Then she had each unit commander—in the order the units had arrived on scene—explain what they saw when they arrived, what their orders were, and what they ended up doing.

Wollf was visibly nervous talking in front of a group. He told our side of the story, and then the stage was turned over to the captain on Engine 25. Engine 25 arrived, laid a two-hundred-foot 1¾-inch line, and sent the driver and one person to the hydrant for a supply. Engine 25's crew kicked in doors on the first floor and then came up to the second after Pickett and I found the fire unit. They masked up and went in behind us. They made it sound as if they were right on our tails, but we were in and out before they even got in.

It was at this point that Eddings mentioned Pickett's burns and asked me to explain what we did inside the fire unit. I told how we'd been stopped short by the heat before we reached the bedrooms, how Pickett had rushed out of the apartment. "Was the fan working when you went in?" Wollf asked me.

"Yes, sir."

"I'm asking the questions here," Eddings said.

"So it was clear inside?" Wollf continued, ignoring her.

"It was clear at first."

"Then what?"

"The air got incredibly hot. Then Pickett got burned."

"Was the fan still running when you came out?"

"No."

"You sure?"

"Yes, sir."

Eddings seemed to miss the significance of the fan getting shut off, because after everybody was finished, she asked if we didn't think the main point here would be to find out why we had a fire department injury and to prevent such an occurrence in the future. The room got real quiet. I thought the cause of Pickett's injury was obvious. Somebody shut off the fan when we were inside.

"Here's what I think," said Eddings, pacing back and forth. "I think Ms. Rideout was responsible for Pickett's injuries."

"That's not fair and you know it!" Wollf said, jumping to his feet. "We just explained how Pickett got burned."

"Just hear me out," said Eddings. "There were a couple of things done wrong here, and Rideout was there each time."

"This is not even how a postfire critique is run," Wollf said angrily. "You said yourself the idea is not to place blame. If a member of my crew needs union representation, you should tell us before you start."

"This is not a disciplinary hearing, Wollf. Don't get excited."

"Look who's talking," whispered Towbridge.

Eddings was angry now. "It seems to me anytime we go into a fire with a probationary firefighter, we need to take extra precautions. In this instance, Pickett went in with a probationary firefighter, and she got lost. While they were separated—"

"I was never lost and we didn't get separated," I whispered to Lieutenant Wollf.

"She was never lost," Wollf said aloud, "and they weren't separated."

"Are you going to keep interrupting, or are you going to let me finish?" Eddings asked.

"Fine," Wollf said. "But she wasn't lost."

"According to Pickett they were."

"That's not what he told us," said Wollf.

I was in the middle of a tug-of-war.

"The way I understand it," continued Eddings, "there was

improper supervision of a probationary firefighter. They went in in front of a hose line. The probationary firefighter opened a window which was not in the fire room, which caused the dynamics of the ventilation to change."

"Can I comment now?" Wollf asked, standing.

"You may not."

"I thought this was a fact-finding mission."

"You can just sit back down."

"Just *your* facts?" There was enough grumbling in the room that Eddings capitulated. Wollf said, "You're right. They went in before the hose line. But the line was charged, and that the hose still hadn't come in by the time they were leaving was not anything they could have foreseen."

"That's why we wait, isn't it?" said Eddings.

"While we're waiting people are dying. They went in on a bubble of perfectly good air and were doing fine. Sure, Rideout broke out a window. But judging by the char on the ceiling, the heat wasn't heading toward that window. It was heading for the front door which became the largest exit after the fan got shut off."

"That's ridiculous," said Eddings. "The place would have been untenable without a fan."

"It *was* untenable," said Wollf. "That's why Pickett got burned."

"Are you saying Engine Twenty-five turned off the fan?"

"Chief Hertlein turned it off."

"That's ridiculous. It probably ran out of gas."

"It wasn't out of gas. We checked."

The classroom grew quiet. "If there's somebody here who wants to back up Lieutenant Wollf, I'd like to hear them, because what you're doing, Wollf, is you're accusing one of our deputy chiefs of compromising a fire operation, and that is a serious accusation."

The room REALLY got quiet.

Even though there were witnesses, nobody was going to back him up.

It was then that we saw Chief Hertlein in the doorway.

"Sorry I'm late," Hertlein said. "Now, what's this about a fan?"

"Lieutenant Wollf seems to think you shut off the fan at Eleventh and Fir," Eddings said.

Hertlein stepped forward, hands clasped behind his back. He was wearing his white chief's shirt and black uniform trousers and had a look in his eyes that would have stopped a cobra. "I think I would remember if I had."

If I'd watched him turn off the fan Sunday night, *I* wouldn't have spoken up. Apparently everybody else felt the same way because nobody said beans.

Afterward Towbridge said, "Don't Chief Eddings look like Miss Piggy in a chief's uniform?" Tow always made everything funny.

35. BINGO, BIDDIES, BUDWEISER, BANK ROBBERIES, AND RIOTS

According to Earl Ward

I know he's working today, but the station is empty every time I drive by.

Jesus. The memories make me sick to my stomach at the same time they get me excited, which is something I can't quite figure. You'd think you saw another guy about to dink your woman you'd want to kill him, but I got so excited I couldn't even watch the whole thing. It's confusing, but most of my life has been confusing. Period.

I slide into the Red Apple parking lot and touch up my lipstick in the rearview mirror. With the red wig and glasses, not even my own mother would recognize me. In fact, she didn't. I inspect the contents of my purse. There's the cash—

seven dollars and twenty-five cents. My ID. Half a pack of gumdrops and a cigarette lighter. Oh, yes. And a pack of ciggies. I found out the hard way it's not enough to have a cigarette lighter and say you were smokin'. You gotta produce smokes.

In the reflection of the windows at the Red Apple I look like a middle-aged babe who was maybe hot at one time. I stroll around the store and catch the eye of a couple of hung-over black dudes who I know right away done time. I shake them off and buy a six-pack of soft drinks, and by ten o'clock I'm driving past Pennington's place. The house is dark. So is the guest house in back.

J's probably out driving the old lady to the opera.

I'm so jittery I can barely read a newspaper article even when it's about me. Mom says I live on caffeine and *Judge Judy,* but that's not true. I eat doughnuts; that's where I get my strength.

This is Friday, and I know from J's letters the old gal likes to mingle with the hoity-toity on the weekends. The symphony. Live theater. She could teach my mother a few things about energy—maybe explain there's more to life than biddies, bingo, and Budweiser.

I drive down to the lake and come up the hill on Fullerton Avenue. I like these lesser-known neighborhoods. Every mile I put on this old Dodge has a purpose. If I don't light up this neighborhood tonight, I'll give it a dose of flash some other night.

When he started the Boy Scouts, Ben Franklin said a smart man prepares for the future. That's what I do too.

Here's what's so cute about me and Mom. The front pages are plastered with my exploits, which she gobbles up like the funny papers, and the whole time she don't even know I'm the one she's readin' about. She knew, she'd shit a brick.

Neither of us ever mentions my time in Salem. Around our house that twenty-five years just evaporates like so much vapor off the roof. One thing Mom's good at is letting things go. Not me. Every little thing I keep thinkin' about. Period.

I park the car on a dark intersection near East Columbia and Thirtieth, and before you can squeeze a chigger I'm taking a catnap.

I wake in a cold sweat. I mean, the brassiere full of newspapers is even wet. My panties are wet. I start up the car and begin driving, turning the heater up full blast tryin' to dry out. It's not midnight yet.

Think about this. For ten thousand years whenever a man, woman, or child got cold, he or she or it could start a fire. In a cave. Under a tree. Beside a rock. Now all of a sudden it's illegal. Why shouldn't I be allowed to start a warming fire when I'm freezing? A small, controlled fire. It's nuts.

In the car I dreamed about the firefighter they lost years ago.

If I'd had any gumption, I would have stuck around, but I was just a kid, so I panicked and ran off to Oregon, which was a mistake from the giddy-up.

I had the $417 I stole from Mom's boyfriend, Mr. Houtz, but even with all that money I got depressed the minute I got off the Greyhound. I got a room and holed up for three days. I met up with Mildred and her friends in downtown Portland, and when she asked me for the twenty dollars and said I could fuck her, why I just naturally felt it would be best to oblige. I never had sex with a woman before that. Actually, I never had sex then neither.

Mildred took me down behind this building and laid herself down on some cardboard in the alley and then laughed when I spilled all over myself taking my pants down. I guess I got a little previous. I wanted my money back and she wanted to keep it, and before I knew it my hands were around her neck and then not too much later I was in the back of a police cruiser.

Bad luck all the way around.

Even in the Portland clink everybody was reading about

the fires in Seattle. The headline I remember most said, "Cowardly Firebug Flees Area?"

It still gets my goat that they called me a coward.

Let me tell you this. Arson is one of the few crimes where the authorities are there just minutes after the fact. I guess bank robberies and riots would be the others. Given that dynamic, you know it takes an extremely brave person to do what I do, brave and smart. Period.

36. HOW AND WHEN

Cynthia Rideout

DECEMBER 17, TUESDAY, 0545 HOURS

I'm here on my bunk too tired to sleep. We caught our one really good fire at 0400 and just now got back to the station and cleaned up our equipment. We've only got an hour and fifteen minutes before the hitch, when we have to get up anyway.

Everybody in the station is jazzed because a crew from *60 Minutes* is following Katie Fryer on B-shift. This morning they were filming her out on the ramp washing the rig. Dolan said Katie was showing off for the cameras and that the water was turning to ice on the ramp, that it was dangerous. I haven't told anybody they asked to film me—or that I turned them down.

I know why they asked me first. I'm a woman, I'm a recruit, I'm an Indian. A poster child for all their liberal biases. But no way do I want cameras following me around while officers and firefighters are spreading rumors and trying to sack me. No way do I want them saying on national TV how two of my brothers are alcoholics. Or showing the shack where I grew up and embarrassing my family.

Katie Fryer was a perfect choice. Outspoken. Colorful. Not a bit shy.

Here's what's been happening.

First, the department cancelled their flyer and alley inspection policy. The last straw was when the rank and file started griping to the national media. Dolan was right. From the beginning it was a feel-good program so the department administration could tell the press they had implemented this program to stop the arsons. It was never going to stop anything and they knew it.

Sunday's paper was full of stories about a dog kennel in Ballard where they lost nineteen dogs in a fire. There were pictures of firefighters giving CPR to dachshunds, along with a sidebar article about the breed. Pickett came in at lunchtime on his way back from the hospital, all bitter over the fact that the dogs got more coverage than he did. Towbridge has been making jokes about it all day.

I've been thinking about that postfire critique. I know Eddings is out to crucify me. I can live with that.

What hurts is all those people who knew the truth and wouldn't speak up.

Those guys can crawl into a burning apartment fire that's 1200 degrees, but they can't talk back to a chief. It's a strange combination of physical courage and moral cowardice.

All weekend I kept thinking about Lieutenant Wollf standing up for me.

Wollf is so deliberate around me, saying only what needs to be said. And yet he's direct and always looks me in the eye when he's talking, as if I'm the only person in the world he's thinking about. I like him so much. Sometimes I wish I *was* the only person in the world he was thinking about.

We got the call for our big fire Friday night when we were parked in the alley near Rainier and Atlantic. Attack 6 got there about the time we did.

There were four houses in a row, all built maybe sixty years ago. All four houses were so close together you could spit out the window of one and into the window of another.

The fire had been set between houses one and two counting from the right, had gone up the wall of house number two, gone into the living and dining rooms on the first floor and snaked up into the attic on the exterior.

When we got there, the front door was open, smoke was pouring out, flame coming out the windows on either side of the house. Wollf told us to do search and rescue. At three in the morning with the front door wide open and nobody in sight it was the obvious call.

Dolan got up on the porch, where he hooked up his face piece. I got myself on air just as Wollf came around the front of the apparatus, clicking his pressurized hose to his MSA mask, giving himself air. Which meant we were all three ready at the same time. On his knees, Dolan tried several times to go into the house, but each attempt was rebuffed by the heat. I wanted to tell him to stay back, that he was going to get burned like Pickett, but Jeff Dolan has twenty-four years in the department and doesn't want my opinion.

"Let's go," said Wollf, who simply stepped over Dolan—no hesitation—and disappeared into the house. Seconds later he was walking in the fire. Walking, not crawling. I saw him in what appeared to be the center of a large yellow ball of flame. Dolan couldn't get in. I couldn't get in. Wollf walked right over us.

At first we thought if *he* could do it, *we* could, but in the few seconds we deliberated, the heat grew more intense.

The smoke closed down again, and a burst of orange flame came out the front door and chased us off the porch, which definitely cancelled any plans either of us had for following Wollf inside.

The crew of Attack 6 was still in the front yard.

"God, he's crazy!" said Dolan, looking into the flames. "He's gonna die."

"We're all going to die," said Towbridge, leaping up onto the porch beside us. "It's just a matter of how and when." It was an expression Wollf used.

A minute later, as Zeke and Slaughter were going through the doorway with the 1¾-inch line blasting, Wollf stuck his head out the second-story window above us, black smoke arching out around him. Over his portable radio he said, "Atlantic Command from Ladder Three. Primary search all clear."

Chief Eddings, who was in the street behind us, didn't reply.

Dolan and I followed Attack 6's hose line inside. They used a lot of water in the doorway. On my way through the living room I stopped and pulled more hose. Again I heard Wollf on my portable. "Atlantic Command from Ladder Three. Primary search all clear. Do you copy?"

After a moment the dispatcher came on the air and said, "Atlantic Command. Ladder Three reports primary search all clear. Did you receive?"

Again Eddings said nothing. A moment or two later she was on the air. "Attack Six. Have you finished your primary search?"

It took Slaughter a moment to drop whatever he was doing and answer. "Negative, Command. We haven't done any searching."

"That's what I thought," Eddings replied, which was both an unnecessary radio transmission as well as a slap in the face to Wollf, who'd already told her the house was clear.

It's dangerous for an incident commander to ignore a radio message. To pretend someone on the fire ground was not being heard. And then to pretend the dispatcher hadn't relayed the message.

If Wollf had been calling for help, would she have ignored that too? It was bad enough she had everybody searching the house a second time.

After the fire was tapped and we were changing our expended bottles for fresh ones, Dolan looked at Wollf. "Man, you tryin' to get killed?"

"If you'd been inside, you wouldn't have wanted me to wait."

"You coulda got killed."

"We're all going to die—"

"It's just a matter of how and when," Towbridge finished.

Wollf's air bottle had blistered from the heat. His helmet was filthy black, the L-3 insignia patch melted and unreadable.

Later, Dolan whispered, "Do we really want to be working with somebody who's got a death wish?"

"I been thinkin' the same thing about you ever since I been on Ladder Three," Towbridge said. We all laughed at the look on Dolan's face.

But I'm beginning to think Jeff is right. I'm beginning to think I'm working for a man who wants to die in a fire.

Not that I wouldn't follow my lieutenant through the back door of hell itself. Because I *would.* But I don't want another partner hurt, and I certainly don't want to see *anybody* die.

It turned out the residents were across the street at a neighbor's house, watching us out the windows—they had no idea people were risking their lives for them.

37. GUARDING THE CAN

While we were waiting for Marshal 5 to show up and investigate, I walked the perimeter of the premises with a battle lantern. Two front rooms had been fully involved when we got there, heat and smoke traveling up the stairs, burning pictures off the walls, charring light fixtures, discoloring mirrors, and ruining the contents of the upstairs closets. The residents had been lucky to escape with their slippers and the cat.

Engine 30 had come in behind us and used their 1¾-inch line to douse the outside of the second house. Slaughter had yelled at them, "You don't attack a fire from outside, you idiots!"

"We're hitting the exposures," one of the Engine 30 guys replied amicably.

"Just don't be pushing the fire onto us when we're inside!"

"That's not what we're doing."

"Assholes!"

At fires everything with Slaughter had to be a contest. When I was a boot, our first fire together had been in an abandoned house. We'd gone in low, him screaming at me the whole way. Finally I turned around and said, "Don't yell at me." I must have intimidated him, because he never did it again. That was about the time he began writing negative reports on me.

Slaughter's yelling wasn't the panicked screaming you got with Eddings. It was more of a bullying tactic he'd copped from his father, long since retired as the driver on Engine 18, an ornery cuss who called anybody who didn't follow his lead a "pussy."

After ten minutes of searching I found what I was looking for.

"Whatcha got?" Slaughter asked. "What's that?"

"It's a Shasta diet black cherry can," I said. "Same as the one we found at the Pennington fire."

"Let me see that," Slaughter said, reaching for it.

"Don't touch it!"

"Don't get your tits in a wringer. I wasn't going to put any prints on it."

"Weren't going to put any prints on what?" Rodney LaSalle approached, followed at a distance by Marsha Connor, who *always* followed at a distance. LaSalle carried a camera, Connor a notepad. Both wore coveralls and rubber fire boots. As usual, there was a wedge of unease between the two fire investigators, just as there was between myself and Slaughter.

I directed the battle lantern onto the container. "You found one of these before?" LaSalle asked.

"Two."

"Why the hell didn't you tell us?"

"I did."

LaSalle knelt and sniffed the mouth of the can. "Nice find. It's piss."

When Connor took a turn at smelling the can, LaSalle laughed and said, "You never smelled piss before?"

She got up and said, "It's piss if they're drinking ninety-one octane. That's gasoline."

"Really?" LaSalle tried to laugh off his mistake. "I burned out most of my olfactory glands smoking Marlboros. Why don't you take a picture?" He handed the camera to Connor. "I'll scout around."

"That's the third one I've seen. There must have been others."

"As far as I know, we got *one,*" LaSalle said.

"But it *is* a signature?"

"Like he's deliberately leaving 'em? Could be."

Slaughter was staring off toward Rainier Avenue. "Back in the late Seventies there was a series of arson fires in this district," I said. "At the time, somebody was leaving Shasta diet black cherry cans at the scene."

LaSalle scratched his head. "Late Seventies was a little before my time. Like twenty years before." He turned and looked at Slaughter. "Steve? Weren't you in FIU in the late Seventies? You remember the arsons he's talking about?"

"Vaguely."

"And?"

"One day the guy just up and disappeared. We never saw him again."

"Didn't a firefighter die?" Connor asked. "Seems to me I remember that."

"My father," I said.

None of them knew how to react. Connor's eyes watered up. Slaughter stared at the street. LaSalle looked at me with undisguised curiosity. "You're kidding. Your father?"

"That's what I said."

"So you two both had fathers in the department? Working at the same time? How did he die?"

I looked at Slaughter. "Ask *him.* I was four years old."

Slaughter looked at LaSalle and said, "I don't recall the details. I do seem to remember something about pop cans."

"Shasta diet black cherry cans," I said.

"We'll look into it," said LaSalle, heading down the street toward Chief Eddings.

"Can you two guard the can for a minute?" Connor asked. "I'm going to get a box to put it in."

When we were alone, I looked at Steve Slaughter. "You never told me you were working in Marshal Five when my father died."

"Do the math. It happened twenty-five years ago. I've been in twenty-seven. A lot of us were around."

"Not in fire investigation."

"We never even had a viable suspect. The arsons stopped. Kerrigan in FIU swore he'd track down the bug and make him pay, spent years on it. He never came up with diddly."

"You must have been frustrated."

"If I saw him now? Tonight? I'd break his goddamn neck."

"You never had a hint who it might be?"

"Nope."

When Connor came back, she gave me a sympathetic look. "You know, what we might have here is a copycat, somebody who knows about those old arsons."

"Either that or he's back," I said.

"Not fuckin' likely," said Slaughter.

38. THE HUMAN GARBAGE DISPOSAL

Eddings found me at the intersection, her bunking coat unbuttoned and flapping, as if she couldn't fit her bulk into it; her bulging lower belly bursting from her pants like the spillage on a boiled egg that cracked during cooking. As she approached, I could see her trying to gather herself together.

"Wollf. I've been meaning to talk to you all shift. It's come to my attention that your reports on Rideout aren't factual."

"I haven't submitted a report yet."

"Maybe not, but you've written three and I read them and they're not right."

"They're still in my drawer."

"Steve faxed them to me. They're not factual."

Ignoring the nugget about Slaughter interfering with my reports, I said, "Which part isn't factual?"

Eddings gave me a look that was maternal and pitiful at the same time, then glanced up the street at the others who were out of earshot. "You say she's strong enough to carry ladders, yet somebody saw her putting a ladder down on the sidewalk Sunday night. You say she doesn't makes mistakes on the fire ground, but we all know she broke out that kitchen window and got Pickett burned. Slaughter says she wanders around at fires like a chicken with its head cut off."

"Slaughter's got his opinion. I've got mine. I'm her officer. It's my opinion that matters."

"You know what I think? I think you're doing everything you can to make sure she succeeds."

"I do everything I can to make sure *every* recruit succeeds. That's my job. It's your job too."

"It would be too bad if you were being influenced by that slinky little body."

"I'll pretend I didn't hear that."

"I don't get this. You fired a woman up at Ladder Eleven."

"She fired herself. I wrote the facts, just like I'm writing the facts about Rideout."

"Maybe you don't understand the politics here, Wollf. You didn't just *accidentally* land in the Fifth Battalion. I had to go over heads, Wollf, but I went downtown and called in some chits. I'm building a battalion here. One I can be proud of. I fought hard to get you, so don't let me down."

"What about letting Rideout down?"

"One phone call from me, and you'll be outta here."

"I don't lie or cheat. Go ahead and make the call."

We stared at each other for a full thirty seconds. Here at last, Eddings knew, was an officer as bullheaded as she was. "You understand you'll be bouncing around the city until Bill Hertlein retires."

"Do what you have to."

"God damn it, Wollf!" Everybody in the street turned around to watch now. "You've got something here. Don't get pigheaded and throw it all away."

"I've been pigheaded my whole life. I can't change now."

All her blather about wanting a good officer on Ladder 3 was just that, blather. I'd been brought in as the axe man. As soon as I got rid of Rideout, I would be expendable. I knew that now. What I didn't know was why Eddings was so bent on firing Rideout in the first place.

"I *really* don't want to see you working at Forty-one's."

I began walking away.

"What's going on here?" Chief Hertlein strode toward us. It was the first we'd seen of him tonight.

"Chief, I want you to transfer this bastard," Eddings said. "Tonight."

"Which bastard?" Hertlein asked. The gaggle of nearby firefighters began backing away like chickens at a dogfight.

Eddings tried to take a deep breath but found her lungs already full. She'd been screaming and holding her breath at the same time. It tended to raise the pitch of her voice. "I want Wollf out of my battalion right this minute."

"What seems to be the problem?"

"He's not somebody I can work with. I thought he was, but I had to counsel him last shift and again tonight. We need to ship him out."

Hertlein turned to me. "I worked on Ladder Three for a couple of years. It always sees a lot of action. I would think that would suit your temperament. On the other hand, I've been thinking of moving you out of there."

"My things are packed."

The comment surprised Hertlein. In the Seattle Fire Department everyone knew there were people who needed to be on engines and there were people who weren't happy unless they were on a ladder company. At Thirty-two's I'd made no bones about it. I was a truckman. Ladders and equipment. Forget the hose lines and the midnight aid calls.

Hertlein looked at Eddings and said, "You went to a lot of trouble to get this man in your battalion. It's been what? Three shifts?"

"This is four," Slaughter said, moving alongside Eddings.

"What do you think about this, Lieutenant Slaughter? You think Lieutenant Wollf is working out?"

"Hey, if the battalion chief wants him out, who am I to argue?"

Hertlein turned to Eddings. "Tell you what I'm going to do." He looked at me. "Since *you* want to leave"—he turned to Eddings—"and you *want* him to leave"—he turned now to Slaughter—"and you obviously don't want him in your station—I'm going to keep him right where he is."

"But you're going to move him?" Eddings whined. "Eventually?"

"To tell you the truth, I kinda like the idea that you don't want him."

Eddings stared at Hertlein in disbelief. As he walked toward his idling Suburban, he scooped up a fistful of cookies off the card table the buffs had set up.

Later, Towbridge said, "Hertlein's a human garbage disposal, ain't he?"

39. LOCAL PARIAH SERIAL-KILLER PERVERT PEEPER PORNO-COLLECTING MURDERER CAR THIEF IN TRAINING

The whitecaps on the lake were taller than my deck, waterspouts crashing over the railing and into traffic on the Mercer Island floating bridge. Gulls hovered nearly motionless over the water.

I was cross-legged on the floor in my living room, the contents of my father's battered black trunk laid out around me, the memorabilia and newspaper clippings compulsively culled by my grandmother, who'd felt an obligation to save anything that contained the family name, no matter how deleterious. Oddly enough, most of our family tragedies had been chronicled in the local press.

My grandfather, who had been ill his last few years, died falling off a cliff while posing for a picture on the wrong side of the safety barriers at Grand Coulee Dam—a snappy little article there. Grandmother followed him with a heart attack two years later—just an obit.

The squabble over whether or not to move me out of Station 6 reminded me of when I'd been a kid and the relatives were trying to decide who would take me next. I'd gotten in the habit of pretending I didn't care, knowing that to acknowledge the hurt was to let it mark you. Except in this instance I *did* care. The pyro working these past weeks near Six's was the pyro who killed my father. I was more and more convinced of it.

I picked up the half-melted helmet—one of the last things my father ever touched. The color was barely recognizable except for the red undersides. It didn't seem fair that this piece of inconsequential plastic could still exist when my father did not.

I pulled a newspaper clipping out of the trunk.

THIRTEEN-YEAR-OLD BOOKED FOR MURDER

SEATTLE—The son of a deceased fire lieutenant who died in the line of duty six years ago has been booked into the King County Juvenile Detention Center on suspicion of murder.

Dead are Alfred T. Osbourne, 29, and Emma Grant Wollf, 32, whose bodies were found in a Belltown apartment rented to Wollf. The suspect, 13, and his brother, 10, are both the sons of the deceased woman. According to neighbors, Osbourne had been living in the apartment for some months and was the mother's boyfriend. Neighbors had complained about loud fights and drinking at the apartment.

According to police, the 13-year-old gave a confused account, while the 10-year-old is believed to be mute. Relatives are debating with the local police about whether or not the boys should be seen by a child psychiatrist. The boy's grandfather has objected to mental health intervention, saying it would be an invasion of the family's privacy.

Police, who are still piecing the story together, say the woman died of stab wounds to the neck and upper torso, while the man died of multiple gunshot wounds.

Osbourne, whose body was found near the front door, was apparently trying to leave the apartment when the 13-year-old allegedly gunned him down. No other details are known.

The 10-year-old has been placed with relatives pending further investigation.

The reference to my being mute brought back some scary moments when I knew my brain was trying to figure out whether to simply stop speaking or to go catatonic. There'd actually been a conscious choice on my part. I have no idea what would have happened if I'd given up and stopped everything. As it was, I ceased talking for three months.

The neighbors painted a picture of the widow Wollf and her two intractable sons that centered the initial investigation on us. It didn't help that Alfred had complained daily to the neighbors about us, or that, after years of no adult supervision, we were as wild as feral cats.

Neil gave them a lot of different stories, which was his habit when confronted by the law.

Their initial reading of Neil was that they had a psychopathic youngster on their hands and they needed to get him off the streets for as long as possible. It didn't help that Alfred had been shot three times in the torso and twice in the back of the skull, or that Neil fought them when the first officers tried to take the empty gun out of his hands. The whole thing looked too much like a new strain of adolescent psychosis.

To make matters infinitely worse, Neil drew an incompetent, alcoholic public defender.

After our mother's death, I lasted less than three months with Grandpa Grant. Then it was off to Uncle Elmo, Grant's eldest son, and his second wife and three children from her former marriage. I was given a spot on the basement couch, my meager belongings stacked beside the couch in cardboard boxes: a few pairs of pants, one pair of shoes, and a suit I'd worn only once. I had a picture book about the American Indian that I carried from house to house like a totem. There was a tiny school photo of my brother—we'd never had the money to buy full-sized photos but each year had copped the samples given out by the photography studio.

At Uncle Elmo's I eventually put a broom handle through their new color television and was packed off to Aunt Valerie's. Valerie was a compulsive gossip, who I learned later had told all the neighbors my brother was doing time for murder. The neighborhood treated me as a pariah. I spent five and a half months on her couch.

And so it went.

After high school I moved into a rooming house in the U District and worked nights at the Boeing Renton plant so I could attend college during the day. Two years later I signed up to take the fire department entrance test.

These days no matter what I did, part of my brain remained in Aunt Valerie's neighborhood in Tacoma, Washington, where the neighbors thought I was the local pariah serial-killer pervert peeper porno-collecting murderer car thief in training.

40. DRY MOUTH

When she returned my call, Vanessa Pennington said she was on her way out and could only talk for a couple of minutes. I told her I had disturbing information about her grandmother's housekeeper I thought she should know about. She seemed interested and said she would call me as soon as she had more time. On the afternoon of the eighteenth she phoned again. "Are you going to be home for a while?"

"As a matter of fact I am."

"Do you mind if I come over for a few minutes?"

My mouth went dry at the thought.

I gave directions, hung up, brushed my teeth, checked my hair in the mirror, made sure the buttons on my shirt were aligned in the right holes, and was sweeping nonexistent bread crumbs from the cutting board with a paper towel when she arrived at my door.

I stared for a moment. "Can I come in?" she asked, laughing, then floated in on a gust of cold air. "I hope you don't mind such short notice. My grandmother just got back from a visit to Guemes Island, and I want to hear what you know about her housekeeper before I talk to her." She glanced around my living room. "You certainly keep a tidy place."

"It's something from my childhood."

"You really are a video buff," she said, standing at the bookshelf next to the kitchen perusing titles while I hung up her coat. She glanced down the hallway at the sturdy cherrywood racks on both walls. "How many videos do you own?"

"Eight thousand, give or take."

"Amazing."

She took in the television screen in the corner of the living room next to the gas fireplace, the single armchair across the room that announced I spent most of my time alone.

"Tell me what you know about Jackie Dahlstrom. I've never fully trusted her with my grandmother, but Nanna seems to like her, and she has so much trouble finding help, once she gets somebody they practically have to set fire to the place before she'll let them go. Oh, God. You don't think she lit those fires, do you?"

"The thought crossed my mind, but actually, no." I tried to explain what I knew about Dahlstrom without confessing to our "date." I told her I knew Dahlstrom had a cache of stolen credit cards and I believed she was a thief and a scam artist.

Pennington walked over to my kitchen window and gazed out at the choppy water. "I just want my grandmother safe. Look, Paul. I'm going to ask you a favor. I'm going to have a very hard time convincing Nanna to fire Jackie. Could you come up there with me now? Or do you have other plans?"

I *never* had plans.

The Pennington house was five minutes up the hill. We took Vanessa's BMW. She'd never driven to her grandmother's from this area, so I gave her directions up the hillside through the maze of side streets. She parked in front and we walked up to the porch. The weather was still cold and windy, the gray skies black along the horizon.

Patricia Pennington was seventy-eight, but shuffling along

in her slippers and mauve dress, she still had a twinkle in her periwinkle blue eyes. Her dyed black hair was mussed in back as if she'd been napping. "So you're the young man who carried my sorry bones out of this house the night they tried to burn me out?"

"I had help."

"First rate outfit, your fire department. I mean that. First-rate."

"Yes, ma'am. I think so too."

"I saw people from your department up in the hospital. They think a lot of you."

"Some do."

She gave me a tour of the first floor, stopping at various photographs on the walls and telling a story about each. Vanessa watched her grandmother's eyes as the old woman spoke.

Pennington was incredulous that I knew all of the actors in the photos, and most of the producers and directors. "George Cukor," I said, at one point. "Geraldine Page. Ronald Colman. There's Dalton Trumbo. What a writer."

"I absolutely adored him," she said. "That blacklist was such a horrible time. But he was constantly smoking. That's what killed him, don't you know?"

We were into the second room of photos when it became clear that the old woman was flagging. "Nanna," Vanessa said, "why don't we sit down?"

When we got her situated in her favorite armchair, she turned on the television with a remote control. Vanessa went to the kitchen to make tea. "So," said Pennington, after Vanessa was gone and the television was warmed up and competing for her attention, "what's this I hear about my housekeeper?"

"She's been seen with stolen credit cards—a lot of them. I don't think you can trust her. I think you should get somebody else."

Staring at the television, she said, "She does a good job here."

"Well, maybe—"

Vanessa returned with a tray of teacups and a teapot. "Nanna, she does a terrible job. You know I had to hire a cleaning service to come in once a week."

"I keep her busy. She wants to be an actress."

"We could go to a job service and find somebody with recommendations."

"I hate to put a young person out of work."

"I'm worried about you up here alone with her. Lieutenant Wollf thinks she's a criminal and might even rob you."

"Do you really think that?" she asked, turning from the television to look at me.

"Yes, I really do," I said.

She looked into my eyes for a long time. "Well, if you say so, I guess I'll have to let her go. I'll tell her tonight."

Vanessa gave me an exultant look and we sat down and had tea. At five o'clock we heard somebody rummaging around in the kitchen. Vanessa took the tea service back into the kitchen, exchanged words with Jaclyn, who I never saw, and came back out to take me home.

We were in her BMW when she said, "Are you planning to eat alone?"

"I was."

"Listen. Let me take you out for a bite. It's the least I can do to thank you for helping me with Nanna, and I'd appreciate the company. It was so hard for me in there. I hate confrontations, and when I went into the kitchen, Jackie was just so sugary sweet I wanted to slap her face."

"I can't imagine you slapping anybody."

"That's the trouble," she said, laughing. "Neither can I."

"Sure. Let's go somewhere."

We drove to B&O Espresso midway up Capitol Hill on Belmont and Olive. Normally I couldn't tolerate silence in a car, especially with a woman I didn't know, but with Pennington somehow it was all right.

The B&O was an eccentrically decorated coffeehouse that

served great food, perfect espresso, and legendary European pastries and desserts. Sitting near a silent elderly couple who looked as if they came often, we ordered and chatted about the weather and other inconsequentials. Pennington had an open, easygoing manner that made me feel increasingly—and uncharacteristically—comfortable around her. It helped, too, that I knew there would never be anything between us other than our mutual concern for her grandmother.

She told me she was divorced. "My ex-husband was a stockbroker. He's out of work now, but he was flying high for a few years. That was his BMW. He took the SUV. I've thought about selling it, but it's paid for."

I'm good at listening, which was probably what kept her going. She was the third of three girls, the youngest by four years, the baby of the family. She'd been raised in Seattle and drove past her old elementary school every day on the way to work at an import/export business. She'd gone to Western Washington University in Bellingham, where she majored in philosophy and English literature. "Two completely useless majors," she added, "but my passion at the time—maybe still."

"How long were you married?" I asked.

"Just under three years. I'm thirty, if you're doing the math."

"I wasn't. I'll be thirty in a few months." We compared birthdays. Birth signs. Neither of us believed in astrology, so that didn't go far. She'd played on two different soccer teams the past couple of years, one coed company team, and one metro-league all-women's team. She loved soccer and jogging. She never got seasick and she hated camping. Day hikes were a passion with her, however, and she quickly gave me an impressive list of local trails she'd hiked.

"Okay. I've told you everything there is to know about me. Now it's your turn." Dead silence. She touched my hand and made a valiant effort to pretend she hadn't noticed. "Also, I want to thank you for helping me with my grandmother. A few months ago I suspected Jackie was dipping into the grocery money. And Nanna's medicines have been coming up short. I don't understand people like that."

I did.

"Now, tell me about yourself," she said.

When it came to my past, what I handed people was an innocuous stew of half-truths, redundancies, and downright fabrications. But somehow I didn't want to lie to this woman.

"My father died when I was young. Then my mom passed away when I was in fifth grade. I lived with different relatives until I got out of high school. I worked at Boeing for a while and went to the University of Washington. I wanted to be a teacher, but I took the fire department test instead."

"How did your parents die?"

"It's a long story. Two long stories." Both guaranteed to evoke pity—which I couldn't abide.

"Have you ever been married?"

"No."

"Ever come close?"

"No." Translation: I either can't commit or there's something wrong with me that keeps women away.

She gave me a look, the one where they're trying to figure out if you're gay. "It occurs to me that there's a movie of my grandmother's playing at the Harvard Exit. *Rogue River Adventure.* I know you've seen it, and so have I, but never on the big screen. It's only a few blocks away, and we just have time to make it if we walk. What do you think?"

What did I think? I thought I liked her. I thought it would be a thrill to sit in front of *Rogue River Adventure* with the granddaughter of the female lead. As we left the B&O, I thought it would be a thrill to go anywhere with Vanessa.

She buttoned her coat against the night chill. "I have a confession. I didn't just think of the movie on the spur of the moment. I planned this." She smiled.

There was nothing to do but smile back.

41. THE SUMMER AFTER TENTH GRADE

Half a block from the Harvard Exit we encountered a beat-up old Chevy double-parked, motor running. A man in leather pants had a woman bent backward across the hood of the car, slapping her. I'd been beat up plenty of times as a kid, so I knew exactly what she was feeling.

They were drawing a crowd, all in all, maybe twenty leery witnesses. He was big and mean-looking, and it was clear nobody was going to step in.

Within seconds I found myself submersed in the feeling I got sometimes, the one that frightened me more than anything else on earth. It didn't come often, but when it did I knew somebody was in trouble. As usual when the feeling came on, I tried to make my mind go blank.

"Oh, my God," said Vanessa.

The only reason I hadn't done anything yet was because my instinct wasn't to stop the beating or to call the police. My instinct was to kill the guy. Also, Vanessa was beside me. Second dates were few and far between when you killed somebody the first time out.

Approaching at an angle, I stood in the blind spot behind his left shoulder, tapped his right shoulder so he turned away from me at first.

When he turned back his jaw met my fist.

His eyes rolled up into his skull and his knees sagged.

Amazingly, he reached inside his coat and fumbled for a small semiautomatic handgun. Before he could get a grip on the pistol, I hit him again, whereupon he flopped into a crumpled heap. Somebody on the sidewalk said, "God, is he dead?"

I kicked the weapon under the car, where it clinked into a street drain. The woman ran down the street.

Moments later Vanessa and I walked to the box office window at the Harvard Exit. "Aren't you going to wait for the police?" Vanessa asked.

"They'll find him without my help."

I hadn't been thinking about the police. I'd been thinking the assailant must have had a jaw like a sack of concrete. I had big bones and large knuckles, and I couldn't remember the last time I got a clean shot at a man and had to hit him twice.

Inside the theater, the wooden floors creaked under our weight as we found our seats. Neither of us spoke.

At least I hadn't beaten him to death.

Once in high school I'd been out drinking with some older guys when Rickie Morrison spit in my beer and called me a "fag." Neither offense was much, but the alcohol laid bare what few mental defenses I had in those days, and in the space of two minutes, before the others could stop me, I beat him up so badly he went to the hospital. My grandmother got the best attorneys available and fought tooth and nail for me until eventually the charges were lost in the system and dropped. Otherwise I might have joined my brother in the juvenile justice system.

I'd always been a scrapper. In eighth grade I'd been the smallest boy in our gym class, yet in a single semester I had six fights, not counting the Jones brothers. You included them, I probably had twenty fights.

At Washington Middle School the Jones brothers made sport out of slapping me around. They were both tall and lanky, both on the basketball team, and either of them could have whipped me alone, though they worked together. They had a friend named Dinkins who they brought along as the court jester. Dinkins always took a turn slapping my face, especially if there were girls in the vicinity. I hated Dinkins most of all. Despite their overwhelming physical superiority, I always fought back, and despite my efforts, I always lost.

I switched schools and between eighth and tenth grades,

grew five inches, put on forty-five pounds, and began lifting weights and studying karate from books and videos. I got smart. I got mean. I got my driver's license. I borrowed my aunt's car and drove back to the old neighborhood. Dinkins was the first one I caught. I thrashed him until two passersby pulled me off, then I thrashed them. I was out of control.

Two days later Merv Jones, the older of the two brothers, saw me coming and caught me in the jaw with a left hook I barely felt. It was the only decent blow he got in. He'd been playing softball with some friends who could only stand and gape as I proceeded to knock out two of his teeth and close both eyes, payback for a dozen beatings at his hands.

I never caught the second brother, but I used up my summer looking for him. Years later somebody told me he'd spent August with relatives in Detroit hiding from me.

That was the summer I decided something was wrong with me. I'd had that feeling a lot, that feeling of loss of control, but until I was sixteen I'd never been strong enough for it to make a difference. It was the summer I had my last drink too. Coming so close to killing Rickie Morrison put me off alcohol, if all those years watching my mother hadn't already.

Rogue River Adventure was about a woman living on the Oregon frontier. Her husband gets gold fever and all but abandons her and their two sons. One of the boys gets sick, there are outlaws after her, and in the end the mother and the remaining boy are forced to raft down the Rogue River for two days fleeing Indians and bad guys in order to get her youngest to a doctor. The father is played by Van Heflin. Barton MacLane injects a fair amount of sexual menace into the bad-guy part.

The flick wasn't as good as I'd remembered, but then, they rarely were.

Afterward, Vanessa and I walked to the Broadway Market complex and found a stand that served pastries and coffee. It was a while before Vanessa spoke. "You really whacked that guy."

"I hope it didn't spoil the movie for you."

"Well, yeah. It was all I could think about."

"I wanted to kill him."

"You're a barely controlled volcano, aren't you?"

There wasn't anything I could say to that. It was something I tried to keep from the women in my life, what few women there'd been. Hell, I lost them soon enough. Not that my rage had ever been directed at a woman. Or ever would be.

"Your grandmother was terrific," I said, changing the subject.

"Did you know the director hated her? They had all kinds of squabbles on the set. When they were filming that fake rafting scene they had to throw buckets of water on her to make it look like they were really running rapids. At first they used warm water, but after a while the director told them to use ice water. She actually got hit in the face with ice cubes. When she complained, he said he wanted her nipples to stand out under her blouse."

"I don't suppose she found that amusing."

"No."

"The night of the fire I saw you in the medic unit with my grandmother. It's hard to reconcile what I saw that night with what you did to that guy in the street."

"He had it coming."

"I suppose he did, but I've never seen anyone do anything like that."

I knew there would be no good-night kiss here. No return phone call. I'd lost another one.

Adios, baby.

42. SIC, SIC, SIC

When I got to the station on Saturday the twenty-first, the first thing I did after the 0800 roll call was dig through the back of my clothing locker, where I'd hidden the report Chief Eddings gave me.

Each shift, a Form 50 was written for probationary firefighters by their overseeing officers to document their performance. At the end of the month a lengthier report was penned, compiled from and reflecting the tenor of the daily reports. Every comment, pro or con, needed to be backed up with objective evidence, observations, or written accounts of the firefighter's activities.

It wasn't kosher to write that a probationary firefighter wasn't strong enough when you hadn't made note of specific weaknesses. Nor was it correct to claim your boot was good at helping with paperwork without noting any instances of that characteristic on the daily Form 50s.

Captain Galbraithe, Rideout's officer on Engine 13, had written, "Rideout doesn't meet department standards with regards to upper body strength. Rideout appears to have trouble carrying a hundred feet of 2½-inch hose by herself." It was one thing to fail at a task. Failure was measurable and demonstrable. But to say someone "appears to have trouble" was an opinion and not likely to stand up in court. A man could be asked to pick up a suitcase full of bricks and carry it across the room. He either accomplished the task or he did not. If he performed slowly, you could time him to document that. If he dragged it instead of carried it, you could note that. These were measurable actions. To say he picked it up and carried it across the room but seemed to have trouble doing it wasn't going to work for the legal department.

In my experience, if somebody had trouble doing a task, you asked them to do it again. And again. At some reasonable point where your average firefighter would keep going, they would fail. Then you wrote, recruit so-and-so failed to perform task X a second or third time.

If Rideout wasn't strong enough for the job, I'd seen no evidence of it.

Eddings had written:

> Rideout came into the staton [sic] with high hopes but we quickly saw her true colars [sic]. She prances around the beanry [sic] acting like she's better than the rest of us. She is slow to obye [sic] orders and displays a fear of fire. She has a [sic] infinite capacity to anger her superiors and does not fit in with the rest of the crew. Capt. Galbraith [sic] found her not strong enough to do the simplist [sic] tasks, such as a 2 ½" nozzle. We doubt she will ever be able to drive a rig or pump affectively [sic]. In short, this recruit will be a bad fit for the department and should be terminated with prejuedice [sic].

The paragraph said more about Eddings than it did about Rideout. In addition there was no documentation they'd ever had Rideout drive a rig or practice pumping, yet she'd been judged incapable of doing either. I'd fired two people in my time and had felt sympathy for both. I saw nothing but antipathy here.

As far as the claim that Rideout had an attitude? I had seen only a good-natured disposition; a recruit who was always ready to pitch in and help with any project; a young woman who maintained a sunny disposition under almost any circumstances; a woman who did what she was told at fires, knew how to listen, and worked as a team member.

I returned the copy of Rideout's November report to my clothing locker and went out to the apparatus bay, where I noticed a fresh piece of tape down the center of the floor,

Gliniewicz to mop on one side, Dolan on the other. In the beanery I found a piece of white masking tape running the length of the wooden table that dominated the room. Towbridge was washing one side of the table, Zeke the other. Gliniewicz wasn't talking to any of us. Slaughter ignored me, while Towbridge and Dolan went out of their way to leave the room when Slaughter came in. Tension in the station had reached an all-time high. I knew there'd always been friction between these two crews, but the arsons and my arrival seemed to have accelerated things.

The engine fielded two or three times as many alarms as the truck, mostly aid calls, and its crew consequently got up more often at night. There were thirty-three engines in the city and they were sent on aid calls before trucks were. With only eleven trucks, the dispatchers needed to save them for fires, so trucks were sent on aid calls only when the nearest engine company was out of service. In a double house, the truckies might sleep all night, while the engine crew might get up two or three times. It couldn't help but spur friction. In most double houses the truckies had learned not to gloat when the engine had a bad night, but that wasn't the case at Station 6.

In retaliation, at night Slaughter kept his rig out of service until they were actually back in the barn, thus increasing the likelihood of the truck catching an aid call, a practice that was against department policy and infuriated Dolan.

The conflict had been further inflamed by Slaughter's fear that Rideout would be assigned to Engine 6 after her truck work was completed.

When I found Slaughter and Gliniewicz, they were outside next to Slaughter's truck, smoking cigarettes.

"Shhhh! Here he comes," Gliniewicz said, enacting a familiar joke around the station.

"Yeah?" Slaughter said, looking in my direction. "What's going on?"

"I thought we might talk. Alone."

"Talk?" Slaughter laughed. "You had your chance for talk."

"With all these fires, I don't want our guys at each other's throats."

"You had your chance."

The two of them began discussing the new tires on Slaughter's truck as if I didn't exist. I'd been aware since I was a recruit on Engine 13 that Slaughter used his size and tirades to intimidate people. I didn't like the way he browbeat Zeke or the way he conspired against Rideout. Most of all, I didn't like the way he ran hot or cold, depending upon whether you agreed with his position at the moment.

43. I AM THE KING OF FLAME

According to Earl Ward

They think they're hot stuff because they caught fire burners in different parts of the city. Retards and drunks. That's who they're catching. Kids, retards, and drunks.

For anybody with half a brain this thing is like stealing coins out of a blind man's hat.

I hate this holiday season, I'm telling you. First, there's Mom. Nothing turns her upside down like Xmas. All she can talk about is how miserable her childhood was and how I always had it so much better and how lousy this Xmas is going to be compared to last Xmas because I ain't bringin' in any money. What I've wanted to know all along, even when I was a kid, is how could Xmas be any lousier than having a mother who sits around all day croaking about it?

Anyways, I got the money thing halfway figured out. You think about it, there's lots of money in my profession. I read where that place I lit on Dose Terrace a couple weeks ago is being rebuilt with $300,000 in insurance money. That's where the dough is. Insurance.

I just haven't quite figured out how to tap into it. I will, though.

One thought was that I could burn down Mom's house and we could collect the insurance, but when I called the agent to ask about the policy, the half-wit practically accused me of *wanting* to burn it down. Maybe I asked the wrong questions. I mighta. There are times when I get a little excited thinking about lighting a match.

Anyways, the gist is there's gotta be a way to make money off my specialty. I seen this all on TV. There are different ways to go about finding a profession. One is to adapt yourself to whatever job pays good money. Another is—and I prefer this—to find something you love doing and figure out how to make *it* pay. An example would be a whore. Some babe likes to screw, so she goes about making a living at it. Like that.

Now maybe I hire myself out and burn down other people's property, help them collect insurance and take a portion of the proceeds. Sound good? Sounds good to me too. Or maybe there's somebody out there who likes fires but doesn't know how to start 'em. They hire me.

The trick in all this would be the advertising, because I can't exactly use the yellow pages. Maybe an ad in the back of *The Stranger*. I bet the cops don't read that.

Another way to make money would be to set up a bank account somewheres and tell people you're going to torch their property if they don't put money in. You don't have to hold anybody up. Maybe two hundred bucks a pop. Enough to pay for Xmas for Mom. The trouble is, you'd need one of them offshore accounts, and I don't know how to do that.

All this aside, I'm pissed. For starters, it's Saturday night, so Mom takes her Dodge and doesn't come back until almost one in the morning. Bingo and beer. Old ladies shouldn't be driving drunk. Now I'm getting a late start. Know what else tweaks me? Them newspaper writers never get it straight.

I mean, I am the most accomplished arsonist in the history of this city. Maybe the world. I'm an expert to end all experts. Period.

I am the king of flame.

Yet all they talk about is the copycats. The papers are so concerned with numbers. A guy sets eight Dumpster fires gets almost the same coverage I do setting one flamer that burns a husband and wife and two dogs out of their house. It's not right.

Tonight is the night I make them forget the copycats.

The night the whole West Coast learns I am the master.

What I gotta do tonight is listen to the scanner and make sure Ladder 3 is in quarters before I set this baby. No way I want to go to all this trouble and not nail the bastard. This was waaaay too much work. It's gotta go perfect. Which is part of the problem with fire. You want to change something after it starts, you better hold your horses, because once it gets goin', you're stuck with what you got.

That's the scary aspect to my profession—how all these accidents happen.

What gets me is everybody knows they're accidents, yet the papers are always trying to say I'm to blame. An accident is an accident. I mean, that's why they call them accidents, right? I give these guys plenty of opportunities to put my fires out, and if they don't, it ain't on my head. They're the hotshots getting paid all that money, driving all those fancy vehicles out behind the firehouse. I'm just driving Mom's old Dodge Dart with the clunking transmission.

This house I found is perfect. To start off with, it looks like somebody lives there. That always gets firemen worked up. Plus there's another house next door that's going to confuse the issue. The best thing about the house next door is that those guys never get home until after the bars close. That's why they never heard me banging inside the first place.

I got the interior filled with boards and old furniture and you name it. I start the fire in the basement, it comes up the stairs, reaches the pile of combustibles right about the time the trucks get there. The fire reaches the middle of the house, it's going to FLARE! I mean FLARE! The hose line will go in the front door, and my guys'll go to the roof with chain saws. That's when the fun begins.

Because I am the king of flame.

After this maybe the papers won't be so full of copycats. Although I do have to say this. Them copycats have kept some of the pressure off me. I mean, as long as they're stumbling around West Seattle and Ballard looking for retards, they can't be in the CD looking for me, now can they?

I drive down along the lake and cruise Lakeside Avenue.

I light a fence. I light some brush, but it's wet and goes out.

I drive to Cheasty Boulevard and I find some garbage in the woods, stuff people've dumped. I light that.

I go to the house on Twenty-first and Stevens. The house I've been prepping. The people next door are home early, but they don't notice me.

I go inside, and I think, This is what happens when you piss me off.

44. NEXT THING I KNOW, I'M RUNNING FOR MY LIFE

According to Earl Ward

I poke through the house one last time, wiping my prints off everything. I'm nervous.

I go downstairs to the basement and wad up two Sunday papers, especially the color advertisements, which give off those beautiful blues and purples when they're hot. I pack the paper under everything in the room, wad it up and stuff it under old chairs, boxes, a rack of clothing.

I light one wad of papers and watch. There's nothing as sweet as a tiny little flame the size of your pinkie turning into a big flame the size of King Kong's ass. Now a single flame licks up the leg of a chair like a rattlesnake, slowly gets the wicker bottom on the chair going with a snap, crackle, and pop. More newspaper wads are igniting. It begins slower than I'd anticipated. I'm getting a hard-on under the dress. One after the other the newspaper stashes catch fire. I should be leaving, but I cannot go just yet. Something this beautiful, it's hard to tear your eyes away from.

The basement fills with smoke. It rises to the ceiling and banks down. Some of it flows up the basement stairs following the draft I've created by leaving the doors open.

There is a sense of luxury in this indoor fire, a feeling that I'm no longer in a hurry. This isn't like outside, where somebody might spot you, where you set it and leave. Nobody's going to spot me here. I sit near the double-bolted basement door and watch my handiwork.

Pretty soon the flame has spread into a series of stacked cardboard boxes. One of the boxes is full of jars somebody has lovingly stored. When the first box gets to burning, a jar slides out onto the floor with a dull pop, juice and broken glass everywhere. Moments later I smell peaches. Smells just like peach pie cooking. And then, almost without warning, the fire makes a big whoosh as it reaches the clothing rack, and the synthetic material on the hangers starts to go up like gasoline.

Godderned, I think, maybe I stayed too long. I tuck my dick into my panty hose and run for the door.

It is only by holding my coat over my face that I get past the flames. I head up the stairs, coughing and choking on the smoke. The air in the stairs is hotter than I thought it would be. It burns my eyes.

Upstairs the place is filling with smoke.

I sit by the back door, one leg of my chair in the kitchen, the other in the hallway, waiting for the rest of it to come roaring up, this creature I've created. My eyes fill with tears.

I don't know if the tears are from the smoke or from the gorgeousness of the whole thing. My work is filling the rooms, making its way upstairs to the second floor, from there to the attic, where I hope everything goes according to plan.

At the top of the stairs, I've piled clothing and bedding and mattresses.

These dumb-ass firefighters aren't going to know what hit them.

Quicker than I thought it would, the smoke compresses down from the ceiling.

Knowing discretion is the better part of valor, I leave through the back door, making sure the lock clicks into place behind me.

In the dark in the backyard I finish my soda, wipe it clean of prints, and set it on the neighbor's porch.

Then alongside the wall of that house I light the pile of clothespins, rope, and garbage. Fire will climb the vinyl siding like ferrets. No need to wait for this one.

I walk back to Mom's car.

I drive down the hill on McClellan and park in the drugstore parking lot. It is late, and Rainier Avenue is practically deserted.

After a bit, I hear sirens. It is torture waiting, but I am a professional and I keep still.

Later, after the fire units have driven past me, I drive back up the hill and park just off Twenty-third. I walk toward the commotion two blocks away. I walk like it's my prerogative. I stand near the fire trucks with the gawkers, cradling a can of soda in my coat pocket.

Pretty soon two firefighters race past carrying a ladder. Their helmet insignia says L-3, so I know things are on track. Wollf will be along in a minute. The ladder tells me he'll be dead soon.

Even though my heart is pounding, I stand calmly and watch with the other women and a couple of men. Pretty soon some bitch in a white chief's helmet comes along and screams at us to move out of the street. That we're in the way.

We're already on the parking strip, but we all take five steps backward until we're ruining our shoes in the tall wet grass in some asshole's yard.

The people around me are watching the firefighters take hose off Engine 13. They're watching the chief. They're watching the drivers running the pumps. I could tell them what each of these firefighters is doing, but I don't want to draw attention to myself. Besides, I have my eyes on the roof.

It seems to take forever.

And then they're up there. One of them is. No. There's another one. They're in the back. At first I cannot tell who is who. I know Wollf is the biggest on the crew. That there's one woman, about my size, who is the smallest. Two of them are walking across the steep part of the north slope. One slips, and my heart leaps in my chest. I don't need anybody to fall off. I want them all directly over the fire. Half a ton of human hope ready to be charbroiled.

They're making their way across the north slope of the roof.

One is starting the chain saw. The other is standing by with an axe. Neither realizes he's on a giant mousetrap. Standing where the cheese should be. A third firefighter makes his way to them. The only thing that would make this better would be if that bitch chief got up there.

They will go through that roof like a satellite dropping out of the sky.

This is going to be so un-fucking-believable.

Standing in the wet grass, I wait with the other looky-loos, my mouth hanging open. I begin to flog the dummy through the hole in my coat pocket.

Funny how things work out.

Next thing I know, I'm running for my life.

45. WE GOT FIRE! WE GOT FIRE!

Going to the roof was arguably the most macho of all truck operations, standing in the dark and the rain and the snow with a roaring chain saw, smoke and flame chasing past your face after you get the hole open. It was also possibly the most dangerous position on the fire ground.

At least the cold snap from last week had blown through. There would be no ice.

"We got fire! We got fire!" Eddings shouted into her radio when she arrived.

"Did you hear that shit?" Dolan asked.

"Settle down," I said.

We were ripping along Twenty-third, maybe five or six blocks away, watching smoke curl up into the sky. These were all residential streets, quiet at night except for the occasional Metro bus. Single-family homes. Wood frame. Brick.

We took Stevens off Twenty-third, turned left on Twenty-second, and found our way blocked by the battalion chief's Suburban. The street was full of smoke, so we saw everything through a gray-black haze permeated by ping-pong flashing red lights and bright wig-wag headlights from the rigs. In addition to the chief, Engine 13 and Engine 30 were already there. We were going to have to carry our ladders and equipment almost a block.

On the apparatus handset I said, "Ladder Three at location. We're going to the roof to ventilate."

Before we stopped rolling, I turned and shouted over the engine noise to Rideout and Towbridge in the crew cab behind us. "You guys take the ladder. We'll follow with the saws and pike poles."

"You want the twenty-five or thirty-five?" Towbridge asked.

"I can't see the house. Better take the thirty-five."

Dolan exited on one side of the rig, I on the other. I was wearing my bunking boots, trousers, and coat. I walked half-way back alongside the compartment doors to my mask compartment and slung a half-hour bottle and backpack onto my shoulders, cinching down the shoulder and waist straps.

From the ladder compartment at the rear of the apparatus I pulled a ten-foot pike pole. I was already wearing a four-pound pick-head service axe at my belt and carrying a six-volt battle lantern on a hook on my chest. On the other side of the rig, I passed Dolan, who was still getting his equipment together. "You bringing the saw?" I asked.

"Both saws."

It never hurt to have a backup in case the Stihl didn't start.

Shabbier than the rest of the neighborhood, two side-by-side houses sat on an embankment, volumes of smoke issuing from between them.

In front of me Rideout and Towbridge disappeared into the smoke as they carried the ladder up a steep paved driveway between the houses. Flame was pumping out a kitchen window at the rear of the house to the south, black smoke jetting out another broken-out window. Three ramshackle pickup trucks blocked the driveway.

Two firefighters hosed down the side of the house to the north.

Engine 30 had been assigned the south house. One of their members was having trouble getting his gear straightened out. His gloves were on the ground, his coat unbuttoned, his MSA backpack straps loose. His main problem, as far as I could tell, was that Eddings was six inches from his face squalling at him like a Marine Corps drill sergeant.

"What the hell do you think you're doing, Smith? Get your motherfuckin' ass in gear! Get into that house with your crew, you worthless pile of shit! My God. My grandmother could . . ." And so forth and so on.

Except for the Pennington fire, all our arsons had been

*out*side buildings, yet the house fire we were looking at to the south had been set inside.

"Where do you want the ladder?" Towbridge asked. I could hear him but couldn't see him in the smoke.

"Around back," I said.

From the basement to the roofline, smoke was coming out cracks in the house to the south. Smoke was leaking between the shingles on the roof. This was the perfect candidate for vertical ventilation.

Dolan was near Rideout and Towbridge now, pulling on the starter cord of a Stihl chain saw.

In the old days truckies went to the roof without masks, often choking on smoke so hot it singed their eyebrows. Unless the wind was just right, they took a terrible beating up there. Then the rule came down that we were to go to the roof with a mask on standby. Now it was compulsory to wear a mask in full operation.

Walking across a steep, slippery roof in the middle of the night wearing a mask that limited your visibility had become a major hazard in itself.

By dint of hand speed and initiative, I finished masking up and got up the ladder first, taking the first chain saw with me. I had to shake my head at the fact that the twenty-five barely reached the roof. I'd told Towbridge to grab the thirty-five.

Our portable radios were crackling with commands. At one point Eddings said, "Ladder Three. Split your crew. I want you to do search and rescue in the fire house and also in the exposure house to the north. Ladder Three? Did you receive?"

"Command from Ladder Three. We're on the roof of the south house. We're about to open it. You want us to cancel?" I asked.

No reply. A few moments later she gave the search-and-rescue orders to Ladder 7, the second-in truck company.

The roof was in two sections. I was on the first section over a porch and sunroom.

Facing me was a flat wall with two windows in it. Above that, the peak of the second, higher roof was running from left to right. I could make the leap up onto the main roof, but it wasn't a particularly safe evolution, given how steep the roof was. Going back to get a roof ladder now would leave the firefighters inside too long without relief. If I could make it, Towbridge, at six-one, the next tallest on the rig, could make it as well. Two of us could punch a hole in a roof.

A hose stream drummed an interior wall below us, water shooting out a window into the driveway in spurts. Broken glass fell onto one of the pickup trucks. A firefighter in the driveway objected loudly to being sprayed. An Engine 13 member gave a radio report saying they'd found victims. It was unclear which house they were in.

The main roof for the residence was a steep eight-twelve pitch. I tied my body loop around the chain saw and slung it over my shoulder to free my hands, then took my service axe out.

I cut a toehold, then another, began making my way to the peak of the roof, stepping in the stirrups as I hacked them out. Each toehold produced smoke. I moved quickly. By the time I was straddling the peak, Dolan was behind me, putting the toes of his boots into the holes I'd cut, the second Stihl in one hand, his own service axe in the other. We were breathing heavily through our MSA face pieces. It was dark up here, and we were on the north side of the house where the moss grew. Each time I tried my foot on the three-tab roofing, my boot slipped.

Straddling the peak of the roof as if it were a giant wooden horse, I scooted along it until I judged we were over the fire.

"Cut here," I said. It didn't take long for Dolan to begin sawing a four-by-eight-foot hole below me, just under the peak. I picked away at the section of roof as he cut the hole. The roof consisted of three layers of old roofing material that came up in chunks. Moments later Rideout was beside me, our service axes swinging in tandem.

Towbridge was below Dolan, his hands on Dolan's hips to keep him from falling. Rideout and I picked off slabs of the roof and watched them slide past Dolan and Towbridge, off the edge of the roof, crashing onto the pickup trucks in the driveway.

Rideout strained to match my efforts. I could feel the sweat in my armpits and inside my face piece.

We cut a hole eight feet long. The black smoke pouring out of the hole wasn't as fast-moving or as hot as I expected. Dolan looked at me; we were both thinking the same thing. There was an intact ceiling between us and the fire.

Rideout started across to get the pike pole she'd left hanging off the west end of the peak, took three or four steps, began to slide, then hammered her pick-head axe into the roof. For a moment I thought she was going off the roof, but she arrested her fall, sitting on her rump, her axe buried in the three-tab roofing material. Inertia was a wonderful thing when it was saving your life. She looked across at me, her brown eyes swollen with worry. Towbridge stepped up to the hole to see if he couldn't reach the ceiling below us with his axe.

I walked west along the peak, a boot on either side in case I lost my footing.

I passed Rideout, retrieved the pike pole, sat, then angled it toward her until she grasped it and was able to make her way to the peak behind me.

In front of us, Dolan and Towbridge were bent over chopping in the heavy smoke. They still hadn't breached the interior ceiling. I slid along the roof, braced myself, and slammed the tip of the pike pole into the bowels of the attic.

A shower of sparks and smoke shot upward past my helmet. Towbridge and Dolan backed off to avoid the rush of heat and sparks.

I slammed the pike pole downward two more times.

Each time sparks shot up past us, Towbridge turned to me and grinned inside his mask. You could only see it in his eyes. I grinned back. Sometimes this job was just too much fun to believe.

It was at that moment that the whole east side of the roof began to shake.

To my horror, the four-by-eight-foot hole we'd cut began disappearing in front of me, as did most of that end of the roof, including the section Dolan was on.

Towbridge vanished into the enlarged hole at the same time Dolan did.

The look of surprise in their eyes would haunt me for years to come.

Even after they disappeared, the roof kept collapsing, folding inward like a row of dominoes, working its way toward me and Rideout. We backed up hurriedly, scooting along the peak. It was slowly gaining on us. We were going in too. And then—

The collapse stopped just short of my crotch.

The whole top of the house continued quivering.

At the spot where Towbridge had been there was only flame and a hell of a lot of smoke roaring out. Hot smoke. More flame. The yellow blaze arched six feet above what was left of the roof, eight feet, ten feet.

"Jesus Christ," I said. The peak sagged under my weight and began dipping into the chasm.

"Get back, Lieutenant," Rideout yelled.

I reached the jagged maw in seconds. I'd just lost two men. Nothing like this had ever happened to me before.

"Stay where you are," I said to Rideout.

"Like hell," she replied, clambering alongside and below me. "We have to get them out."

I could feel the sheathing bounce with her movement.

"We don't need the extra weight," I yelled, but she was at the lip of the hole, as was I. The roof bobbed like the end of a diving board with a fat man on it.

I keyed my portable radio and said, "Mayday. Mayday. This is Ladder Three on the roof. We've just had a cave-in. Two men fell through. We need hose lines in the attic. Now!"

46. SOLE SURVIVOR

Cynthia Rideout

DECEMBER 22, SUNDAY, 0219 HOURS

Tonight has been a little piece of hell. I'll start at the beginning.

We had two side-by-side houses on fire. The fire on the north house was mostly on the exterior. The fire in the south house, the house we tackled, started in the basement.

Our assignment was to go to the roof of the south house, cut a hole, and ventilate so the guys inside didn't suffocate when they applied water. So they could see. So they wouldn't get burned.

Wollf orders us to get the thirty-five, but when I go to the back of the rig, Towbridge has the twenty-five out. Easy to figure why. It's lighter. In fact, it's considered a one-man ladder, while the thirty-five requires at least two people to carry it. This is so like Towbridge, who, even around the station, is always trying to work some angle to make things easier.

"Wollf said the thirty-five," I tell him.

"I know. It's okay."

So we carry the *twenty*-five down the street, over hose lines, past firefighters, up an embankment to the house, and then I see the look on Towbridge's face when he realizes it isn't going to reach.

Wollf sees our predicament and tells us to take the ladder around back where the roof might be lower. We find ourselves squeezing past these three old trucks in the driveway. It takes forever. At one point we set the ladder across the bed of a truck and walk around to the other side and pick it up again. Wollf has a spot picked out in the backyard. The ground is lumpy and dark, and we move cautiously.

Towbridge and I are both so winded we can hardly talk. Towbridge moves fast, but he pays for it. So do I when I'm working with him. We are both still trying to catch our breath when Dolan climbs the ladder.

We get our masks on, Towbridge looks at me, and we both know neither of us wants to go first. If you go second, you get that extra time to breathe. Carrying that ladder down the street and up into this backyard while wearing fifty pounds of equipment has winded us.

I'm the boot, so I start climbing.

I get to the flat part of the roof, turn around, and steady the ladder for Towbridge. He jumps to the second roof, while I'm forced to crawl onto it and to keep crawling until I get to the toeholds somebody cut with an axe.

We're cutting the hole when the roof caves in.

Dolan and Towbridge disappear into the fire together.

I scream, but the noise is inside my mask and nobody hears me. Oh my God, I think. They're dead. Or will be in a matter of seconds.

Then Wollf is leaning over trying to spot them and he has his head in the flames and I think he is going to die too. Which will leave me alone on the roof, the sole survivor of Ladder 3. I've never been more frightened in my life.

After a while Wollf reaches down into the smoke and hauls a bundle of yellow out like it's a sack of dirty laundry. It's Towbridge.

It's a long time before we find out what happened to Dolan.

47. WE'VE LOST HIM

Below me is a caldron of flame and hot, boiling smoke. Every once in a while a haphazard tongue of flame forces me back. You feel the heat through your turnouts. We don't have an inch of bare skin showing, but still, you feel it. We might as well be pigs on a spit.

I put my left leg into the hole we've cut, searching until I find a board strong enough to support some weight, then reach out and grab the pike pole, which is sticking straight up. I feel the heat crawling up my pant leg.

"Mayday!" I repeat on the radio. "Mayday!" No reply.

Rideout yells, "Dolan! Towbridge!"

And then, before I can lower myself into the fiery attic, a yellow helmet comes into view three feet from my face, a firefighter facing the other direction, blindly backing toward me.

I grab the shoulder strap on his backpack and yard him out of the hole backward. He is incredibly heavy, and thrashes about like a struggling swimmer. Rideout grabs one of his legs when he throws it up over the roof.

Towbridge.

Remarkably, his air is still working and he appears not to be too badly injured.

I grab the pike pole and begin poking around in the smoke at the point where I'd last seen Dolan. Jabbing the pole anywhere he might have fallen, or rolled, or crawled. Or died. Prodding for anything soft.

A hose stream comes out of the smoke and smacks me in the face, hard, almost knocks me off the roof. A moment later it shoots straight up into the night sky. Then it is gone and we can hear it drumming on wood and plaster inside the house. Another stream shoots up into the sky.

"Where's Jeff?" I ask Towbridge.

"I don't know. Man, what happened? One minute we're here and the next minute everything is black and it's hotter than shit."

"You were in the attic. Lucky you didn't go through," says Rideout.

"I musta landed on the planks. It was weird. I was just walking around down there."

"Jeff?" I call. "Jeff?"

"Hey, Dolan. Hey, buddy," yells Towbridge. "Come on outta there."

I keep probing the darkness with the pike pole. The smoke turns to steam as the engine crew below us gets more water on the fire. Towbridge takes the pole and, braced by Rideout, fishes around in the hole. One of his gloves is missing. I drop down chest-deep in the cavern and begin walking around, holding on to the edges of the hole, feeling tentatively with my boots.

As we search, another truck crew arrives on the roof from the front of the house. Their weight, the four of them, over half a ton of men and equipment, begins sagging the roof even more. I am afraid Dolan is under them. That they are crushing him. I say as much. They back off.

When I see flashlights and firefighters below on the second floor, I ask them to pass up a hose line, which they do. It is hot and damp in the attic space, but I feel relatively confident in my footing. It is so hot I might as well be putting my head into a chimney. I pull up twenty feet of hose and begin hitting the remaining hot spots in the attic. My greatest fear is that he is burning to death while we are farting around.

Rideout says, "Oh God. We've lost Jeff."

I am sick to my stomach, straining to peer through the smoke around me.

I pour water into every nook and cranny of the attic, into all the closed spaces under the collapsed roof. I still can't find Dolan.

Then I get an idea. I shout down to the firefighters who handed up the hose line.

"Did somebody fall through there?"

"What?" A firefighter below is craning up at me.

"Did somebody fall through here?"

He steps back and shines his flashlight on a crumpled firefighter on the floor sitting amidst a pile of burned plasterboard. It is my driver, Jeff Dolan. He's passed straight through the attic to the second floor and landed only a few feet in front of the hose crew.

"You okay?" I shout.

"I guess so."

"Are you okay?"

"I broke my leg. Do you have the chain saw?"

"I don't know where it is."

"Don't lose that saw."

"Why? You want me to cut your leg off?"

He laughs through the pain. "No. I don't want to have to explain to Stan down at the commissary how we lost it."

"You just worry about your leg."

Moments later as they begin to move him, he hollers.

"Remember you're carrying a hero," Towbridge shouts from above. "Don't be messing with no hero."

48. SHOOTING CHIEFS OUT OF CANNONS

Cynthia Rideout

DECEMBER 22, SUNDAY, 0340 HOURS

Whining like a baby the whole while, Dolan got patched up by the medics. Wollf, myself, and Towbridge stood at the back of the medic unit, the doors open. The medics cut most of Dolan's clothing off. Towbridge and Wollf made it harder for Dolan the way only men can make it harder for each other.

"Jesus," Wollf said. "Don't you ever clean your toenails?"

"I clean 'em every morning right before I leave for the station. Then I come to work and have to wade through all the bullshit. That's bullshit. Smell it."

"No, thank you," Wollf said.

"He's hurtin' pretty bad if he thinks somebody's gonna

smell his toes," Towbridge said, laughing. Towbridge had minor burns on both wrists. Not enough to get laid off, but enough to ride up to the hospital with Dolan. How he got out of that attic without getting fried is something none of us have figured out. We came so close to losing two people.

Jeff's leg is going to keep him out for at least six weeks.

There's more. Katie Fryer made a rescue! Go, Katie.

She was working a trade on E-13, and they were sent to the second house, where they found two drunk civilians. The man managed to get out on his own, but the woman collapsed inside the front door.

Katie Fryer and one of the regulars from Thirteen's kicked open the front door, and Katie dragged the woman out.

Later, the news crew from CBS showed up and began interviewing her, lights, camera, action. The civilian she rescued was on the heavy side, and during the interview Katie made the mistake of saying it was a good thing she'd been only a few feet inside the front door, because they couldn't have dragged her much farther.

Eddings, who had been watching, called a halt to the interview and placed Fryer inside her Battalion 5 vehicle, where she began chewing her out for admitting she wasn't strong enough to make a rescue. Eddings told her it was not only bad PR, but it was plain stupid. More than anything, Katie hates being told she's stupid.

After the fire, the whole top of the house to the south looked like a collapsed angel food cake. Wollf and I went inside. Upstairs we talked to one of the guys on Ladder 7, who said, "It was a miracle you guys didn't fall through sooner. Somebody sawed through the rafters in the roof."

"The roof was booby-trapped?" Wollf asked.

"Sure looks that way," said Fendercott, the Ladder 7 lieutenant.

I don't think I've ever seen Wollf so mad. Everybody was backing away from him.

We went downstairs, walked through both floors and then the basement, tracing the evolution of the fire.

We found the fire investigators, Connor and LaSalle, poking through the basement, where the fire had been set. From there it spread up to the first floor, then to the second story, where most of the heat had been trapped until we popped the roof.

Three hose crews had gone inside. It was the crew from Engine 10 who ended up taking the worst beating. "Jesus," one of them said later. "As soon as he fell through the ceiling, we could feel the relief."

Wollf laughed. "Maybe we should do all our ventilation that way. We could mount a cannon on the rig. Shoot firefighters through the roof from down the block. We'll shoot chiefs first."

Outside, Wollf and I took off our face pieces.

I followed him around the house and found him staring at a can of Shasta soda on the back porch next door.

"Stay here," he said. "Make sure nobody touches this can. Marshal Five is going to want prints." You could see he was still pissed about the roof. I was too, but not like him.

Somebody tried to kill our crew.

Before long everybody on the fire ground was talking about it.

Marsha Connor came over while Wollf was gone. "Hey. I heard you guys had some excitement."

"A little."

"These fires are giving them fits downtown. Last night there were twelve arsons. Tonight we've got four to look at. Everybody's working overtime. It's a mess."

It's a shame so many people pick on Marsha. She's one of the nicest people in the department. True, she isn't in such great physical condition; in fact, God only knows how she dragged herself through drill school. But she treats everybody with the same respect she needs so desperately and almost never receives. LaSalle is especially rough on her, making monkey faces behind her back, belittling her to her face. Sometimes I want to slap him.

"No Shasta products in either house," Wollf said, returning. "I saw the owner in front, and he said all they drink is Schlitz and Michelob Light."

"You better leave the interviews to us," LaSalle said, coming out of the house next door.

"Yes, sir," mocked Wollf.

I had to turn around real fast so LaSalle wouldn't see me laughing.

It was three in the morning. Our fires had generated a fair-sized crowd, neighbors, looky-loos from other parts of town, local news network cameramen and commentators. Down the street, the CBS guys were interviewing Katie Fryer again.

While we stood in the street waiting for orders, Wollf looked past my shoulder and shouted, "Hey, you!"

He was looking at a cluster of six or eight women, one in a belted tan raincoat, a redhead.

Suddenly the redhead took off running.

Wollf blew through the onlookers and chased her along the side of the house across the street and into a backyard. He was still wearing his mask and all of his gear.

As she ran around the corner of the house, he pitched a ten-foot pike pole at her, threw it like a javelin, as if he wanted to kill her.

It almost did—kill her—it sailed through the folds of her raincoat and penetrated the sod.

Half a minute later the redhead raced out from between some houses down the street and turned south on the sidewalk. Wollf came out too, having dropped his MSA bottle and backpack somewhere in the darkness. He still had the pike pole, though.

All the firefighters in the street watched in astonishment. Nobody tried to stop him.

Wollf wasn't somebody you tried to stop.

49. CHASING WOMEN IN THE DARK WITH SPEARS

I knew she was the woman who'd run from me at the Red Apple weeks earlier, the middle-aged woman with the heavy makeup.

The woman Towbridge told me had visited the station to have her blood pressure taken. She had red hair tonight.

Running like that after standing around for so long with my bottle on, I was stiff, which was the reason I missed with the pike pole.

I lost her in the dark in the backyard.

I came out from between the houses to the street again and spotted her running south down Twenty-second, coattail flapping in the breeze, red hair hanging off her head like a piece of torn carpet.

She had a block lead on me and was running as if she already knew I was going to kill her. Which I was.

As I ran I realized several things. One was that Chief Eddings was calling my name from behind. Another was that I was losing bits and pieces of my mind. That I was beginning to move into a familiar hypnotic state. It was a form of mania. I'd done this prior to every bout of violence. I knew I was going to kill this woman. I knew also that I was going to lose everything over it.

The worst part was, I couldn't stop myself.

At the corner of Winthrop and Twenty-second my prey turned left.

Without checking traffic, she bolted across Twenty-third Avenue South, a main arterial. A lone car crossed behind her.

Despite the turnouts and big rubber boots, I was gaining.

She crossed onto the property of an elementary school that took up half a city block, slowed, looked around desperately for somewhere to hide, then dashed behind the buildings.

By the time I reached the school, she'd vanished in the darkness.

I'd thought about killing the firebug for a long time, but over the years, my fantasies had centered around killing a man. Not a woman.

The building was long and ran north and south. Beyond the building was a small, fenced playground. Beyond that, woods.

I walked alongside the rear of the east wall behind the building, double-checking any nook or cranny that might harbor a fugitive. Anyplace from which an ambush could be launched.

So far my prey had done nothing but run, but I had to think that was over now, that I'd either cornered her or worn her out.

I wasn't worried about hand-to-hand combat. I would win hand-to-hand. Even had I been chasing a man, the money was on me. If I didn't win on size and strength, I'd win on rage. But what if she had a gun? Now that we were in the dark and blocks from the fire, she might get away with killing me. I would never get away with killing her, but she might murder me and skate.

Behind the single-story buildings that comprised the bulk of the school, I found a large, concrete play area encompassed by trees and a cyclone fence. I keyed my radio. "Dispatch from Ladder Three. I'm at Twenty-three Avenue South and South Winthrop. Behind the school. I need the police. I have a suspect."

I don't know why I was on the radio. I had no intention of doing this legally.

It was half a minute before the dispatcher said, "Twenty-two Avenue Command? Did you receive? Are you asking for additional resources?"

"That's a negative. Forget that transmission." I recognized the voice on the radio as Eddings.

I said, "Dispatch from Ladder Three. Repeat. I have a suspect at Twenty-three South and South Winthrop. Send SPD."

I was still talking when she darted out of the shadows fifty yards in front of me, galumphing along like a water buffalo with a sore hoof, charging across the playground.

She used her good-sized lead to hit an opening in the cyclone fencing, ran behind the fencing, perpendicular to and in front of me. Instead of following her to the opening, I decided to intercept, thinking there would be another gap in the fence somewhere along the way, a gap I could reach first.

Then, as I ran and scanned the dark fence in front of me, I realized there weren't any more openings. I couldn't go back. I was committed. I would soon arrive at the inside northwest corner of the fence, which meant I would have to run the long way around the wing of the fence to reach her. Which meant she was going to escape.

There we were, jogging side by side, a sheet of cyclone fencing between us. Every once in a while she slapped into a wet branch that jutted out from the woods on her side. I could hear her breathing heavily.

Neither of us had spoken since the beginning.

It was eighty feet before we were at the corner that would box me in and free her. I raced ahead hoping to find a gap in the fencing.

I reached the inside corner and *did* find a hole, not nearly large enough for me to get through, made by kids. I had about two seconds before she would pass.

Our pike poles were constructed with fiberglass shafts and a steel tip formed into a point-and-hook arrangement for pulling ceilings. I inserted the point through the hole.

She was coming up fast, traipsing along the dirt path years of children had laid down, her hair wet and bedraggled, her face spotted with rainwater and perspiration.

When I shoved the pike pole through the opening, the shaft caught her mid-chest and took her down, the wind knocked out of her.

For an instant I thought she might have a skull fracture, but I gave up that hope when she tried to move. I stabbed at her viciously in the dark. She grabbed the shaft, and for a split second we wrestled with the pole.

Then I pinned her against an old tree stump.

The steel tip wasn't sharp, but she held on to the fiberglass pike pole anyway in an effort to keep me from pushing it through her lungs.

I pressed it against her, telling myself over and over not to kill her. Knowing that in the end I wouldn't be able to stop myself.

I was trying to talk myself out of something I'd spent twenty-five years talking myself into.

I knew from experience once my brain clicked over on a decision, there were no second thoughts. My brother said it was a criminal's mind, that the joint was full of people who thought like I did. But what was wrong with taking revenge on the person I believed had tried to kill me and my crew, the person I suspected had murdered my father?

Still, I was having second thoughts.

Extraordinary.

On the other hand, maybe I was only trying to prolong the pleasure.

It made me laugh.

She looked at me as if I were insane.

We stayed like that for a minute, me on one side of the tall cyclone fence, she on the other in the shadows. Me in what passed for light. She couldn't get up, but I couldn't leave either. Not if I wanted to hold her.

Finally, with one hand I reached down and switched on the department issue flashlight dangling off my chest, put the beam on her.

She was a mess. Torn nylons. Dirt-smudged dress. Wig twisted to one side, lipstick smeared down one side of her cheek and chin.

"You're hurting me," she gasped, trying to work the pike

pole away from her chest. In the light I could see her hands. They were a man's hands.

"Hurting you is what my program's all about tonight, friend. Just like hurting us was what your program was all about."

I had no doubt I'd broken ribs, perhaps ruptured internal organs too.

"I gotta . . ." She was gasping like a dog hit by a truck. Going down. Knowing it. "I gotta get . . . some air." I put more force on the pole.

"Don't kill me. Please don't kill me." The voice had changed as it strained to suck in air. It was a man's voice now. Tears poured out of the mascara around his eyes. "Don't kill me. You're Lieutenant Wollf, aren't you? I was there the night your father died."

I eased up just enough so he could talk.

"How do you know my name?"

It took him four or five shallow breaths before he could get the words out. "You want to hear how your father died?"

Nobody had ever been able to tell me anything about my father's death. It was one of the Seattle Fire Department's best-kept mysteries, probably because it represented one of the biggest fuckups in department history.

"Keep yapping."

"Your father was Lieutenant Wollf? Right?"

"I'm not answering the questions. You are."

"In 1978 your father worked on Engine Seven. Out of Station Twenty-five."

I pressed the pole so hard both his feet came off the ground. "Stop," he gasped. "Stop, or I don't tell the rest." I eased up. "Okay. Okay. Your father died in a fire in 1978. Here's what happened. I was walking down this alley minding my own business when this guy shows up and starts hassling me. Pretty soon he's beating the crap out of me. That's when your father shows up. Your father saved my butt, 'cause I think that other guy was planning to kill me. That's the truth, man. Your father saved my life."

"Tell me about the first guy."

"I never knew his name. He was in civilian clothes, but he was a firefighter. Your father knew *him,* and *he* knew your father."

"Keep talking."

"This guy caught me outside this basement fire, only he didn't know it was a basement fire. Didn't know I'd set anything. All he knew was I was in the vicinity. So he grabs me, shoves me up against a wall and beats me. I was just a kid, man. I was only nineteen.

"He said I set them fires. I never did. But he said I did. He was trying to beat a confession out of me. He didn't seem to realize we have a bill of rights in this country. This country was founded on—"

"Get on with it."

"He knocked out one of my teeth. That's when your father showed up. He told your father to go back to his rig. That he was arresting me. But that's not what he did. He dragged me over to the fire and tried to throw me in. Can you imagine? You meet a stranger in an alley, you beat him up and throw him into a fire? I mighta done some bad things in my life. I'm not saying I have or I haven't. But I've never done anything like that."

"What about my father?"

"Your father tried to stop him. Finally, this guy hit your father. That's when your father went into that window well. Headfirst. Just kind of slid into the window. He never came out."

"How big was the fire at this time?"

"Not big."

"What'd you guys do?"

"We watched."

"What else?"

"We just watched. After a while you could see your father trying to find a way out. But then the fire took off, and he was still in there."

I began leaning on the pike pole. He resisted for all he was worth, the strain of it evident on his face.

"The other firefighter? What'd he do?"

"He didn't do nothin'."

"He must have done something."

"That's just it. He didn't. He just stared. That's how I got away."

"You telling me my father was in a burning basement and this cop or fireman or whatever . . . just stood there?"

"That's what I'm saying."

"You're lying."

"I ain't. The Shasta cans. You know who I am."

"You set the fires tonight?"

"On the outside of the house. I admit that. The other one. I don't know how that happened."

"Jesus, you must think I'm stupid." We looked at each other for a moment or two. "What'd the guy in civvies look like?"

"That was a lot of years ago."

I jiggled the pike pole. "And you've had a lot of time to think about it."

"I'm being honest here, man. The more I thought about what him and your father looked like, the harder it was to bring their faces back. Right now I couldn't tell you what he looked like if my life depended on it."

I leaned on the pole. "Let's pretend it does."

"Ow. Ouch. Oochee. Okay. He was big. Like I said. Mustache. Glasses."

"White? Black? Asian? What?"

"He was white."

"Taller than you?"

"A lot taller."

"How tall are you?"

"Five-eight. Okay. Five-six and a half. I'm taller in shoes. He had a voice like a football coach. He scared me."

"You hear either of them call each other by name?"

"Naw."

I leaned into the pole.

That was when he rolled and twisted away. By the time I got around the end of the fence, he'd vanished.

50. GREEN CHEESE IN THE PARSON'S HAT

Cynthia Rideout

DECEMBER 22, SUNDAY, 0800 HOURS

Last night I thought Wollf had gone nuts.

Thirty minutes after taking off after that woman, he came back looking exhausted. As if he'd had some sort of epiphany out there in the dark.

Oddly enough, he wasn't even mad at Eddings.

Maybe he's come to expect backstabbing from her.

The rest of the night he acted as though nothing mattered. It was like he was on laughing gas. *Everything* was funny.

Then, before we left the scene, Marshal 5 questioned him for half an hour.

Wollf said the suspect was a white male, unimpressive except for the mauve dress. LaSalle believed this was our perp, while Connor remained unconvinced. She said, "Why would he be in a dress and a wig? I don't get it. You're talking two different pathologies here."

LaSalle snapped, "Why was he in a dress? Why does he light fires? Why does he stand around and watch us put them out? His head's screwed on backwards, that's why. He probably bays at the moon and shits green cheese into the parson's hat."

Wollf's chase was already the talk of the department. Opinion was divided among firefighters. About half thought Eddings's negligence allowed the firebug to escape; the other half thought Wollf was losing his mind. Personally, I thought he'd found the bug *and* was losing his mind.

Towbridge said, "You gonna recognize this guy when he's dressed like a man?"

"I don't know. It was dark. He had makeup smeared all over his face. He was crying."

"You made him cry?" I asked.

51. IDIOT'S DELIGHT

After the shift where the roof caved in, we had two days off. A Sunday and a Monday. I spent most of Sunday recovering, sleeping, reliving Saturday night's confrontation with the perp, and watching old movies with a cup of hot chocolate next to the chair. My favorite of the day was *Duel in the Sun* with Jennifer Jones, Gregory Peck, and Lionel Barrymore. The Jones part was so overacted it was uproarious and never failed to keep me in stitches. Especially the part at the end where she takes about two weeks to crawl up the hill to Gregory Peck, who she's just shot, and who's just shot her, so she can declare her everlasting love for him and he can do the same for her. They kiss. He dies. Fade out. Wonderfully overwrought movie pap. It almost made me forget how close I'd come to killing a man the night before.

I spent Sunday night and most of Monday trying to contact my brother's wife, Susan, or Mitzi as she now preferred to be called. She'd lost her place, but I talked to her former neighbors and called coworkers from her last job. Nobody seemed to know where she was.

Except for Neil, she was the only family I cared about, and I desperately wanted to spend Christmas day with somebody I loved. Our shift was scheduled to work Tuesday night, Christmas eve, so I would be free all day on Christmas.

At an import shop on Capitol Hill I'd bought her a pair of earrings from Uganda to add to her collection of jewelry from exotic locales.

I'd sent a package to my brother in Walla Walla. Two SFD T-shirts, which he said were a status thing in the joint, and a box of chocolate chip cookies, which he was addicted to—when he wasn't addicted to other things.

Monday night I had nightmares about going to prison with my brother.

Eventually I got out of bed and sat in the big chair in my living room and watched Clark Gable and Norma Shearer in *Idiot's Delight.*

Tuesday morning I rewound my tapes, shaved, showered, and walked to work. There had been no fires in our district since Saturday night, proof to me that I'd maimed the bastard and that he was having trouble getting around.

I'd been thinking about what he'd said after he slipped out of my reach.

"Your father was a dick," he said. "He deserved to die. And that other asshole should have gone with him. And you and your whole crew. You're all dicks."

Clutching his ribs, he'd hobbled into the dark woods on a path kids had made. He'd tried to say something to hurt me, but what he *didn't* say was that his story about my father was a lie. For a few minutes he thought he was going to die, and when he escaped, the invective simply spewed out. Had the earlier story been a lie, surely he would have said so then. Guys like that, they pull the wool over your eyes, they want you to know it.

After he left, I ran around the long end of the fence and followed him into the woods, but after ten minutes I knew I would never find him.

I'd lost the man who tried to immolate me and my crew; the man responsible for my father's death twenty-five years ago. The man responsible for my mother's fall into depression and drunkenness. The man who'd destroyed my childhood and my brother's life.

The man I'd been dreaming of killing since I was four.

It was ironic because, had I slain him, I would have certainly lost the second half of my life to the man who'd stolen the first half.

With Dolan gone and stories circulating about how close the department had come to losing our whole crew, the antagonism between the engine and the truck at Station 6 seemed to lose momentum.

It was a relatively quiet shift. Crapps from Engine 13 was riding Ladder 3 with us, Towbridge driving, Rideout behind me. Dolan and Pickett were both home nursing their injuries.

Around eight that evening Slaughter came out of the phone booth in the beanery and said he had to take his father to the hospital. Eddings okayed it, and thirty minutes later somebody from Station 28 came in to fill for him. The guy from Twenty-eight's put his gear in the tailboard spot, and Zeke moved up to the officer's position, a prospect that made Zeke visibly nervous.

"You gonna be gone all night?" Gliniewicz asked.

"No point in coming back," said Slaughter. "There's no telling how long it'll take."

"I hope he's better."

"I hope he's better too," I said.

"Thanks." Slaughter addressed Gliniewicz and did not look at me.

The engine had only three runs that day, all aid calls. We had a service response to an assisted-care high-rise to rescue three blind women from a stalled elevator. The same women had been stuck in the elevator a month earlier, and one of them had a crush on Towbridge. I'd always thought it was his good looks that made him irresistible to women, but even blind women were chasing him.

It was just after midnight when the main phone rang. Gliniewicz had the night watch, so it was his job to answer. Two minutes later I heard Engine 6 being fired up.

The apparatus doors closed behind them with a heavy metallic bang.

I stepped into my bunking boots and trousers.

In the watch office there was a paperback war novel next to Gliniewicz's pillow. His uniform was carefully folded over a chair. Gliniewicz was overweight, sedentary, out of condition, yet he took obsessive care with his hygiene, and his uniforms always had razor-sharp creases.

Curious as to what sort of run they'd been called to over the main phone, I checked the daybook, but Gliniewicz had made no notation.

I turned on the television and sat in front of another holiday showing of *It's a Wonderful Life,* one of the featured players Donna Reed, who, before she died, had lived nearby on Mercer Island.

Seven minutes later the main phone rang.

"Station Six. Lieutenant Wollf."

"Lieutenant?" It was Zeke's deep voice. "Uh. You better get down here. We found Slaughter's truck."

"Get down where?"

"That house where we had the fire a couple weeks ago. With the antique cars? The movie star? We found Steve's truck, but we can't find him."

"Did you check the guest house?"

Gliniewicz got on the line. "Just get down here, God damn it! We need a ladder."

"You want the police?"

"Hell, no. He said not to call the cops."

"Who said?"

"Steve. He called the station. Said he was handcuffed to somebody's bed."

52. UGLIER. HEAVIER. CRAZIER. YEEHAA!

Lt. Stephen Slaughter AU6/C-3

You gotta love firefighter groupies.

After she called the station, I took a quick shower, changed my underwear, slapped on some Aqua Velva, and told the guys I had to take my dad to the hospital, half expecting this to be a joke Gliniewicz was pulling. But when I slid into the driveway, there she was at the back door of the mansion.

Jaclyn flirts like a ten-dollar whore, but then when I show up she wants to sit around and talk. The movie star's off somewhere for Christmas. There's a tree in the corner with phony ornaments and a manger scene.

So far we've had three shots each of the old lady's vodka. Jaclyn tells me she's headed for Hollywood, but as far as I know, most of the wannabes in Hollywood end up hooking and I tell her so. She says only, "Lieutenant Slaughter, you're funny."

"I ain't kiddin'."

She's definitely on her way out the door. There's a stack of suitcases in the kitchen.

Which means tonight is probably my last chance to tap into this.

I figure if I sleep over, I can get it again in the morning. Whatever else happens, I gotta be outta here before eight, showered and smelling like me. I get home on Christmas morning reeking of vodka and cheap perfume, and Connie's going to hit the roof. That's just what I don't need on Christmas day.

I can't believe how woozy I am.

"We ever going to fuck?" I ask, slurring the words.

"You cut right to the chase, don't you?"

"You bet I do."

"If that's how you want it."

She heads for the stairs, walking just out of reach. She smells great. So do I. We glide up the carpeted stairs to the second floor, and I'm thinking she's going to stop, but we just keep going to the third floor, where she escorts me into a huge bedroom with a canopied bed and tells me to make myself comfortable. Lie down. Relax. Get naked. She'll be back in a minute.

Talk about a perfect Christmas.

I kick off my shoes, step out of my boxers, and strip nekid. That's how we used to say it in the Navy. Nekid. Yeehaa. Oh, I am a dirty old man.

I'm also one sleepy little buckaroo.

I crawl under the covers and prop myself against the pillows. I can see the light under the bathroom door. Can see the shadow of her moving around in there. Getting undressed. Probably putting her diaphragm in. Geez, I hope she don't think I'm going to use a rubber. I don't eat chocolate cake through a wool hat either. No sir.

I'm barely awake when she comes out.

She stands at the end of the bed. "You're still dressed," I say, only it comes out something like, "Ooo still dwesst."

"You're a tough nut, you know that?"

"I thought you were gonna give me a poke."

"Don't worry. We'll have some fun. Just wait here. I've got a phone call to make."

"Oh, come on, baby. You ain't give me nothin' yet. Break out them puppies. Let Daddy see 'em before you go."

She smiles and lifts up her blouse, shows me the goods, and real loud like, I shout something along the lines of, "Yeehaa!"

"I'll be right back," she says.

It takes me a while to figure out where I am and what's going on, but now that I'm awake I realize the lights are off. The house is like a cave. Drafty as hell. I'm alone in this big bed, trying to remember did we have sex? I can't recall exactly what happened. Jesus, I haven't been this drunk in years.

The cold was what woke me.

If she'd pulled the covers over me I'd be asleep still, but she didn't.

I have a lulu of a headache. And a gut ache to boot. Hell of a way to start off Christmas morning. I cut a fart and most of the gut ache goes away. I try to look at my watch to see what time it is, but my wrist isn't where it should be. In fact, my entire left arm is pulled around at an unnatural angle.

Jesus. I'm handcuffed to a thick post in the bed board. My wristwatch is missing.

"Jaclyn? Jaclyn? Where are you?"

Except for some movement downstairs which might be the wind, the house is silent. I don't have a clue what time it is. My glasses are gone and I can't see much in the dark.

I rattle the handcuffs, but they are tight and the bed board is solid.

"Jaclyn? Come on, now. I can hear you down there. This isn't funny. You're going to have to let me go sometime. Come on, Jackie. You hear me?"

Then, for just a moment, a shadow fills the doorway.

"Jaclyn?"

The doorway empties.

It's spooky as hell. Moments later I hear somebody going down the carpeted staircase. My eyes aren't that great, but I have a feeling it isn't Jaclyn. In fact, I'm certain it isn't.

I rattle the bed again, but all that does is tighten the manacle around my left wrist.

The only thing I can reach is a lamp on a side table. I turn the switch, but the bulb is burned out. I can barely hook my toes under the chair where I left my clothes. Even without a light, I know my money is missing. My credit cards are gone.

I use my bare foot to pick the fleece vest off the back of

the chair. It is heavy enough I know she hasn't found my cell phone. Jesus, I'm like a monkey now, picking shit up with my feet. I'm buck naked and chained to some old lady's bed.

Jesus. Talk about humiliating.

Grabbing the bedposts with both hands, I shake for all it's worth. It would take a team of gorillas to take it apart. Jesus. My credit cards. Now I'm going to have to waste Christmas making phone calls to cancel them.

I squander another four or five minutes trying to shake the bed apart, but this thing was built to withstand a nuke. I can't get out of the handcuffs either. Shit. Shit. Shit.

"Hello?" I yell. It's a weird sound, my own voice, because except for the bed rattling, it's the only real noise I've heard since waking up. "Hellooooo. Jackie? Is that you?"

Somebody is standing just beyond the bedroom door out of my sight. It occurs to me that I'm a prisoner.

"Ma'am. I'm Steve Slaughter of the Seattle Fire Department. I've got myself into a predicament here. Remember me? I'm one of the guys helped save you a coupl'a weeks ago. If you could get a hacksaw, I could just mosey on outta here."

This is when I hear the propane torch. You can hear the hiss of gas, the poof when the striker ignites the tip. There is light too. Just beyond the doorway. The light a propane torch makes when you fire it up.

"Hey. I had a date with Jackie. I'm not a burglar. I'm not here to rob anybody. Can you help me out here?"

She steps into the room holding a torch. Is it the old Pennington woman? Looks more like that Norman Bates guy dressed up as his mother in *Psycho.* Bad makeup. Ill-fitting dress. Shoes too big.

There is only the light from the torch casting shadows on her face.

She steps into the room with the torch held out in front of her. Oh, God, I think to myself. This bitch is crazy.

"Get away from me with that."

Now she has knocked the chair aside, is reaching for me, holding the flame out toward my buttocks as I arch away.

Then it hits me and I scream.

Instinctively, I kick at her, not a solid blow, but it is unexpected and knocks her backward. She staggers and the torch rolls onto the floor. Jesus. If she starts this place on fire, no way I can get out of these cuffs.

I push the correct sequence of buttons on my phone and hide it under one of the pillows on the bed. I wait until I think the connection is made. All this time the woman is coming back.

I try to gather up the bedspread and wrap it around one of my legs. Anything for a buffer.

"Station Six. Gliniewicz."

"Gliniewicz? I'm at Thirtieth and King. You know the place. You gotta get out here. I'm on the third floor. You gotta help me."

"What?"

She is moving in on me, Anthony Perkins in drag, uglier, heavier, crazier. The torch aimed at my butt cheeks again. The bedspread's all twisted around. I can't get it out from under me. I scream.

Somewhere in the distance I hear Gliniewicz's tinny voice on the phone asking if I'm all right.

53. PARDON, SIR? BUT ARE THOSE BLOWTORCH BURNS ON YOUR ASS?

"This isn't a real call, is it?" Towbridge asks. We are driving with red lights but no siren; stealth mode, as Towbridge likes to call it.

"No," I say.

"The movie star's crib? She in trouble?"

"I don't know."

"Oh, I get it. The housekeeper."

"Gliniewicz called. They're up there looking for Slaughter."

"Slaughter? What the hell?"

In front of Pennington's house, Gliniewicz, Zeke, and the detail from Twenty-eight's are standing next to the engine. To stave off the cold, Zeke and the detail wear full turnouts, boots, pants, and coats, even their helmets. Gliniewicz wears only his boots, bunking pants, and a department sweatshirt, and is puffing away on a Salem cigarette. Despite a cold breeze rushing at us from the south, he is sweating. He's bouncing around like a gerbil on speed. All of a sudden I've become his best friend. All the eye contact I haven't been getting around the station is here in spades. The guy loves me. Keeps touching me as we talk.

"His truck's around back. He sounded bad, man. Real bad."

"You try to get in?"

"Everything's locked up tight. But there's an open window up there on the third floor. Our ladder won't reach."

"You knocked?"

"I did," says the detail from Twenty-eight's, a man named Moscowitz. "I think I heard somebody screaming."

"Put the stick up," I say to Towbridge.

"I don't think it was somebody screaming," Gliniewicz says hopefully.

But I am already moving. "How long ago?"

Moscowitz says, "Three, four minutes."

I tell Towbridge to place the tip of the aerial just under the open window on the third floor, then I take Crapps around the house with our forcible entry kit. I carry the Halligan tool and flathead axe combination.

The back door is even stronger than the front. In the driveway in back I spot Slaughter's truck.

When we go back around front, the aerial is just stretching up to the window on the third floor.

Gliniewicz is preparing to climb. "Not on your life," I say, pushing him aside. Rideout is already on the apparatus, having donned a mask and bottle in standby position.

"You don't have to do this," I tell her.

"I know."

"We'll use channel seven," I say to Towbridge. I scramble past the control tower and head up the ladder. "Put two people at the back door. And guard the front."

"Why?"

"Just do it."

I reach the window before Rideout.

It is a bedroom window at the peak of the house, Pennington's master suite. I have visions of the old lady huddled under her blankets with a pistol, blasting away as I approach. I pick up the pick-head axe out of its slot on the aerial and shine a flashlight through the window. A haze of light smoke lingers in the room.

When I force the window up, the room stinks of burned flesh.

On the floor near the bed a plumber's torch is lit and hissing, scorching a hole in the carpet.

On top of the bed, in a sort of a stupor, Steve Slaughter gives me a dead look of incomprehension and bewilderment. I can't tell if he is alive. One arm is handcuffed to the bedpost. His naked body is softer and less toned than it looks in clothing. In fact, without his glasses or clothes, he looks like a turtle that has been pulled out of his shell.

"She just left. God. You saved my life," he says.

Carrying the axe and battle lantern, I work my way down through the house, down two flights of stairs. I'm on the second floor when I hear the back door open and close. When I get there, our firefighter guards are nowhere in sight. Neither is anybody else.

I walk through the house and open the front door, motioning for Towbridge to bring a hacksaw. Upstairs, Rideout has thrown a blanket over Slaughter and turned on the lights. They are talking about the weather as if there was nothing at all odd about the circumstances.

Rideout has turned off the blowtorch.

"I hope you had your gloves on," I say.

"You're not worried about fingerprints?" Slaughter exclaims. "Jesus Christ! You didn't call the cops?"

"Didn't call anybody."

"Don't. 'Cause I ain't talkin' to anybody. I'm fucked up, man. I'm drunk and I got a headache the size of Cincinnati."

Slaughter stares at Rideout until I motion her out of the room. "Look, Paul. You're not going to tell anybody, are you? I got twenty-seven years invested in the department—twenty-two in my marriage. I got a wife and two girls. The department finds out I took emergency leave and was up here bangin' Jackie, I'll be in deep shit."

"You're burned."

"I been burned before. I can explain burns to my old lady. This other I couldn't explain to the tooth fairy."

"What happened?"

"I don't know. I woke up and some old bitch was tryin' to barbecue me."

"Not Patricia Pennington?"

"I don't know. It was dark."

Towbridge comes into the room with a hacksaw, looks at Slaughter in disbelief, then at me. I make a sawing motion. He cuts the manacles off Slaughter's wrist, then the bracelets off the bed. Slaughter dresses quickly, stuffing his boxer shorts into his vest pocket. I watch him gather up the contents of his wallet.

"She rob you?"

"Yes. But you call the cops, I'll deny I was here."

"I want to hand that torch over to LaSalle and Connor. The prints might come in handy."

"I told you I'm not testifying against anybody."

"Humor me."

"Fuck you." He thinks better of his anger and places his hands on my shoulders, squinting through his glasses. "Look, we been having trouble, you and me, but when it gets down to the crunch, one firefighter will always take care of another. You proved that tonight. I won't forget."

Gliniewicz bursts into the room, breathing hard from the three flights of stairs. "What happened?"

"Not a damn thing," Slaughter says.

Slaughter rides to the station on Attack 6 while somebody ferries Slaughter's truck. The crew will nursemaid him and tend his burns until he's had enough coffee to drive home. I call LaSalle. Then I call Vanessa Pennington.

She arrives before LaSalle and parks in the courtyard. Rideout is beside me. Towbridge and Crapps are in front of the house on the rig. Vanessa is more than annoyed.

"You just had to come back, didn't you? She told me you were after her."

"This isn't about me, Vanessa."

"Of course it's about you. You knew this was her last night here, didn't you?"

"Jaclyn?"

"Who else would you come here to see?"

"Lieutenant Slaughter."

"Who?"

"Steve Slaughter. She handcuffed him to your grandmother's bed."

Vanessa is silent for a moment. "Is Jackie here?"

"Not that we could tell. If I were you, I'd get the locks changed. Let me show you what happened." She follows me into the house.

We climb four or five steps before Vanessa says, "I'm sorry about the way I came at you. Jackie told me . . . well, it doesn't matter what she told me. I don't know why I listened."

"No problem."

"I really *am* sorry."

I take her upstairs and show her the burn marks on the carpet and the scratched bedpost.

"I'm sure glad Nanna is in Idaho."

Five minutes later LaSalle arrives, takes in our story, picks up the blowtorch in a plastic bag and says, "What am I supposed to do with this?"

"You might want to dust it for prints."

"We'll see."

54. CRIMINAL ERASURE OF A MOST EXCELLENT PHONE MESSAGE

I spent Christmas day alone, same as I had for the last ten Christmases except those when I'd been at work. Funny how much I'd looked forward to those holidays surrounded by my built-in family—firefighters.

Christmas morning I took a ten-mile walk along the path on Lake Washington and through Seward Park. The weather was cloudy, with wind from the south pushing against my back most of the way home. The roads were devoid of cars except for the occasional family driving to see relatives, cargo areas laden with presents.

The walk gave me a chance to think.

My description Sunday morning of the man made up as a woman wasn't of much use to Marshal 5. They'd asked me to describe him for a sketch artist, but the drawing we made wasn't very good.

Judging from Slaughter's brief description of the woman with the blowtorch, his assailant was the same person I tried to kill Saturday night. I couldn't even guess what the pyro had been doing inside Pennington's mansion. It made me worry for Pennington. If it was the same person, that would make it twice now that I'd come within a hair of nabbing him.

The story the pyro spun gave me a lot to think about. It might have been a lie he'd made up to stall me, but on the other hand, if what he said was true, my father's last act saved the pyro's life.

I wouldn't make the same mistake.

Besides my father, the original pyro was thought to have been responsible for at least two civilian deaths. Now he'd tried to kill me and my crew.

After all these years, I'd been expecting some hunchbacked monster, while the reality was nothing more than a mild-mannered wimp. I should have known. Arson was a crime practiced in secret, a crime that started off small and grew, but only after the perpetrator was safely offstage. Arson was the crime of a sneak. Still, I'd been taken with how ordinary he'd seemed. Even in women's clothing and makeup, he could have passed for any of half a dozen simple-minded twits we ran into every day.

I was watching Clark Gable and Loretta Young in *Key to the City* when the phone rang. I especially liked the bumbling fire chief played by Frank Morgan, of *Wizard of Oz* fame. "Will you accept a collect call from Neil Wollf?"

"Yes, operator. Put him on."

"How you doin', little brother? You a chief yet?"

"Another couple of weeks. How are you?"

"Got over that cold finally. God, you know, one guy in here coughs and five minutes later six hundred peckerwoods have pneumonia. Thanks for the cookies and stuff."

"You're welcome."

"What are you doing for Christmas?"

"Watching a video."

"You seen Susan?"

"I called around, but she must be out with friends."

"Jesus. You know you get to be a certain age, you just stop bouncing."

"I know. I'll drive over and look for her again after we hang up."

"Will you?"

"Yeah."

"So. What else is going on in your life?"

"I talked to the pyro."

"You're not still on that kick, are you?"

"Listen to me, Neil. I talked to him. It's the guy! He was standing right next to our father when he fell into that basement."

"He fell? I had the impression he went in looking for victims and got trapped."

"He told me there was another fireman there. They had a fight." I fleshed out the details.

"You believe him?"

"I think I do."

"Did you hurt him?"

"Not bad. He got away."

"So why don't you talk to this other firefighter?"

"I don't have a name. Besides, that was twenty-five years ago. Most of those guys are long gone."

"You know what, Paul? I been in the joint most of my life, and I'd rather be dead than be where *you* are now and end up where *I* am now. Don't do him that favor."

"What makes you think I can control it?"

"Don't give me that shit. Don't trap yourself with a vow of vengeance."

"Hey. I'll drive past Susan's place right now. Talk to the neighbors. See what I can pick up. You don't hear from me, I didn't get anything."

"Thanks."

Two hours later I carried two boxes full of her things into my condo. She'd been evicted months earlier, and a neighbor had been holding a few of her possessions. I should have kept tabs on her. Having a brother in prison was bad enough, but losing track of his wife whom you'd promised to watch over was worse.

When I got home I found a message on my answering machine. "Paul? I wanted to apologize again for what I said last night. I just . . . well, I shouldn't have said it. And thanks for calling me. I'm going to follow your suggestion and have the locks at Nanna's place changed." After a long pause she added, "I was thinking we could do something together, see the Kurosawa film at the Seven Gables maybe? It was just a thought. Or if you want to talk sometime. Call me . . . or not."

I wanted to call her. God, how I wanted to call her.

I finished the Gable video, made some dinner while listening to the news on the radio, and spent the next few hours on the Internet looking up anything I could find on arson, fire investigation, and pyromania. I'd done this before. It was almost a fetish. I kept returning to a couple of old newspaper articles about Captain William Kerrigan, the fire investigator who said he'd never stop looking for my father's killer. A Web search turned up a William Kerrigan residing in Sequim, a small town on the Olympic Peninsula two hours from Seattle. The listing said he was seventy-six. That seemed about right. I phoned and got his wife, who told me he was retired from the Seattle Fire Department. I made an appointment to see them Monday morning after my shift.

In the morning I listened a second and a third time to the message Vanessa left on my machine. I was falling in love with the sound of her voice, if not with Pennington herself, and I knew if I wasn't careful I would lose my mind standing next to the answering machine. I could never have a woman like her and I knew it.

Feeling a large hole open up inside me, I erased the message.

55. GHOST IN THE BASEMENT

Sunday morning while we were waiting for the freshly waxed floors in the station to dry, I fabricated a list of boneheaded excuses to telephone Vanessa Pennington. I was almost hoping she wouldn't answer so I could chalk up the call to good intentions and bad luck.

Secreted in the small study room at the base of the stairs, I dialed her home number from memory. "Hello?"

"Hi. This is Paul Wollf—"

"Paul! How nice to hear from you. I got the locks changed on Friday. No sign of the 'J' person. Nanna won't be back until Tuesday, so I'm going to pick her up from the airport and help her get settled. Actually, I have the whole week off, so I'll probably spend some time up there. I'm so glad you called."

She knew from our earlier meetings I was no conversationalist, and I could tell she was trying to make it easier for me by yakking a mile a minute. Either that or she was as nervous as I was. Not likely.

You didn't know better, you might have thought she was happy to hear from me.

"Do you have plans for tomorrow?" she asked. "Maybe we could meet for lunch somewhere . . . if you'd like."

"I'm going up to Sequim tomorrow morning when I get off work. I don't know. Maybe you'd want to take a day trip to the peninsula?" I couldn't believe the words had come out of my mouth.

"Sure. That sounds nice. Would you like me to drive? Then if you have a rough shift tonight, you can sleep in the car."

"That'd be great. I'm shooting for the eight forty-five ferry."

"How about I meet you at the station? What time do you get off?"

We talked for half an hour longer, which, except for the evening we'd gone to the Harvard Exit together, easily made this the lengthiest conversation I'd had in ages with a woman I wasn't about to screw. After I hung up I was floating on air. Not that anything was going to come of this.

The shift passed uneventfully until 0223 hours, when we were sent to a garage fire at Twenty-ninth Avenue and East Pike Street. Attack 6 and Ladder 3. No other units. Flames showing.

Gliniewicz made a right-hand turn off Martin Luther King Jr. Way onto Union, thinking he would make another left on Twenty-ninth. Except Twenty-ninth didn't connect to Union. A minute later Towbridge chuckled when we got to the location first.

Despite the fact that they weren't on the right street, Slaughter radioed the dispatcher, "Attack Six at Twenty-nine and East Pike. We have a single-story single-car garage fully involved. Laying a preconnect. Ladder Three, help with the lines."

"They ain't even here," Towbridge said.

"He knows nobody listening on the radio knows that," I said. "Except us."

The fire was in a concrete-walled single-car garage with no vehicle inside, flames lurching out a missing window on the south wall. Massive amounts of smoke had already filled the street.

When Attack 6 finally rolled in behind us, Zeke climbed out of the crew cab and pulled the preconnect while I motioned Rideout to help.

Slaughter had promised things would be better after we cut him out of those handcuffs, but things had grown worse.

"God damn!" Slaughter yelled, walking around behind the hose line where he could bark into Rideout's ear. "That hose is for enginemen. Are you an engineman?"

"Sir, I'm a firefighter," Rideout barked back, holding the nozzle tightly. She'd stolen it from Zeke the way a lineman steals a dropped football. "I adapt."

"You adapt. Jesus Christ!"

"We would have put it out earlier, sir," Rideout said. "But our engine company got lost, and we had to wait for them."

Feigning disgust, Slaughter walked away. He hadn't been expecting sarcasm from a recruit, and it disturbed him as much as it pleased me. Most bullies grew uncomfortable when somebody stood up to them, and Slaughter was no exception.

The garage was on a dead end amidst rows of Monopoly houses on either side of the street. The only exposure was an old apple tree. It was a fun fire. No risk to occupants or firefighters. No screeching chiefs.

As a matter of course, I surveyed the street for looky-loos or perps, but, except for a couple of homeowners peeking out their windows, the street was empty.

When Slaughter walked past me, he said, "You probably don't even know how close we are to the basement where we found your old man."

"You were there?"

"Afterwards I was."

"Why didn't you ever say anything?"

Slaughter took a long while to reply. "It was an ugly fire. It was hard to talk about."

"You going to tell me where it is?"

"There's nothing you can do about it now."

Before either of us could take a breath, I had him against the driver's door of Ladder 3, his bunking coat in my fists. I could see Slaughter registering shock.

"Okay, motherfucker," he said. "It's across the street."

I let him go. "The green house?"

"It's turquoise, you fuck. You don't know what you're messing with here."

The homeowner, a thick-chested black man with a sliver

of a mustache, met me on the front porch in collapsed slippers and pajama bottoms. “Hey, man, was that another arson?”

“We think so. You mind if I look around?”

“Be my guest. You think he’s still in the neighborhood?”

“Could be. You got a basement?”

“Yeah.”

I walked around the house, switched on my flashlight, and swung the beam around the backyard. Last Sunday the perp talked about an alley, but I didn’t see an alley.

I did see a basement window.

I was standing over the window well wondering if this was even the right house, wondering whether Slaughter was shining me on, when the homeowner opened the door to the basement from inside and let me in.

It was smaller than I’d imagined—concrete walls on three sides tapering to a crawl space that smelled of damp and dirt. Except for the washer and dryer, it contained only a hot water tank, a lawn mower, and a discarded Christmas tree dripping tinsel.

“Years ago there was a fire down here,” he said. “Hell, we were just kids. They rebuilt it, but you can still see a couple of spots where there’s char.” He pointed to a floor joist in a corner above the washing machine and dryer.

My father had probably died within ten feet of where I was standing. I couldn’t escape the emotions piling up on me. As I stood there thinking about it, it occurred to me that had we not caught the garage fire across the street, I might never have run across this. Slaughter might never have told me.

Which made me wonder if the fire across the street hadn’t been set for my benefit.

“Did you know a firefighter died right here in this basement?” asked the homeowner.

“You know where?”

“I always thought it was in that corner.” He pointed. “I got the newspaper article upstairs. You want me to get it?”

"Please."

After he was gone, I tried to imagine what it must have been like to tumble into the darkness, to fight your way toward the exit, to feel the heat on your skin, to know you were never getting out. To call for help and know somebody was standing outside but wasn't helping you. We were taught when lost to find a wall and follow it. The basement was almost empty now, but had it been full of junk, moving around would have been next to impossible.

"You okay?"

"Pardon?"

"You look like you're getting sick."

"I'm okay."

"I got that article."

Same as my own copy, this one had aged to sepia. If the homeowner realized I was the spitting image of the man in the photo, he didn't say anything. The picture frame trembled when I handed it back.

"You believe in ghosts?" he asked.

I believed. I believed because I could feel my father in the corner. I could feel him looking at me. I could feel him wondering why it had taken me so long to get here. I could feel him begging me to find his killer. Begging me to avenge him.

I had never been this close to my father. Wearing the same uniform and gear he wore. Wearing his old bars on my collar. Standing next to the spot where he died.

My legs felt weak as I walked up the crude basement steps to the backyard, the steps they'd carried my father's body up.

"Just out of curiosity, was there an alley back here at one time?" I asked.

"There was, but it's all grown over."

I could feel the blood draining out of my head. For a moment I wondered whether I was going to faint. I didn't.

In the moonlight in the side yard I was greeted by Towbridge and a tall, curly-haired civilian with heavy glasses and an Adam's apple that should have been on Mount Rushmore, a camera slung around his neck. He warmed his hands by cupping his palms to his face.

"You Lieutenant Wollf?"

"That's right."

"My name is Webber. I'm with *The Seattle Times*. You *are* Paul Wollf, aren't you? The one whose father died in an arson fire twenty-five years ago."

We were in the middle of the street, and I knew this buzzard would have a cow if he found out we were in front of the address where my father died or that there was a possibility the garage fire had been set to draw me here.

"There's a rumor going around that the arsonist setting these fires might have been the one who killed your father," Webber said. "How would you feel if it *was* the man who killed your father?"

We stared at each other for a moment. Then, sensing peril, he stepped back. "I assure you the chief of the department has given me permission to speak to firefighters in the field."

"*I* didn't give you permission."

"Lieutenant. Your father died fighting an arson fire, and here you are working in the same part of town. Same kind of fires. Don't you find that uncanny?"

I turned my back on him and walked away.

56. BAPTIZING HOUSEGUESTS

Vanessa Pennington

When I picked up Paul at the station Monday morning, it was obvious he hadn't gotten much sleep. It was just as obvious that something had happened during the night that he didn't want to talk about. I wonder how often that happens to a firefighter. I wonder too whether he might have opened up if he knew me better. It must be strange to see people dying or injured every time you go to work. Different from what most doctors and nurses deal with, since a firefighter is generally right there in the home or at the accident scene moments after the worst has occurred, surrounded by the victims, the fresh blood, the broken bones, and their worried relatives.

We drove down the hill to his condo listening to the radio in the car. At least I listened. He was focused on something else.

"I just need a shower and quick change," he said as we walked the corridor to his unit.

When he put his key into the door, we heard music and voices from inside. He gave me a look that told me to remain near the doorway. I sensed trouble.

Scattered about his living room were newspapers, coffee mugs, and empty beer bottles, a pair of men's striped trousers on the carpet like a popped balloon, dirty dishes and take-out food containers on his immaculate counters. In the back room I heard a woman talking. Music that sounded East European playing.

In the hallway there was a bearded man wearing a dingy V-neck T-shirt and a pair of sloppy socks and absolutely nothing else. He had Paul's white hutch open and was manhandling a digital camera, snapping pictures of the walls and video racks. At his feet were two videos, the tapes ripped out. He didn't seem to mind that Paul and I were there and made no attempt to cover his nakedness. I had the impression he was on drugs. Suddenly I had a sick feeling in the pit of my stomach. This whole scenario was so at odds with what I had glimpsed of Paul's private life the first time I was here. Was this man a friend of Paul's or an intruder? I wasn't sure which possibility was more disturbing and didn't know how to react. Paul certainly didn't give me any clues.

He calmly took off his coat and hung it in the hall closet, then took mine and hung it up. I still didn't know what to think, but I knew one thing: If this man was a friend of Paul's, I wasn't about to stay alone with him while Paul took a shower.

Paul walked across the living room to the glass doors on the deck, gazed at the water for a moment or two, then opened the doors wide so that the condo began filling with cold air off the lake. The sun was coming up over Lake Washington, turning the sky pink and orange. He walked back to the man in the corridor, took the camera out of his hands, then reached up toward his head and walked him very quickly to the deck. It took me a moment to realize he'd grabbed the man by the ear.

The man hit the lake with a thunk that sounded like a large rock going in. I saw a life ring hanging on the deck railing, so I tossed it into the water next to the stunned swimmer. It's pretty easy to drown when you hit water that cold, and the man had looked to be in a mental fog.

Paul didn't seem concerned about what happened to him after he hit the water. He found a second man in the next room wearing trousers and no shirt, shorter and stouter than the man in the water. I thought for a minute he was going to put up a fight, but Paul grabbed his ponytail and dragged him past me and onto the deck, where he pitched him into the lake next to the first man. Neither man had had much of a chance against Paul. It was as if he were casually throwing garbage out. Which, I now realized with some relief, was in fact the case.

The two men began dog-paddling toward the dock next door with the life preserver between them.

It was about that time that a woman in panties and a camisole top came flying down the hallway and out the front door behind us, a bundle of clothing in her arms, her white thighs flashing. "I'm sorry, Paul," she shouted over her shoulder, to my astonishment. "I must have lost track of time."

"Susan, come back."

But she didn't come back. There was an uncomfortable silence in the condo after she left. Paul was so embarrassed, and I didn't know what to make of any of this. I still had no idea whether these people were burglars or neighbors or what. One thing was certain. He knew the woman.

He did a walk-through of the apartment, gathering up all the loose clothing he could find, and handed the bundle to a police officer who showed up at the door a few minutes later. It turned out a neighbor had called in a noise complaint. "They're gone now," Paul told the officer. "They've left."

"Where'd they go?" asked the officer.

"A couple of them are out there in the lake."

After the policeman left, Paul set the destroyed videotapes aside, showing remarkably more emotion over the tapes than he had over throwing the men into the water. When he excused himself to take a shower, I began to rethink whether I wanted to spend the day with this guy. It wasn't his fault if he'd come home to find three strangers in his condo, was it? On the other hand, he'd known the woman's name and she his. I'd been too stunned by the events to ask him for an explanation, and I sensed that he wasn't yet prepared to give me one. Now I would just have to bide my time until he got out of the shower.

The aftermath of this violence was the same as that evening in the street when he caught the wife-beater. My stomach was tied in knots, but with him, it was as if it hadn't happened. He had shown no visible excitement. No adrenaline rush that I could detect. It was just housecleaning. I'd never known anyone even remotely like this.

I made coffee and closed the windows, which he'd left open to rid the place of the stench of spilled beer and B.O. There was so much that was contradictory in Paul Wollf. At times he could barely talk to me, but if I brought up the subject of films, he was right up there with the sharpest critics around. There were so many times when he seemed unsure of himself. Yet, when something physical came up, like rescuing Nanna or taking care of these two guys, he moved without hesitation.

After a long shower, he changed clothes and came out. "You must think I'm a lunatic," he said.

"Who were those people?"

"The woman's name is Susan Wollf. She's my brother's wife. The guys I never saw before."

"What were they doing here?"

"I believe they were having a party."

"Do you share this place with her?"

"No. She has a drug habit that comes and goes. My guess is she's trying to clean herself up. She goes on these benders, and right before she pulls out of them she likes to rub it in our faces. Near as I can tell, the shame helps her hit bottom so she can resolve to turn herself around."

"Why did she run?"

He poured himself a cup of coffee. I already had one. "I don't know."

"Where's your brother?"

"He's in Walla Walla."

"The town or the prison?"

"The prison."

Despite the delay, we managed to reach the ferry terminal in time for the 9:35 run.

It was a bright winter day. From the stern of the ferry we watched Seattle grow smaller, and then, when we were thoroughly chilled, we went inside and bought espressos and carried them to an empty booth against the tall north windows. In some ways I wondered what we were doing together, but in another sense I felt very comfortable and safe around Paul Wollf. Maybe that was what I'd been wanting my whole life, to find a man I could truly feel safe around. My father, while a good provider and a fine man, had always given off an air of incompetence in all things physical. He couldn't fix his car or change a tire, and he never went out after dark, even though we lived in a comfortable middle-class neighborhood with almost no crime.

The trouble was, there wasn't a whole lot I really knew

about this guy. Getting facts out of him was like digging for water in the desert.

"The news said there are orcas this year," I said. "Maybe we'll see some."

He smiled. "Let's hope so."

As had been the case when he knocked out the man in the street, I couldn't get over the sudden flash of violence I'd seen in him this morning, the impassivity with which he dispensed it, or how quickly he settled back into seeming normalcy afterward.

As the Seattle side of the sound receded, I noticed a distant tanker headed in our direction. Drenched in fresh snow, the Cascades lined the eastern horizon like a heap of lace curtains, while Mount Rainier loomed in the southeast corner of the sky. It was truly one of the most breathtaking ferry rides there could be.

After a while his weariness got the best of him, and he lay lengthwise on the hard plastic bench seat.

"How did your brother end up in prison?" I asked as he closed his eyes.

He kept his eyes closed and spoke softly. "He used to steal people's mail, get their bank account numbers. He'd make fake IDs, print out checks, and pass bad paper. He was pretty messed up on drugs, otherwise he never would have got caught. He's very smart when he's not doping."

He began to drift off. I don't know why, but I crawled under the table and came up on his side. It was an ungraceful move, crawling under the table, but I did it on impulse, without thinking about how it would look or how he would react. He was so unlike anybody I'd ever known, and yet, underneath it all, I felt he was more like me than he would ever admit.

I picked up his head and slid my thigh under it. It took him a few moments to get over the surprise and then a while longer to relax completely. A few minutes later he was asleep. I was convinced that, for a man who did everything in his power to keep people at bay, he had an undeniable little boy quality hidden under the surface that would accept love almost without question.

57. A SHED IN THE RED

Kerrigan's homestead was west of town on a flat piece of land just off the highway, the Strait of Juan de Fuca and Vancouver Island to the north, foothills with wind-battled misshapen trees to the south.

The locals up here fished the strait in small boats, and every once in a while one of them got lost in the fog or dropped a motor and blew out to sea.

Mrs. Kerrigan greeted us at the door of a modular home. The years had thinned her limbs like stick taffy and given her a watermelon middle. A man in his seventies with kindly eyes appeared behind her.

"Bill Kerrigan," he said, giving me the death grip so many retirees used on the young. "You couldn't be anyone but Neil Wollf's son. You're the spitting image of your old man."

"And this is your wife?" Mrs. Kerrigan asked.

"This is my friend, Vanessa Pennington."

"I'm Grace. Vanessa, why don't we go off to the kitchen and let the men talk?"

"I'd like that," Vanessa said, though I knew she wanted to hear our conversation.

When we were alone, Kerrigan turned back to me. "He was a wonderful man, your father. He had a way of talking to a man like he was the only person in the world who counted. He didn't have an enemy in the world."

"There was *one.*"

Kerrigan was a tall, vigorous man with well-defined features and pink skin that complemented his swept-back white hair. He sat in a recliner that featured a pair of reading glasses perched on one arm, while I sank into a couch across from him. "You're bigger than your father. Hell, you're bigger than most people. You play ball?"

"No, sir."

"That's a pity. What'd you do in school?"

"Mostly I fought and got kicked out."

"You couldn't have fought *much*. There aren't too many people dumb enough to take on somebody your size."

"I got my growth late. I took some lickings before that."

"Tell me, what brings you up here?"

"I believe the arsonist who killed my father is working again."

Kerrigan gave me the kind of eyeballing people give you when they're trying to decide whether you're bonkers. "What makes you say that?"

"The Shasta cans are back. Plus, he told me."

"He told you? What do you mean, he told you?"

"It's a long story."

Kerrigan mulled it over. You thought about it, it *did* sound preposterous.

"I was hoping you'd tell me about the night my father died."

"At the time we hadn't lost a firefighter in quite a few years, so it shocked us." Kerrigan looked out the window wistfully. I could see the emotion welling up in his eyes. My father's death had been the seminal event in this man's career, just as it had been the seminal event in my life, though I couldn't recall the emotion the way he did. "Your mother, Emma? At the memorial service she lost all the strength in her legs. She got so weak, she practically had to be carried. Watching her about tore my heart out. I never seen anybody suffer so much."

"She suffered for a long time."

"What a damn shame," he said, shaking his head. "I hate to hear that. Anyway, this arsonist started working, and before we knew it we had copycats. We figured about six of 'em. Are you in FIU? Is that why you're here?"

"No, sir. I'm on Three Truck. I'm here because he killed my father and he's in our district, playing cat and mouse. Getting closer all the time. Last week he booby-trapped a house so the roof would cave in. Two of my guys almost got killed."

"Jesus. That don't sound good."

"No, sir."

"What it boils down to is they start fires because they like to. Pyromaniacs. They're weak personalities, ineffectual in the real world, the kind of people who get laughed at. Screwups who blame their problems on others."

"Can you tell me about the night my father died?"

"It was wintertime . . . God, I remember you both at the memorial service. Were you the older one?"

"The little guy."

"Sure. You kept taking off your clip-on tie. A woman kept putting it back on."

"That would have been my grandmother."

"The night your pop died, Engine Seven had maybe twelve, fourteen calls. Running from one to the next. He used matches or a cigarette lighter. He had a tendency to set two or three small fires in a vicinity. While we were fighting those, he'd wander off and set more. Mostly he worked the Central District. Once in a while Capitol Hill. He left these Shasta diet black cherry cans. One night your father left his crew while they were working a 'shed in the red' on Thirtieth and Pike. The crew figured he was scouting for more fires. Maybe ten minutes later somebody spotted smoke a block away. Your father still hadn't come back, but Engine Seven took the run anyway. It was close enough, they figured your father would see the rig. It turned out to be a basement fire in a little crackerbox house."

"Twenty-ninth and Pike, right off Union?"

"That's the place. It was coming out the windows by the

time they spotted it. You couldn't even see the floor. Shit piled to the ceiling. The old lady lived there was a pack rat."

"You ever figure out how my father got in that basement?"

"Nobody ever did. Engine Thirty was helping with the overhaul, dragging smoldering material out. Mattresses. Furniture. He'd been missing about an hour when Stanley Bumstead began wading around down there. Bumstead found your dad all curled up into a ball with his back to the wall like somebody waiting for a bus."

Kerrigan's eyes began to water over. I was touched by how much of this he'd taken personally. I wished he'd come around when we were kids. It would have meant a lot to know this gentle and thoughtful man had been mourning our father.

Kerrigan sat upright. "We hoped he went fast. It's always hard to know for sure. I guess the fire was rolling around in there for a good little while. I think he realized he wasn't getting out and just went over to the corner and sat down."

The thought of my father panicking in that tiny basement chilled me to the quick. You get lost. You get burned. You panic. No way around that. I actually began to go into shock thinking about it. I wanted to tell Kerrigan to stop talking, that I thought I was going down, but I didn't do either one. The last time I felt this woozy I'd been hit in the back of the skull with a hardball by Billy Winston. Tenth grade.

"I've talked to firefighters who came close to burning to death. Both of them went into a sleeplike state, so I don't think after the beginning he was hurting much."

I figured this last was a fiction Kerrigan had been telling himself over the years to make himself feel better.

For twenty-five years I'd wondered about my father's last minutes. By the time I was eight, Neil had instilled in me a legend of our father as the city's biggest hero. Then, between ourselves, we propagated a religion of hatred, vowing revenge against the pyromaniac.

Pyromaniac. I was six when I learned the meaning of that word.

58. HE'S GOING TO DIE ANYWAY

"Was my father wearing a mask?" I asked Kerrigan.

"Naw. We had them on the rigs, but you were a sissy if you went for a mask before you'd taken your share of smoke. The second-in group might use them after the first crew knocked the fire down. The thinking was, the extra forty or fifty seconds it would take to put your mask on would let the fire grow too big. Of course, what they found out later was that you go in there without a mask, choking and puking, you weren't going to put out much fire. You took that extra minute to put your mask on, then you could breathe and think and the fire went right out. It turned out being macho was the worst thing to do, but none of us knew that back then."

"Did you ever think maybe he surprised the firebug as he was starting a fire and got blindsided?"

"There was no way to know one way or t'other. We took pictures of the crowds. We interrogated several young males but never got anywhere."

I told him about the cross-dresser I'd chased. I told him the story of the second man in the alley. I told him our pyro said my father fell into a basement window well after getting into a fight with another fireman. "Is there any possibility he's telling the truth?"

"Whoa now. You're not thinking a fireman pushed your father in?"

"That's what our suspect told me."

"The only firefighters in civvies would have been in fire investigation. Myself and a few others, and most of us had been downtown until after they found the body."

"Who else was around from FIU that night?"

"Dan Traffic. Carl Whitney. Steve Slaughter."

"Lieutenant Slaughter?"

"Steve, yeah. He was there."

"You know where these other guys are?"

"Traffic is dead. He had a heart attack six months after he retired. Whitney is living in Europe. He got pissed off at the federal government and left the country. Slaughter's still around. Isn't he something?"

"Oh, yeah."

"Whooo. Of all the unfinished business in my life, that's the thing I'd give my left nut to have turn out different. Your father."

"Did Steve know my father?"

"Hasn't he told you any of this?"

"No, sir."

"Your father was Steve's first officer. Your old man nursed him through his probation up at Twenty-five's. He worshiped your old man. You didn't know that?"

"No."

Kerrigan stared at the floor. "So this cross-dresser gives you some song and dance. Do you have any reason to believe him?"

"At the time, he thought I was going to kill him."

"Were you?"

"Yes, sir."

"You're going to spoil the rest of your life for some asshole's going to die anyway?"

"We're all going to die anyway. It's just a matter of how and when."

Kerrigan remained silent for a moment. "If he thought you were going to kill him, he might have been making up stories."

"Maybe."

"Whatever you think, there's nobody your father could have been fighting that night except the arsonist."

On the way out the door, Bill said, "I meant to tell you how sorry I was to hear about your mother. That was a bad way to end. I thought about you boys when it happened. I know that was a long time ago, but I *am* sorry."

"Thanks."

It wasn't until almost two hours later when we were sunning ourselves on the windswept deck of the Bainbridge ferry that Vanessa said, "Do you mind if I ask about your mother?"

"I don't mind. Actually, I'd like to tell somebody. I never have."

59. I WASN'T ALWAYS THE NICE GUY YOU SEE IN FRONT OF YOU TODAY

Vanessa looked at me with stark expectation in her gray-blue eyes. It was true I'd never told anyone this story before, and a part of me wondered why I was telling her now.

"My mother was raised by the Captain Queeg of fathers. She eloped at seventeen basically to get out of the house. That marriage lasted four months. Our father, her second husband, had not been the love of her life so much as a second ticket out of the house, which she'd been forced to move back into after her first marriage failed. She didn't really fall in love with our father until a few years later. He knew she didn't love him when they got married, but he'd been determined to win her over. And he did. The only thing he wouldn't do for her was quit the fire department.

"After a year of marriage my brother, Neil, came along. Three years later I was born. When my father was at work, my mother didn't like being alone at night with two babies in the house. She didn't like the stories our father brought home about crispy critters or the guys he worked with or the things he'd seen. I remember a dog we used to have named Gibbs who got hit by a car when our dad was at work, and I remember my mother crying like a baby over it for days.

"Not long after my father made lieutenant, an arsonist began setting fires in the Central District. At one of the fires, my father got trapped in a house and died. My mother fell apart. It was just like Gibbs getting hit by the car all over again, only this time she didn't stop crying for a year. These days they would call it clinical depression. A couple of years after my father died, our mother began drinking. She just . . . when my father died, something broke inside her.

"She loved Neil and me, but she couldn't cope and couldn't take care of us the way she should have. My brother and I got into trouble. We used to steal stuff. Neil got a BB gun and he must have broken out every car windshield in a radius of two miles. In the end, our mother fell in with this man named Alfred T. Osbourne. Alfred lived with us maybe six weeks before he got into one last drunken fight with my mother and ended up killing her."

"Oh, no."

"There's more. If you lived in town you might remember the thirteen-year-old who got sent up for murdering his mother's lover?"

"It doesn't sound familiar."

"I was ten. The thirteen-year-old was my brother."

"Oh, no," she said again. "But this man killed your mother. Surely it was justifiable."

"Neil ended up with a court-appointed attorney who drank. It's a long story."

"So you went to live with your grandfather?"

"Right. He was a disciplinarian, and I was the kid raised by wolves. We didn't get along."

"What happened to you?"

"I became a firefighter, rescued a famous movie star, met her granddaughter, and we took trips." I grinned.

"No, really."

"I lived with my grandfather and grandmother for a few months. Then I lived with my uncle Elmo, where I lasted until I was almost twelve. Back to my grandparents for a month. I got passed around like a bad cold. I guess I deserved it. I was a jackass. I used to steal things. I guess what I'm saying is I wasn't always the nice guy you see in front of you today."

She laughed at my lame joke.

60. PEOPLE SAY YOUR MOTHER WAS A WHORE

Katie Fryer was working a trade for Zeke on the tailboard of the engine. It was January 2.

"What did you say?"

"I asked if your mother was really a prostitute," Katie said.

"Where did you hear that?"

"They're talking about it in the beanery."

"Who is?"

"Everybody. Haven't you seen this morning's papers?"

The irony was that until today I'd been relentlessly scouring every local newspaper for news of the arsonist, listening to news on a transistor radio as I walked to work, checking the wire services and the websites for the local papers four and five times a day. The arsons had been an enormous ongoing threat to the city, and each day the letters-to-the-editor columns and radio call-in shows were flooded with exhortations for more investigators, along with threats of renewed vigilante patrols, talk of recalling the fire chief and the mayor. It was unlikely any new angle would not be seized by the dogs of the local media. I began to get a sick feeling *I* was that new angle.

I knew whatever was in the papers was bad by the way the lieutenant I replaced that morning stared. Joe Williams wasn't sensitive enough to have figured out on his own that I would be wounded by the articles; somebody must have told him, which meant they were all in the other room talking about my feelings. The idea made me cringe. "Hey," Williams said cautiously.

"How's it goin'?"

"Fine."

Moving through the early morning routine on the apparatus floor, I could feel adrenaline pumping through me in amounts it never did on a fire alarm. Much as I wanted to dash into the beanery and read the newspapers, I'd learned long ago not to let anybody know I cared.

Eventually, I sequestered myself in my office with an armful of papers. There were two articles in *The Seattle Times,* one of which began on the front page. I recognized the author: Anthony R. Webber, the reporter who'd found me at the garage fire the other night.

Webber started by recapping the events of the past few weeks, the injuries to civilians and firefighters. He theorized freely that, because of the injuries and roof collapse, my crew was being targeted by the arsonist. When he asked Deputy Chief William Hertlein about it, Hertlein said, "No targeting, just inexperience. Some of our younger officers haven't gained the skill to handle certain situations that come up."

It was a public slap in the face from a man I'd KO'd in private.

Hertlein, who had burned Pickett and screwed us in Pennington's mansion by turning off our fans, now claimed *I* lacked experience.

Further on, Webber drew a connection between my father's death at the hands of an arsonist and the fact that his son was now a lieutenant in the SFD fighting a similar string of arson fires. "In 1978 Wollf's father, who hadn't been wearing an oxygen mask, was found dead in a burning basement." Oxygen mask? Our tanks contained compressed air. Pure oxygen could make dirt burn.

The *Times* chronicled the fires my father fought twenty-five years ago, comparing that arson string to ours, comparing his career to mine. There were side-by-side photographs of my father and me. The head shots we'd each had taken for our fire department ID cards. We might have been twins in some sort of time-travel experiment.

Apparently the father-son-arsonist triangle wasn't enough of a story, because there was also a sidebar about my mother's fall from grace and her untimely death at the hands of Alfred T. Osbourne. About how, after my father's death, she had turned to drink and ultimately to men to drown her sorrow. They made it seem as if she went from the funeral directly to the tavern, failing to mention the eighteen months when she didn't leave her bedroom.

"Without Wollf's calming influence, Emma Wollf soon became an habitué of the local tavern scene, sometimes bringing home paying customers to the cramped apartments where her two young boys were sleeping."

Paying customers? I couldn't help but wonder if this peculiar slant on the story hadn't come about because I'd refused to give Webber an interview.

In another sidebar titled THE BROTHERS, the *Times* capsulized our school records, including my expulsion from three different high schools for fighting. They listed Neil's incarcerations, beginning with the one for the murder of Alfred T. Osbourne. They chronicled my career in the fire department, inserting quotes about me from unnamed sources inside the department. "Few close friends," said one. "One of the most aggressive firefighters I've fought fire with." "Has problems with authority."

My life had been lived in a shell, and now the media crows had broken it open on the rocks of journalistic integrity.

I sat in the chair for a long time trying to breathe. Deep, heavy inspirations. Purposeful expirations. It could have been worse. There were things nobody knew about, things that mercifully would never appear in any paper. For instance, nobody knew about my drunk mother passing out on the freeway with two boys in the car; nobody had witnessed Neil reach over her shoulder to steer the car to the shoulder until we could revive her.

All morning I hid out in my office futzing about with paperwork and rereading the articles. Just after nine I got a call from a columnist with the *King County Journal,* the major paper serving the growing population east of Lake Washington. "When can I come out and interview you? I want to ask about the arsonist."

"You can't." I hung up.

Next came a television producer who wanted me to drive downtown and appear on the noon news. I refused that too. I was rude to them all. I couldn't help it.

At ten I knocked on the office next door. "Steve?"

"Yeah." He had a dressing on his left wrist, where the handcuffs had marked him a week ago.

"Your burns okay?"

"What d'ya want?"

"I spoke to Bill Kerrigan on Monday."

"Who?"

"Kerrigan. Retired Fire Investigation."

"Yeah, Bill. Sure. I used to know him. Hell of a fisherman."

"He said you knew my father."

"A lot of guys knew him."

I was in the doorway, Slaughter at his desk about seven feet away. The thick glasses. The shock of hair. The Fuller brush mustache. That way of holding himself that told you he knew what the world was about and had licked most of it.

"Your dad meant a lot to me, Paul." His eyes began watering over. "Your old man showed me the ropes. He took me up into my first attic fire." Slaughter stared at his desk, his elbows looking like flesh-colored fudge as they pressed into the glass-covered desktop. "I always had a warm spot for you, Paul. Because of your father. I tried to look out for you."

"The way I remember it, you were on your way to firing me."

"I didn't want you to get hurt like your old man." He looked up at me. "Nobody even knew he was down there. That was the worst part."

We looked at each other for a few moments before the bell hit. Aid tones. It was for Attack 6. Slaughter brushed past me, and I knew we would never speak of it again.

61. IT'S MY PARTY AND I CAN CRY IF I WANT TO

We parked Ladder 3 across the street from Station 10, a four-story concrete station on the corner of Second and Main in Seattle's historic Pioneer Square area. A gaggle of tourists traipsed down the sidewalk on their way to view what was left of the Seattle that had been buried after the great fire in 1889.

Parked in and around the intersection outside Ten's were four or five television trucks with antenna dishes pointed at the sky.

Eddings greeted us in the lobby, her eyes as bright as hot marbles in grease. Her nostrils whistled when she breathed, and when she opened her mouth to speak, a foul smell hit me. It occurred to me that carrying all that extra weight couldn't be healthy, not after you added in the stress she shouldered as a fire department battalion chief.

Gripping my arm tightly, Eddings escorted us to the elevator, which we took up to the second floor, where the firefighters' living quarters were. She walked me past the beanery, the TV room, and the handball court, past the weight room and down the corridor to the large windowless meeting room clogged with reporters. A current of electricity buzzed through the room.

The chief of the department, Hiram Smith, was standing next to the podium at the far end of the room, as was Chief Hertlein, who caught my eye with a mixture of triumph and surly smugness.

The room grew hushed. Somebody whispered, "Here he is." All heads turned. For a split second I was confused.

Eddings pulled me along to the front of the room, where I immediately slipped into a panic.

Chief Smith was a jovial man with dozens of dirty jokes at his disposal at any given moment and the W. C. Fields nose and spider face veins of a longtime drunkard. He was easy-going and the troops loved him, as did the press.

Chief Smith looked at me and said, "Thanks for coming."

Hertlein knew enough about me to realize privacy was what I treasured most. If he hadn't engineered this spectacle, he'd had a hand in it.

It took Smith a few moments to silence the room. "Excuse me? People? It has lately come to our attention that one of the four or five identifiable arsonists working in the past few weeks has a modus operandi nearly identical to an arsonist who, as far as we know, set his last fire in the late Seventies. We lost a good man back in the Seventies. His name was Neil Wollf. I knew him. He was a fine fire officer. His son is standing beside me today. Ladder Three's own Lieutenant Paul Wollf."

They began asking questions without prompting. "Lieutenant Wollf. How are you reacting to all this publicity?" For the first time, I realized what Eddings had dragged me into. They expected me to give a press conference!

"The publicity? I'm not sure how to take it," I stammered.

"Is any of this bringing up old wounds?" The question came from Tony Webber, who was standing in front, his Adam's apple bobbing. "Do you believe this is the same arsonist who killed your father? And if so, in light of what happened to your crew the other night, do you think he's trying to kill you too?"

I stared at Webber for ten seconds, fifteen, twenty. When it became clear that I wasn't going to reply, Chief Smith turned to me and said, "The man asked you a question, Lieutenant."

Thirty seconds.

I could see where they were coming from. They'd been riding this story for weeks, and the news had been the same. There was a fire. The fire department put it out. There was another fire. There was X number of dollars of damage. A few injuries. The pyro was still out there. No suspects. Copycats were discovered and some were arrested, but the fires continued. Now suddenly there was a new angle. The pyro was being linked to the man who'd killed my father twenty-five years ago. And here I was, Paul Wollf, battling fires in the same part of town where my father had died. There was definitely a new twist to it. You almost couldn't blame them for adding in all that crap about Alfred killing our mother and my brother killing Alfred. After all, the best headlines were always written in blood.

As the silence lengthened, other reporters began peppering me with questions. "Are you still in touch with your brother?" "What was the domestic disturbance on the police blotter at your address this past week?" The last question came from Tony Webber. As long as he had the protection of the pack, I could see *his* contributions getting nastier and nastier.

Flashbulbs had been going off in my face sporadically since I'd come into the room, and there were at least four video cameras focused on me. My throat was dry, my armpits wet. When it became clear that I was not going to answer, Webber shouted over a flurry of other questioners, "What do you remember about the morning your mother was murdered?"

His words muted the assembly like a cannon shot. The room grew so quiet I could actually hear the motor in one of the cameras. Eddings's nostrils whistled with the inhalation and exhalation of each breath. I turned to her. "Chief, I'm taking emergency leave. I'll be gone the rest of the shift."

I walked to the back of the room and out the doorway, followed by Towbridge, Rideout, and Crapps, the detail. On the way down to the apparatus, Towbridge said, "I wouldn't have answered any of that shit either."

I found his comment strangely comforting.

At the station I signed myself off duty in the daybook, retrieved my lunch from the refrigerator, got my jacket, and left.

The phone was ringing when I got home. I picked it up, listened for a moment, and racked the receiver. It rang all morning and most of the afternoon. In a funk, I watched *Raintree County* with Montgomery Clift, Elizabeth Taylor, Eva Marie Saint, and Lee Marvin. I watched *National Velvet* with Mickey Rooney and a young Elizabeth Taylor. The latter movie never failed to move me to tears. I'd noticed that whenever I was depressed, I turned to early Elizabeth Taylor movies.

Vanessa called, and I hung up before I realized who she was. I thought about calling her back but didn't.

At six Vanessa phoned again. "Paul? I called earlier, but we got disconnected."

"I'm kind of in a bad mood right now. Maybe we could talk later."

"Sure. I saw you on the news. I thought you might want somebody to talk to. Call if you change your mind."

I wasn't going to call.

I'd been on a John Wayne jag recently, so I watched *The Searchers, The Shootist,* then fell asleep in the middle of the black-and-white version of Patricia Pennington's *Duel at Water Creek.* There was something soothing in the black-and-white moralizing of a B western. A little after nine P.M. the phone rang for maybe the fiftieth time since I'd come home. "Will you accept a collect call from—"

"Yes, operator."

I'd just slipped my copy of *The Graduate* into the video recorder, thinking to myself I'd chosen that particular movie because it was about a young man journeying from a summer of numbness into a life of genuine feeling, while in my own life I seemed to be reversing that journey.

"Neil. How're you doing?"

"I saw you on the news. How are *you* doing?"

"Fine."

"Why aren't you at work?"

"I made a trade."

"You're sitting in the dark watching old movies, aren't you?"

"No."

"Don't shit a shitter. Listen to me, Paul. This isn't the end of the world. I know how private you are. But you can blow this off."

"Did you read what they wrote? They practically called our mother a goddamn hooker!"

"You got two options here. Blow it off or let it eat your heart out. I say fuck 'em."

"Don't give me that prison psychology crap, Neil."

"Listen to me. Nobody rents out space inside your brain but you."

"You talk the talk, but look where you are." The line was silent for a few moments. "I'm sorry. I didn't mean that."

"No. You're right. Where I am is a direct result of thinking I didn't have any control over my thoughts and feelings."

"Neil, I had no business saying that. I know damn well it was an accident of fate that you're where you are and I'm where I am. I think about it every day."

"What do you mean?"

"I mean it could just as easily have been me going to Echo Glen for what we did to Alfred."

"Don't ever say that! I did the time and it's over. You understand?"

"Neil—"

"Hey. This is what I'm going to tell you, and then I'm going to hang up. Listen close. Somebody says something about our family, tell 'em to go take a flying fuck at a rolling doughnut. Around here people are already wiping their butts with that newspaper."

62. ROCKY IN THE PARKING LOT

By six in the morning my machine had collected twenty-two messages. It took twenty minutes to listen to the first eleven and clear them. Most were from the media, including one from Tony Webber, who seemed to be under the illusion there was a bond between us. "Lieutenant Wollf. I'm guessing you probably weren't happy about everything you read yesterday. I'm free for breakfast, so this'll be a chance to give your side of the story. I'll call in the morning and we can arrange a time and place."

I erased it and moved to the next. "You and your newspaper buddies. You think you know everything." That was all it said. I was pretty sure it was the pyromaniac.

There were a lot of ways to kill somebody with fire, and if you were trapping firefighters who were already putting themselves at risk in fairly predictable patterns, the task was that much simpler.

Apparently the newspaper coverage hadn't pleased him any more than it had pleased me. What his gripe was, I could only guess, but then, people who set fires and jacked off in public were not easy to understand.

There was a TV truck in the parking lot, which I had to assume was there to ambush me, so instead of going out front to collect my papers, I read *The Seattle Times* and the *Seattle Post-Intelligencer* on the Internet.

SEATTLE FIRE LIEUTENANT REFUSES TO COOPERATE WITH MEDIA.

The *PI* was the primary offender today, as if they needed to catch up after yesterday's greater discretion.

They made it sound as if my mother had been a linchpin in a circle of lowlifes who drank and drugged and partied and tricked and neglected their kids and did God-knows-what-else. Maybe some of that was true, but our mother had never taken drugs and never tricked, and she'd loved us right up until the morning Alfred plunged the kitchen knife into her throat.

When I'm hurt, bored, or in trouble, I clean.

I scrubbed the bathroom, mopped the kitchen floor, did three loads of laundry, articles of bedding I thought Susan and her friends might have touched the other day. I washed up and prepared a vegetable omelet, using a recipe I'd found on the Internet. I took my time with all of this, hoping the day would go faster if I slowed things down.

It was noon when I thought to turn on the television. Our local cable channel carried a crime network piped in from Atlanta. I was in the kitchen fixing a cup of tea when a big-eyed, bleach-blond news anchor named MacKenzie began speaking to an on-the-scene reporter in Seattle named Rocky. I recognized Lake Washington in the background before I realized they were broadcasting from the parking lot outside.

"Rocky. There have been new developments in Seattle over the past twenty-four hours. Tell us more about what's going on."

"Well, MacKenzie. There's been one primary pyromaniac working Seattle for several weeks now. And that's what they call them out here on the West Coast, MacKenzie—pyromaniacs. Now I looked up pyromania in the dictionary as I was preparing this piece, and it is described as an excessive desire to set fire to things. That's certainly what's been going on here, MacKenzie, because over the past two weeks there have been over a hundred and fifty arson fires, and even though most of those fires were caught in their incipient stages and put out by the fire department, or tapped, as they call it, some of them got going pretty good, and so far the damage estimate, including overtime for police and fire investigators, is well into the millions."

"Rocky, there's more than one arsonist working. Isn't that correct?"

"That's right, MacKenzie. They're not sure how many. They have the primary arsonist, who's working in the Central District, a part of town that is mostly poor and African American. Then they have at least four other firebugs, who are thought to be copycats and have been active in other parts of the city."

"What's the thinking on the relationship between the primary arsonist and this fire lieutenant, Paul Wollf?"

"Well, MacKenzie, even the local reporters are finding this man, Wollf, to be something of an enigma. We do know this. He's been in the Seattle Fire Department a little under nine years. Three years ago he became a lieutenant. MacKenzie, after that the record gets a little murky. It is said that he had the top score on the promotional register, but on the other hand, his personal relationships with his superiors have sometimes been, let me say, on shaky ground. In fact, there's been a pretty strong rumor circulating in the fire department over the past few months that Lieutenant Wollf actually got into a fistfight with a chief and knocked him out. I haven't been able to get any official comment on this, but it's widely thought to be true.

"Also, local reporters have dug up some interesting information. His father was likewise a lieutenant in the fire department and lost his life in an arson fire twenty-five years ago. MacKenzie, the locals here now believe the pyromaniac working the Central District is the same pyromaniac who set the fire in which Lieutenant Wollf's father lost his life."

"Rocky, you're not suggesting Lieutenant Wollf is fighting fires set by the same man who killed his father twenty-five years ago?"

"MacKenzie, that's exactly what a local wag suggested in one of the Seattle papers yesterday morning. And that brings us to some of the more bizarre aspects of this already bizarre case of fire-setting and murder. At this point in time we have no idea what the lieutenant or the arsonist knows about the other. We *do* know that when this lieutenant was ten years old, his mother was killed by her live-in boyfriend, and then the boyfriend was killed by Wollf's brother in a bizarre incidence of domestic violence."

"It is bizarre. Rocky? What does Lieutenant Wollf say about all this?"

"That's just it, MacKenzie. At a hastily called press conference at fire department headquarters yesterday morning, Wollf refused to answer questions."

"Rocky. We have a tape of that news conference. Let's air that now."

I hadn't seen myself on a video camera since the last time I walked through a television store and wasn't especially happy with the way I looked then. This was worse.

"It's a sad case all around, MacKenzie, and getting sadder each time there's another fire. Meanwhile, the men and women of the Seattle Fire Department continue to battle on valiantly."

"Rocky, is there any chance you might speak to Wollf in the near future?"

"We're outside his condo right now, and we're sure going to try, MacKenzie."

"Thank you for that update, Rocky."

63. TESTING THE WATERS WITH A BAD BOY

At four-thirty I picked up the receiver when I heard Vanessa's voice on my answering machine. She was right. I needed somebody to talk to. It was hard to believe how good it was to hear a friendly voice.

"Hey. Listen. I know you said you'd call if you wanted to talk, but I just happened to be in the neighborhood to visit my grandmother when I thought of you."

"Vanessa. You're not that good of a liar. You called to cheer me up, and I'm glad you did. I have to warn you, though, I'm in a pretty lousy mood."

"After all that crap in the papers, who wouldn't be?"

"Since you just happen to be in the neighborhood anyway, maybe you'd like to stop by for a while? I could use some company," I said, feeling grateful I could get the words out.

"I'll be right over. How about if I pick up some groceries and make dinner?"

"I don't know if I feel like eating, but that sounds fine."

She arrived at my door thirty minutes later with two grocery bags, droplets of rainwater from the drizzle outside highlighting her hair and coat like dust under a diamond polisher.

I checked to see if anybody'd followed her, then locked the door behind her.

"Expecting company?" she asked.

I grunted.

"By the way. Did you know there are news people standing in your parking lot like buzzards on a fence? I mean *birds* on a fence. Did I say buzzards?"

I laughed for the first time in two days.

She slid the bags onto the kitchen countertop. "How long have they been out there?"

"I spotted them this morning."

"What happens when you try to get to your car?"

"I don't."

"No wonder you're in such a bad mood."

Vanessa began working on a stir-fry with chicken and rice. I stood at the sink, where I diced a tomato and chopped onions, a bell pepper, a cucumber, then washed lettuce for a salad. Neither of us spoke. She'd kicked off her shoes and lost her coat. After I cut my finger and swore, she told me to sit down. I turned on the gas fireplace and flopped on the couch in the living room near the windows to the deck. I have no idea how long I sat staring at the fireplace.

Vanessa, sensing I was in no mood for chitchat and out of reach of meaningful dialogue, kept to herself in the kitchen. That we could be together without speaking to each other for thirty minutes at a pop spoke volumes to me about our relationship, which felt as though it had progressed from casual acquaintance to the sort of deeper friendship I'd read about and seen in the movies, yet had never partaken of; certainly not with a woman.

In high school the few relationships I had with the opposite sex were with girls who wanted to be around a bad boy, one-night-stand girls, flirts I met at city dances and never saw again. Looking back on it, I must have had a certain roguish charm, swaggering about in my battered motorcycle jacket, eager to fight any local bully. I looked older than my age and began picking up adult women, usually heavy drinkers. Once, I even had to go down to the King County Public Health office to take the cure.

It was the killing of Alfred that had resurfaced to bother me the most. I'd shoved it into one of those unused recesses we all keep in the deepest part of our gray matter, where things we do not, cannot, or will not think about are kept until such time as we might drag them out into the sunshine for scrutiny.

We had lost our mother in the ugliest way possible and slain a man minutes later. My brother and I. Two skinny-ass, rail-thin, ragamuffin boys nobody in the neighborhood had ever thought two licks about had been involved in the most bizarre double-killing in a decade. We'd killed a grown man. He had killed my mother, but that never made me feel any better about what we did to him.

I hadn't thought about any of this in a long while.

These were the events that resigned me to a life crowded with isolation.

64. THE OCCUPATION ARMY

Vanessa stepped into the living room. "Dinner's ready, but you don't look hungry."

"Sorry."

She sat down beside me. "It's okay. We'll put it in the fridge. You can have it tomorrow."

"I've been thinking about the night we killed Alfred Osbourne."

"I notice you always say 'we,' but the way I understand it, it was your brother who killed him."

"He's the one who went to jail."

"What brought this on? "

"Unconnected dots. Connect the dots long enough and you start seeing what you've missed before. I've been trying to understand things the last couple of weeks, but I've been trying to understand the wrong things. I've been trying to understand why I am the way I am."

"I'm not sure I know what you're saying."

"You've seen me go off."

"You mean your anger?"

"That's part of it."

She sat beside me on the sofa, and the closeness of her body slowed my thought processes and renewed the sexual tension I'd felt between us from the first night I saw her. "I've been wondering why I'm so angry all the time. I thought my problem was brain chemistry. Now I think it's deeper. The point is, I don't want to be walking around with all this anger. With this inability to connect."

"Tell me what happened the morning your brother killed Alfred."

"Well, this is what the police found when they arrived.

Two boys standing in the living room in a pool of Alfred T. Osbourne's blood. Our mother in the kitchen stabbed seven times. Five bullets in Alfred. Three in his left lung. Two in the back of his head, one fired from so close the muzzle blast set his hair on fire.

"The cops get there, and my brother's covered in blood, my mother's and Alfred's and maybe a little of his own. He's waving the pistol around. The first two cops point their guns at him. It was a bad minute or two. After they got the gun out of his hands, they cuffed him and searched us. In my pockets they found a blue see-through spinner yo-yo and twenty-five cents. In Neil's pocket they found one of Alfred's fingers that had been shot off when he put his hand out to fend off the attack. Neil hated him so much he was going to keep it as a souvenir. That was when Neil told them he killed Alfred."

"So he confessed."

"He lied."

"What are you saying?"

"I was the one who shot Alfred."

"What?"

"Neil took the rap for it, but I did it. I shot him once, and he looked up from my brother and said, 'I'm going to make you eat that, you little bastard.' Meaning the gun. Then he came around the end of the couch and I fired again. Twice. He dropped to his knees. After that, all he wanted was to get out of the apartment. He started crawling toward the door. Didn't say anything, just changed his angle and headed for the door.

"He was crawling when I shot him in the back of the head. Remarkably, he kept on moving, so I put the gun against the back of his skull and pulled the trigger one last time. When the cops got there, my brother took the rap. I think he wanted to believe he was the one who fired the shots. Later on I found out about paraffin tests that can determine if you've fired a gun. But they didn't test us."

"That must have been terrible. Your mother, Alfred, all of it."

I wanted to say something further, but instead of speaking I began crying. It came on so quickly I didn't have time to head it off. It wasn't the boohoo blubbering kind of weeping, but more the slow, teary, eyes-dribbling variety where your face falls and your brain goes numb and your limbs go weak and you don't think it will ever stop and you don't care who's watching or what happens, because if this isn't the end of the world, it's certainly the end of *something,* and you are overwhelmed with this ineluctable sadness; you think this is perhaps the greatest sadness anybody on earth has ever tasted. Later, when you ponder it, you realize no matter what the trigger, you were really feeling sorry for yourself, for your miserable existence and for your own end, which is the last sadness any of us will ever feel and which is the underlying conceit in all gloom.

It went on for a while. For reasons I couldn't decipher I felt no shame. Vanessa had seen me grouchy; she'd seen me in Terminator mode; and now she'd seen me crying.

Aside from the times when I sat alone in the dark watching a movie—*National Velvet* came to mind—I could not remember the last time I'd wept. I'd stopped crying over real events about the time I started using my fists at school.

For a moment or two I was afraid she was going to leave, but she shifted her weight, moved closer, and put her arm around my shoulder.

I was crying for a lot of things.

I was crying for my lost childhood. For my tortured adolescent years. For the hardness that had taken over my soul. I was crying for the eons Neil had spent in lockup, for the druggie he'd married, who might have had her own life if her stepfather hadn't raped her. For the things that were within my grasp that I would never be able to reach. For the lives that could have been so wonderful but had gone so miserable. For my father's ending. For all those years my mother chased the bottom of a bottle and allowed herself to be seduced by boozehounds and eventually murdered by one. For the timidity that had crept into my life, for my fear of women, for my craving for something higher and better.

Then suddenly something came over me. A sense of hope. A feeling you get when you're being beaten senseless by the town bully and you know you at least have to try, that you can't go down without at least trying.

I turned toward Vanessa. When you pined for an impossibility, you were destined for disappointment, and my life was full of disappointment. Once more wasn't going to change anything. I wiped my eyes and kissed her.

She seemed surprised—no—astonished.

She pulled back and looked at me, and for a second I couldn't decide whether she was going to slap me or call the vice squad. Instead, she kissed *me.* It wasn't the sneaky guerrilla kiss I'd planted on her either, but more of a long-term-occupation-army kiss, one that knew it was welcome and would stick around for as long as needed, put up barracks, build roads, and buttress the economy.

The thing about a kiss that makes it so wonderful is not the touch of warm moist flesh on warm moist flesh, although that produces undeniable electricity, but the mere fact that the other person wants to do it. Wants to be there with you, has nowhere else to be other than holding you and letting you hold them. Even if the commitment is only for a moment, it's a commitment, and more than I ever thought I would get from this woman.

65. DOG DOOR GIRL

Dinner grew cold while we kissed on the sofa, colder still while we lay entangled in each other's limbs, a haze of perspiration on her brow, my cheek next to hers, the gentle rise and fall of her breathing beneath me. Maybe *she* wasn't in heaven, but I sure as hell was.

It was a strangely chaste encounter.

When I made a move as if to shift my weight, she whispered, "Don't go. I like you right there."

"I thought I might be too heavy."

"I like it."

After a few moments she said, "You've told me so many things about your life. I mean, so many things that didn't go well. Would you like to hear something that happened to me?"

"I would."

"I don't want you to think I'm telling you this because I think it's in any way comparable to the things you've told me about your life, but I haven't thought about it in years, and it just sort of popped into my head."

"I understand."

"You're going to think this is funny, but it wasn't when it happened."

"I'm not going to think it's funny."

"Yes, you are. I was a sophomore at the U. My best friend, a girl named Dilys Marlheiser, was from Wenatchee, a former Apple Blossom Princess. We did everything together. I had this boyfriend named Bud Hogan. Bud and I had been going together six months, and we were at a party and I got to talking with some people and lost track of Bud. I went to ask Dil if she'd seen him, but I couldn't find her either. Finally somebody said I should look in Mark Hager's room in the basement. Mark was Bud's best friend.

"I should have known something was up. I went down there and the lights were off. I heard noises, so I fumbled around and found the lights. All Bud had on was socks, and all Dil had on was her bra. We just all looked at each other, and then I turned the lights back off."

"This is terrible."

"It gets worse. After the lights were off I began to think maybe I'd imagined it. You know how you see something and you have to double-check? I turned the lights back on. They were these fluorescent lights that took a few seconds to blink on. Neither of them had moved an inch. They were looking at me like owls. I turned the lights off again and ran through the basement in the dark. I ended up at the back door in this little storage room. I tried the door, but it had one of those locks you can't open from the inside without a key. There was a little doggy door, and I thought if I put one arm up above my head and the other one down at my waist I might be able to wiggle through. That way I wouldn't have to face Bud and Dil, and I wouldn't have to run through that party crying either."

"Oh, no."

"Oh, yes. I got about halfway through the doggie door and got stuck. I mean really *stuck.* I yelled, but the music was too loud for anybody to hear me, so I just lay there crying. I was stuck maybe twenty minutes when the lights came on and I heard voices behind me. The voices went away, and a few minutes later I could tell the room was filling up with people and they were talking about me. Finally somebody opened the door with a key. When it swung inward, I swung in with it. There were maybe fifteen people staring at me, including Bud and Dil. Bud said, 'Jesus, Van. Have you gone crazy?' "

We talked for a while longer. I'd never conversed with a woman like this, and I'd certainly never kissed a woman this way without it leading to sex. It was a novel experience all around. I remember Towbridge once saying as a joke that if you really wanted to get a woman hot for you, cry. There was some history behind that statement, but I wasn't going to hear it from Tow any more than he was going to hear about tonight from me.

I said, "I guess I made an ass of myself."

"Don't be silly. Everybody needs to cry now and then. And it's natural to feel bad about killing Alfred all these years later."

"I never said I felt bad about it."

"But you do."

For reasons I cannot fully explain, her attitude infuriated me. Maybe it was her tone of voice. Or the fact that she presumed to know what I was thinking. Maybe I thought she was trying to own me. Alfred had "owned" me. My grandfather had "owned" me. Maybe I was so private I didn't want anybody knowing what I was thinking unless I told them. Of course she was right. I felt horrible about killing Alfred, and had since it happened. Still, I couldn't abide her telling me that. It was adolescent and immature, but it was me. I got up, feeling the poison stirring in me. "I'm *glad* we killed the bastard. I'd kill him again tomorrow. I'd kill him right now."

"How can you say that? It must have been a freakish—"

"Don't tell me what to think!"

Maybe it was the shame of having cried in front of her. Maybe I thought she was patronizing me. Maybe I didn't want to get close to her only to have her dump me later. Maybe I couldn't stand the suspense.

"I was . . . I was only trying to . . ."

I walked to the window and faced the water. I waited a long time without moving. A very long time. The wind picked up outside, and I could hear the waves slap at the pilings under the condominium. I didn't turn around. She spoke to me twice, and twice I didn't reply or turn around. Nobody could go mute like I could. Later, I heard her getting her things, heard the front door open softly and close just as softly.

Only somebody like me could twist something like what we'd had into something like this.

Later, much later, I dialed Vanessa's number, thinking to put an apology on her voice mail, something along the lines of, I've had a lot going on in my life and I really liked her and wanted to keep seeing her, but . . .

"Hello . . . Is that you, Paul?"

I hung up.

It was a wonder I hadn't mucked things up sooner. People talked about free will, but if there was such a thing, I didn't know where to find it.

66. BLOWTORCH WOMAN

Marsha Connor called at noon to tell me there'd been a huge break at FIU.

"Paul. You didn't hear this from me. Understand? Because this is all top secret, and I'd probably lose my job if anybody found out I was talking to you."

"Nobody'll find out."

"Swear?"

"My lips are sealed, Marsha. What is it?"

"They caught that blowtorch woman in Oregon. I believe she was going by the name of Jaclyn Dahlstrom. They caught her and some guy using one of Steve Slaughter's credit cards. I guess he cancelled the others, but he forgot a JCPenney card, and she tried to max it out in the jewelry department. They're holding her on outstanding warrants for fraud."

"And?"

"We sent two people down to interrogate her, and guess what?"

"Keep talking."

"She was seeing some guy up here. He came up from Oregon after he got out of the penitentiary. Earl Ward. We double-checked Ward against a list of people they interviewed twenty-five years ago around the time your father was killed. We had to get the case notes from a retired firefighter. Guess what?"

"Marsha, can you just tell it?"

"I'm sorry. FIU interviewed Ward twenty-five years ago. Two different times they caught him in neighborhoods where they'd been having fires. One of those fires was at Twenty-eighth and Jackson."

"That's just a few blocks from the Pennington place."

"Right. His mother used to work for Pennington. They're looking for him now. But check this out. A few hours ago his mother said she caught him all dressed up in her clothing. So they're not sure if they're looking for a man or a woman."

"Where does he live?"

"Now don't go getting any ideas. He's not home anyway. His mother says when she told him we were nosing around, he took her car and she hasn't seen him since. I can't believe we have the pyro."

"What was he in prison for?"

"He killed a fifteen-year-old girl in Oregon."

"When?"

"You'll love this part. A week after your father died. That's why there weren't any fires for twenty-five years. Because he was in the cross-bar hotel. He might have gotten out sooner, but he was linked to a series of fires inside."

"Thanks, Marsha."

By three o'clock it was on the local news. While there were plenty of pictures of Earl Ward as a man, there were none of him as a woman, nothing except the composite I'd cooked up with a police sketch artist. Using his makeup skills and a new wig, Ward could easily change his appearance again.

By seven I'd learned that Earl Ward's mother lived near Station 33 close to the Renton city limits. I knew I had the right place, because as I drove past it I saw a city vehicle parked out front. A stakeout. They didn't have him yet.

67. SORTA HANDSOME PYROMANIAC SEEKS BIG-BOOBED NYMPHO

According to Earl Ward

The day gets worse as it goes on.

My feet have blisters from all that running in heels. My chest continues to ache where the guy poked me with the pole. There are black and blue marks that have begun to turn yellow and purple. It's pure-dee nasty what Wollf did to me. I don't know how these people can call themselves civilized.

I can't get over the feeling of impending doom. It horrifies but also impels me to greater exploits.

Today starts off like every other. I wake up to hear my mother nagging that she's already had lunch two hours ago and I need to find a job. I check my wounds, have breakfast while perusing the papers, and borrow Mom's car on the pretext of following up on a job application to Boeing. Mom seems to be the only human being in the Northwest unaware that Boeing is laying off by the thousands.

It's almost six-thirty and plenty dark by the time I put two dollars worth of gas in the car and read *The Stranger* whilst sitting by the window in the Starbucks at Twenty-third and Jackson. I'm two blocks from his fire station. The fire trucks come by while I am there.

It is almost impossible to quantify just how godderned exciting it is to be this close to all those big, strong, mustachioed firemen. And women, although only a few of the women have mustaches. Ha ha. Old Earl can still make a joke. Just like that bastard who was trying to kill me. I've heard them laughing together.

I love to watch those powerful machines drive by, the

sounds of the sirens blasting against the buildings in the street. Mom says when I was small I used to wake up crying every time the sirens came past our house. That was the thing about the joint. Twenty-five years without a siren.

He was planning to kill me. Lieutenant Paul Wollf. So I'm treating it just like the joint. You find yourself with a mortal enemy, you eliminate him before he eliminates you. Wollf is a dead man. Period.

I check out the sex ads in the back of *The Stranger* but don't find anything I can afford in terms of either emotional commitment or finances. I might place my own ad. How about this? "Redheaded cross-dresser seeks hot sex with psycho mama who can appreciate an experienced heating expert."

I climb into Mom's Dodge Dart and wheel around the neighborhood looking for targets, setting the good ones hard in memory when I spot them.

Somehow I end up in front of the old woman's place. She spots me out the window, her dyed hair in the doorway now. I walk up the steps to the porch, where she is opening the front door. "Ma'am. I'm a friend of Jaclyn's. I just stopped by to see if she was in attendance."

"Jackie left a long time ago."

"Pardon me?"

"I had to let her go. She doesn't live here anymore."

"Do you happen to know where she went?"

"I've no idea. Now, you're going to have to go. I only came out to tell you to move that car."

Jaclyn gone? Was it possible?

Driving aimlessly, I while away the next two hours scoping out targets, then I go home and park in front of the house. I enter and sniff the fetid odor of cats.

"What have you done now?" Mom asks.

"I told you. I had to check up on that job application. If you don't come in once in a while, they forget about you."

She glares at me. "No. Not that. The police called. They want to talk to you."

The veins in my brain begin pulsing. "To me? Why?"

"All I know is they want to talk to you."

"Which police, Mom? "

"Don't you grab me."

"I'm sorry. Okay." I let her go. I had to have more information. This could be something as easy as my parole officer getting a bug up his butt, or it could be worse.

"Which police? You have to tell me."

"Some man wanted to know if they questioned you twenty-five years ago about some fires. I said twenty-five years ago you were in prison."

"How long ago did they call?"

"Why, just before you walked in."

I dig through her purse and take all her money. Her cigarettes. I grab a handful of clothes, my bag of makeup, two wigs, then I make a U-ey in the street. When I get to the top of the hill, I check the rearview mirror. I believe I see a pair of headlights stop in front of our house, but they might be at the neighbor's.

There is a liquor store and U.S. Post Office at Twenty-third and Union. I park two blocks away on a side street and walk to the liquor store. I don't have to wait fifteen minutes before some lunkhead leaves his motor running while he goes in to buy a bottle. It is a Ford Exploder. By eight-thirty I have another set of plates on the Exploder and have transferred my personal belongings from Mom's car.

It is time to put the finish to all of this. It isn't like I don't know who I need to stop.

I've been a nice guy up until now, but now they have nobody to blame but themselves. Period. I can kill, I can maim, and by golly, they've got my dander up, so I'm going to do both. Maybe I'll go down, but I'll go down in a blaze of glory. You betch'er butt.

This is for sure.

No more little fires. From now on they're only going to see big fires from this heating expert. Period.

68. BATTALION GOSSIP

Cynthia Rideout

JANUARY 6, MONDAY, 1259 HOURS

This morning everybody was talking about the firefighter in Ballard who slid off a wet roof, fell two stories, and broke her back in two places. She may end up paralyzed. Dolan almost died. Tow could have died with him. It sure makes you think about the job.

The other news is Chief Hertlein turned off another fan. Up north. It was a house fire, and apparently it was real smoky. The word was firefighters were bailing out windows and doors left and right.

Wollf convened a station meeting this morning. He said it was true his brother was in prison, his mother had been murdered, and his father had died in a fire in 1978. He said it was also true he didn't want to talk about any of those things. He said he wouldn't be answering any more personal questions after the meeting, so if we had any, we'd better ask now. Towbridge said he'd been called at home by a couple of media people and what did Wollf want him to say? "My friends won't say anything," Wollf told him.

Gliniewicz said, "Let's be frank here. Everybody read those articles the other day. I mean, didn't we? So what's the big deal?"

"Anything else?" Wollf asked.

Slaughter turned around and left the room. After the door closed, Zeke spoke in that mellow voice of his. "I have a question."

"What is it, Zeke?" Wollf asked.

"Well . . . uh . . . you talked to this person, didn't you? Didn't you talk to the torch workin' our district?"

"I did."

"Did he say he was planning to quit?"

Towbridge laughed. "He ain't gonna quit, Zeke. He ain't never goin' to quit."

"Why not?"

" 'Cause he's a fruit loop, that's why not. He can't stop hisself."

"I don't understand why he don't get tired and quit," Zeke persisted. "It's a lot of work, what he's doin'. It don't make sense."

"No shit, it don't make sense." Towbridge laughed. "That's why he's a fruit loop."

Somebody said, "But they have the guy's name. Surely it's only a matter of time before he gets picked up. His face is all over the TV. I saw it this morning on CNN."

"Maybe he ain't a *guy,*" Towbridge said. "When the lieutenant ran him down, he was wearing a dress and a bra."

"I didn't see a bra," Wollf said. We all laughed. Wollf was in a bad mood, but he was funny too.

Later in the morning Lieutenant Wollf went over last month's report with me. He gave me above average marks and told me to stick with it. Yaaaaay!

JANUARY 7, TUESDAY, 0046 HOURS

I can't sleep. I've been thinking about a phone call I received from Gwen Verdings. Gwen works at Thirteen's on the other shift, so she's plugged into all the battalion gossip. Her chief told them that our chief, Eddings, had just had a lawsuit filed against her by a woman from the class in front of mine. It seems Eddings used to visit this firefighter after lights-out, that she used to sit on her bed and touch her. She asked Eddings to leave, but Eddings said—and this is Gwen's quote, "It's just us girls here," which is what she said when she was touching me.

Gwen said Eddings asked her to sign a statement saying

she'd never done anything like that to her. "Are you going to sign?" I asked Gwen.

"I don't know. The trouble is two years ago she did do something like that to me. I don't know if Eddings forgot or if she wants me to lie for her or what. Maybe she doesn't think visiting your bunk and touching you is wrong."

"She did it to me too," I said.

"Can you imagine what would happen if a male officer did that? He'd lose his job in a heartbeat. You think this suit has a chance?"

"If we both stepped forward and testified against Eddings, it would."

"For a long time I didn't understand why they don't give her a desk job. But then I overheard a couple of chiefs talking about it. They think she's less of a liability to the department if they leave her in operations. Out where she might get somebody killed. Isn't that a hoot?"

"It's not a hoot if you have to work with her. Gwen, what are you going to do?"

"I haven't decided. I don't want to lie, but I don't want to get dragged into this lawsuit either."

It's become clear why Eddings wants to fire me. I'm just one more female firefighter who can confirm allegations of sexual harassment against her. But if I get canned, it will look like anything I say is sour grapes.

69. THE DOSIMETER

Right away you could tell these fires were different.

Same guy. Same technique. Same materials.

But you could tell now he was trying to hurt somebody, whereas in the past, excepting the night where Dolan and Towbridge went through the roof, the fires in our district had been pretty much haphazard targets of opportunity. You could see in our first three calls today the goal was to create confusion, tie up rigs, to hurt people.

Ladder 3's first call was to a U.S. postal box at Twenty-third and Union outside the post office door. We took it on a single. Smoke was pouring out of the box. We tore the door off the box and retrieved the unburned mail. There wasn't much, but it was a federal crime and we needed to keep the site secure until the feds arrived, which took us out of action for the next forty minutes, during which Crapps, our detail, went ballistic listening to the sirens all around us.

"Shit. We're missing everything," he said. Rideout and Towbridge exchanged weary looks. There were some people who never got enough action, and rangy, basketball-playing Crapps was one of them.

During the hour we were out of service, our section of the city had four more arsons.

While we waited for the postal inspectors, I thought about Vanessa. I'd been thinking about her for days. Thinking about how nice she was to me, how accepting of me. About how good she made me feel when we were together. Thinking about the way I'd frozen her out. The way I'd hung up on her. The way things were but didn't have to be. The way things always ended up.

I thought about it all morning, and then when we were on our way back from the Red Apple, I had Towbridge stop the rig in the bus zone while I dashed across Twenty-third to the flower shop at the corner on Jackson. I bought flowers and had them sent to her work. I tore up three cards trying to get my apology right. I finally settled for saying I was sorry I'd acted like a jerk, that she was the best thing that ever happened to me, and that I hoped she would give me a second chance.

It would be nothing short of a miracle if she would.

By ten o'clock at night, when I still hadn't heard from her, I realized she was either waiting for me to call or she didn't want anything more to do with me.

When we finally got put back into service, all the units around us were out on alarms. "Damn it. We missed all the fires," griped Crapps.

"We usually catch up," Towbridge said, laughing.

"I don't get it," said Rideout. "They have his picture. Hasn't anybody seen him?"

"Maybe he's wearing a different shade of lipstick," said Towbridge.

The city was on hyperalert. People were out looking for the firebug, groups of young men and women on almost every corner. Twenty-third and Cherry had so many people cluttering the sidewalks it looked like the early stages of a riot.

We parked on the ramp. There was no point in backing the rig into the station. I signed us into the daybook and was headed toward the computer in the inspection room to write my fire report when I saw Rideout and Crapps in the beanery staring at the large message board under the TV. Somebody had scrawled across the board, *You basturds!!!! feel my rath tonight!!!!!!!*

A long red arrow pointed from the message to the chalk tray, where we found a small tubular object that looked like a fountain pen, dingy and worn from handling. No one else seemed to know what it was, but I knew at once.

"God," said Rideout. "What if he's still in the station?"

"I got a gun out in my car." Crapps made a run for the basement stairs.

"Call the dispatcher," I said to Towbridge. "Put us out of service and tell them we think the pyro has been in the station. We need SPD and maybe a dog team."

"How did he get in?" Rideout asked.

"I can think of at least two ways to get into a fire station without leaving a trace," I said.

"What if he has a gun?" Rideout asked as I launched a search of the building.

"He couldn't possibly have enough bullets," I replied. I

could feel the same poison I'd felt the night I was seventeen years old and beat Rickie Morrison half to death in less than a minute.

I searched the officers' quarters first, then worked my way around the floor in a counterclockwise direction, opening closet doors, checking bathroom stalls. By the time I got to the basement stairs, Crapps was pointing a .357 Smith & Wesson at my chest. "What the hell are you doing? You know you can't have a gun in the station," I said. "Get rid of that."

"Jesus," said Rideout.

The SPD dog team arrived, and a German shepherd named Otto went through the station like a blur.

"What's this?" asked a police officer, picking up the tubular object that had been left on our chalkboard, holding it by the edges.

"It's a dosimeter," I said. Everyone in the room looked at me. "To measure radiation levels. Years ago department members used to carry them." I'd seen one among my father's effects.

This one had SFD stamped on it as well as a department ID number. Everybody in the department had a four-digit number that followed them to retirement. The number went onto all your personal paperwork and was inputted to the computer each morning to tell the dispatchers who was working on which rigs.

When Attack 6 returned, Slaughter walked into the beanery. "What?" he said. Gliniewicz and Zeke piled up in the doorway behind him.

"We had a visitor," I said.

Crapps pointed to our message board.

"You ever see this before?" I said.

"It's a dosimeter," Slaughter said.

"It's *your* dosimeter. That's your number."

"We turned those in years ago."

"Somebody found an old dosimeter and decided to print your number on it?"

"I guess. I don't know."

LaSalle and Connor, from Fire Investigation, came through the door.

I said, “We think the pyro was in our station sometime in the last hour. He left this.”

“He coulda got it anywhere,” Slaughter said. “Who knows what the department did when we turned them in? Probably threw them in the trash out behind Station Ten.”

“So he goes through the pile, saves one for twenty-five years, and it turns out to be yours?” I asked.

“He’s a psycho.”

“Wouldn’t it be more likely you had some sort of contact with him and you dropped this? He picked it up?”

“You’re full of shit.”

“He told me a firefighter in civvies beat him up the night my father died. That wouldn’t have been you, would it?”

“Abso-fuckin’-lutely not.”

We stared at each other. I knew there was a reasonable chance Steve Slaughter was the man who put my father into that burning basement.

The main phone rang. Zeke picked it up in the watch office, listened for a moment and said, “Can the truck go in service?”

I nodded.

Zeke spoke into the phone. A moment later we began hearing the tones on the radio scanner. A fire call. It was 0122 hours. As Slaughter and I left the room, LaSalle said, “You know what I think?”

I turned back. “What do you think?”

“I think this asshole is self-destructing. I think he knows he can’t go home and he’s going to do it all in one big last fling. You guys watch yourselves.”

70. RUB-A-DUB-DUB

According to Earl Ward

Tonight I drive over to Cherry and park two blocks away for a good getaway, then go into The Harvey through the side entrance. Two young men step out and hold the door for me. My disguise fools them. I hobble in, making them wait.

When I get to Hollywood, my talent is going to be appreciated. Producers will pay for my meals. I'll get blow-jobs from groupies in the back of taxicabs. Jaclyn will come crawling back. I may even give her a part in my first feature.

I check my supplies on floors one and two. Paint thinner. Discarded furniture. I've got the oily rags all set to go in the basement. I was so lucky to find this place. The ongoing remodel and the fact that they ran out of funds and had to stop was perfect. Two units are empty on floor three, one right over the main entranceway. This is godderned perfect.

I climb stairs that smell like barbecued ribs, sawdust, and urine. When two women come out of a unit on two, I pass them in a hitching gait. I tell you, there's no respect in the country for the elderly. Absolutely none. Ha ha ha. I walk past the sawhorses and the tools in the top floor apartment, past the items I've separated for my own use, the sacks of mortar mix and paint cans, the turpentine.

I take my lock off the unit and go inside.

Sometimes when I think about what I'm about to do, I feel like my bowels are going to cut loose. It scares me, but then these people haven't given me much choice, have they? In minutes I'll start the ball. Then we'll dance, Mr. Wollf. We'll dance and I'll settle me some scores. Period.

First, I check the babies in the tub. Wrapped in pastel pink and blue blankets. Three very quiet babies.

The scanner tells me Ladder 3 and Attack 6 are both in service.

I dash downstairs to the basement, passing the young women on two. I light the oily rags and race back upstairs screaming, "Fire! Fire!"

The two young women take up the call and begin skipping up and down the hallway pounding on doors, shrieking, "Fire! Fire! Fire!"

As soon as two clears of people, I step back downstairs and light the vacant apartments, one at either end.

Now all I have to do is sit in my window with my babies and wait. Oh, yeah.

71. BABY TAKES A DIVE

The radio is giving out the call information when I climb up into the apparatus, only to be greeted by a brain-splitting sound—Attack 6's air horn. Gliniewicz has stomped on the button and kept his foot on it, trying to punish a driver who was stalled behind a Metro bus at the bus stop just south of the station. Because of the blast, I miss a good portion of the run information.

I switch the radio to channel one, the fire channel, as Attack 6 launches off the ramp. We head into the pall of gray diesel smoke behind the engine.

I am thinking about the dosimeter. It is a confirmation of what Earl Ward told me about my father struggling with a second SFD member the night he went into the basement. Slaughter had been the firefighter in civilian clothes that night. They struggled, and my father tumbled into the basement. Then, according to Earl Ward, Slaughter didn't raise a hand to help him.

The fire call is on East Cherry at Twenty-sixth.

"The Harvey," mutters Towbridge as he swings Ladder 3 wide on Twenty-third to pass cars.

"What's The Harvey?" I ask.

"It's an apartment house. Three stories. Tall ones."

I hear the bells on the MSA air masks in back as Rideout and Crapps slip into their shoulder harnesses and open the main valves. They will be ready when we arrive. The second-in units should have been Engine 25 and Ladder 10. Instead, we were getting Engine 2 from downtown, Engine 8 and Ladder 6 from the top of Queen Anne Hill. They will be lucky to get here inside of ten minutes.

"Attack Six," says the dispatcher. "Be advised. We've had several callers on this. Heavy smoke showing from an apartment house. One caller says she sees jumpers."

"Attack Six, okay," says Slaughter.

All the other nearby units are on other calls. It is us and Attack 6 only. This is going to be a bitch.

I review our options. We are eight blocks away. An apartment house. Middle of the night. The life hazard will be appreciable. Virtually everybody will be home.

We see smoke before we round the corner onto Cherry—quick-moving, dense black smoke that signals a structure fire, one that probably has a good toehold.

"Jesus Christ!" blurts out Crapps from the crew cab behind us. "Would you look at that?"

"Listen up, people," I say. "We'll put the stick up. We'll take whoever we see first, then we'll do a systematic search inside. Stay calm and don't get distracted. You can do a whole building in minutes. Start near the fire and work your way out. Got it?"

"Got it," says Rideout, her lips dry with anticipation.

"Jesus Christ!" exclaims Crapps.

"We got overhead trolley lines," Towbridge warns.

"I know. Is there an alley behind?" I ask.

"I don't know what's in back, but it ain't no alley," says Towbridge.

"Jesus Christ!" says Crapps again.

Our fire is on the right side of the street, a skinny brick building, the tallest for several blocks in either direction. A simple rectangle, the long side facing the street. Smoke is pouring from the front door and from windows on the second floor.

Gliniewicz blows his air horn to move the gawkers. He loves that horn. Slaughter gives his radio report before they come to a full stop. "Attack Six at twenty-six zero one East Cherry. Heavy smoke showing from the front door of a three-story apartment building. We're laying a two-and-a-half through the front door. Second-in engine, give us a supply. Passing command."

As we close in, I see one face in a window at the west end of the building. A second face hanging out a third-floor window over the main entranceway, an elderly black woman waving a hanky. While there is heavy smoke elsewhere, there is only light smoke behind her.

As we pass the entrance, three civilian men stumble out the front steps. None of the onlookers in the small cluster at the bottom of the steps moves to help these men. Some are watching the fire engine. Others are holding their collars or scarves over their faces to filter the smoke.

When the engine stops in front of us, Towbridge looks at me and I signal to keep moving.

I instruct Towbridge to angle the aerial apparatus at the east end of the building, far enough off Cherry to avoid the power lines and trolley wires, but close enough so we can shoot the stick up along the face of the building if need be. We can also access the east end of the roof from here.

I turn to the two firefighters in the crew cab. "Go inside. I saw one person on the second floor and one on the third.

"Put up the stick," I say to Towbridge. I get on the radio. "Ladder Three *at*. We have a three-story residential apartment complex approximately eighty by two hundred feet. We're initiating search and rescue and putting up the aerial on side B. Passing command."

When the dispatcher doesn't acknowledge, I repeat the message. Around the corner I hear Gliniewicz revving the pump engine. Several teenage girls in front of us are screaming. When the dispatcher doesn't respond to my second message, I say, "Dispatch from Ladder Three?"

"Ladder Three, switch to channel two."

Damn. Most fire responses are on channel one, but tonight the channel is full, so they've sent us on channel two. I missed it back at the station in all the noise of the engines and Gliniewicz's air horn. I'd heard Slaughter's report due to the scanner feature on the radio. Losing precious seconds, I repeat my report on channel two.

I slip my MSA backpack and bottle out of the compartment and walk around the corner to evaluate the situation. Zeke and Slaughter haven't gone in yet. Across the street LaSalle and Connor are hauling a long section of four-inch hose toward a second hydrant down the street. They've followed us from Station 6 and found an opportunity to be useful. The closer hydrant is blocked by a car.

There are no other fire department vehicles in sight. Just Ladder 3 and Attack 6 and the FIU Suburban.

Rideout is heading up the stairs at the front of the building, but Crapps is on the sidewalk looking up. The elderly black woman in the third-floor window appears to be in danger of falling out. In her arms is a baby wrapped in a blanket.

Crapps is yelling at her, but I can't hear what he says over the sound of Engine 6's motor. I'm sure the old woman can't either. She offers the bundle out the window as if to drop it. More smoke is pushing out the opening behind her.

"Don't do it!" Crapps yells frantically. But she's old and confused, and anybody can see she is about to drop the baby.

Next thing I know the baby blanket and whatever is inside is sailing through the air. My brain is racing. Below, Crapps has dropped the axe and battle lantern and has stretched out both arms.

Crapps is just over six feet, muscular, a star ball player,

according to the guys at Thirteen's, a man who can dunk a basketball one-handed. If anybody can catch a baby, it is Crapps.

The bundle hits his arms and knocks him down, exploding across his legs in a burst of gray material. Dust spreads around Crapps's supine figure in a small mushroom cloud.

I get to him just before Rideout does. "Oh, God!" Crapps says. "I think it's broken."

"What? What's broken?" I ask.

"My leg. I think my knee's broken. Oh, God!"

"Where's the baby?" Rideout asks, unfurling the plaid baby blanket and finding nothing but a ripped-open sack of cement. All three of us are choking in the dust. I reach down and palpate Crapps's right leg gently. It's broken, all right.

"Where's the baby?" Rideout asks.

"There's no baby," I say. "It's the pyro."

Together we begin dragging Crapps out of range. We get about eight feet when the second sack of mortar mix, this one without a blanket, splatters behind us. We feel the sidewalk shudder with the impact. "Look out!" Rideout yells.

Together Rideout and I park Crapps in front of Attack 6, where the first-in medic unit will find him.

"Let's go search," I say to Rideout. The window above us is empty now.

Before we go up the steps, I collar Gliniewicz and tell him to warn incoming firefighters about the cement bags. He hears me, but I cannot tell if it's registering. He is watching LaSalle and Connor at the hydrant across the street. His supply lines are still flat.

As we are going in, two civilians emerge from the building. A man and a woman, mid-twenties, tattoos and body piercings, barely dressed, barefoot. I tell them to go left, that somebody is throwing things out of the windows to the right. Once outside, the woman screams, "Save them. Aren't you going to save them?"

When I go back out to see what she's pointing at, I spot

two African American males in a window, one of them bloody, probably from breaking the window. They are waving a dish towel, holding their shirts over their faces, heavy black smoke billowing out behind them.

"Change of plans," I tell Rideout. "Ladder."

As Rideout and I walk around the ring of gray dust on the sidewalk, I hear more sirens in the distance. I yell to the two men in the window that we are getting a ladder for them.

We secure a thirty-five, carry it at waist height, and throw it up. I get behind while Rideout grabs the halyard and raises it, then we drop it against the building. Rideout scrambles up while I foot the ladder to keep it from walking out. She uses her axe to clean the glass out of the window, then brings the first man down, her arms grasping the beam of the ladder around him.

She goes back up immediately. "You all right?" I ask the man, who wears only a pair of black jeans. Both forearms are covered in blood. He is staring at something behind me. When I turn around, I see Crapps lying in the street on his back, his head propped on his helmet. He has a .357 pistol gripped in both hands and is pointing it at the third-floor window where the old woman had been. I can't see anybody in the window, but that doesn't mean Crapps can't. The revolver is cocked.

Across the street a red Suburban with Battalion 5 plates on the doors comes to a screeching halt. Kay Eddings leaves the siren on for a moment after she parks, deafening anyone nearby. I see Gliniewicz, aka Mr. Airhorn, at the pump panel shaking his head over the siren. Rideout comes down the ladder with the second victim.

"What now, Lieutenant?" Rideout asks.

"Keep an eye on the windows for more victims."

Heavier black smoke is coming out the front door now. Two medics appear from behind Ladder 3. One asks if anybody needs help. The other stops in her tracks, staring at Crapps and his Magnum.

Eddings comes across the street toward me in a fast waddle. "Wollf? What the fuck's happening here? The second-in unit is supposed to take command. Shit! You know that!"

When I reach Crapps, I bend down and put my gloved hand between the hammer and the frame of the pistol, then pull it out of his hands. "Give that back," Crapps says. "That old lady's going to kill somebody."

The medics come in while I let the hammer down on the pistol and walk toward our rig with it. Before I can reach the apparatus, somebody grabs my shoulder and tries to spin me around. Chief Eddings. "What the fuck do you think you're doing with a gun? You know we're not allowed to have guns in uniform. You stupid shit!"

A second engine finally shows up just as the supply line from the hydrant to Attack 6 begins filling. The crew from Engine 2 is climbing off. Smoke is beginning to pour out the east end of the building near our truck now.

"Attack Six reporting a basement fire," says Slaughter over the radio. "We're getting water on it now."

"It's a basement fire," Eddings says, looking at me. "I want you to ventilate so all these people can get out. Put fans up. Now!"

"There's more than one fire. The fans aren't going to help."

"He said it was a basement fire. Now ventilate this motherfucker." Eddings heads toward the front door of the building to intercept Engine 2's crew, who are hooking up a hose line to Attack 6. A policewoman who'd listened to Eddings's tirade gives me a look I wish I could save on videotape.

As I watch Eddings walk, I realize she is heading through our war zone. "My baby. My baby," shouts the old woman above us.

It is almost comical to watch Eddings turn around in a complete circle and then finally look up. The figure above has another package wrapped in a blanket.

Judging from the contents of the first two drops, I am confident our "victim" is about to throw a forty-pound bag of concrete mix at Chief Eddings. Three stories isn't far, but it's enough to kill someone. From this angle I see a man in blackface dressed as a woman. He looks at me, and a spark of recognition passes between us. He smirks.

It is Earl Ward.

By now two men from Engine 2's crew are alongside Eddings under the window.

The baby blanket is teetering on the lip of the windowsill. The firefighters below the window are each more eager than the next to make the catch, to be the hero.

As the package slowly begins to roll over the lip of the windowsill, I sprint. Hertlein, who's shown up from nowhere, sees what I am about to do and steps in front of me. I sideslip him. Later, I realize he thinks he is keeping me from saving the baby, that he doesn't want me to get the glory. I take three long running steps toward the trio under the window and hit them broadside with my body, Eddings first, the other two behind her. We go down like bowling pins, bodies, bunkers, plastic helmets, and compressed air bottles all clattering to the sidewalk.

A fraction of a second after I hit them, the bag explodes in the tangle of our feet.

Above us Ward has disappeared in the smoke.

The collision has broken Eddings's glasses. She is trying to get out from under somebody's legs, shrieking that I am an idiot and deserve to be fired, that I am on suspension as of now.

Having seen the event from start to finish, Chief Hertlein discounts her rants and says to me, "Nice move. I want you to get in there and ventilate that building. Right now, mister! Get your troops moving."

"You're going to have to assign the next-in truck. We've got rescues. Nobody's searched yet."

"You ventilate that place and the rescues'll take care of themselves."

"The hell they will. We've only got a few minutes. Maybe less." It is usually true that a well-ventilated building is easier to search, but this building is already like a sieve. It has too many openings for the fans to work effectively. Or at all.

"Chief! God damn it, Chief. You gotta get us more teams in there," says Slaughter, interrupting. "We don't have any backup, and we've got one helluva basement fire." Slaughter's face piece is dangling around his neck, his reserve bell ringing. He is furious.

"Nobody's been giving us a lick of help. We were in that basement all by ourselves! We took a beating you wouldn't believe. You don't do something fast, you're going to lose the whole goddamn building!"

Flames and heavy smoke are coming out at the east end. Heavy black smoke is being pumped out the center window on floor three, where the old woman had been.

"I'm going to call this a defensive fire," Hertlein says. "I want all our personnel out now."

I move toward Ladder 3, signaling to Rideout with my eyes that I want her to follow. Behind, I hear Eddings screaming my name, cursing like a sailor. The others know it, but she is too angry to realize I've just saved her life.

72. RESCUING HALF-WITS

Rideout and I cover and jog up the painted concrete steps in front of the building, stepping over hoses, feeling more secure as we get under the fascia over the entranceway, where at least we don't have to worry about sacks of cement falling out of the sky.

I can't help but wonder why Earl Ward is still in the building. Why he's throwing projectiles at us like a man in a besieged castle. Usually he's long gone after setting a fire. Is it possible he's stuck in his own trap? It's obvious from the smoke patterns that he's set multiple ignitions. There is too much smoke on two and three for a lone basement fire.

We are alone inside. The crew of Engine 2 is on the sidewalk, and Zeke and Slaughter are outside getting fresh air bottles. I can only guess why they ran out of air so quickly. The fire has been declared a defensive battle, which means hose streams will be directed from the sidewalk rather than from inside. We aren't supposed to be in here, but I am not going to leave possible victims to fend for themselves while we squirt water through the windows from the sidewalk.

We search two apartments using the thermal imager; both units are filled with smoke and empty of inhabitants. At the west end of the floor, flames lick out a doorway that leads to the basement. Farther down the hallway near the center of the building we locate another stairwell. It is a long upward flight and is clogged with dense smoke.

Despite the fact that we can't see the walls, we manage to search the entire first floor in less than two minutes, kicking in locked doors, dashing through each apartment in search of the young, the old, the inebriated, the handicapped, anybody in need of rescue. Some of the apartments have only light smoke in them. Others have smoke down to the floor. Midway through our search we run into two incoming members from Engine 2 who are looking for the basement fire. We point them in the right direction. Apparently they haven't gotten word that this has turned into a defensive fire. That, or Hertlein has changed his mind.

We hear a phone ringing in one of the apartments. Except for two televisions left on, the first floor is devoid of life. Oddly, one of the smoke-dimmed televisions displays live video of this very building from the KIRO TV chopper. It is shocking to see the thick column of smoke above us.

The secondary stairwell to floor two is located at the east end of the building. The door at the top has been removed, and I see flame. It sounds almost as if a natural gas pipe has broken and ignited. I pray that floor two is vacant, because we aren't going to make it up the stairs.

"Oh, shit," says Rideout, peering up the stairs alongside me. "If you think it's a go, I'm with you."

I grin at her, but she can't see it inside my mask. She doesn't know we aren't going up, but she is game to try. This will look good on her report.

Up the stairs we can see flame boiling paint off the broken door, plates of wallpaper curling off the walls from the heat. We can see beyond the top of the stairs, where the flame is blue and purple and deep red. The flames are incredible. I can *almost* understand why Earl Ward sets fires. I want to stay and watch, but I have a job to do.

Going up the stairs at either end of the hallway would have been foolish without a hose line. Even if we made it through the flames and found somebody to bring down, anybody in civilian clothes coming down those stairs would be burned beyond recognition.

Channel two is busy with conflicting messages. It appears Hertlein and Eddings are both trying to run the fire, quite possibly from different sides of the building. I press the button on the remote microphone clipped near my collar. "Command from Ladder Three. Primary search on floor one complete. All clear."

Interfering radio traffic cuts off any answer. The fire ground is filling with firefighters and equipment, and channel two is bogging down as fresh units confirm assignments and request orders. Engine 8 arrives. Ladder 6 announces they are putting up ladders to the front of the building.

As we walk back toward the main entrance we hear a loud burbling over the radio. It is Eddings's voice, though her words are indistinguishable. This is probably the biggest fire she's ever presided over—it certainly rivals anything I've been to since the Armitage Furniture Warehouse. Perhaps because of this, she's once again lost her composure, if not her mind.

When we go outside, two crew members from Ladder 6 are throwing up a thirty-five-foot ladder near the entranceway. I advise them that floor one is clear and to keep an eye out for the asshole who's been throwing bags of concrete out the windows. This is the first they've heard of it.

At the corner, I spot two civilians above me. The first is a middle-aged Caucasian female on three. Oddly, she is peering down at us as if there is no peril at all. Her apartment lights are on, revealing a modest amount of smoke in the room. Directly above her on the roof stands a figure in a wig and a dress. He has a blowtorch in his hands and is staring at me. It is as if he's challenging me to come up and get him.

As we climb the five vertical steps to the base of the aerial on the back of Ladder 3, I turn to Rideout. "He's trying to kill us. You stay clear."

"I want to go."

"Then stay behind me."

Towbridge is moving the tip of the aerial ladder to the third floor, where the victim in the window seems about as concerned with all the activity in the street as if she were watching it on television. For that matter, maybe she is.

I climb toward the victim on the third floor. Ward has disappeared. When I reach the window, I motion for Towbridge to move the tip a few inches to the left. I take my service axe out of the scabbard and break out the glass. The resident acts frightened, as if she's being stalked by a very large and very dangerous cat.

"You alone?" I am speaking across the now-clear space between us.

Moving as if her knees are splinted, she backs away.

"Seattle Fire Department. Lady, your building is on fire."

The bottle on my back catches on the window frame as I climb through. The resident, who appears to be in her late forties or early fifties, is smoking a cigarette.

"Ma'am. We're going to have to walk you down the ladder. Can you do that?"

"You get on out of here now."

"Your building's on fire. You'll have to come down with us."

"They told me it was a false alarm."

"Who told you?"

"Some man running up and down the hall in a dress."

"This is no false alarm. Where do you think all this smoke is coming from?" The aerial jiggles as Rideout climbs toward us. Before I can stop her, the woman fumbles open her front door, but her plan backfires as a column of filthy black smoke marches in and overwhelms her, knocking her to her knees.

I close the door and remove the cigarette from her hands. I lift her up and walk her toward the window.

When she and Rideout are ten feet down the ladder, the abandon-building signal sounds in the street, a loud high-low siren on the chief's buggy. Over the speaker on the tip of the aerial, Towbridge says, "Lieut. They want everyone out of the building."

"Has somebody else searched floor three?"

"Far as I know, you're the only one up there."

"Then I'll be searching."

"You know you're not supposed to be up there without a partner."

"Leave the stick where it is."

"Oooookay."

The corridor on three is filled with hot smoke, like a dense fog, growing hotter by the minute. I can hear the fire crackling at the far end of the hallway. Using my six-volt battle lantern, I manage to see the walls and doors in some spots, but I can't see dick in others. I no longer have the thermal imager with me.

I kick in the next apartment door and wander into an apartment almost as murky as the corridor. There is no fire, but I run into a wall of smoke. No people—only mussed beds that tell me they fled in haste.

The next two units are vacant. The door is off one, ajar on the other. Both are on fire. In the second apartment the fire has banked up and is starting to rip out the door and burn along the ceiling. I crawl close, reach around the corner into the heat and buy some time by pulling the door closed. The heat abates instantly.

I travel less than two-thirds of the way along the corridor on my hands and knees before I am forced to turn back. There is fire below me, fire behind me, and maybe even fire above me. I am alone and have no hose line. Nobody knows where I am. If I'm not careful, I'll end up in the same situation that killed my father.

73. WHAT'S BLACK AND WHITE AND FLIES AT NIGHT?

As I crawl back to the end of the corridor, temperatures abate somewhat so that I am able to stand. I hear thumping on the roof above me. We haven't put anybody up there that I know about.

There is more noise above me now. Footsteps.

How he thinks he is going to get off that roof is a mystery. But then, with a pyro, thinking ahead isn't always a specialty.

If the interior access to the roof is on this side of the building, I will go up and surprise him. If not, I will ride the aerial up . . . and surprise him. Surprising people is *my* specialty.

I don't normally get jacked up at fires the way a lot of people do, but every time I lay eyes on the pyromaniac, I find myself ready to explode. I've seen him three times tonight, and each time I feel blood pounding in my ears. It's as if all my plasma has converted to adrenaline. My need to kill him has outrun everything else.

Setting fires is a cutthroat hobby, but when you sit down and think it through, you are forced to admit the actions involved are fairly passive. You light a match; you walk away. There is nothing inherently violent about it. It isn't like clobbering somebody with a baseball bat. Girl Scouts light matches every weekend. People light wood stoves, debris piles, fireplaces. The crime is in what you touch the match to and what happens afterward.

Tonight he's turned violent. Even a mouse will bite when cornered.

As I work I hear Eddings's voice on the radio requesting firefighters to abandon the building.

I push my mike button. "Ladder Three primary search complete on east half of floor three. All clear. Somebody needs to search the west half of three."

My report is answered with an indecipherable caterwauling. After thinking about it, I realize she's said, "Ladder Three, you cocksuckers get your butts down here now! Get your asses out now. Now! Now! Now!"

The stairwell to the roof is on the third floor, around a corner at the end of the corridor, narrow and steep. I climb the stairs, but the door at the top won't budge.

The smoke is so thick even with a flashlight I have to place my face against the door to ascertain the lock has been broken. The door *should* open. I know this much—without a mask and air bottle, he isn't coming down through here. Without compressed air the entire third floor is untenable and getting worse by the minute.

I shoulder the door and push. The door shifts a fraction of an inch, then slams shut. He's piled something against it. Taking my service axe out, I brace my legs against the inner wall and push with all my might.

I pop through the doorway and onto the roof, roll, and come up with the axe in my gloved hands. Moving on adrenaline and twenty-five years of hate, I've taken the door completely off its hinges. A huge gush of gray-black follows me onto the roof, which is already smeared with smoke from several sources. The stairs are a natural chimney and now act like a smokestack for the building.

All along the roof, smoke is seeping through the tar roofing material. The smoke in the sky over the front of the building reflects the flashing red lights from below.

I am on a flat, black, torch-down tar roof with a knee-high parapet around the edges, a small penthouse enclosure at the east end to accommodate the doorway I've come through. The roof has a smaller footprint than you would think.

Not a soul in sight. There are stacks of roofing materials and racks of five-gallon buckets tall enough to hide behind. He might be in the smoke. Or behind me on the far side of the penthouse door housing.

The roof under my feet is spongy and I stomp as I walk, feeling the tremors move through the roof, listening for footsteps behind me and trying to guess how much fire is under me. The danger here is falling through. A danger that escalates every moment we're up here.

The smoke on the west end of the roof is thicker.

The plastic skylights are melting.

What I don't need is to become the second Lieutenant Wollf this bastard kills. I don't need to let him sneak up behind me and push me forty feet to the street.

At the west end of the roof I find the tip of a fifty-five-foot ground extension ladder fully extended. As I approach the top of the ladder, a long fold of black smoke curls up from below the parapet and envelops the entire west end of the rooftop. When I look down, four men are pulling the ladder out from the building. It is easy to see why. Huge ragged gouts of flame are roaring out the windows below me.

Then I hear the screams on the roof. Two in quick succession.

I am in the smoke now, heading east, stepping around stacks of roofing materials, TV antennae, guy wires, and vent pipes. Black smoke is oozing out the broken door I came through. Somebody is in trouble. I wonder if some of the building occupants came up here to escape the fire.

As I approach the stairwell housing, a firefighter steps over the high doorsill onto the roof, glancing around in the smoke. It's Rideout.

As our eyes meet, a blur of movement comes from behind the stairway housing and knocks Rideout down the stairs and into the smoke. A figure follows Rideout, and they tumble down the stairs together until they are out of sight.

The figure is in a paisley, ankle-length dress. He is in blackface. Has a blowtorch in his hands.

I dive in after them.

Once inside the stairwell, I can't see a thing. Not until I draw close. Rideout is on the floor, Ward straddling her with the flame from the propane bottle held at waist height.

When he sees me, he stabs it at my face.

The impact of my first blow is dulled by my gloves.

He flies sideways and rebounds off the wall, the propane bottle rolling to the side. I pick up Rideout with one hand and drag her away.

"You all right?" I ask.

"I sprained my ankle."

I toss the propane bottle up the stairs onto the roof.

Then I pick up Earl Ward, the material of his dress ripping in my gloved hands. I grab him and propel him up the stairs. "Get up there, you sorry sack of shit."

He starts coughing as soon as I let go. When I am certain he is on his way to the roof, I walk Rideout back through the hallway and make certain she is safely on the aerial.

"You going to be okay?" I ask.

"Aren't you bringing him down?"

"He'll be down in a minute."

I key my intercom. "Tow? I'm going back to the roof."

"They moved all the hose lines outside, Lieut. I don't know how long this rig can stay here. The paint's peeling off." He laughs. Towbridge loves conflict. To be the centerpiece of an incident where we burn up a fire truck will produce a humorous tale he can spin for years to come.

"Use your judgment. I'm going to the roof. I'll need a way down."

"I'll put it up there for you."

The warning bell on my MSA is ringing as I head back up the stairs. In order not to give my presence away in the smoke, I remove the low pressure hose regulator from my face piece and turn the bottle off at the knob behind my hip until the bell no longer rings, then proceed up the stairs. I suck dark smoke all the way up. It tastes like the undercarriage of a fertilizer truck might.

I won't be able to take much of this. Very quickly the chemicals in the smoke will incapacitate me: carbon monoxide, cyanide gas, the rest of it.

Ward lies in a heap twenty feet from the doorway, coughing spasmodically. His nose is broken and is leaking blood onto his dark makeup. He's lost the wig.

The propane torch has rolled to a spot between us and is burning a hole in the roofing material. Not that it matters. Flames are coming out of one of the skylights in the center of the roof now. In various spots around us the tar is bubbling. In one area thirty feet away the gases from the tar have ignited and are burning lazily.

I kick the torch off into the smoke.

When I walk over to him, he says, "I didn't mean for this to get so big."

"Bullshit. You meant for it to get exactly this big."

"I'm so sorry. I'm so sorry."

"What's black and white and flies at night?"

"Huh?"

I pick him up and start running him through a mushroom of smoke toward the edge of the roof.

I release him in a perfect trajectory for the street in front of the building. He will land just about where the concrete sacks hit. He is moving so fast he can't stop. He keeps running, arms flailing. Half a step before the edge of the roof, he cracks his leg on a vent pipe and sprawls onto his face against the bottom of the parapet.

I'm not a murderer yet. Not yet.

As I watch him curl up in agony, something in me changes. I don't know exactly what it is or how long it has been coming on, but it's like a jar has shattered inside me and all the murky waters have filtered to the ground at my feet. It is very odd. I am watching his pain, and I'm not happy that I caused it. In an instant I know that no matter how much I detest this man and no matter what he's done, I am not the person to mete out his punishment. I will bring him to justice, but I no longer feel the incredible passion to kill him myself.

Just like that. It is gone. I'm sane again. Maybe for the first time in my life. Maybe it is because I've lived through the act, essentially, of killing him, even though he survived.

I'm having one of those epiphanies we get three or four times in our lives—if we're lucky. I've lived my life thinking this man was the cause of all my troubles, but he wasn't. My primary source of problems throughout my life has been my own hate, a hate that filled me with tension and anger that boiled over at inopportune moments and in brutal ways. Hate always destroys the vessel that carries it. I remember other epiphanies in my life. The night I decided to try out for the fire department. The night I almost beat Rickie Morrison to death and decided I wasn't going to drink again. The morning my mother was murdered and I shot Alfred, the morning I realized they were taking Neil away from me.

What I did to Earl Ward felt wrong in a way that it never had in my fantasies.

I hadn't felt anything like this since the morning I put five bullets into Alfred. I *could* kill Ward the same way I'd killed Alfred. In fact, here on this roof I would probably get away with it. But I wouldn't be my father's son. And whether I wanted to admit it or not, I needed to be my father's son. I was in *his* uniform, holding *his* rank, doing *his* job. I'd never known my father, really, but I wasn't going to betray him now.

What makes this all so sad is that it was only a freak accident that saved Ward's life.

As these thoughts wash over me, the strangest feeling of peace takes hold.

I pick him up. He thinks I am going to pitch him off the roof and struggles until I throw him back toward the center. Behind, I hear men and machines in the street. Another skylight begins burning through with a Rice Krispies sound; flames emerge and disappear as the physics of fire plays tricks inside the building. I will never get another chance like this. Once they lock him away, Ward will be out of my reach forever.

"Wha'dya got there?" It's Steve Slaughter, his face piece off and dangling on a strap around his neck. He's breathing hard from a combination of the climb up the aerial and the smoke on the roof, dripping sweat off his nose and out of his helmet, walking toward me in that peculiar John Wayne gait. I look behind for his partner, but he is alone. "This him?"

"This is him."

"You like fire?" Slaughter asks Ward. "Sure you do."

"I don't," says Earl Ward, without meeting Slaughter's eyes.

"You always miss the best part, don't you? *We* get the best part. Come here. I'll show you the best part."

Grabbing him by the collar, Slaughter drags him until they are beside the nearest burned-out skylight, torrents of hot smoke rushing skyward from the four-by-four-foot opening where the skylight had been.

"No. Noooooooo." Fitting the nape of his neck into his gloved hand, Slaughter squeezes him like a struggling fish, then pulls him over to the opening and pushes his face into the smoke. "Don't do this," Ward begs. "Please don't—"

Ward's sentence is cut off by a coughing fit. He chokes. It

is as if Slaughter is holding his head underwater. He gags and finally vomits.

Slaughter brings him back into relatively fresh air on the south side of the hole, allows him to regain his equilibrium, then pushes him back into the smoke. Ward tries to hold his breath again, but it doesn't last. He is coughing violently when I say, "Stop it."

Pulling Earl Ward out of the smoke, Slaughter tosses him to one side, where he flops like a sparrow that's hit a window.

"I'm taking him down."

Slaughter grins. Nearby another skylight melts through and we hear the fire on three. I am surprised the roof hasn't collapsed. Smoke rushes out of the skylights with a woofing sound that could only be described as dogs walking on marshmallows. Lots of dogs. Lots of marshmallows. Lots of smoke.

"Fuckin' bastard." Slaughter looks down at Earl Ward and kicks him hard in the kidneys. Ward rolls over and curls into a fetal position. "This is Attack Six on the roof. I'm bringing down the Ladder Three officer and one civilian."

Slaughter's made it sound as if *he* were rescuing *me,* putting it out over the air that way so the whole city will get a false picture of what is happening up here. "You go ahead," he says. "I'll follow with him."

"Not on your life. I'm taking him."

"Listen here, asshole. *I'm* the senior officer. You just trot on along."

"Jesus, man. We can't argue about this. The roof is going to cave."

"That's why you need to move along."

Slaughter and I watch each other warily. I know he will come down alone. It is the perfect out for me. Let somebody else get rid of Ward. Take it off my conscience and push it onto Slaughter's. This is why fictional heroes keep psycho tough-guy friends. So the psychos can dispatch enemies while the hero's conscience remains clear. But if you think about it for two seconds, that is all smoke and mirrors. It's for suckers. If I allow Slaughter to bring Ward down, he will kill him and we all know it, all three of us. He'll say Ward fell off the roof or Ward ran away in the smoke, but Ward will die. Slaughter will be responsible. But so, too, will I.

"I'm not going to let you do this," I say.

"Like you have a choice. Move, dickhead."

"Fuck you. Hand him over."

"It's him!" Ward is pointing at Slaughter. "I know that voice. He's the firefighter I told you about. He's older and fatter, but that's him."

"This ain't fat," Slaughter says. "I been liftin' weights."

"You killed this man's father."

"What are you talking about?" Slaughter boots him again. Hard. Ward rolls over and groans.

I step between them.

"You're the one who knocked his father into the fire."

"Bullshit!" Slaughter tries to chase Ward, but I block while Ward scoots across the tar roof on his side, moving closer to the skylight and the smoke rushing out.

"Wait a minute." I hold Slaughter in front of me.

"Keep your goddamn hands off me."

"You were there, weren't you? The night my father went into the basement. He's telling the truth." Perhaps because he is too weary to hide it any longer, he wears guilt like a beard.

"I recognize the voice," Ward says.

It is true Slaughter has an idiosyncratic voice.

"What happened that night?" I ask Slaughter.

"I wasn't there, so I don't know. What I *do* know is this bastard set the fire, so he's responsible. He pushed your father into that basement and then stood outside and watched him burn. Didn't even help. Just stood there."

I step toward Slaughter. Slaughter is big, but I am bigger and younger, and we both know I am crazy. "What happened that night?"

Slaughter is barehanded, so when he reaches into the thigh

pocket on his bunking pants, I think he is reaching for his gloves. Instead, he tears the Velcro flap open and brings out a silver knife so large it looks like a joke prop. It is a knife he carries as a tool. He flips the blade out and points it at my navel.

"I told you he was the one," Ward says, without getting up.

"Shut up," says Slaughter. "You're just trying to save your own butt."

"I wish he was," I say. "This is the same story he told me two weeks ago. That's how he got your dosimeter. Twenty-five years ago you dropped it when you were fighting my father."

"So I was there. So what? It was an accident. I didn't cause it. Listen, stand back. You've already struck one superior officer. All I have to do is tell them you were coming at me."

Water from a hose stream drums loudly on the parapet thirty feet away. Dollops of cold water shoot up past the roof and arch down, where they hit us like dirt clods.

"*You* killed my father."

"Don't be an ass. This jerkoff set the fire. *He* killed him. You know the law."

"You were wrestling with him. *You* were responsible."

"He wanted to save this asshole. Check it out. I was right and he was wrong. It's as simple as that. Look at all the grief this asshole's caused since your father let him go. I was going to throw this guy in the basement is what I was going to do. Your father thought it was un-fucking-ethical. So tonight I'm going to do what I should have done twenty-five years ago."

"No, you're not."

"God. You're just like your old man."

"I hope so."

Before he can reply, we hear screams, the same screams I heard as I was crossing the roof a few minutes ago. "Help me! Somebody help me!"

Flames begin shooting skyward at the west end of the

parapet, reaching up over the wall. A hose stream shoots up over the parapet. More flames. More hose streams. The various fires below are melding into a single conflagration. Inside the building the fire is burning in rooms and hallways where exterior hose streams will never reach.

The voice is coming from the burned-out skylight Slaughter had been pushing Ward's face into.

I grab Ward's arm and look at Slaughter. "You going to do something about that screaming?"

"You're the truckie. You make the rescue."

I head for the aerial ladder at the east side of the building, taking Ward with me. "Steve. At least yell down at that guy and tell him help is on the way. Tell him not to move."

"Fuck you."

On my way past, I grab the knife out of Slaughter's unsuspecting hands and sling the weapon over the side of the roof into The Harvey's backyard all in one smooth movement. While I'm doing this, Ward slips away from me and vanishes into the smoke.

Then, before I reach the aerial, a small piece of the roof caves in.

74. HOW TO GAG AN ARSONIST

I stride through the smoke feeling the sticky tar under my boots. In places the roof sways with my weight. With bottle, mask, bunking suit, and tools, I come in at two eighty. Fortunately this isn't new construction or it would have collapsed long ago.

Every aerial in the city has tools mounted on the top section so they can be accessed by firefighters—a pick-head axe, a pike pole, and a roof ladder.

Balancing the roof ladder on my right shoulder, I move

through the smoke, taking care lest I bump into Slaughter or Ward and sweep either or both into a skylight. I haven't backed off from murdering Ward just to kill him by accident.

Showers of cold water shoot over the parapet at the front of the building, smack my helmet, and make my ears ring. Ward and Slaughter are nowhere in sight.

When I get to the skylight where I heard the screaming, salt and soot trickle into my mouth along with water. I peer into the murky depths using the flashlight on my coat. Volumes of hot, black smoke rush into my face, singeing my eyebrows and nostrils.

"You still down there?"

He doesn't reply, but I can hear someone coughing.

"I'm letting down a ladder."

"Hey, man . . . Where are you?"

"On the roof. I'm going to let down a ladder. Don't climb until it's solid."

This skylight accessed the east end of the corridor on three, the same end I'd searched, which meant I either walked past this person or he's made his way through a wall of smoke and fire I've deemed impassible. In either event, he's down there because I screwed up. I feel bad about this.

Opening the ladder hooks, I begin to angle the butt end of the roof ladder into the square opening. After some maneuvering, I feel somebody grabbing the base of the ladder. "Don't pull," I say. But he can't help it. He is in a panic.

I wrestle the ladder against his efforts until I feel the butt on solid footing, take out my utility loop, a three-foot-long piece of webbing every Seattle firefighter carries, fasten it quickly around the top rung, the other end over a nearby vent pipe to stabilize the ladder.

By the time I finish the knot, he is climbing. I can hear him coughing and spitting the way people do in smoke.

When his head appears, I grab him under the shoulders and help him up. He is a heavyset man who is probably suffering from carbon monoxide poisoning. This is confirmed when he reaches out for me and misses twice in succession; his coordination is kaput. It is a wonder he made it up the ladder.

"Anybody else down there?"

He shakes his head. His teeth are peppered with particles of soot, his eyes bloodshot and rimmed with tears, a telltale ring of soot marking his mouth and nostrils. I've spoken to CO patients who told me they were fine and then died eight hours later. This man is headed for the hyperbaric chamber at Virginia Mason Hospital for treatment, and if he's very unlucky, from there to the morgue.

He is in shorts and a sweatshirt, barefoot, and before I can warn him, he crawls away from the smoky orifice into the bubbling tar. He picks up one hand and one knee and howls in pain.

I grasp him around the waist, carrying him like you would a large dog until I think we are at a spot where the roof isn't hot. The roof wobbles under our combined weight. I escort him to the tip of the aerial and call Towbridge over the intercom. "One victim, Tow. He's going to need help."

"How many more are up there?"

"Including me, three." I'm still breathing hard from carrying the victim.

"They got hose lines on me, but we already blew a tire. You want me to get your T-shirt out of the cab?" I knew that last was a joke, the thought that he might try to save my T-shirt while a half-million-dollar fire truck burned up.

"He's got tar burns on him, Tow."

"Right."

Towbridge scrambles up the three-story ladder quicker than I've seen anybody do it all night. When he looks at me, I see something in his eyes I've never seen before. It takes a moment to realize he thinks he's looking at me for the last time.

"Ain't you comin' down?"

"I have to get somebody else."

Towbridge glances down. It is easy to forget how high we are. Forty feet. High enough to die if you fall. And if you don't die, high enough to make you wish you had.

A breath of hot air rises into my face. I wonder how much carbon monoxide I've taken tonight, how much toxin is contaminating my bloodstream.

I don't want to cross the shuddering roof again, but I need to locate Ward and get him down. I know from experience the roof is about to give way. My legs feel weak. I haven't been this beat up since the Armitage Furniture Warehouse fire eight years ago.

I circle the penthouse. "Steve. Hey, Steve. Where are you guys?"

It occurs to me that the skylights are almost flush with the roof, so that in the smoke they will be easy to step into. I head along the south side of the roof, sweeping my flashlight in a large swath, stopping when I find myself blinded by smoke. At one point I look up and glimpse a black column rising into the sky. Smoke boils off the roof from all sides now, as well as from the skylights and vent pipes.

Carbon monoxide poisoning comes on quickly. It limits your ability to think and deceives you into believing you're all right. I now have enough CO in me to blunt my reactions and my agility. I am holding on to my sanity like it's my last nickel. For a moment as the smoke thickens, I wonder why I don't turn around and go down the aerial myself. But I don't.

Halfway along the south rim of the roof, I come upon a stack of roofing materials. The smoke shifts for a split second and I see movement on the other side of the stack, a man hunched over, working. Below us I hear food cans exploding in somebody's kitchen. In another room, stored ammunition pops off like firecrackers.

One of the skylights at the other end of the roof begins spitting flame, illuminating the area around me. The extra heat starts to draw smoke away from the surface and pull it into the sky.

The increased visibility reveals Steve Slaughter thirty feet away, one boot on Earl Ward's back, pinning him down. In his free hand he holds the blowtorch. Before I can reach them, Slaughter applies flame from the torch to the back of Ward's ear.

Ward struggles and kicks frantically but cannot escape. Strangely, he does not yell. I wonder why he isn't screaming, until I see Slaughter has torn off a piece of Ward's dress, jammed it into his mouth, and secured the gag with a fire department body loop wrapped around Ward's head. If the world got any crazier, I'd put a photo of this in our training guide and caption it, "How to gag an arsonist."

Before he realizes I am there, I bat the bottle out of Slaughter's hands. My hand speed is proving too much for him tonight. The torch flies over the parapet and into the darkness of the backyard. Slaughter glowers at me. "Are you fuckin' insane?"

Slaughter presses on Ward's back with his boot until Ward screams through his gag.

Slaughter reaches down and slugs Earl Ward in the back of the head with his fist.

He is preparing to do it again when I step over Ward's body and push up against Slaughter's chest. We are face-to-face now, toe-to-toe. He cannot hit Ward, but he can hit me. "Let's get off this roof," I say.

"This is the SOB burned me when I was handcuffed to the bed."

It isn't often you can point to one moment during which your fractured persona congeals into a single entity, but later on I will point to this moment, right here, face-to-face with Steve Slaughter. It is even more central than not killing Ward. I've been conflicted my whole life about who I am and what I need to do in life, yet at this moment I know exactly who I am.

I *am* my father's son.

My father defended Ward against vigilante rage, and I will too.

"I'm not done with him," Slaughter says. I can feel the spit from his words hitting my eyes as a wave of hot smoke engulfs us. "He burned me. I'm burning him. It's simple justice."

We hear the cracking and buckling of timbers as the center of the roof begins sinking. For a split second I think about leaving these two to their destiny. On my own I could make it around the perimeter to the aerial before the roof caves in. But I don't move.

The pallet of roofing materials begins to slide away from us as the roof slowly begins sloping toward the center. A small hole opens twenty feet away while the area around the hole dips down like the walls of a funnel.

We slide, all three of us, toward the hole as a sheet of flame roars out. I can feel the heat on my back. The sudden light illuminates Slaughter's face like a flashbulb.

Slaughter doesn't seem to realize what is happening.

"I could have finished this fuck twenty-five years ago, but *some*body got in my way. That's not going to happen here."

"So you admit you killed my father!"

"It was an accident. He tried to protect this fuck."

Suddenly the old rage rushes back. This man staring me in the eye, this man who is so cocksure of everything in life, this bastard destroyed my family. My mother. My brother. Alfred. It all started here. For a few seconds I am confused. I can live my father's dream. Or I can avenge his death.

I lean toward Slaughter to counter the sinking roof behind us. Ward is beneath us. We continue to straddle him, Slaughter facing the flames, my back to them.

Without another word, I shove Slaughter; he backs up, stumbles, and lands on his rump.

The fire flares up and a fusillade of sparks shoots into the sky behind me, along with twenty or thirty feet of flame. I duck down on top of Ward to escape some of the heat and to cover him. The radiant heat has already penetrated through the layers of my bunking coat and trousers to my wet T-shirt and jockey shorts, where I am being scalded.

The roof creaks like a huge rusty hinge and grows steeper. Slaughter is holding on to the parapet, but Ward and I are being held in place only by inertia and the sticky tar surface of the roof.

Eddings has been screeching at us on the radio for the past minute, but now the dispatcher takes over in a calm voice. "Ladder Three. Attack Six. Do you read? Ladder Three? Attack Six?"

From below it must look like we are all dead.

Another large section in the center of the roof caves in and more flames shoot skyward. At this point about a third of the roof collapses with a staggered series of crashes.

Slaughter gets up from his crouch, catches his balance, and rushes me football style, as if to grasp me around the waist or push me into the hole behind us. He doesn't seem to realize we are *all* on the verge of sliding in.

I knot up my left fist and crack him across the jaw.

The blow sends him reeling onto the pile of roofing material that is teetering on the lip of the maw. As soon as his weight settles onto it, the pile flips into the hole, the hole that is becoming a giant oblong funnel, sucking in everything in its path.

Twenty-five years ago Lieutenant Wollf and a firefighter named Slaughter fought over what to do with an arson suspect. Tonight Lieutenant Wollf and Slaughter fight over what to do with that same suspect. Tonight the positions are reversed. Tonight Slaughter falls into the flames. Wollf remains outside.

Without thinking, I move.

Holding a vent pipe with one arm, I grab the sleeve of his coat as he continues to slide in. The roofing material disappears, producing a glorious shower of sparks. Slaughter would have gone with it had I not grabbed his sleeve.

For five long seconds his gray eyes hold mine, the blind anger in them replaced by supplication. He sees the same irony I've seen. That if I let him go, I am doing what he did to my father. That he will burn to death like my father. That the simple justice he was talking about a minute ago will be served.

All that is left is a strip of roof five or six feet wide on this side of the building along the parapet wall, all of it tipping steeply toward the maw.

"Don't let me die," Slaughter gasps.

"You let my father die."

"God damn it. I was scared. I didn't have my bunkers. It was too hot. I didn't know what to do. I was scared."

"You miserable coward."

He slips farther in as the roof folds under him. Flame creeps up his backside and tickles my face.

Is this poetic justice? Has God handed me this situation as a gift? Or is it something else? A test perhaps? I forget about fate and go with my conscience.

Using every available ounce of strength, I try to pull him upward. He doesn't budge. Feeling the flame against my face, I am tempted to let go. Finally, I pull him onto the lip. He crawls up swiftly under the parapet and puts his back against the parapet wall. He's been burned. I can't tell how badly because I've been burned too.

All three of us are going to cook if we don't start moving.

Now that he is safe, I let go of Slaughter's coat sleeve and pull Earl Ward over to the parapet wall too.

The enormous dimple in the roof continues to enlarge, softening at the edges, snapping off section by section. Earl Ward stares at the flames. Earl Ward is incapable of locomotion. It is clear if I leave him he won't budge—that he will eventually slide into the fire without a struggle.

His whole life he's had a special relationship with fire, but tonight that relationship has gone rancid.

The fire has brightened the roof until it is almost like a summer afternoon.

I pull the body loop off Ward's head and remove the spit-soaked gag. Even though his hands aren't constrained, he is afraid to remove it on his own. He's lost a shoe and his sock has holes in it. For the first time in my life I realize what a wretch he is. Burned on the back of his head and his ears from the blowtorch. Dazed. Weeping.

I stand him up, take his arm, and walk him briskly around the roof, behind the penthouse, where flame is shooting out of the doorway, to the tip of the aerial, which, blessedly, is still there. Towbridge is my hero. The descent will be dicey; flames are encroaching on the rungs near a third-floor window below. We'll need hose support.

Stepping up onto the parapet and onto the aerial is a potentially dangerous move; if you slip, you may fall into the street.

Because I want to be below him, I climb onto the aerial, then reach for Ward.

I have his hand, like a father holds a child. The image freezes in my mind—as repellent as it is ironic.

As he steps over the parapet wall, a figure approaches from behind Ward. I've been focused on saving Ward, while Slaughter has been focused on getting rid of the only witness who could positively tie him to my father's death.

In an instant he's knocked Ward over the parapet.

Because I still have his hand, I nearly go over with him.

I hold on as his body swings violently below the aerial. The movement and his body weight almost tear my arm from its socket.

I am doubled over the side rail of the aerial, trying not to let go, while he swings limply, his hand softening as if it's a poorly tied knot coming apart. He is actually looking down to see where he will fall. Where he will die.

He mutters, "Let me go."

"Let him go, dickhead!" says Slaughter, leaning over the parapet.

I feel the aerial shuddering and know somebody is climbing up behind me.

When you're doing something that pushes the limits of

physical endurance, you come up with tricks to extend the operation, holding for ten seconds, shifting your position slightly and telling yourself you can hold for another ten in the new position, tricks to con yourself into persevering just a little bit longer than you thought possible. Each millisecond stretches the window for help to arrive.

We might have gone over together if I hadn't jammed my left leg through one of the rubber-coated aerial rungs. It hurts like hell, but it is keeping us alive. Should Towbridge decide to extend the aerial, perhaps to lift me and my victim, the scissors movement of the rungs will amputate my leg. I want to look back to warn him, but I don't dare. Nor do I dare remove my leg from between the rungs. Not if I want to keep Ward alive.

I lean farther over the railing and grasp him with both hands, the move multiplying by a factor of ten the odds of my falling with him. A collective gasp arises from the crowd below.

Slaughter leans close. "Come on, dickhead. You think he wouldn't drop you? You'll still be a hero."

My torso is folded over the aerial's tall steel guardrail, and the squared guardrail is cutting into my ribs. I feel something in my lower leg burst, and the pain becomes almost unendurable. It is no longer a question of whether I'll drop him; it's now a question of whether we'll both fall.

I can't yard him up, because we are both too far over the edge. All I can do is hold on and hope my leg doesn't snap. If I really work at it, I can hold another five seconds. When five seconds is up, I make myself hold another five.

I know that if I let go now people will say I've made a valiant effort. That I've done my heroic best. Hell, I'll get a medal.

Slaughter looks at the climber behind me. "Get the fuck out of here!"

"Go yell at your own crew." It is Towbridge. "What do you want me to do, Lieut?"

The crowd below begins screaming when we start. First Earl Ward, and then the crowd below. The lights from the TV cameras are blinding.

The idea is to get Ward swinging, to gain momentum like a pendulum and swing him up to the edge of the aerial railing, where Towbridge might grab him. With two of us, we might be able to roll him over the rail and onto the bed of the ladder.

It takes four or five swings before I have Ward moving, each swing taking him farther toward the building, each eliciting a gasp from Ward and a roar from the peanut gallery below. We are both being burned now, he more than I.

On the second long swing toward the building, his dress bursts into flame. There is nothing I can do about it.

I slap him up against the aerial, where Towbridge gets a grip on his dress, then his waist. Towbridge begins slapping at the fire on the dress. I am twisted around at an awkward angle, bent like a horseshoe, my leg still locked under a rung.

I give Earl Ward over completely to Towbridge now and wrestle the rubber boot and my leg out of the gap between the rungs.

"You got him?" I ask Towbridge, who is still slapping the fire out on Ward's dress.

"I think so."

Together we roll Ward over the railing and onto the aerial bed. His dress is smoking.

"You fuckin' heroes make me sick," says Slaughter from above.

75. DWI

Cynthia Rideout

MAY 9, FRIDAY, 1201 HOURS

Things have begun looking up since I got permanently assigned to Ladder 3. I'm taking the place of Pickett, who retired after he came back to work and promptly fell through a floor at another fire.

Slaughter's gone.

In light of the lawsuit against Eddings and the fact that four women are now accusing her of sexual harassment, Eddings has been transferred to the Seventh Battalion in West Seattle. I guess the department thinks there aren't any women working in the Seventh, or that they won't have any fires while Eddings is there—that her problems will melt away if they move her.

I've decided to testify against Eddings if the case goes to court.

The night of the fire at The Harvey was wild.

Including the pyro, there were nine rescues. The people around here tell me I'm not likely to see that again anytime soon. Nobody died, which was a minor miracle.

All three guys on the roof came down with burns. Slaughter's were the worst. Wollf was burned on his wrists, neck, and legs. He also had a stress fracture of his tibia.

Except for the principals, nobody knows for sure what happened up there.

Later that night, Slaughter, Hertlein, and Chief Smith approached the three of us as we sat on the front bumper of Ladder 3. Tow had rolled the rig two blocks up Cherry, where the shop mechanic was changing the flat tires.

Chief Smith wanted to know why Wollf hadn't allowed

Slaughter to make the rescue. Slaughter was standing beside Smith.

For a moment I could feel Wollf tense up the way an animal tenses up just before it pounces on its prey. He could barely walk, was full of smoke, and had a strained shoulder—we had to help him take his bunking coat off—but just for a moment I thought he was going to take Slaughter apart.

"Slaughter had no intention of rescuing Ward," he said calmly. "He tried to kill Ward. He wants him out of the way because Ward saw Slaughter push my father into that basement fire twenty-five years ago."

Talk about a conversation stopper.

Slaughter chewed his mustache and stared at Wollf.

Although his retirement wasn't official until months later, by the next afternoon Slaughter had vacated the station. Three weeks after that he was involved in an auto accident in Maple Valley we were told would keep him in the hospital for at least a month. To make matters worse, his wife left him and he got ticketed by the State Patrol for driving under the influence the night of the accident.

It must have been a bizarre experience to be involved in a firefighter's death and sixteen years later have that firefighter's son show up on your doorstep as a probie.

No wonder Slaughter wrote bad reports on Wollf. He wanted Wollf transferred to another station as quickly as possible. But then the Armitage Furniture Warehouse fire came along, and Wollf was suddenly bulletproof.

76. THE DEAD SQUIRREL

As the weeks and months pass, it becomes clear that my life has been a botched performance. I've grown up hating an invisible enemy, thinking all my troubles stemmed from the pyro who killed my father, when in fact most of my troubles, my anger, my isolation, were of my own manufacture. It didn't help that I'd murdered a man when I was ten years old. That I'd never had counseling. It didn't help either that I'd never spoken of it, had in fact put the entire event out of my mind until recently.

It wasn't until I passed up my chance to kill Earl Ward that I began to find peace. My old self would have been outraged that Steve Slaughter was going to get away with his actions against my father, but I was determined not to let hate rule my thoughts. If he got away with it, he got away with it. I wasn't going to let him rent space in my brain. It wasn't easy to pass up such a splendid opportunity for revenge, but I was gaining ground on my feelings.

If I could control the impulse to kill my father's murderer, I could do anything.

In the days and weeks after The Harvey, I found it amazing to realize how much all that barely submerged hate had compromised my ability to lead a normal life, how it had inhibited me from revealing myself to others.

After being out of touch with Vanessa for a week, I phoned her. This time I didn't hang up when she answered.

"Hey," she said. "How've you been?"

"I've been fine."

"You were all over the news. They said you were being treated for smoke inhalation and burns. They said you had a broken leg. Are you all right?"

"I'm fine. My leg was only a stress fracture and some bruising."

"I thought you did very well on the interviews."

"I was nervous."

"It didn't show."

"I called because I'd like to take you out to dinner."

There was a long silence. "I don't think so, Paul."

"I've turned a corner in my life. At least let me tell you about it."

"Paul, I'm going to be honest here. I've felt attracted to you from the first time I met you, but your anger and volatility worry me. I just don't see how the two of us have any kind of future together."

"I've changed."

"I don't think so."

It was the most effort I'd expended for a "nice" girl in quite a while, maybe for any woman ever. I was crushed. I understood what she was thinking, but I was crushed. Then again, getting crushed is part of being alive, and I was now truly alive for the first time.

In the past few months things have settled down. Neil calls collect and we talk. He says he can't get over the change in me.

I've spoken to SPD detectives repeatedly, but they aren't going to charge Slaughter with anything, least of all complicity in my father's death. The evidence, they say, simply isn't strong enough to take to court. Ward's testimony against Slaughter is worthless. Oddly enough, they aren't going to charge Ward in my father's death either. Still, he'll be in prison the rest of his life.

"Slaughter told me he did it," I told the SPD detective. "When we were on the roof, he confessed."

"That's a little problematical," said the detective. "At the time he was about to slide into the fire. The way he sees it, he was telling you what you wanted to hear, hoping you'd save his ass."

For weeks I reviewed every conversation I'd ever had with Steve Slaughter, searching for clues he might have inadvertently dropped. For a time I let it eat at me. As infuriating and frustrating as it was to realize Slaughter had gotten away with killing my father—whether through malice, because of an accident, or sheer incompetence—I was determined to suck it up and live with whatever the justice system divvied up for him. A year ago I would have driven out to Maple Valley and run him down with my car. Or shot him. At one point

I might have beaten him to death without thought of the consequences.

What I'd learned was that sometimes you had to let things go. Even big things. That you can't exact revenge or find justice for everything in life. I knew this much: If I could help it, I was *never* going to have another man's death on my conscience.

Earl Ward sits in the King County Courthouse awaiting trial. For reasons I can't fathom, he sends me postcards with pleas for money and gifts, his missives scratched out in a barely legible scrawl. I can't imagine why he thinks I will help him. I read the cards and throw them in the trash.

The morning after the fire at The Harvey, statewide newscasts played videotapes of Chief Eddings in front of the building screaming at firefighters and citizens in an uncontrolled manner. Editorialists wondered aloud why she hadn't been given a desk job, but the department had no answer for them. There were a lot of things the department couldn't answer for, and Chief Eddings was only one of them.

Three months after the fire at The Harvey, Hertlein was transferred to a desk job in a position that effectively removed his power to interfere in my career or anybody else's.

Jeff Dolan's broken leg healed up and he came back to work. Towbridge continued to swoon the women and make jokes. After his burns healed, Mike Pickett returned to work and within a week fell through a floor at a house fire and retired to live on his boat near Anacortes. Rideout took Pickett's spot. Slaughter retired.

I'd about given up on ever seeing Vanessa Pennington again when one night her grandmother's new housekeeper called 911 at four in the morning. Attack 6 and Ladder 3 were dispatched on a Med 7, along with a medic unit and an aid car. The housekeeper thought Patricia Pennington was having a heart attack.

On the way into the house, Towbridge and I spotted a dead squirrel in the front yard, a fresh one, each of us mentally marking it for later.

We ran all the tests on Patricia Pennington, helped the medics put their twelve leads on her, and watched her heart on the Lifepak monitor. It turned out she had only fainted on her way to the bathroom, having gotten out of bed too quickly.

After the medics told us Pennington didn't need to go to the hospital, I dashed outside while the others picked up equipment. A few minutes later at the rig, Towbridge said, "I coulda swore I saw a squirrel in the yard when we went in."

"Me too," I said, grinning. I'd had barely enough time to climb into the cab of Attack 6 and perch the dead animal on the console, where it would be facing Gliniewicz when he got in.

Towbridge looked at me. "A dead squirrel could be real handy around a fire station."

"You think?"

"Let's go," said Dolan. "I need to get back to bed."

Ignoring him, I walked around to the front of Attack 6 as Gliniewicz climbed into the cab to catch some sleep before the others got there. Half a minute later Gliniewicz opened his left eye and saw all four members of Ladder 3's crew lined up in front of his window staring at him. Gliniewicz must have seen something in our eyes, because he sat bolt upright and looked around inside the cab.

None of us actually saw his face when he started squalling, but he must have been within inches of the dead rodent. Gliniewicz was still screaming when he leaped out of the apparatus and sprinted across the yard. "Jesus H. Christ!" he said from behind a nearby tree. "What the hell was that?"

By then the four of us were laughing so hard Towbridge actually lost control of his leg muscles and rolled into the grass.

We knew the gag would run for weeks, if not months. Squirrel cartoons would show up on Gliniewicz's food locker. Stray acorns would be found on the beanery table. Nuts on the hood of his car.

We were still laughing when Vanessa Pennington pulled up in her BMW, got out, and said, "What's going on?"

We must have looked like lunatics.

I stopped laughing and walked her to the front porch. "It's just a silly practical joke. The main thing is your grandmother's going to be okay. The medics are pretty sure she just fainted. They're not even suggesting she go to the hospital, although maybe she should see her doctor tomorrow."

"I broke every speed limit on the way here. The housekeeper called me right after she called nine one one."

"You shouldn't have worried. These are probably the best medics in the world."

We looked at each other for a few moments. We hadn't seen each other in months and hadn't spoken since she'd refused to go out with me. "You're looking good," I said.

"So are you."

"I've thought about you. I feel like I had a shot at the majors and blew it."

She smiled, embarrassed. "That's an interesting way to put it. I've thought about you too."

"I know I was volatile before. I've changed."

"What happened?"

"I grew up. I'm not done, but I'm on my way. I would still like to take you out to dinner."

She evaluated me for several long moments. "Why don't you come over to my place? Tomorrow night? Say around seven? And maybe you can tell me about the joke."

"See you then."

We both knew she was savvy enough to have placed our meeting on neutral ground if she'd wanted to, yet she'd invited me to her apartment. It was a good sign. A very good sign. Things might or might not work out between us, but I was a solid citizen of the world now, and if I didn't hook up with Vanessa, I'd hook up with somebody else, and eventually I'd have a wife and family. Just as in the past I'd known it would never happen, I now knew it was sure to. Life had turned around for me, and nothing could stop it, least of all myself.

Read on for a sneak peek at
Earl Emerson's next thriller,

THE SMOKE ROOM

Coming in hardcover in June 2005
Published by Ballantine Books

1. HOWLING IN THE DEEP BLUE TWILIGHT

Experts estimated the pig fell just over 11,000 feet before it plunged through Iola Pederson's roof.

The lone witness had been snitching cherry tomatoes from a pot on his neighbor's front porch when he looked up and spotted the hog as it tumbled through the deep blue twilight. Whether the hog had been howling because he was delighted with the flight or because of the rapidly approaching earth, nobody ever knew. Ultimately the critter pierced Iola Pederson's roof with the sound of a man putting his foot through a rotten porch.

The pig's demise pretty much signaled the end of all my ambitions.

My name is Jason Gum. Just call me Gum.

At the time, I was twenty-four years old and had been a Seattle firefighter just under two years, but was already studying to take the lieutenant's examination in another year. I was aiming to be chief of the department. It was ambitious, I know, but the way I figured it, you need goals if you are going anywhere in life—goals and a straight and narrow pathway.

Engine 29 runs out of a sleepy little station in a residential district in West Seattle. Four people work off the rig: an officer, a driver, and two of us in back. On the day we got the call to check out Iola Pederson's roof, I was working B shift. Stanislow had less time in than I did, and I could tell she was looking to my lead as we raced toward the scene of what the radio report said was a rocket into a house. I knew not to get too worked up until we'd evaluated the scene ourselves.

"I wonder if it's an accidental firing from the submarine base across the water," said Stanislow. "Christ."

"It's probably nothing," I said.

As we sat in the back of the crew cab watching the streets unfold behind us, Stanislow and I slipped into our MSA harnesses. They'd also dispatched two more engines and two aerial ladders, a chief, a medic unit, and probably an aid car; yet even with all that manpower, Stanislow and I would be first through the door. Life on the tailboard. Cash money couldn't get a better seat to every little bizarre extravagance of human behavior.

The address was on Hobart Avenue Southwest, a location drivers from stations outside our district were going to have a hard time finding.

Siren growling, Engine 29 moved through quiet, residential streets until we hit the apex of Bonair Drive, where we swooped down the hillside through a greenbelt that was mostly brown now—Seattle enjoying the driest August on record.

The slate-blue Puget Sound was spread out below us like a blanket. West over the Olympics the sunset was dead except for a few fat razor slashes of pink along the horizon. A hawk tipped his wings and bobbled on air currents over the hillside. Above us a small plane circled.

The house was the only single-family residence on a street of small apartment buildings. The lieutenant turned around and said, "Looks like smoke. I want you guys to lay a preconnect to the front door."

The driver placed the wheel blocks under the rear duals and started the pump, while I jumped down and grabbed the two-hundred-foot bundle of 1¾-inch hose preconnected to an outlet on the rig and headed toward the house, dropping flakes of dry hose behind me. Behind us the officer busied himself on the radio, giving incoming units directions to our location. Because the driver on this shift was noted for filling the line with reckless speed, I moved quickly, not wanting the water pressure to knock me down the way it had Stanislow at her first fire.

In front of the house a man with one of those ubiquitous white Hemingway beards you see on so many old guys sat cross-legged on the turf, covered in blood. Behind him, the living-room windows were broken out, pieces of plate glass littering the lawn like mirrors and reflecting distant city lights, a twilight sky. The roof had a hole in it the size of a duffel bag. All I could think was that the man on the lawn had been burned and wounded, possibly in an explosion.

"Anybody inside?" I asked.

"My daughter," he gasped. "My daughter's in there! I *think* she's in there. God. I'm confused."

Stanislow stooped beside the victim. "What happened?"

"I'm not sure. It might have been a bomb."

"A bomb," Stanislow said. "Did you hear that, Gum? What if there's another one?"

"You got any explosives in the house?" I asked.

"Just a few bullets. But *I* didn't do this. It came from up there." He pointed toward the sky.

Powdery material that might or might not have been smoke drifted out of the hole in the roof. Later we determined it was creosote dust being distributed by the kitchen fan. The broken window frames were drenched in a wet substance that appeared remarkably similar to entrails.

As I neared the doorway and the cotton-jacketed hose started to harden at my feet, I clipped my air hose to my face piece and began inhaling compressed air. Stanislow caught up with me but stopped near a gore-festooned window frame. "Jesus. Look at that."

I pushed the front door open with my boot.

"You think that's his daughter?" Stanislow asked. "You think that's her guts?"

"Only one way to find out."

"There's no telling how bad he's bleeding. I better stay out here and take care of him."

"Okay. I'll go in. You take care of him."

I picked up the nozzle and went through the front door, keeping low the way we'd been taught, not crawling but not standing either. When I switched my helmet light on, hundreds of thousands of black motes wafted in the yellow beam. I could see maybe ten feet through the nebula.

It had been close to 90° Fahrenheit when we left the station, and experts estimated that under normal working conditions the microclimate inside our turnouts was close to 150°. It was probably higher tonight, which kept me sweating profusely in the heavy, all-encapsulating turnout clothing.

It didn't occur to me until I entered the structure that I'd been listening to howling for some time now, the noise obscured by the roaring of Engine 29's motor and pump. The noises might have been coming from an animal. More likely it was a second victim. Most of the ceiling in the main room was on the floor, plaster and broken boards underfoot. I moved through the blackness, at times forced to feel my way, dragging the hose even though there was no sign of heat or fire.

"It's okay," I said. "I'm here to help."

She was hunkered on the floor. The black ink in the air had settled on her like broken spiderwebs. The floor was gooey, and as I reached her I slipped to one knee. When I tipped her head up and peeked through the blood and the black residue covering her face, I was greeted by the most startling blue eyes I'd ever encountered.

"You all right?"

She blinked but did not move.

"What happened? Are you all right?"

"There's a head over there."

"What?"

"A head."

"How many people were here?"

"Just me and Daddy."

"So whose head is it?"

"I don't know. Maybe somebody came in the back. All I know was he was huge."

The furniture had congealed into vague, elusive lumps swathed in plaster and rubble. On the floor in front of the kitchen sink I found a large animal's head. It took a moment to ascertain the head had belonged to a hog and the material surrounding it was an animal cadaver, half-empty, the entrails spewing this way and that like grotesque Halloween ornaments strung up by a lunatic.

"Am I going to die? Please don't tell me I'm going to die."

"You'll be okay." My Emergency Medical Technician training taught me to start with what we called the ABCs: airway, breathing, and circulation. She'd been making noise, so she had an airway and was breathing. As far as the circulation and bleeding went, she was covered in gore, so I had no way of knowing whether she was bleeding or not.

Speaking into my portable radio, I said, "Command from Engine 29 team B. No sign of fire. There's light smoke in the structure. We've got a second victim inside. I'm bringing her out."

"What happened?" she asked, as I took her arm and stood her up. "Who did this?"

"I don't know. Let's get you out of here. Can you walk?"

Apparently not, I thought, as she sagged against me.

One arm under her shoulders, the other under her knees, I lugged her through the ravaged interior of the house. As it turned out, she was a full-grown adult, almost as tall as I was—five-eight—and while I wasn't the strongest firefighter in the department, I managed to get us out the doorway and onto the lawn without either of us falling on our butts.

Outside, Stanislow and our earlier victim were gone.

I set my victim down on the lawn away from the broken

glass and got my first good look at her in the twilight. In addition to the blood and guts, she was covered in soot. I took off my helmet, shut down my air supply, and removed my face piece.

"Oh, God," she said, holding her arms stiffly away from her body. "Can't you do something? Oh, my God. This is disgusting. Get it off me."

I yarded the hose line out of the house and cracked the nozzle until water poured out in a limp, silvery stream. "Here."

She cupped water in her hands and splashed it on her face, picking at her hair. "Oh God. Just pour it over my head. It's all in my hair. It's everywhere."

"It's going to be cold."

"I don't give a damn. Get this off me."

I opened the nozzle on flush, giving her what amounted to a cold shower. Underneath the gore and soot she wore a T-shirt and jeans. The cold water emphasized the fact that she wasn't wearing a bra.

Is Daddy all right?" she asked, after we'd sluiced the last of the blood and soot out of her hair. "Have you seen Daddy?".

"He's over by our engine. Anybody else in there?"

"Just that god-awful head."

As I turned the Task Force nozzle around and screwed up the pressure to knock the crap off my rubber boots, she looked up at me, suddenly bashful. "I must look hideous."

"No. I think you look terrific."

Her name was Iola Pederson, she was maybe twenty years older than I was, and although I didn't know it then, she was the initial nail in my coffin.

2. THE FIVE F'S

As firefighter and police investigators dissected the wreckage, the mechanics of the destruction were slowly unraveled. Contrary to expectations, we found no bombs, no exploded water heaters, no downed rockets, and no fallen airplane engines. Clear and simple: an animal had fallen out of the sky, later identified as a breed of hog known as a Chester White. The hog had penetrated the Pederson homestead, punching through the roof, the attic, the second floor, and then had exploded against the concrete subfloor under the living-room rug.

Accompanied by his owner and his brother, the animal, having just won two ribbons at a county fair on the Olympic Peninsula, had been returning home to Ellensburg, a small college/farming town east of the Cascades. The pig's owner had modified his Cessna 210 to transport livestock, altering the door, removing the last four seats, and jury-rigging a wooden pen in the rear of the plane. The floor of the pen was lined with straw, old blankets, corncobs, rutabagas, and stale doughnuts to keep the hog occupied during the flight. Despite the fact that their passenger tipped the scales at nine hundred forty-seven pounds, total weight for the three of them was still under the allowable payload for the plane.

During the originating flight from Eastern Washington the hog had become airsick and thrashed about in his pen, his movements tipping the plane from side to side. Fearing another bout of airsickness on the return flight, the pilot laced a bucket of apples with Stressnil and fed it to the creature. If he'd been paying attention, the pilot would have seen the hog spit out the tranquilizers, ingesting just enough to doze off after they prodded him into the plane, but not enough to keep him asleep.

Because he'd already weakened the slats of his pen on the initial flight, it took only a minute of thrashing about before he broke the enclosure.

Without hesitation the hog rushed forward and nuzzled the back of the pilot's seat in a desperately friendly move, thrusting the pilot up against the yoke. The weight shift sent the plane into a shallow dive, which prompted the pilot to shout at his brother. "Goddamn it. Help me here. I've got half a ton of pork crawling up my ass."

"I'm trying," said his brother, whose seat was also rammed up against the instrument panel. Despite their efforts to discourage the airsick hog, the plane's dive grew steeper.

"Open the door!" said the pilot.

"Are you kidding? He'll jump. You know how hard it was to get him in here."

"Okay, then you jump!"

"Are we crashing?"

"What do you think? Open the goddamned door!"

They plummeted almost 5,000 feet before the pilot's brother got the door open, before the cabin filled with cool air and scraps of flying straw, before the hog seized his opportunity and, with a snorking sound, heeled around and dove into the evening sky, all four legs splayed out, headed for Iola Pederson's roof.

It was one of those misadventures that got picked up by wire services around the country, the kind radio personalities wore out and schoolkids embellished and re-enacted for each other on the playground.

What our officer had mistaken for smoke turned out to be creosote-impregnated soot that had accumulated in the attic over a period of thirty years, and disgorged into the house when the pig went through the rooms and broke the conduit for the kitchen fan. On final impact in the living room, the animal exploded, plastering the main room of the house in animal matter.

Amateur psychologists talk about the fight or flight response, but it's not an either/or situation. Behaviorists have determined that when threatened, all mammals respond in five predictable patterns, the five F's: fight, flight, freeze, fidget, or faint.

The man we found sitting on the lawn, having gone for his gun and staggered outside, had run through three of them: fight, flight, and fidget—the latter being just another name for confusion. Iola had limited herself to one reaction. Freeze.

Despite the media flurry over the event, Iola and Bernard Pederson declined all requests for interviews. Iola explained it to me weeks later when she turned up at the station with a plate of cookies.

"It's not a question of being camera shy," she said. "It's a question of whether you want your worth defined by the fact that a pig destroyed your home. We're not about to be painted by the media as the latest freak accident victims."

The flying pig was my first but not my last brush with celebrity. A firefighter who's lucky gets one sure-fire story among the thousands in his career, a nugget of liquid gold he can spin at parties and bars and standing in the sunshine after church; a tale that entrances at the same time it hypnotizes, a yarn he can tell in his sleep and not screw up; one he can hand strangers the way a rich man pushes five-dollar bills at panhandlers to surprise and delight them, a story that is so certifiably unbelievable it simply has to be true.

The falling pig was the beginning of such a tale for me, yet in the end it was a tale I dared tell no one.